TARGET
PRACTICE

D0311116

Other Rex Stout titles
available from Carroll and Graf

Her Forbidden Knight

The Great Legend

Under the Andes

A Prize for Princes

TARGET PRACTICE

Rex Stout

CARROLL & GRAF PUBLISHERS, INC.
NEW YORK

First Carroll & Graf edition 1998
Carroll & Graf Publishers, Inc.
19 W. 21st Street
New York, NY 10010
ISBN: 0-7867-0496-9
Manufactured in the United States of America

CONTENTS

TARGET PRACTICE

TARGET PRACTICE

T HE MAN LAY ON A COT NEAR A WINDOW IN ONE
of the wards of the French army hospital at Toulon. Dr. Dumain, who was showing me through
the hospital and who had been called away to attend a
delirious patient in another ward, had told me that the
man's name was Bonnot, and that he had shot himself
in the breast two days before in the barracks at the fort.

I had started after the doctor, thinking to take advantage of the opportunity to make my escape—I had had
enough of hospital for the day—and had nearly reached
the door, when a hoarse, agitated voice sounded from
behind.

"Monsieur!"

I halted. The man on the cot had turned his head to
look at me with eyes that positively startled me with
their expression of poignant, intense suffering.

The outline of his body under the white sheet and the
knotty appearance of his arms, which lay outside,
showed him to be a big, muscular fellow; his bare shoulders were brown and massive. His chest and neck were
swathed in bandages; but these details did not enter my
consciousness till later.

My whole attention was centered on his eyes, that
burned like twin fires of agony; and I told myself that

no physical pain could produce so keen a torment. As I looked, one great, brown arm was outstretched toward me.

"Monsieur, s'il vous plait," he murmured.

I walked to the cot. "What is it—a drink of water?"

He shook his head. "No. I am not thirsty, *monsieur*, except here—" he laid his hand on his breast—"for death." The eyes flashed. *"Monsieur* is English?"

"No. I am an American—a war correspondent. Is there anything—"

"So much the better," he interrupted. *"Monsieur*, will you do me a kindness? I dare not ask anyone here—they are all French—they would laugh at me in scorn—"

"But you yourself are French," I observed, considerably mystified.

"No!" he shouted with sudden fierceness. Then, glancing quickly at the three patients at the other end of the ward, he lowered his voice to a savage murmur.

"No!" he repeated. "Or, if I am, I am Bonnot first. You will understand when I tell you, and I must tell you—I must tell some one. It is a long story—the doctor may return soon. Will you listen, *monsieur?"*

I nodded, wondering. And that is how I came to hear the story of Joseph Bonnet.

Before I go further, I want to say that it is made public with the full and free consent of his poor old mother, whom I saw a week later at the address in Paris which he gave me. I can really see no disgrace in it for him, nor for anyone else.

As nearly as possible I shall tell it in his own words; but if you would realize to what degree the story affected me, you must remember the bare, dreary hospital ward, the white sheet and bandages, the great, brown arms tossed about in feverish gestures, the burning eyes, intense with suffering.

Throughout, his voice was low and hoarse, packed with feeling; now and then, when he paused to clear his throat, the muscles of his face jerked with pain from a self-inflicted wound.

But he kept steadily on to the end. As I remember it, I did not once interrupt him.

I was born in Alsace (he began), in the town of Colmar, about fifteen miles from the French border. We were both born there—my brother Théodore and I. I was six years the elder.

When Théodore was only ten months old our father died—he was a carpenter, I don't remember him very well—and our mother was forced to go to work. She was never very strong, and she had a hard time of it.

So when some German friends, who had been very kind to us, decided to return to Frankfort and offered to take Théodore along as their own son, mother let him go. He was a little over a year old then.

Not long after that she and I went to Paris, walking all the way. There she did a little better, and managed somehow to send me to school; she could never get enough together to send for Théodore, hard though she tried.

Finally I went to work. But I always hated Paris, and I never got along very well.

Once mother and I made a visit to Germany, and found that Théodore was a student at a university. We saw that he was happy and well fixed, and didn't try to get him to return with us. But it was curious how well I seemed to remember him. He was a fine young fellow, and I was proud of him. I thought it strange that my own brother should talk with a German accent.

I think it was in 1909 that Théodore came to Paris. I mean the last time; he had been there to visit us several times before. I was twenty-nine then. He never explained his business any further than to say he was sent by the German government to conduct some sort of scientific investigation. I never caught on to things very well. He stayed two years, till August 1911.

Once I found a lot of maps and plans in his room, with names of Paris forts and suburbs and roads scattered all over them; but I didn't think anything of it. In fact, I didn't know what they were at the time.

Those two years were happy ones for all three of us. Théodore was even kinder to mother than I was, and so jolly he used to make the tears run down her face from laughing so hard. I don't think a man ever loved another man better than I loved him. I guess there were tears on my face, too, the day he left Paris.

In 1911, just after Théodore returned to Germany, I joined the army.

At last I found a job that suited me, though it didn't pay very well—just enough so mother didn't have to work after taking a little out for myself. Théodore was sending her money then, too.

Six months after I enlisted I won a prize for artillery marksmanship; in a year I was made a corporal and was sent to Boulogne. I was transferred to Toulon in April 1913, and in the very first target practise I came out the head of the list.

You know, *monsieur*, they anchor a small fleet of boats carrying a low, mud-colored sail about the size of a torpedo boat. I hit it ten times at five kilometers without a miss.

They made me a sergeant for that, and put me in charge of Battery No. 3 on the second tier of the main embankment. You can see it from the window there—

just under the flag on the right of the middle traverse.

So, you see, I was doing pretty well, getting a hundred and fifty francs a month and studying to take the examination for chief gunner, which is a fine job.

This summer, in July it was, three months ago, I began to get ready to send to Paris for mother, so she could be near me here in Toulon. She never liked Paris any better than I did.

But then the war came and I had to give that up.

A day or two after war was declared, about half the force at the fort was transferred to the field division and sent to the front. Every man of us wanted to go; but, of course, some had to stay.

We had enough to do. The colonel gave us target practise every other day, and set up double watches everywhere; so we barely had time to sleep and eat.

But nobody grumbled. All we talked about was how we'd like to get a chance at the Germans. I caught the fever from the rest of them, and every day at morning quarters I was hoping I'd be picked out to go to the front. I knew I was the best gunner in the whole battalion, and I couldn't understand why I hadn't been sent before. It was just chance, I guess.

It went on like that for two months, and every day we were getting more excited, what with the despatches from Lille and Rheims and Louvain, and the little speech the colonel made every morning at quarters.

What spare time we had we'd sit around in the barracks singing the "Marseillaise," and our talk was bloodthirsty.

One morning—last Monday it was, the 5th of October—the orderly came to the gun room where I was to say that there was a visitor in the office asking to see me. I followed him, wondering who it could be.

It was my brother Théodore.

I had not seen him for nearly a year, and we embraced each other joyfully. I thought he had been to Paris, and asked about mother, but he said he had come straight from Frankfort, through Switzerland. He said he hadn't seen any of the fighting, having passed south of the lines.

"It was the only way I could make it," he explained. "And since I had to pass within fifty miles of Toulon on my way to Paris, I thought I might as well make a detour and see you. I was drafted for the German army a week ago in Frankfort, and I had a hard time to escape."

As he said this his eyes refused to meet mine; but I thought it was because he had to confess being a deserter, though I could see no shame in that.

Could I blame my own brother for refusing to fight against France?

Of course the first thing I thought of was that he should enlist in the coast defense here in Toulon in my company. But he refused, saying that he wanted to go to Paris first and see mother, and that when he did enlist he wanted to go to the front.

I could understand that well enough, so I didn't press the matter. We talked for an hour or so about the old days together, then I asked if he wouldn't like to look around the fortifications.

"Yes, that would be amusing," he replied, without showing any particular interest.

I went off to get permission of the officer of the day, who happened to be Captain Janvour, a good friend of mine.

"You know, Bonnot," he said, when I had saluted and made my request, "the colonel has given very strict orders about visitors. Everyone is under suspicion in time of war. But I suppose—you say he is your brother?"

"Yes, sir. My brother Théodore."

"You will vouch for him?"

I hesitated a moment; after all, Théodore was from Germany. But I shook the thought off impatiently. Bah! My own brother!

"I will vouch for him, sir," I replied.

"Then it's all right. You are a man to be trusted, Bonnot. Here, orderly! Give Bonnot a ticket."

It so happened that I was free till the two o'clock watch, so we had plenty of time. I took him first to Embankment A, the one on the right with the disappearing guns.

It didn't seem to me at the time that he was very much interested, asking very few questions and talking mostly about the old days in Paris; but I remembered afterward that his eyes kept darting from one side to the other like a searchlight.

From there we crossed the traverse over to the main embankment, stopping to look at the new orillons that have been built in since the beginning of the war. He asked some questions about them, and I explained how they had been substituted for the old extension of the bastion face to guard against an enfilade of the second tier of gun rooms.

By eleven o'clock we had been all over the fort from one end to the other, even including the decoy embankment by the—but that is not for you to know, *monsieur*. I took delight in explaining everything, for Théodore had always been so much brighter than I that I was proud to show I knew something, too.

I telephoned to the barracks to arrange for him to eat with me at the gunners' table, then we went to my gun room to wait for noon mess.

There are three 42-centimeter breech loaders in the room under my charge. They are the kind with the Reffye mechanism—the best guns in the fort, *monsieur*. I had two gunners and five privates under me, and we had the best record in the battalion.

I explained the guns to Théodore, unlocking the breechblock and showing how the projectile and charge are lifted from the loadingcarriage and inserted in the bore.

He got upon the sighting platform and looked through.

"Good Heavens!" he exclaimed, "I had no idea they were so big! Why, a man could crawl in there, and he wouldn't have to wriggle much, either."

"Not I," I replied, laughing. "I've tried it. But you might."

You see, *monsieur*, Théodore was a little fellow compared to me; for I am of a good size.

Then we climbed upon the parapet together like two boys, and looked out across the sea with my glass. Just as we jumped down again into the gun room I heard a footstep at the door, and looked up to see Chanin, a gunner from Embankment A.

He looked a little surprised at sight of Théodore, then turned to me.

"Been looking for you all over the barracks, Bonnot. The captain has sent orders to stack up in the magazines for two o'clock practise. Come on if you want to finish before noon."

Chanin trotted away, grumbling something about the captain always finding a job just before messtime.

"What's up?" asked Théodore, grinning.

I explained that we had to prepare the ammunition for afternoon target practise. "It won't take long," I added; "half an hour at the most. You can come along if you want to."

He said he would rather wait for me in the gunroom,

so I went off alone after promising to return to take him to mess.

In the magazine I found a squad of privates and three or four gunners filling up the loading-carriages and wheeling them into place.

"Who's your friend?" asked Chanin, as I crossed to the projectile rail and began loosening the hold screws.

I told him it was my brother from Paris.

"Your brother? Didn't know you had one. How long is he going to stay?"

I swung a projectile into place as I answered:

"Till this evening."

"Well," said Chanin, who was a good-hearted fellow, "if I had known that I wouldn't have bothered you. We can handle this alone, can't we, boys? You go on back, Bonnot, and visit with your brother. I'll load your carriages for you."

I protested a little just to be polite, but he insisted; and some of the others did, too.

So I got permission from the lieutenant in charge, put on my shirt and jacket, and went back to join Théodore. I had been gone about ten minutes.

I was a little surprised to find that the door of the gun room was shut tight, for I was certain that I had left it open when I left. But, not thinking much about it, I pushed it back and entered.

As I did so I heard a little cry of surprise. It came from Théodore.

He was standing in the corner by a block of concrete, facing toward the wall, only his head was turned to the door. His face was flushed, and there was a queer expression in his eyes. One hand was thrown back against the wall, and in the other—the right—he was clutching something white.

Something—I guess it was the look in his eyes—

seemed to tell me everything in a flash. And then suddenly they changed, and I saw that he was aware that I knew.

For a long time we stood looking at each other in silence, neither one of us moving a muscle. He looked straight in my eyes, and I looked straight back; but I felt something coming up into my throat and choking me, and he seemed to be a long way off.

When I spoke my voice sounded strange and queer.

"Théodore," I said, "what have you got in your hand?"

He didn't answer. I made a step or two forward, then stopped. All the time we were looking straight at each other. His cheeks had gone white, and his lips were drawn tight together. Then suddenly his face relaxed, and he came forward, holding out his hand.

"There," he said calmly, "you may as well look at it."

I took it—a small pad of white paper with a leather back. A glance was enough. There were notations and abbreviations in German, but I understood the diagrams and figures: "3-35×10—4-20×8—30 paces—6-25×15—40 paces—7-15×15." And so on. Two pages of the pad were filled.

I remember that even then I was conscious of a feeling of wonder that he could guess so accurately, for of course he had had no opportunity to measure anything, since he had not been alone for a second except in the gun room.

It was a long time before I could raise my eyes from the pad of paper. I felt as a man must feel when he reads his own death sentence. I knew that Théodore was looking at me, but I could not look at him.

Then his voice came:

"*Bien?*" He had always had a funny way of saying

that. *"Bien?"* Like a child impatient and amused and angry all at once.

"Bon Dieu, Théodore!" I cried, half sobbing. "You— a traitor!"

At that he drew himself up. "I am no traitor," he said proudly. "I am an officer of the German army."

"You are a spy!" I exclaimed fiercely. "And you come here—you betray me, your brother—At least you try, for you have failed—"

Théodore crossed to my side and laid his hand on my arm.

"True, I have failed," he said. His voice trembled a little. "But listen, Joseph. If anyone is a traitor it is you. No—wait—I do not say you are one, but neither am I. Were we not born in the German empire, subjects of the Emperor William? Do we not rightfully owe him our allegiance? You joined the French army merely because you happened to be in Paris and could find nothing better to do. If you had been in Berlin you would be in the German army instead.

"Listen, Joseph; I am an officer—a captain. Come with me, go to Strassburg with me, and I'll have you made a lieutenant. Come, isn't that better than this gunner business?"

I think, *monsieur,* if he had not said that it would have been different. But it made me angry to have him think I could be a traitor.

"Théodore," I said, looking him in the eye, "I have made an oath to defend my country, and you are an enemy of France. You came here as a spy; you have tried to use me as a tool. I owe no allegiance to the emperor of Germany. I am here to perform my duty."

Then he understood, for he drew back and changed color.

"Joseph—" he said, and stopped.

Then there was another silence, while we stood looking at each other.

I do not know how it was, *monsieur;* but there seemed to be no room for pity or affection in me. It was the war, I think, and rage at Théodore that he had tried to make a fool of me. Day after day we had heard nothing but France, France, France, until I believe everyone in the fort was crazy. May the good God forgive me, I had a feeling of pride that I was strong enough to do the thing I meant to do!

"Monsieur," I said—I was theatrical, I called him *monsieur*—*"monsieur,* I am a soldier of France, and I must perform my duty. By your own admission you are a spy of the German government. You will understand why I prefer not to arrest you myself. I shall lock you in this room and report your presence to the officer in command."

I started to back away; and then suddenly I weakened, when Théodore smiled, just as he used to smile in the old days together, and he spoke calmly; there wasn't a trace of anger or reproach in his voice.

"Joseph," he said, "I am a soldier, too, and I would be the last to blame you for performing your duty. But this means death for me, you know; and, after all, I am a Bonnot—I am your brother. Here is the pad—you may search me, I have nothing else—and let me go."

I shall never forget the way he smiled at me as he said that, *monsieur.* It went straight to my heart. I took a step away from the door.

"Théodore, my brother!" I cried, and opened my arms.

But as I did so the sound of voices reached my ears from without, rolling over the parapet and echoing throughout the fort. A hundred voices raised all at once.

It was my comrades singing as they marched to the barracks for noon mess:

"Allons enfants de la patrie,
Le jour de gloire est arrivé!
Contre nous de la tyrannie,
L'étendard sanglant est levé—
L'étendard sanglant est levé.
Entendez-vous dans ces campagnes
Mugir ces féroces soldats?
Ils viennent jusque dans nos bras
Egorger nos fils, nos compagnes—"

We stood in silence while the song swelled to its climax. I felt my heart bursting within me. My arms dropped to my side.

When the last echo had died away I turned without a word—without a look, without a sign, *monsieur*—walked out of the gun room, locked the door behind me, my brother a prisoner, and started for the office of the officer in command.

I never saw Théodore again—but yes—wait—

Just as I reached the door of the office Captain Janvour appeared on the threshold. I fell back a step and saluted.

"What is it, Bonnot?" he asked pleasantly.

And then, *monsieur*, I realized that I couldn't say it. "My brother is locked in the gun room. He is a German spy." The words would not come out.

I hesitated, confused, feeling my face grow red while the captain looked at me.

"Nothing sir," I ended by stammering.

"Nothing! What the devil did you come here for?"

"Why, sir—to ask—may my brother go to mess, sir?"

"Certainly! You know it wasn't necessary to ask that."

The captain gave me a queer look before he walked off in the direction of the officers' quarters. When he had gone I sighed with thankfulness and relief, and tears came to my eyes.

Then the next instant I was cursing myself for a weak fool.

I tell you what, *monsieur*, this war has made us all crazy. Nobody is the same. The men at the fort eat like hogs, like wild beasts, and they yell around at night, and the officers smile and say it's the fighting spirit.

I went to the mess room in the barracks, trying to think what to do. I sat down at the table and ate with the rest of them. Chanin asked me where my brother was, but I didn't answer. They were all so noisy they didn't notice my silence.

After the meal I went out to the yard and lit my pipe and walked around a long time—half an hour, maybe. I couldn't decide what to do.

Then suddenly I thought of mother—somehow I hadn't thought of her before—and then I turned and ran through the yard and barracks and over the traverse to the gun room. My fingers trembled so I could scarcely unlock the door, and I stumbled and nearly fell as I sprang inside.

Monsieur, the gun room was empty! Théodore was not there. I could not believe my eyes.

I called his name in a low tone, then louder, but there was no answer. I couldn't understand it. Of course, he could not have left by the door, locked as it was, with the key in my pocket.

The only other way of escape was to climb the ladder to the parapet, walk along that till he came to another gun room, and then slide down. But I knew the doors of all the gun rooms were kept locked; so he couldn't have got out.

I mounted the parapet and ran along the ledge, looking in each gun room as I passed. There was no sign of him, and all the doors were closed tight. In several of the rooms were gunners and privates getting ready for target practise, and they were surprised to see me on the parapet and asked what I was doing, but I paid no attention.

I ran on to the end, where the bastion face breaks off and the new orillons are placed. From the edge of the parapet to the first orillon there is a space about eighteen feet wide, and the trench is thirty feet deep. A sentry is supposed to be stationed there, but I couldn't see him anywhere.

Had Théodore leaped the trench and escaped over the wall on the other side? It appeared to be impossible, but there was no other solution.

Then, struck by a sudden thought, I ran back along the parapet to my gun room and slid down the ladder. I ran to the corner where I had dropped the pad of paper. It was gone.

I swore at myself then. If I had only taken it with me when I went to report to the captain! But had Théodore really escaped? I could not think it possible that he had leaped that trench, and there was no other way.

But, then, where was he?

I was half crazy, *monsieur*. I told myself that I had betrayed my country.

I see now that I exaggerated everything. After all, he had nothing but a scrap of paper with a few figures on it, and of this fort, too, which could never be attacked except from the sea. But you know what the war fever is; and besides, I was enraged that he had outwitted me.

I started to climb the ladder to the parapet, thinking to look through the other gun rooms again.

As I did so I heard the door open behind me. It was some privates bringing the loading carriages with ammunition for target practise.

"Hello, Bonnot!" they called. "Come and give us a hand!"

I slid back to the floor.

"Mon Dieu!" exclaimed one of them—Biron—looking over at me. "What's the matter, man? Your face is white as a German's liver!"

I mumbled something—I don't know what—and began to help them wheel in the carriages. It took us quite a while to get them forward and in position.

Captain Janvour came in to ask if everything was ready. I said we hadn't loaded yet.

"Why the devil don't you hurry up, then?" he said. "We're waiting for you. Signal when you're ready. The blue pennant is yours. Ten rounds at five-minute intervals, using only one gun. Get a move on."

For the next ten minutes I forgot everything but my work, and I kept the men at it so that by the end of that time everything was in place.

I hadn't oiled up my mechanism that day, and so I hadn't decided which gun to use. I think I told you there were three in the room. I climbed up to No. 1, opened her up, and looked down the bore. It looked rough, so I went on to No. 2, but she was even worse.

When I climbed up to No. 3, I saw that the breech-block was swung half open.

That doesn't mean anything to you, *monsieur*; but you're not a gunner. I knew I hadn't left it that way, for I take better care of my guns than any other man in the fort.

I opened her wide and looked down the bore.

It was black as night! Completely choked up. I couldn't understand it.

One of the men handed up a candle, and I poked it in. It took me a few seconds to get it set right on account of the reflection; and then, *monsieur*, I saw what made me start so that I nearly fell off the platform.

It was the top of a man's head, covered with curly brown hair. It was my brother Théodore. There he was, like a rat in a hole!

I felt the blood leave my face, and my hand shook so that the candle knocked against the steel and went out. For ten seconds I stood there without breathing.

My first thought was to close the breech and use one of the other guns. Then suddenly my head grew hot, as though my brain were on fire; and then, quite as suddenly, I felt cool and calm as ice.

I thrust my arm farther into the bore to see if there were room for loading, and my fingers brushed against Théodore's hair. Then I drew my hand out and turned to the men below.

"We'll use No. 3," I called out in a steady voice. "Here, quick! Up with the lever, Biron." It would ruin the gun, I knew—

Biron leaped up beside me, and together we raised the projectile from the loading-carriage and inserted it. Then the charge and primer.

He jumped down. I swung the breechblock to and turned the translating-screw, then twisted the locking screw till she was closed tight.

The cold steel felt warm to my hands, and I felt drops of sweat coming out on my forehead, but I worked steadily and calmly.

Calling to Biron to press the signal button, I mounted the sighting platform and began turning the side crank. Off across the water I could see the mud-colored target, tossing up and down on the waves; and to the right, at the end of the embankment, a group of officers and privates were gathered around the foot of the pennant staff.

I worked the lever slowly and firmly, with my eye glued to the glass.

"Take your time, *mon vieux*," came Biron's voice from below.

Suddenly a blue pennant went fluttering up to the top of the staff. I gave the lever one little turn to the right, locked it, dropped my hand to the guard—then closed my eyes tight and pressed the trigger.

I heard nothing and saw nothing after that, *monsieur*. My brain seemed to be on fire again, and they say I fell from the platform to the floor and was picked up senseless.

Anyway, that is my story. You understand now what I meant when I said I was not French. It was not I who killed my brother, *monsieur*; it was France. I am of no nation; I am Joseph Bonnot.

You will see my mother—you will tell her what I say—I love her, *monsieur*, and I love my brother Théodore, but I hate war and I hate all nations—*all*.

As he uttered the last word Joseph Bonnot's head sank back on the pillow and his arm, raised in a menacing gesture, fell across his breast. I sat for some time pondering on what he had said.

Finally I was aroused by the arrival of Dr. Dumain. As he saw the still and inert form on the cot a look of comprehension entered his eyes. He stepped to the side of the cot and placed his ear against the gunner's breast.

After a minute he looked up with solemn eyes, shaking his head sorrowfully.

"The end," he said in a low voice. "I wonder," he added reflectively, "what possible reason a fine, strong man like Bonnot could have to commit suicide?"

THE PAY YEOMAN

PAYMASTER GARWAY ROSS, ATTACHED TO AND serving on board the United States steamship *Helena*, possessed in an eminent degree all of the qualifications mentioned as appertaining to his position.

He also possessed one or two of the flexible virtues and a bitter knowledge of the sourness of the fruit of life. This last it was that drove him to seek the salty masculinity of the wardroom.

On a certain day of the year Paymaster Garway Ross, moved by the inherent laziness of man and a careless irresponsibility peculiar to himself, did a very foolish thing. He gave the combination of the office safe to his yeoman.

The pay yeoman, generally speaking, is the man who does the work of the paymaster. Particularly was this true in the case of Yeoman James Martin and Paymaster Garway Ross.

To the latter a monthly statement was a fearsome labyrinth and a quarterly return a snare of the devil. Also, he hated to count money, always having had so much of his own that he had never been under the necessity of counting it.

Finally, after a year of growing confidence in his yeoman, he entrusted him with the daily balance of the cash and sighed with immense relief.

For two years all was harmony. Paymaster Garway Ross read novels, wore out the lounge in the wardroom, invented mysterious and tantalizing cocktails, while Yeoman Martin wrote and ruled in the pay office two decks below.

Then, on a day in August (the *Helena* was at dry dock in New York), Martin announced his intention of applying for a furlough. The paymaster heartily approved, though he realized it meant a temporary burden on his own shoulders.

By a tactful word to the captain he got Martin's week of liberty extended to two; and in his effort to show his appreciation of his yeoman's services, even went so far as to present him with a treasury note of poetic denomination.

This gift, however, Martin steadfastly refused, seemingly on the grounds of personal dignity. The paymaster pocketed the note with great reluctance and waved a cheerful *au revoir* as Martin went down the gangway.

About three o'clock on the following afternoon the paymaster, by a tremendous effort of the will, lifted himself from the wardroom lounge, proceeding to the pay office, made an entry in the provision return, opened the safe, and balanced the cash.

That is, he tried to balance it. It was eight thousand dollars short.

For the remainder of that day, and the whole of the next, Paymaster Garway Ross was thoroughly stunned.

He was conscious of an immense incredulity. This was not based on any real knowledge of Martin's character or belief in his honesty, but originated in and proceeded from the paymaster himself. His mind, limited by its own habits, was incapable of registering so sudden and complete a reversal of conception.

In short, the thing was incredible.

But when, on the morning of the third day and for the fortieth time, he checked up the contents of the safe and found the shortage actually existent he forced himself to recognize the truth and prepare for action.

Owing to certain of the naval regulations, his dilemma was a curious one, for had it become known that he had entrusted the combination of the safe to his yeoman the paymaster would have been court-martialed and probably dismissed from the service; so runs the rule. Obviously, therefore, he could not expose Martin's guilt without at the same time admitting his own.

But the paymaster's sympathies had been smothered by an overwhelming fact—he disliked, as he expressed it to himself, being made the goat for anyone. For a long hour he sat perched on the edge of the office stool, smoking a huge black cigar, revolving schemes innumerable and rejecting each in its turn.

Exactly in proportion as his helplessness became apparent his anger increased, and the cold anger of a brain slow to conceive and strong to retain is to be feared.

It was well for Jimmie Martin that he was many miles away from the berth-deck of the *Helena* when Paymaster Ross emerged from the pay office and mounted the officers' ladder to his own room.

The following morning he visited his bankers in Cedar Street, and in exchange for a personal check received eight hundred ten-dollar bills. These he took to the ship and placed in the safe, after which he balanced the cash. He then drew forth a private account-book and turned to a clean page, which he headed, "James Martin."

Beneath this he wrote: "To experience supplied—$8000."

He knew nothing of bookkeeping, however, and the sense of the entry appeared to be somewhat obscure. Accordingly, after a minute of thought, he wrote in the middle of the page in pencil the words: "Account not closed."

One hot June morning the United States steamship *Helena*, with her shining decks and her rakish stack, boomed forth a salute to the commandant and weighed anchor in the harbor of San Juan.

Within half an hour her boats were lowered and her starboard gangway made fast, and a few minutes later the steam launch glided away, headed for the naval station wharf.

The passengers were the captain, paying a call to the commandant; the surgeon, whose errand was personal; and Paymaster Garway Ross, in search of fresh meat. The commissary was paying for a little indiscretion by reposing in solitary grandeur in the brig.

For two years and six months, since the disappearance of Jimmie Martin, the *Helena* had roamed the seas and paraded the coast. She had escorted a floating dry dock from Cherbourg to Norfolk, honored a New Orleans Mardi Gras with her presence, twice attended the annual maneuvers at Guantanamo, and made herself generally handy and useful. She was at San Juan in obedience to an order to relieve the *Chester*.

More than two years ago it was that the new pay yeoman had placed a big red "D" opposite Jimmie Martin's name on the crew payroll, for Martin's furlough, already extended by himself from two weeks to thirty months, seemed likely to become permanent.

Perhaps some day some country deputy would appear at Norfolk or Brooklyn with Martin in one hand and an expense list in the other, and, pocketing the reward for apprehension of a deserter, leave Martin to be sentenced for three dreary years to the prison ship at Portsmouth; but he remained as yet on the list of the wanted. His billet had been filled, his bag and hammock sold at auction, and he had become but a vague and unrecognized number to the roll and the crew of the United States steamship *Helena*.

With one exception.

Paymaster Garway Ross did neither forget nor forgive. Perhaps it would be not exactly just to call him vindictive; yet he desired revenge. Almost unconsciously he nursed his anger and the wish for vengeance.

It had never taken the form of active investigation or pursuit. But it was there, smoldering, waiting; just as, according to the scientists, we each harbor within us the sleeping germ of insanity, ready to be raised at any moment to dreadful activity by something that is not within us.

In his search for fresh meat the paymaster followed his nose in and out of three smaller shops before he found the way to the large establishment of Hernandez y Hermanos. Here he found what he wanted.

The elder Hernandez, smiling, courteous, recorded his order for ten hindquarters and the same number of fores, promising immediate delivery and the freshest beeves. Then he turned to a clerk and beckoned sharply.

"*No!* Mendez! Drive to the storage and bring this," he said, handing the clerk a duplicate of the paymaster's order. "And, going, you may take the scales to the hotel."

"But there are the jars of Señor Martin—"

"Go, fool!" the excitable Hernandez shouted. "Bah! Señor Martin can wait."

An electric thrill, indefinable, illusive, passed through the brain of the paymaster. He decided to disregard it, but it was insistent. He turned to Hernandez.

"Señor Martin?" he said half indifferently. "Who is this Martin?"

Hernandez was glad to oblige the paymaster.

"*Americano*," he replied. "Coffee planter this side— a little—of Caguas. A very good man, I believe, but small. He pays very well."

"I think I know him," said the paymaster. "What is he like?" He understood that the "small" applied to the fortune, not to the person.

"I have never seen him, señor," was the reply. "Never does he come to San Juan. He sends money by the carrier and a writing. Every month—sometimes two."

"Do you keep the orders? Could I see them?"

"Certainly, señor."

Hernandez trotted to the office at the rear, and after some minutes reappeared with an old letter file. From this he took some papers which he handed to the paymaster.

The paymaster was curiously excited. Whether it was the spoken name of Martin or an awakened recollection of something he had once said about Puerto Rico, or merely the effect of intuition, may not be known; but he was actually quivering with eagerness—the eagerness of bruin roused by the odor of the hidden sweet.

The first paper showed him his mistake. It was an order for three chairs and some glass jars and was signed "S. Martin." He gazed at it blankly.

"Pardon, señor," said the courteous Hernandez, "but that was written by the señora. For many months she has written. But there are some—"

He rummaged in the pile of papers, drew one forth, and handed it to the paymaster.

And then the face of Garway Ross turned pale and his

eyes closed to a narrow slit. Perhaps, after all, he was vindictive. As for the paper—that handwriting! The books of the pay office of the *Helena* were full of it.

The next morning but one found the paymaster, mounted on a short-haired native pony, proceeding leisurely along the white, level road that leads from San Juan to the foothills of the Sierra de Luquillo. Feeling sure of his quarry, he had taken his time. He had not questioned the carrier for fear of a possible communication and warning to Señor Martin; but the courteous Hernandez had furnished information of the exact whereabouts of Martin's plantation.

The paymaster's intentions were extremely hazy. Strapped about his waist under his coat were two ugly Navy revolvers; yet he was no Corsican. He told himself that they were meant purely as a defense; he certainly did not premeditate murder. In the meantime there they were.

He did not intend to expose Martin or arrest him; that would have been to expose and betray himself. Nor had he an idea of forcing a material restitution. The loss of the money had been but a slight and temporary annoyance; furthermore, it was to be doubted if Martin had it in his power to repay even a small part of it. Apparently, then, his journey was purposeless.

But still his heart was hot with anger; indefinable, and therefore reasonless. He was not a lover of justice, an avenger of the law, a crusader for the right. He was simply a man with a grudge.

The pony, unlike its rider, was little inconvenienced by the glare of the road and the heat of the tropical sun. For four long hours he trotted on unwearyingly, stopping now and then to rest in the shade of a grove of palms, or to drink from one of the bubbling streams dashing toward the foothills below.

At eleven o'clock he turned from the road into a path at the foot of a ridge of limestone cliffs, and three hundred yards farther on came within sight of a low rambling house set at the edge of a small clearing.

This was the home of Señor Martin.

Paymaster Garway Ross stopped his pony and for some minutes sat gazing at the house in silence. Afterward when the scene rose in his memory, he wondered at the rare loveliness of the setting—the charm, even, of the house itself.

In the immediate background was a grove of tillandsia, fragrant and cool. On either side appeared long rows of coffee trees, brilliantly white with their innumerable blossoms; and beyond, at the foot of a sloping valley, could be seen a somber purple patch, relieved here and there by a gorgeous scarlet of nature's most beautiful parasite.

Over all was the heavy fragrance, the droopy languor, of the land of the lotus.

But for the present the paymaster was conscious only of his immediate emotions. For the first time he realized that the enterprise contained an element of real danger.

Martin might even now be observing him from one of those shaded windows; possibly have recognized him. Thinking thus, the paymaster wheeled his pony about and retreated out of sight round a bend in the path.

Here he removed one of the revolvers from the hidden belt and placed it in his side coat pocket; after which precaution he returned to the clearing and rode boldly up to the door of the house.

He had scarcely halted his pony when the door opened and a woman appeared on the threshold.

The paymaster dismounted, lifted his hat, and bowed.

"I want to see James Martin," he said.

The woman looked up quickly and for a moment was silent.

Then she spoke in a low, rather harsh voice:

"What about?"

The paymaster bowed again.

"I had rather tell that to Mr. Martin himself," he said. "Is he here?"

"No." A faint gleam of interest flickered across the woman's face as she added, "Were you a friend of his?"

"Yes," said the paymaster inwardly thanking her for the tense, while he wondered at it. "When will he be at home?"

The woman did not answer. Instead after a moment of silence, she turned and called sharply, "Miguel!"

Another moment, and a slouching blinking *hombre* appeared in the doorway.

"Take the pony," the woman said shortly.

Then, motioning to the paymaster to follow, she started round the path encircling the house toward the grove of tillandsias in the rear.

The paymaster guessed intuitively what they were to find.

It was in the air, in the woman's tone, in her very silence; and he as silently followed her through the shady grove across a quivering log bridge, and into a second grove more deeply shaded than the first. She halted abruptly by a giant tillandsia, and the paymaster approached and stood at her side.

He had guessed correctly. At their feet was a slender mound of earth covered with coarse grass; and at its farther end was a rude block of limestone bearing this inscription:

JAMES MARTIN
Died December 22, 1907
Age 24

The woman sat on the trunk of a fallen tree and gazed at the stone impassively, in silence. Finally the paymaster turned to her.

"So," he said, "six months ago."

The woman nodded.

"I am Paymaster Ross, of the navy," he continued presently. "Perhaps you have heard him speak of me. I knew your—him—"

"My son," said the woman dully.

At this the paymaster felt a slight surprise; somehow he had never thought of Martin as having a mother. He knew that he ought to speak, to say something; but he felt that there was nothing he could possibly say, nothing worth saying.

Finally, "He was a good boy," he observed awkwardly.

Again the woman nodded.

"I suppose he was. He spoke a lot about you. He always said you was kind to him. I suppose I ought to thank you."

"Won't you tell me more about it?" said the paymaster. "I mean about him, and how he came down here, and how he—about the end."

Then he seated himself beside her and waited.

She began with a grim smile.

"There was a time then I could have talked all about it," she observed. "Somehow I don't feel like it anymore. And it's all Jimmie's fault. Maybe you're right. Maybe he was a good boy and all that; but somehow he never seemed to get anywhere."

She paused and sighed heavily, and the paymaster rose to his feet and stood looking down at the grave.

"He was just like his father."

As the woman continued, her voice held a new note of bitterness, and the paymaster shuddered.

"He died when Jimmie was twelve years old and the others was babies. He always was a fool, and Jimmie was just like him. Then, after I'd starved and slaved to death nearly, Jimmie got that money from the navy.

"He called it a bonus. I never understood about it. I never wanted him to go in the navy anyway; but then that was all right. And then, when he got all that money, he made us all come down here, where it's only fit for niggers.

"And Annie and Tom are always sick, too. I used to wonder about it and I wouldn't be surprised if he stole it. Annie and Tom are the others. You didn't see 'em as you came in from the road?"

With an effort the paymaster turned to face her and shook his head.

"No. But he—he was a good worker."

His own words sounded in his ear hollow, inane. Here all was dust and ashes. Words were useless.

"Perhaps," the woman continued. "But when a woman like me has had her whole life spoiled by a man and his son, she can't think very well of either of 'em. He should have given me that money; I'd earned it. But he talked about Annie and Tom, and what he'd do for 'em, and brought us all off down here where it's only fit for niggers.

"And now he's gone and I can't get anybody to stay here, and the niggers won't work, and we're worse off than ever. He ought to stayed in the navy. At least, we got forty dollars a month from him then."

The paymaster forced himself to speak.

"But the place seems to be in good condition. Couldn't you sell it?"

The woman laughed—a harsh crackling laugh that gave the paymaster an involuntary shiver of disgust. Then she waved a hand toward the long stretch of white blossoms on either side of the house.

"They look pretty, don't they?" she said with infinite sarcasm. "Yes, they look pretty all right. But they're all eat up with worms. There's something wrong with 'em inside. Of course, I tried to sell out as soon as he was gone. He might have done it himself."

Again the paymaster made a weak attempt to probe beneath the crust.

"But he was a good boy, Mrs. Martin," he said. "And from what you say, I judge that he gave you all he had. He did everything he could. And now—now that he is gone—"

For a moment the woman stared at him almost wonderingly. Then she gave a short laugh.

"That's a fool notion," she said. "I guess I know what you mean. It sounds just like him. What's the difference if he's dead? He's better off than I am. But then, of course, you was his friend."

She stopped abruptly and sat gazing at the paymaster in a sort of stupid antagonism.

But the paymaster was silenced. The fruit of life! And he—not knowing—for what had he come? His eyes, as he turned them for the last time on the grave of Jimmie Martin, were eloquent and—if that may be—tender.

But the dust of the grave has no ears—perhaps! He wondered and turned to go.

The woman made no motion to follow or to speak. Was she somehow aware that her harsh and gloomy note had been used by the poet to complete the rhythm of a scheme awful and beautiful? Had she played her part knowing and yet helpless?

She barely glanced up as the paymaster passed her. He moved swiftly. At the log bridge he turned and looked back. She was sitting as he had left her, her head bowed forward, and he shuddered as he conceived her likeness to the hovering form of the bird of death.

It was a week or so later that the pay yeoman of the *Helena* was seated at his desk, striving valiantly to bring order out of chaos. He was trying to strike a balance from the vague and cryptic entries of a private account-book which the paymaster had asked him to check up.

The paymaster was seated on the edge of the desk, smoking a huge black cigar.

"I don't know," said the pay yeoman, scratching his head in perplexity. "Which are receipts and which expenditures?"

"Why, they're in a sort of chronological order," said the paymaster vaguely. "But it must be mostly expenditures."

The yeoman sighed hopelessly and turned over some half-dozen pages. Then he gazed at the book reflectively, tapping his teeth with the end of a penholder.

"Now, here, for instance," he said. "Here's an entry: 'James Martin. To experience supplied—$8000.' Does that mean you gave him eight thousand, or did he give it to you?"

The paymaster did not reply. Instead, he leaned over the yeoman's shoulder and gazed at the page for a full minute in silence.

Then he took the book from the yeoman, erased something written on the page in pencil, and taking a pen from the desk, printed across it in big black letters the word "Paid."

Then he returned the book to the yeoman.

"But was it a receipt or an expenditure?" persisted the other. "That doesn't mean anything."

"It means a good deal to me," said the paymaster.

"And," he added to himself as he turned to leave the office, "to Jimmie."

SECRETS

I WAS FIRST ATTRACTED TO HER BY HER ATTITUDE toward the picture.

Taken altogether, it measured up better than that of any other person who had been submitted to the test. I can see even now her gaze of frank interest and curiosity and her quick questioning glance at me as I sat watching her out of the corner of my eye, finding an unusual difficulty in regarding her with that attitude of calm and impartial analysis which, in my opinion, a lawyer should always maintain toward his client.

First of all, perhaps I had better explain about the picture.

It was my own idea. From the day that I opened my law offices on William Street I had been keenly conscious of one of the greatest handicaps under which an attorney labors: the difficulty of getting a line on the character of the client.

This is more important than a layman would suppose—and particularly so with lawyers like myself, who make it a rule never to defend the confessedly or obviously guilty. In many cases it is next to impossible to form a sensibly correct judgment.

When a man is placed in a position where he finds it necessary to seek legal advice and aid, his mind is usually so disturbed and disarranged by his perplexities that all ordinary tests for the reading of character are rendered useless.

The picture was more a happy accident than any result of my own ingenuity or wisdom. I came across it by chance in the studio of an artist friend who was possessed of an extravagant interest in the bizarre and unique.

Its subject has nothing to do with the story, and I shall not attempt to describe it. It is enough to say that it portrayed with frank naturalism and a taste of genius one of the most fundamental of the elements of human nature and experience, without being either distasteful or offensive.

No sooner had I seen it, and realized the effect of the shock which I had felt in every corner of my brain, than I knew that here at last was the very thing I wanted. My friend was loath to part with it until I explained the reason for my desire; and then, flattered by my recognition of its peculiar merit, he wished to make me a gift of it.

The thing was incredibly successful from the very first.

The chair in which I seat my clients is placed directly at my elbow on the right, in front of the arm slide on my rolltop desk. I placed the picture inside the desk, opposite this chair, so that it was invariably the first thing that caught the eye of the visitor after being seated.

The effect was always interesting and profitable; in some instances even startling.

A study of the different sensations and expressions it has caused to appear on the faces of my unsuspecting clients would fill a volume. Frank or affected modesty, involuntary horror, open curiosity, sudden fear—it has shown them all. I became an adept at reading the signs—the temperature of this human thermometer.

By its very crudity, its primality, the thing was infallible, never failing to shock the mind into a betrayal of its most carefully hidden secrets. Of course, its main strength lay in its unexpectedness. I believed then, and I believe now, that no will, however strong, could have held itself neutral against the test without being forewarned.

And yet—I often wonder—how could she possibly have known?

On the morning of her first call I was alone in the office, having sent James uptown on some errand, while it was too early for the stenographer to have arrived.

Thus it was that I myself greeted her in the outer room, and inquired the nature of her business.

"I came to see Mr. Moorfield," she said in a voice which, naturally gentle and refined, was rendered rough and harsh by a very evident anxiety and uneasiness. "I wish to see him concerning a personal matter. It is very important."

You will have some idea of the manner of her appearance and bearing when I confess that they almost persuaded me—me, the coolest and least impressionable lawyer at the New York bar—to forego what I had come to call the "picture test," and interview her in the outer room. Would to Heaven I had!

As she stood by the door looking up into my face with a half-hopeful, half-fearful expression, her rich, cherry lips trembling with the emotion she could not conceal, her eyes glowing and moist, her figure swaying in mute appeal—well, the angels themselves have seen no more delightful picture.

I can see her so now when I close my eyes.

However, I managed to retain my professional sense as I ushered her into the inner office and placed for her the chair before the desk. She sank into it with a murmured "Thank you," and then, as I seated myself beside her, I saw her gaze light upon the picture.

As I have said, her conduct was very nearly perfection. When the first rush of conscious thought returned—after the inevitable shock produced by the picture—I could observe none of the signs which I had come to regard as unfavorable.

There was no tightening of the lips, no dilation of the nostrils, no widening of the eyelids. It is true that I missed the most important moment, as immediately after her glance of curiosity at myself, I had become suddenly aware of the fact that I was holding a lighted cigar in my hand, and turned aside to throw it in the cuspidor.

It fell instead on the floor, and I stooped to pick it up. Thus I missed three or four valuable seconds which, however trifling they may seem to the average mind, will be recognized as all-important by the student of crime and character.

"Now, madam," I said gravely, turning to her, "what can I do for you?"

She was regarding me with a look of appeal and helplessness that was well-nigh irresistible.

"I have come," she said in a low tone, "to ask your help. I am—I am in great trouble. As soon as I discovered—"

"First," I interrupted, "why do you come to me? It is usual in such cases for one to consult one's own attorney."

"I know," she said hurriedly, "but I have no one. Besides, Mr. Moorfield surely knows his own reputation too well to be surprised at such a visit as mine."

For the first time in my life I found a compliment a thing not to be despised. I smiled in spite of myself. When I looked up she, too, was smiling bravely through her tears.

The story she told me I shall attempt to reproduce in her own words:

"My name," she began, "is Lillian Markton. I am living in New York with my uncle, William Markton, of Riverside Drive. There is nothing in particular to tell you about myself unless you care to ask questions. The whole thing is so—so absurd—"

She hesitated, regarding me nervously.

"Go on," I said encouragingly.

After a moment of silence she continued: "It happened only last night. Uncle Will came home late, looking worried and uneasy, but I thought little of it, for he has had many business troubles, and it was really nothing unusual. You know, he is cashier of the Montague Bank. Well, when I got up this morning he was nowhere to be found.

"We usually ride in the park at seven o'clock, and after I had waited half an hour for him I went up to his room. The bed had not been disturbed. At nine o'clock I went to the bank and found"—her voice sank till it was scarcely audible—"that he had been arrested— charged with stealing fifty thousand dollars from the vaults."

"Was he arrested at home?" I interrupted.

"No—at the station. He was boarding a train for Chicago."

"Did he have the money with him?"

"Of course not!" Miss Markton exclaimed indignantly. "Do you think I would be here if he had?"

"My dear madam," I observed, "I was merely seeking information. But, after all, it is useless to question you. I must see Mr. Markton."

My visitor eyed me for a moment in silence.

"That, too, is useless," she said finally. "Mr. Markton has confessed."

I admit I was taken aback.

"Confessed!" I cried. "Confessed what?"

"To the theft."

"Then what the deuce do you want me for?" I demanded.

Miss Markton rose and stood facing me.

"Mr. Moorfield," she said, "I came to you because I have heard you mentioned as a man who, in addition to ability, possesses both sympathy and discernment. If my informant was mistaken—"

"But he was not," I hastened to assure her. "Pray forgive me and proceed."

With a nod of thanks and approval, and after a slight hesitation, she continued:

"My uncle's confession was peculiar," she said. "He admitted taking the money, but declares that he does not know where it is. It seems that the bank officials have been watching him for some time. He says that he brought the money home last night and locked it in the safe in the dining room; that when he went to get it early this morning it was gone, and that he was leaving New York with only a few dollars of his own.

"The money has not been found. There was no one else in the house but the servants and myself—Uncle Will is a bachelor—and none of the servants could possibly have opened the safe, to which I carried a key. That is why I have come to you. I am suspected of having—stolen—"

She suddenly gave way to sobbing, her head falling forward on the desk.

And I, overcome by a choking sensation that was entirely new to me, and wholly uncomfortable, sat regarding her hungrily, longing to take her in my arms and comfort her. I did not understand it then, and I do not now.

As soon as Miss Markton regained her composure she continued, speaking hurriedly and in a low tone:

"As far as Uncle Will is concerned, he must know I am innocent. They will not let me see him. It is the bank—I suppose they believe me to be an accomplice. They—I saw—" she hesitated, her eyes full of fear and appeal. "A man followed me here to your office. What am I to do?" she cried. "I am all alone! There is no one!"

Many times before had I heard such appeals—but they had left me unmoved and cold. Now it seemed that every fiber of my being trembled in response to this woman's cry.

My blood leaped and sang—I could see nothing but her tears, hear nothing but her voice. As well as I could I restrained myself; I took her hand, lying before me on the desk, and patted it gently. Words refused to come; but with that gesture I committed myself, and she felt it.

For upward of a quarter of an hour I questioned her, but without gaining any further information. Evidently she had told me all she knew. With my businesslike assumption of responsibility she gradually grew more calm, even cheerful; and as she rose to go she glanced at the picture before her and then looked up at me curiously.

"Someday," she said, "you must tell me the story of that picture. It is—I can't describe how it makes me feel."

She shrugged her shoulders prettily.

"I am sure it must have a history?"

"None whatever," said I, smiling. "It serves merely to hide the dust."

"Then we must give it one. Ugh! It looks as though it might hide much more than dust."

I bade her good-by at the door, assuring her that

everything would turn out all right, and advising her to pay no attention whatever to the man who was following her. At parting she took my hand in hers and pressed it gently. When I returned to the office I could still feel the thrill of that contact through every inch of my body.

Once alone I attempted an analysis of the facts she had given me; but I found it impossible. Her voice, her face, her figure, filled my thoughts to the exclusion of all else.

My dry light had deserted me, and I found myself swimming, or struggling rather, in a sea of sentiment and emotion. Finally, angry and impatient at my inability to formulate my thoughts, I started for the Tombs to see William Markton.

Markton received me sullenly enough, but when I told him I represented his niece, his face suddenly blazed with an almost maniacal fury. I recoiled involuntarily from his wild expression of rage and hate, while he burst forth into cursing and swearing, declaring that it was the fault of his niece that he had been caught—that she had taken the money, and that she would "pay for it in hell."

In vain I expostulated and argued with him—it was all to no purpose. The man seemed absolutely convinced that Lillian Markton had taken the fifty thousand dollars which he himself had stolen from the bank; but when I pressed him for proof or evidence he had nothing to say.

Finally, however, I got an explanation of what I had considered the chief difficulties in Miss Markton's case, though her uncle had no idea that he was thus aiding one whom he considered his worst enemy.

He explained that when he had first discovered that the money was missing from his safe he had had no suspicion of Lillian. Instead, he had suspected a friend and accomplice, who he knew had had many opportunities of obtaining duplicates of his keys—and he had gone to the railway station, not to make his escape, but to watch for his confederate. But when pressed for the man's name he refused to give it, saying merely that he now knew he had suspected him unjustly—and launching forth again into curses and oaths against his niece.

I found it impossible to get anything further from him, even any reason for his own confession; and he sullenly refused my offer of legal aid, declaring that he would have nothing to do with anyone connected with his niece. I admit I was relieved at his refusal of my offer, which I had made solely for the sake of Miss Markton.

I emerged from the Tombs with a confident belief in Lillian Markton's innocence. In Markton's story of the suspected confederate I placed no credence whatever— the thing seemed to me to bear all the marks of a hasty fabrication. Also, in the same breath with which he had accused his niece, Markton admitted that he had not even awakened her when he found the package of money missing.

His accusation of and bitterness toward her made it impossible to consider Miss Markton as an accomplice— for if she were holding the money in collusion with him it would be to his own interest to have her movements free. There was only one possible explanation: that Markton himself had removed and secreted the money.

From the Tombs I went directly to the Montague Bank—but the president was not in, and since the theft had not been made public I hesitated to confer with any other of the officials. Accordingly I returned to my office, leaving word that I would call again the following morning. I wanted, if possible, to get a trace of the money before seeing the president, knowing that to be the easiest way to clear Miss Markton of the breath of suspicion.

That evening I called on Miss Markton at her home.

To all outward appearance it was merely the counterpart of any other New York apartment of the better class; but her presence invested it with a distinct charm and attractiveness.

As I explained to her, I really had no excuse for calling; I had done nothing conclusive, having been unable to get the slightest trace of the missing money; and the only real news I had—that of her uncle's hostility toward her—was both unwelcome and unimportant. I ended by asking her if she could guess at any possible reason for Markton's confession.

"That," she said, after a moment's hesitation, "is easily explained. Uncle Will is the most lovable man in the world, but he has always been weak and somewhat of a coward. It was simply what you would call lack of nerve. That is why I find it almost impossible to believe you are right in supposing he has the money, or knows where it is.

"Of course they have tried every means to force him to tell, and I don't see how he could hold out against them, if he knew. And yet," she continued after a moment's thought, "where can it be? Perhaps you are right, after all; at any rate, I hope you find it."

"And I, too," I said earnestly. "You know, Miss Markton, I am interested in this case as I have never been in any other. It is not only that I wish to prove you innocent; your name must not even be mentioned—that is, publicly. It is to that end that I am working—I trust, successfully. It is the greatest pleasure of my life to be allowed to help you."

Miss Markton rose suddenly and walked to the window. When she turned back again her eyes were moist with tears and the hand she held toward me trembled as I grasped it in my own.

"Really, Mr. Moorfield," she smiled falteringly, "I

am very silly. You must forgive me; but I have never had a great deal of friendship, and yours is very sweet to me. And just to prove it," she added with a brave attempt at gaiety, "I am going to be very kind and send you home to bed!"

She finished with an adorable little smile that haunted me long after I reached my own chambers, which, for the first time in my life, seemed lonely and bare and cheerless.

How little, after all, do we shape our actions by reason, when once the senses feel their strength! The lightest perfume of a woman's hair is sufficient to benumb the strongest brain; the slightest glance from her eyes is blinding, fatal. And how hideously ugly does the truth appear when our senses have forced us to nurse a lie!

It would have been strange indeed if I had not succeeded in ridding Lillian Markton of the suspicion that had fallen upon her. I had set my heart on it; I felt in my heart that she was innocent; and I expended all my faculties and energy in her assistance.

I soon gave up all hope of finding any trace of the missing money. Markton remained firm in his statement that he had placed it in the safe, and that when he went for it he found it gone. A careful search of the apartment revealed nothing. I attempted to communicate with the confederate whom Markton had mentioned in his confession, but found that the police had exhausted all inquiries in that direction, and without success.

The money seemed absolutely to have disappeared from the face of the earth. I learned that the police had spread their net in all directions; that every possible clue had been unearthed and developed—in vain.

At last, in despair, I made a long-deferred call on the president of the Montague Bank.

"I have been expecting to see you," said the bank

official as I entered his office, "since you left your card on Tuesday. Pray be seated!"

I came to the point at once without preliminary.

"I have come," I said, "as the representative of Miss Lillian Markton. For the past week her every move has been spied upon—wherever she has gone she has been followed, presumably by detectives in your employ. Further, she has every reason to fear that she will be publicly accused of complicity in the theft to which her uncle has confessed. As a result she is almost in a state of nervous collapse. The thing is monstrously unjust, sir, and you must know it."

As I spoke the bank president was walking up and down the floor. When I stopped he turned and regarded me uncertainly.

"Mr. Moorfield," he said, "I thoroughly appreciate your feelings and those of your client. But what are we to do? We owe it both to ourselves and to others to exhaust every possible effort to recover the stolen money, and certain facts point strongly to the possibility of your client's complicity.

"As far as Miss Markton personally is concerned, I have a high regard for her; she has been a friend of my daughter; and to tell the truth, she would have escaped all annoyance if it had not been for the importunities of my fellow directors. But until the money is found—"

"Which will possibly be never," I interrupted. "Or, at least, not before William Markton has served out his sentence. I fully believe he knows where the money is, and no one else."

"Perhaps so. But can you blame us for trying every possible means for its recovery?"

"No," I said, "that is your right. But surely you have no desire"—my voice was raised almost to appeal—"to persecute the innocent? And you must know—since you know her—you must feel that Miss Markton is not guilty."

For a minute there was silence, while the bank official gazed through the window, lost in thought. Then he turned to me with a gesture of decision.

"Mr. Moorfield," he said, "I'll tell you what I'll do. The proceeding is a little irregular, but that is our own affair. I know—who does not—that you are one of the most conscientious men at the New York bar. I know what your word is worth.

"I know that you would never have taken Miss Markton's case if you had not been absolutely assured of her innocence. You know her story, of course."

"Of course," I agreed.

"Well," he spoke slowly and distinctly, "if you will stake your reputation on Miss Markton's innocence; if you will give me your word that the evidence you have has persuaded you of it, she will be absolutely freed from any further annoyance and from the slightest suspicion."

"But—" I began.

"I know," he interrupted, "that you will be assuming a certain responsibility. But so will I. The point is—that we are both desirous that this girl should be freed from anxiety and trouble. I am merely asking you to do your part."

I hesitated, but only for a moment.

There rose before me the vision of Lillian Markton as I had seen her the evening before, happy and grateful at my assurance of success—her eyes, tender and appealing and trustful, lifted to mine—to me a most perfect picture of innocence and purity. What harm could there possibly be in staking my reputation, even my honor, on what every throb of my heart, every pulsation of my brain proclaimed as an undeniable fact?

Still, as I walked out of the bank and down the street

a few minutes later with the words of my pledge to the president ringing in my ears, I felt a vague uneasiness that would not be reasoned away. I had placed myself in a most peculiar position—I could only trust to the future to justify it.

As for my motives, they were indefinable. I merely felt that I had been pushed on by some irresistible power that had left me helpless and weak before it; and I was weighed down by a sickening sense of impending disaster.

That evening, as Lillian Markton pressed my hand with tender gratitude, I felt my fears disappear as though by magic. With her at my side, cheerful and lighthearted at the news I had imparted to her, my doubts and misgivings of the morning seemed absurd.

At noon of that day, she told me, the espionage of her movements had ceased; and, she added, "I really didn't know how horrible it had been until it was over! Oh! how good it is to feel that there is someone who—who—"

"Well?" I said hopefully. "Who what?"

"Who is a friend," she said, laughing at my eagerness. "Only you aren't much of one or you wouldn't be running off to a business engagement just when I want to talk to you. But there! You know how grateful I am!"

I walked on air and rode on the wings of the angels as I went downtown that night.

The following evening—for the first time—I dined with her at her home. During the day I had made an important decision—to me. I had decided to ask Miss Markton to be my wife. I could no longer conceal from myself the fact that I loved her—indeed, I no longer had any desire to conceal it.

It may be asked why I hesitated at all. I put that question to myself impatiently—and I could find no answer.

No answer—that is, in reason. But always there was in my heart that strange foreboding of evil—something inexplicable that tried to restrain me in spite of myself. I ignored it.

A dozen times that evening I tried to declare my love—to ask Lillian Markton to marry me—but the words somehow refused to come. In fact, I believe it takes a great coward to propose marriage—no man could possibly have the courage.

Miss Markton's mood may have had something to do with it. All her gaiety and cheerfulness of the evening before were gone; but when I attempted to rally her she declared that it was merely a reaction from the strain of the past week, and that all she needed was rest. At my earnest expression of sympathy she rose and crossed slowly to where I sat, resting her arm on the back of my chair.

When I looked up at her I was surprised to find that her eyes were wet with tears.

"Mr. Moorfield—" she said, hesitating, her voice strangely tender. Then, after a long minute of silence, "But no—not tonight," she continued, as though to herself.

She let her hand fall to my shoulder, then hastily drew it away and returned to her own chair.

"If there is anything I can do," I began uncertainly.

"No," she said hurriedly, "there is nothing."

For several minutes we sat in silence. When she spoke again it was to make what I then considered a rather strange request.

"I wish," she said, "to see that picture again—the one on your desk. I wonder—may I call on you tomorrow morning?"

"Certainly," I said; "but it seems—if you wish, I can bring the picture to you instead."

"No," she answered; "if you don't mind I would prefer to see it—to come to your office. Of course, I know that what I am saying sounds queer, but tomorrow you will understand. You don't mind, do you?" she smiled.

For another hour we sat, talking trivialities, and by the time I rose to go Miss Markton was almost cheerful. She accompanied me to the door and stood looking down at me as I descended the stairs, and as I paused at the bottom I heard a faint, tender "Good night."

I have heard it many times since—in my dreams.

The next morning I arrived at the office early, after a bad night. I was in anything but a pleasant mood, and I am afraid I made things rather uncomfortable for one or two callers and for James and the stenographer, who seemed relieved when I dismissed them for the day, saying that I expected someone with whom I wished to be alone.

It was an hour later when the door opened to admit Miss Markton.

"You see," I smiled as I ushered her into the inner office, "I have cleared the way for you. Here is your chair. It was just ten days ago today that you first sat in it. Things have changed since then, haven't they?"

"Yes," said Miss Markton slowly, "things have changed. No," as I took a seat on the window ledge, "sit here—in your own chair. I want to talk to you— that way."

I did as she requested, and drew my chair up in front of the desk, close to hers, while she sat regarding me intently, even wistfully.

Then, as she turned and looked at the picture in front of her, her eyes hardened, and when she spoke it was in a cold, lifeless voice that was new to me.

During what followed she did not look at me once, but gazed steadily at the picture.

"Do you know," she said, "what that picture has done to you—to us? I want you to promise me," she went on before I could speak, "that you will hear me through in silence. That whatever I do or say you will say nothing—till I have finished. Will you promise?"

"But surely—" I began, bewildered.

"No. You must promise."

It was my professional training, I suppose, that led me to nod my head gravely and listen calmly as she continued.

A lawyer grows accustomed to the unusual.

"I have seen that picture in my dreams," she went on. "It has haunted me night and day. I could see your surprise when I asked about it every time I saw you. I knew it was dangerous, but I couldn't help it. Somehow I enjoyed it—I suppose just as a child likes to play with fire. But before I go on—"

She stopped suddenly and, bending forward in her chair, thrust her hand behind the picture and drew forth a package wrapped in paper. Placing it on the desk at my elbow she broke the string and, tearing off the paper, placed the contents before me.

One glance was enough—involuntarily I uttered a cry of amazement.

It was the fifty thousand dollars stolen by William Markton from the Montague Bank!

Opening a large handbag she had carried with her, Miss Markton picked up the package of money and dropped it inside.

"There," she said, patting the bag, "is the money you have been searching for, Mr. Moorfield. I shall keep it. Heaven knows I have earned it!

"You may wonder," she continued as, scarcely hearing or comprehending, I sat with staring eyes set straight before me, "why I did not remove the money without your knowledge. It was because I felt that I owed you an explanation.

"I took the money from Uncle Will's safe ten minutes after he had put it there. At first it was my intention to return it, but after I opened it and saw—well, I am not making excuses. When I found that Uncle Will had been arrested, I saw plainly that I, too, was in danger.

"They were absolutely certain to search the apartment, so I went home to get the money, and started downtown with it, having no idea of where to go. Then I saw that I was being followed, and, thoroughly frightened, came to your office merely by chance, although I had heard something of you. Almost the first thing I saw was the picture and, hardly knowing what I did, I thrust the money behind it when you stooped to throw away your cigar. It was only afterward, when your manner told me that it had not been discovered, that I realized what an excellent hiding place I had chosen.

"You know the rest. You know why I feel myself safe in telling you. And yet you do not know all. There is one thing that such a woman as I am has no right to say to such a man as you. If I had the right"—the hard voice faltered ever so little—"I would say it. Heaven knows it is true. No—let me finish!

"I have fooled you and cheated you enough. I am speaking now simply that you may know me for the thing I am. If I could only—"

Here her voice broke, harsh with pain. As I sat with my head bowed between my hands I felt a breath, the merest touch, on my cheek. A moment later the door closed. She was gone.

* * *

I have never found her except in my dreams.

Perhaps it is just as well.

I seem somehow to get along better with my memories than most men do with their wives; and the passing years have given me philosophy.

As for the picture—I returned it to my friend who painted it, and who later sold it for quite a handsome sum.

Sometimes even memories are sharp-tongued.

ROSE ORCHID

ACCEPTING AS POSTULATES THE ASSERTIONS THAT human beings are pegs, and that Lieutenant Commander Brinsley Reed, U.S.N. was a human being, it follows with certainty that he was beautifully fitted for his particular hole.

He was third in his class out of Annapolis. By the time he attained his two full stripes he had successfully dominated three junior messes and been the subject of unusual commendation in two wardrooms; and before he had advanced halfway up the list he was known as the best deck officer in the North Atlantic.

Four different captains applied for his services as executive when he passed into the next rank. But Lieutenant Commander Reed, who had ideas of his own concerning the proper discipline of a ship, and who was lucky enough to possess a key to a certain door in the bureau at Washington, disappointed them all by obtaining for himself the command of the gunboat *Helena*.

For the two years that followed, every man who had the good fortune to be transferred from the *Helena* to another ship swore at every chance, with violent and profane asseveration, that the *Helena* was a "madhouse."

"The old man's a holy terror," they would say. "Bag

and hammock inspection and fire drill twice a week.
Abandon ship three times a month; and when he can't
think of nothing else it's general quarters. For a seagoin'
hat it's ten days in the brig. And brasswork? Say! Why,
this is a home!''

All of which meant to indicate that Lieutenant Commander Reed was one of those persons who illustrate
and justify the rather curious order of the words in the
phrase: an officer and a gentleman.

He had at one time believed in the Bible; but it had
long ago been discarded for the Blue Book, which is
officially known as ''Navy Regulations, 1914.''

In the third winter under his command, at the conclusion of the annual target practice and maneuvers at
Guantanamo, the *Helena* was ordered to San Juan to relieve the *Chester*, which was returning to go into dry
dock at New York.

Lieutenant Commander Reed was much pleased at
this, for two reasons: first, it would remove him from
continual subordination to a flag officer; and second, he
would have an opportunity to visit a boyhood friend
whom he had not seen for many years, and who was
now the owner of a tobacco plantation in Puerto Rico.
The *Helena* had lain at San Juan for a month the previous spring; but the lieutenant commander had not then
known that his friend was on the island.

After all, the visit proved to be disappointing. I will
not go so far as to say that Lieutenant Commander Reed
had lost all social instinct, but the fact is that in his
endeavor to perfect himself as a military machine he had
forgotten how to be a man. He found his friend dull, and
his friend found him insufferable.

For two days they made a pretense of amusing each
other. On the third morning the lieutenant commander
begged his friend to take no notice of his presence, but

to follow his own inclinations; the guest would amuse himself.

"Very well," the other agreed, "then I shall ride over to the north enclosure; the carts should arrive today. You won't join me?"

The lieutenant commander refused, and spent a miserable day lounging in a hammock between two giant cedars, drinking crushed pineapple and reading some ancient copies of popular magazines. That evening he announced his intention of returning to the *Helena* at San Juan on the following morning.

"But you were to stay a week," his host protested rather feebly. "And a rest will do you good. It's not very amusing out here, but I'd be glad to have you. What's the hurry?"

"Confound your politeness," said the lieutenant commander, who regarded bluntness as an untainted virtue. "It's no good, Dick; we don't cut in. We're only in each other's way—and I want to get back to the ship."

Accordingly, at four o'clock in the following afternoon (the start having been postponed some hours on account of the midday heat), the lieutenant commander mounted his little native pony that had carried him from San Juan to Cerrogordo in six hours, waved a last farewell to his host, and departed on his journey of forty miles across the mountains, through the foothills and down the long plain to the sea.

As he turned into the white wagon road that leads through San Lorenzo, the lieutenant commander felt a pleasant sense of relief.

He understood himself perfectly. Stern, passionately fond of authority, conscious of but one code of morals and of conduct, and supremely happy in his power and ability to enforce it, he was utterly unable to breathe in any other atmosphere than that of his cabin. As his pony carried him forward, past the wonderful blue limestone cliffs and innumerable rushing streams of the southern slope of the Sierra de Luquillo, his mind was thirty miles away, on the decks of the *Helena*.

It dwelt on a score of petty details: the independence of Ensign Brownell, the return of Quartermaster Moran, the disgraceful condition of the pay storeroom at the last Sunday inspection. He considered these matters at some length; he liked their flavor; and he earnestly desired to deal out justice—according to the code.

At Caguas, where he stopped for a cooling drink and a few minutes' rest, he was advised to postpone the continuance of his journey.

"It is dangerous, señor," said the proprietor of the little shop. "See!"

He pointed to the northeast, where, above the top of the dim, blue range, a black cloud was proceeding slowly westward, like a giant treading ponderously from peak to peak.

"Well, what of it?"

"It means a storm, señor; you will be drenched. And the trail over the mountains—at night—"

But the lieutenant commander stopped him with a gesture, mounted his pony, and departed.

He was very nearly in the center of the range, within two miles of the village of Rio, when the storm finally broke. It began with a mild drizzle; and the lieutenant commander dismounted long enough to unstrap the rubber poncho from his saddle and put it on.

He had not proceeded a hundred yards farther when the rain began to descend in torrents. At the same moment the fast-approaching darkness came like a blanket over the narrow trail; and the traveler found himself fighting blindly against whirling sheets of water and the impenetrable blackness of a tropical night.

He soon gave up the attempt to guide his pony; it required all his strength, bending over close against the animal's neck, to maintain his seat. The roar of the wind and the descending torrents seemed terrific; he was incapable of thought or movement.

Something brushed violently against his body, and he felt the pony sway and stumble; then a jar, a feeling as though he was being hurled violently through space. . . .

The lieutenant commander sat up, glanced round, and cursed long and variously. He wanted to know where in the name of the Seven Seas—Then he remembered.

He started to rise to his feet, and suddenly became conscious of a sharp, stinging pain in his left arm; and, trying to raise it, found that it hung helpless at his side. With another oath he stood up and stamped vigorously to assure himself of the seaworthiness of his legs, and gave an involuntarily grunt of pain as the shock communicated itself to the broken arm.

The storm was past.

Overhead the stars gleamed with the soft brilliance of the South. About and above him the thick foliage waved its broad fingers mysteriously in the gentle breeze, and through a rift to the left could be seen the uncertain white outline of a limestone cliff. Toward this the lieutenant commander made his way, thinking to find the trail. The pony was not to be seen.

For perhaps half an hour he searched for the trail, stumbling over roots and fallen branches, occasionally brought to an abrupt stop by a growth of shrubbery and vines too dense to penetrate.

At every step a shiver of pain ran through his body from the injured arm, and his head felt faint and dizzy.

Suddenly he found himself in an open clearing, at the farther end of which he saw a light shining from the window of a cottage. He staggered to it painfully and hammered on the door.

The door opened; the floor seemed to rise to meet him; and once more all was darkness.

When he awoke it was to a feeling of the most delicious warmth and weariness. For some minutes after he became conscious he kept his eyes closed, merely through the lack of desire to open them. Suddenly he heard a voice at his elbow. The words were Spanish.

"No, beloved, he is still asleep."

Another voice, a man's, came from across the room.

"But are you sure?"

"But yes. Really there is no cause for worry. Except for the arm, there is no injury."

"All right. Come here, Rita."

The lieutenant commander opened his eyes. It was broad daylight; evidently he had remained unconscious, or had slept, for many hours. He noted a small bamboo table placed close by the couch on which he lay, an American wicker rocking chair, a homemade palm screen; then his gaze wandered across the room, where stood the owners of the voices.

The girl was directly in front of the man, disclosing to view only the outlines of his figure. Suddenly she moved to one side; and the lieutenant commander gave a start of surprise and closed his eyes involuntarily.

Then he opened them again, slowly and cautiously. The man's face stood out clearly in the light from the open window; and there could be no mistake.

"Decidedly," thought the lieutenant commander, "I'm in a devil of a hole. The wonder is I'm still alive."

Then he lay silent, feigning sleep, and overheard the following dialogue:

"Well, I must go," accompanied by a masculine sigh.

"But, Tota! I've been waiting for you to say that; I've seen it in your eyes. This is our holiday; you promised it."

"Now, little one, don't be unreasonable. How could I foretell the storm? And those *hombres*; you know what they're like. If it were not for the little trees—"

"Very well; then do you go. I shall not miss you; I shall amuse the stranger. I shall sing to him, and prepare for him the little yellow *bisca*, and perhaps—"

The voice ended with an indescribable tone of teasing suggestion.

"Rita! What do you mean?"

There came the sound of feet scurrying across the floor, a sigh, a little breathless laugh, then:

"Oh, Tota, my beloved! Well then, kiss me, kiss me! Ah!"

There was a pause, then the man's voice: "And now—"

"Now you may go. But I shall go with you to the spring. And I want—but come, I'll tell you on the way."

The lieutenant commander heard them go out, leaving the door open behind them; and he opened his eyes and thought swiftly.

He understood at once that he had not been recognized; which was easily accounted for by the facts that he was in "civilians," and that in the past six months he had grown a beard. But there still remained some danger; and this position of insecurity and helplessness was extremely unpleasant. Decidedly, he must get away at the very first opportunity. The first thing to do was to find out about his pony. He would ask the girl when she returned.

Then, suddenly, the lieutenant commander became aware of the fact that he felt exceedingly comfortable. Only his poncho, coat, and boots had been removed, he was covered only by a coarse cotton cloth, and there was a dull, aching pain in the injured arm from wrist to shoulder; still he felt unaccountably easy and contented.

The room, which he now noticed for the first time, though uncarpeted and with bare walls, had an indefinable air of coziness, even of refinement. The light entered with a soft glow at the window opposite, which he surmised to be toward the west; over the other window a green shade was drawn, to exclude the tropical sun.

Two or three wicker chairs, an American sewing machine, and a table or two were all the room contained; yet such was its effect that the lieutenant commander, who had never noticed a mere room before in all his life, found himself studying it with interest and appreciation.

He was roused by the sound of approaching footsteps, and looked up to see the girl coming up the path toward the open door. In her arms was a huge bunch of rose orchids.

She entered the room silently and placing the flowers on a table, tiptoed to the side of the couch. Then seeing that the lieutenant commander's eyes were wide open, she smiled brightly.

"Ah! The señor is awake."

"Yes." In spite of himself, he smiled back at her.

"Well! But you have slept a very long time. And the arm—does it pain you greatly?"

She carefully drew back the coverlet, and the lieutenant commander perceived for the first time that the sleeve of his shirt had been slit to the shoulder and his arm encased in rude splints and bandages.

"Why—I didn't know—" he said, "thanks to you, it is really comfortable."

"That is well. We did the best we could. Oh, but I was so frightened when the señor tumbled in at the door! I thought you were dead. And Tota—Mr. Hurley—that

is, my husband—he thought you would never—but oh!''
She stopped short, and a look of real horror appeared on
her face.

''What is it?'' the lieutenant commander asked in
alarm.

''Why, the señor must be starved!'' she cried. ''And
here I stand and talk like an old woman.''

She turned without another word and fled into the
kitchen.

From thence, for the following fifteen minutes, there
issued a series of most tantalizing sounds and smells.
The lieutenant commander had not realized it before, but
he was hungry—incredibly so.

''Will the señor use the goat's milk?'' Rita called
from the kitchen.

''No; make it black, please,'' he replied.

He was served on the bamboo table, drawn up close
to the couch. Rita, saying that she had work in the next
room, instructed him to call if he needed anything. Then,
struck by a sudden thought, she bent over the table and
cut his meat into little squares, broke the hard bread into
small pieces, and separated the sections of grapefruit,
saying:

''I forgot about the señor's arm. Of course, you are
helpless—like a baby.''

Despite the difficulty of eating with one hand, he
found the meal incredibly good. There were alligator
pears, broiled ham, a spiced omelet, black steaming coffee, and several kinds of fruit.

When he had finished Rita appeared and, after asking
if he smoked, cut off the end of a cigar and lighted it
for him! He lay back on the couch and puffed away in
glorious content, thinking of nothing.

The morning passed. Rita tripped in and out, lightly,
her little sandaled feet gliding noiselessly over the bare

floor, stopping now and then to inquire if the señor was comfortable.

She arranged the rose orchids in a red jar and placed them near him, on the bamboo table. Once she appeared in the doorway to say that her husband had found the señor's pony, unharmed, in the grove of tillandsias over near the trail. She had forgotten to tell the señor before.

"Ah!" said the lieutenant commander. He ought to have been pleased by this information, and perhaps he was. But he made no comment.

Early in the afternoon Rita, having completed her household tasks, sat down in the wicker rocking chair and began to talk. She had brought in a pitcher of pineapple juice and offered a glass of it to the señor, who leaned back against a heap of cushions and sipped luxuriously.

"The señor was going to San Juan?" said Rita abruptly.

The lieutenant commander nodded.

"Ah! It is a wonderful city—San Juan. I used to live there." She sighed, and clasped her hands back of her head. Her form, small and wonderfully graceful, was outlined against the back of the chair like the "Sibyl" of Velásquez.

"It was very gay. The music at night, and the promenade, and the little chairs that used to fall under the weight of the big Americans. And how we would scowl when we were forced to stand while they played the— what you call it?—the 'Star Spangle Banner'!"

The lieutenant commander sipped away in silence, watching her.

Rita sighed again.

"Oh, it all seems so very long ago! And yet it is only a few months. And perhaps, some day I shall see it again."

"Are you lonely—out here?"

The lieutenant commander realized with surprise that he was really interested to know her answer.

He read it in her eyes. They grew large, and glowed with eloquent negation.

"No, no! How could I be, with Tota?" Involuntarily, as she pronounced the name, her voice softened with tenderness. "That is my husband," she continued proudly.

"You have not seen him. He is an American, too. And one thing is hard—it is that I never can talk about him. Even my mother—she was angry when Tota took me away. I suppose that is why," she threw at the señor a glance at once ingenuous and reserved, "I want to talk to you."

The lieutenant commander felt uncomfortable.

"So you are married," he observed foolishly.

Rita frowned. Then the frown gave way to a little, amused, happy laugh.

"Why, what does the señor think? But then, you Americans are all alike. That is, all except Tota. He will be here soon; he wants to see you. He is a very wonderful man, and so good, señor."

"I have no doubt of it," the lieutenant commander said dryly.

"Yes. We came here but nine, ten months ago, and already we have many acres of coffee trees. There were some—that was in May—already in bloom. Have you ever seen them, señor? The little white blossoms that look like tiny stars, they are so very white? Tota says he prefers them brown, like my face," and she laughed delightedly at her Tota's stupid joke.

Of this chatter the lieutenant commander was hearing very little; but he was looking at Rita—her soft brown, slender arms, her lithe form, full of nervous grace, her dark, glowing, ever-changing eyes. I have not attempted to describe her, and I shall not; you must use your imagination. You may judge a little of her charm by the fact that, as he sat and looked at her and listened to her voice, Lieutenant Commander Reed, for the first time in his life, had emotions.

For an hour she rattled on, mostly of Tota, and the señor sat and sipped pineapple, now and then interposing a nod or a word. He became utterly unconscious of everything in the world but her presence and his delight in it, and he felt a distinct and disagreeable shock when the door was suddenly opened and a man appeared in the room.

It was Hurley.

Rita sprang from her chair and ran to him.

"Tota!" she cried.

Hurley folded her in his arms and kissed her.

"Well, little one, I kept my promise." Then he turned to the señor, "You must excuse us," he smiled, utterly unabashed.

Rita had an arm about his neck and was clinging to the lapel of his jacket with the other hand.

The lieutenant commander was experiencing a curious and hitherto undreamed-of sensation. A lump in his throat was choking him, and he felt a tight gripping in his chest. But his mind was working rapidly; and he made his decision almost without hesitation.

"I've been waiting for you," he said to Hurley. "I understand you found my pony. Bring him up."

At the tone of command the man started and glanced keenly at the lieutenant commander, who remembered too late that he should have attempted to disguise his voice. He thought of his broken arm, and braced himself for whatever might come.

Hurley walked over to the couch and stood looking

down at him in silence. The expression in his eyes was distinctly unpleasant; but the lieutenant commander perceived that it was alloyed with doubt.

"Have I ever seen you before?" Hurley said finally.

The lieutenant commander achieved a smile of surprise.

"What makes you think so?" he asked.

"Why did you speak to me—like that?"

The lieutenant commander, being rather clever, did not make the mistake of apologizing. Instead, his tone was one of irritation as he said: "How do I know? Do you expect a man with a broken arm to get up and bow?"

For another minute Hurley stood above him, eyeing him keenly. Then he turned.

"I don't know," he muttered. "I'll bring up your pony. Come, Rita; you come with me."

They returned shortly with the pony, saddled and bridled. Hurley, sending Rita to another room, helped the lieutenant commander put on his coat and boots, placed the injured arm in a sling, and strapped his poncho back of the saddle. Then he steadied him with both hands, carefully, while he mounted.

"You ought to be in San Juan by seven," said Hurley, standing in the doorway. "That's a good hour and a half before dark. The trail runs over there," pointing to the west, "by that first blue cliff. You can't miss it. And I guess I made a mistake in there," he continued, a little awkwardly. "I meant no offense, sir."

For more reasons than one the lieutenant commander made no reply. He started the pony as gently as possible out of respect for the broken arm, and nodded a farewell. As he met the trail under the cliff he turned and looked back. Hurley and Rita were standing together in the doorway.

*   *   *

Lieutenant Commander Reed was a man of decision. Whenever he met a problem he liked to face it squarely, analyze it thoroughly, and decide it quickly. This he had always done.

But the problem which was now before him defied analysis. It seemed somehow intangible, fleeting, ungraspable. He tried one after another of his cherished rules, and found that none of them fitted.

For the first three hours of the last stage of his journey to San Juan his mind was in an uncomfortable and entirely unique condition of flexibility. As might have been expected, the weight of habit preponderated and he decided in favor of duty.

Owing to the broken arm, the four hours' ride was slow and painful, but he suffered no further mishap. As Hurley had predicted, exactly at seven o'clock he climbed from the naval station wharf at San Juan into the commandant's gig.

On board the *Helena* all was confusion and despair. They had not expected their commanding officer for another four days, and they were having the time of their lives.

The first luff, who was an easygoing, good-natured fellow, who possessed a hearty dislike for his skipper, had taken advantage of his absence.

There had been no inspections or drills of any kind, the brasswork had not been touched, the decks had received merely a gentle flushing with the hose, and every classed man on the ship had been granted shore liberty.

You may imagine the effect of this state of affairs on Lieutenant Commander Reed. Within two hours after his arrival every man and officer on board was ready for insubordination or mutiny, or worse, and the first luff heard his skipper's voice in his dreams.

At eleven o'clock the following morning Lieutenant Commander Reed sat in his cabin, holding a pen in his hand and gazing thoughtfully at a pad of official memorandum paper on the desk before him.

He had got his disordered ship and crew in something like a presentable and tractable condition, and was preparing to put into effect his decision of the afternoon before.

He frowned and sighed at intervals, and finally rose, walked over to a porthole and stood for some time gazing out on El Morro and the rocky coast.

Finally, with a gesture of decision, he returned to the desk, arranged the pad of paper, and wrote as follows:

Ensign G. J. Rowley, U.S.N.,
U.S.S. Helena.
Sir:

You will take four men and proceed at once to the village of Rio, twenty miles from San Juan on the Caguas road.

Two miles beyond Rio, in a cottage three hundred yards to the left of the trail, you will find James Moser, Chief Yeoman, a deserter from the U.S.S. *Helena*.

He has assumed the name of Hurley. You will arrest him and deliver him on shipboard. You are advised to proceed with caution.

> Respectfully,
> Brinsley Reed,
> Lt. Comd'r., U.S.N.,
> Commanding.

He read the order through slowly, and pushed a button on the desk for his orderly. Then removing the order from the pad, he reread it more slowly still, while a deep frown gathered on his forehead.

The decision had been made.

Suddenly he opened a drawer at the side of his desk and took from it—a rose orchid!

I have no idea where he got it; possibly he had taken advantage of Rita's absence while she had gone with Tota to fetch the pony.

But then that is scarcely possible, since the lieutenant commander was the last man in the world to be swayed by any weak sentiment.

"Did you ring, sir?"

The orderly's voice sounded from the doorway, and his commanding officer actually blushed as he hastily slipped the orchid back into the drawer.

Then he turned to the orderly:

"Learn to stand at attention till you're spoken to!" he roared. "No, I didn't ring! Get out of here!"

It is little wonder that Ensign Rowley failed to carry out the order, since it was no part of his duty to go searching about in his skipper's wastebasket for torn bits of paper.

THE INEVITABLE THIRD

I HAVE NEVER BEEN ABLE TO ACCOUNT FOR JIMMIE'S success—in a particular way—except on the theory that a Divine Providence protects the weak. How many of us, after getting what we want, are able to hold onto it? It is not an unusual thing to see even a strong man knocked on the head by a detached chunk of what he had taken to be his astral glory, when his stars begin going sideways instead of pursuing their proper and natural courses.

Now and then we find an Avier or a Prometheus, able to stand unmoved and hurl defiance at Fate, but the best that most of us can do is to shut our eyes and dodge—quick.

That is what Jimmie did.

Jimmie was one of those disquieting creatures who are able to extract an astonishing amount of happiness out of a clerkship in Wall Street, a Harlem flat, and a wife. They make us wonder if we are not very silly indeed to worry about lost tribes and the ruins of Philæ and the value of post-impressionism.

Jimmie was abnormally happy. He took an immense pride in filling the flat with all sorts of horrible things known as modern furniture, for of course he was entirely without taste. He spent just a little more than he should on presents for his wife, and he fitted up the little room on the left of the kitchen as a den for himself.

Once, in a moment of unguarded optimism, he purchased a small white-enameled crib. It stood unused in a corner of the second bedroom, as a constant reminder to him of the only blank in Jimmie's life.

Jimmie liked his job at the office, and it showed in his work, so that his salary was raised regularly every six months. He came to have a room of his own, with a rolltop desk and a stenographer.

Certainly, Jimmie thought, he was getting on, and he began to be a little proud of himself. This lasted three years.

Still the little white-enameled crib remained unoccupied; and this, if only Jimmie had known it, was dangerous. A vacuum is as abhorrent to a woman as it is to Nature. Jimmie should have taken care to fill it up himself—at least with sympathy—instead of leaving it to the first one who should perceive it.

But Jimmie was undeniably a fool. He was not aware of the peculiar shades imparted to a word by the flicker of an eyelash, the moistening of lips, the tremulous closing of a hand. He knew merely that he loved his wife, and saw no reason why she should be otherwise than perfectly happy, since he always came directly home from the office and found pleasure in nothing without her.

He did not perceive the necessity of finding a new interest to take the place of the natural one, which had been denied her. In short, he was not versed in the workings of a woman's mind, as was the inevitable third.

The name of the inevitable third was Mason.

He came from somewhere across the Atlantic, and his chief business in life—though neither Jimmie nor Nell knew this—was picking up one or another of the Ten

Commandments that had been shattered by somebody else, and amusing himself by fitting together the broken pieces in bizarre patterns of his own.

Nell met him at an afternoon recital in the tea-belt, and described him to Jimmie at the dinner table that evening as "the most interesting man she had ever met." Jimmie nodded absently and helped himself to another piece of steak.

He was in the middle of an intricate mental calculation which had to do with his wife's approaching birthday.

Nell grew quite eloquent in her eulogy of Mason, ending with, "What do you think of that?"

"Eh? What?" said Jimmie.

"You weren't listening at all!"

"Right," Jimmie admitted, laughing. "I was thinking of—er—an important matter. What were you saying?"

"Nothing."

"Come now! I was thinking of you."

"It doesn't matter. You wouldn't understand, anyway. All you know is your dirty old office."

Jimmie whistled.

"What the deuce—" he began, but his wife promptly burst into tears, and he spent the next thirty minutes trying to comfort her.

Twice during the following week Jimmie returned home from his office at half past five to find his wife absent.

The first time she answered his question with a brief "At a matinée"; the second, she told at some length of having spent the afternoon at the Museum of Art with Mason. Jimmie looked nonplused for a moment.

He stood in the doorway leading to the kitchen, his hands in his pockets, watching his wife as she busied herself among the pots and pans. Then he walked through the flat to the windows in front and stood looking down on the street, his brow puckered into a puzzled frown; and finally he returned to the doorway.

"Who is this Mason?" he asked.

"I told you the other day." Nell was slicing big, ripe tomatoes that were no redder than her lips. "I met him at Osborne's."

"I know—but who is he?"

"He is a gentleman."

"Oh," said Jimmie vaguely. He stood for a moment regarding his wife uncertainly, then continued: "But I say, Nell—"

"Well?"

"Nothing," said Jimmie.

He went into the front room, seated himself, and picked up a newspaper. But when he was called to dinner a half-hour later the paper remained unread.

That was, of course, the proper time for an explanation. But how could Nell explain something which she didn't understand herself?

She felt an incredible, an insatiable longing for something—but what? Jimmie bored and irritated her, and the very sight of her neat kitchen became hateful to her. Add to this the fact that she was both secretive and ignorant—in a restricted sense—and the curious conclusion at which she finally arrived loses much of its strangeness.

Its result was that she spent every afternoon of the following week riding or driving with Mason, whose sympathy and tenderness were never-failing, and curiously satisfying.

She lied to Jimmie. She told him each evening that she had spent the entire day at home, and that she was feeling under the weather.

"Want a doctor?" Jimmie would ask solicitously.

"No," she would answer, "it's just a headache."

Then she would go to bed and cry herself to sleep,

while Jimmie sat in his den staring at the wallpaper and wondering what the devil was the matter.

It was on Saturday that Jimmie's married sister found herself shopping at Tenth Street round noon and decided to take lunch with him. She telephoned his office.

She was ten years older than Jimmie, and had two children; and she felt that he needed advice. Besides, being a woman, she had a right to be curious. She came to the point at once.

"Who was Nell riding with yesterday?"

"What?" said Jimmie blankly.

"I asked," repeated his sister with emphasis, "whom Nell was riding with yesterday."

Now Jimmie knew perfectly well that his wife had remained at home all of the previous day, for she had told him so. Therefore, it was obvious that she had not been riding with anyone. Still, he knew his sister. She usually knew what she was talking about.

Jimmie rose to the occasion like a gentleman.

"A chap named Mason," said. "A friend of mine. Why?"

His sister eyed him shrewdly.

"Lord save us, Jimmie, you can't fool me," she declared. "You're in trouble. What is it?"

But Jimmie turned the question aside, and many other similar ones, and, freeing himself as quickly as possible, returned to the office. He sat at his desk for two hours, chewing up unlighted cigars and gazing at the wall before him in a sort of hurt surprise.

It was Jimmie's first glimpse of hell, and he didn't at all understand it. Finally he put on his hat and went home.

He found no one there. He wandered to and fro through the flat a dozen or more times, then pulled a chair up close to the window and sat down to wait—and watch. For a full hour he sat, silent and still, his eyes glued on the street below; and gradually cold fear filled all his veins and chilled his heart.

Perhaps—the thought formed slowly—perhaps she would never return. Even now she had gone—

Perspiration covered his brow, and his face was white. He felt no anger, but a most potent and terrible fear. When Nell saw his face through the window as she came up the street ten minutes later she hardly recognized it.

"What's the matter?" asked Nell calmly, as she entered the door which Jimmie had opened.

Jimmie folded his arms about her.

"Thank God!" he said devoutly. "Oh, Nell, I thought—"

Nell struggled from his embrace.

"Well? You thought?"

Then Jimmie stammered an incoherent account of his meeting with his sister and what she had told him.

"Of course," he finished, "I didn't believe her, but I thought—you might—so I told her it was Mason."

There was a pause, then: "It was Mason," said Nell calmly.

Jimmie gazed at her for a full minute, frankly disbelieving.

"But you told me—" he began.

"I know," Nell interrupted wearily.

She hesitated, and looked at her husband uncertainly, then, clenching her hands and advancing a step toward him, she began to speak hurriedly and in a low tone.

She spoke of Mason. And when she had finished, and ended by sinking down onto the floor and bursting into tears, Jimmie stood as one stunned, watching his little world crumble and fall about his ears.

And yet the very worst of Nell's conduct was the telling of a lie—not exactly an unique sin. But Jimmie could not perceive this. Being what he was, he was unable either to judge or consider—he merely *felt*. And Nell no longer loved him.

As she sat on the floor at his feet, her face buried in her hands and her body shaking with convulsive sobs, Jimmie actually felt that *he* was the one who needed sympathy and counsel. He trembled weakly and stared at his wife in a miserable silence.

When Nell had become calmer she rose and seated herself on a chair and spoke again, in a tone of weariness and despair. She explained that though she no longer loved Jimmie, she did not want to leave him. Not from a sense of duty, she simply preferred to remain.

No doubt it would be very hard for both of them, but she thought that was best. As for Mason, she would continue to regard him as her friend. He had been very kind to her, and Jimmie would never understand, and men were beasts anyway, and she didn't want to leave Jimmie, and she wanted to be left alone.

So Jimmie left the house, and returned two hours later to a silent and tasteless dinner. As soon as it was finished Nell went to bed, complaining of a headache; and Jimmie sat alone until late in the half-lighted dining room, fondling his misery.

A week passed by. Jimmie, racking his brain for an explanation or a solution, failed entirely to realize the meaning of the catastrophe. He was conscious only of the pain—the dull aching pain that filled every thought and movement and ate his soul. A stronger man would have dominated the situation—and the consequences would have been extremely unpleasant. Jimmie was fortunate enough to be helpless.

Each evening, as he returned home from the office, Jimmie determined to have the matter out with his wife, he perceived that he was being made ridiculous, which is of all things most intolerable to a man. And each evening, seeing Nell's white face and averted eyes, his courage failed him, and the words would not come.

He spent two afternoons sitting on a bench on Riverside Drive, both fearing and hoping to see Nell with Mason, and feeling a curious sense of disappointment when his quest failed. He wanted very much to see Mason, and he feared him—horribly.

Then, one evening, he found a note on the mantel in the dining room, addressed to Nell, who had evidently been at no pains to conceal it. It was from Mason, and contained the information that he would call at her home on the following afternoon.

Jimmie read it over twice, and found himself studying the handwriting with a sort of detached curiosity, when Nell entered from the kitchen. She stopped short, glancing at the note, then at Jimmie's face; and for some moments they stood looking at each other in silence.

When, a few minutes later, they seated themselves at the table, Jimmie, controlling his voice with difficulty, said simply:

"Have you answered it?"

"Yes," said Nell. The meal proceeded in silence.

It was this that at last roused Jimmie to action. He decided on the weakest possible course—and the wisest.

After six hours of tortured thought and painful indecision, he sat down on the edge of his bed at three o'clock in the morning and wrote a farewell letter to his wife. It was a curious performance.

He declared that he had always loved her and always would, and she would never hear from him again, because she would be happy, and it was her fault, but he forgave her, and he knew that what he was doing wasn't manly but he couldn't help it, and he had never seen Mason anyway (he repeated this three times), and he didn't believe that she had ever loved him, and God bless her.

This he folded and sealed and left on the table in his own room.

At seven o'clock, while Nell was still asleep, he left the house with two full suitcases, which he carried to an express office and there ordered delivered at the home of his married sister.

Then, after an attempt at breakfast in a lunchroom, he wandered about the streets aimlessly until time to go to his office. He didn't at all realize what he had done, and he felt a curious sense of relief and freedom.

At one o'clock that afternoon, while Jimmie was standing at his thirtieth-story office window, staring with unseeing eyes at the antlike throng in the street below, Nell was sitting on the edge of her husband's bed, holding in her hand an open letter which she had just read for the third time.

She had found it only a half-hour before, and she was trying to reconcile the moisture in her eyes and the uncomfortable lump in her throat with the fact that there was now nothing—apparently—between her and her desire.

She understood Jimmie's action perfectly, and she felt that he deserved to be despised for his weakness. But she was conscious only of an intolerable pity. She refolded the note and placed it in the bosom of her dress.

She was, of course, glad that Jimmie had gone. But somehow—

In the meantime Mason was to come at three o'clock. Yesterday this thought had filled her with a keen pleasure. Now she experienced an unaccountable feeling of revulsion, and she hated herself for it.

If there had been nothing irrevocably wrong in her

relations with Mason, it was more through good luck than her own wisdom; she had been willing to surrender everything except the hollow shell of outward appearances; and now that the shell was gone, she saw the naked folly, the common ugliness of the thing, and she shrank from it.

She contemplated the Nell of yesterday with an indescribable contempt, and wondered why. Then she threw herself, face downward, on the bed, and remained so, silent, for a long time.

When the doorbell rang she did not move. It rang again and again. During the pause that followed Nell heard her heart beating loudly, as it seemed, in protest.

Then the bell rang once more, long and violently—and then silence.

As Jimmie approached the entrance of his married sister's apartment that evening he felt an almost uncontrollable impulse to turn and run. He had had a whole day in which to consider his conduct, and he was beginning to be very much ashamed of it.

At the moment, it had appeared to be merely the means of escape from an intolerable situation; its desperateness and finality were only now beginning to be apparent to him. In short, he was in a very fair way to repent at leisure.

His sister met him at the door. She looked startled at the sight of his face. It was white and drawn, and his eyes were red.

"What's the matter?" asked his sister. "What has happened to you?"

Then her face became stern and her lips set in a straight line.

"No," said Jimmie. "Not that, sis. But, for God's sake, tell me what to do."

It was an interminable and considerably tangled story that he told her, after she had taken him into her own room, but his sister had no difficulty in understanding it. She sat in grim silence while he explained his part of the marital wreck, and confessed his utter inability to understand his wife's conduct.

When he had finished his sister rose without a word and, going to her wardrobe, began to put on her hat and gloves. Jimmie rose of his feet in alarm and opened his mouth to protest. Before he could speak his sister said:

"You keep still. You've said enough."

"But—where are you going?" stammered Jimmie.

His sister completed her preparations in silence. At the door she turned.

"Jimmie," she said, "if you are my own brother, you're a perfect idiot. Why, in the name of Heaven, didn't you tell me before? You know very well you never had any sense—I've told you so. All this could have been prevented. Now maybe it's too late. I'm going to see Nell, and I want you to follow me in two hours. I want to see her first alone. Remember—two hours—don't come sooner."

"But I say—" began Jimmie.

The door slammed in his face.

Jimmie sat down in a chair and wondered why she had called him an idiot, and how it could "all have been prevented," and what she could possibly say to Nell. Then his brother-in-law arrived and insisted on Jimmie dining with him. Jimmie protested that he wasn't hungry, but was finally dragged away.

"Is Nell sick?" asked the brother-in-law as they seated themselves at the table. He had been told that his wife had gone to see her.

Jimmie mumbled a negative.

"Anything wrong?"

"No."

After which the brother-in-law remained discreetly silent, while Jimmie strove valiantly with a fierce desire to tell him everything, being restrained only by a sense of the weakness and folly of his own conduct.

He pretended to eat, fingered his napkin and knife and fork nervously, and looked at his watch every two minutes. As the brother-in-law pushed back his coffee cup and lit a cigar a maid appeared in the doorway.

"You're wanted at home at once, sir," she said to Jimmie. "Mrs. Thrawn just telephoned."

Jimmie jumped to his feet and, without a word to the astonished brother-in-law, rushed through the hall, down the stairs, and out of the house.

"Say," shouted the brother-in-law, "wait a minute! You forgot your hat!"

But Jimmie was already out of sight.

As he stepped from the car, which had made an incredible number of stops and had seemed to go forward at less than a snail's pace, and approached the door of his own flat, Jimmie slackened his gait and finally halted.

There were so many possibilities behind that door that his heart stood still at the bare thought of them, and he hesitated, both dreading and longing to go on. His knees trembled disgracefully as he ascended the stairs. At the top he found his sister, who placed a finger on her lips to enjoin silence and led him into the front room.

"Where's Nell?" Jimmie's voice was harsh and unnatural.

His sister pointed toward the bedroom within.

"Sleeping. Goodness knows she needs it," she said grimly. "You've worried her nearly to death."

At the first word Jimmie had started for the bedroom, but she barred the way and pushed him back into a chair. He sat and glared at her.

"I worried her?" he said weakly. "What have I done?"

His sister appeared to consider.

"I suppose it's been hard for you, too," she said finally. "Your ignorance amounts to a positive crime, but you've had to suffer for it. How long has she known this Mason?"

Jimmie reflected. "About a month."

"I thought so. Now, you listen to me—then go in and see her. There's a certain period in a woman's life, Jimmie, that no man will ever understand. Often we don't understand it ourselves—Nell didn't. We are filled with an impatient longing, a dissatisfaction, and a sort of haunting fear. It is indescribable.

"While it lasts we need sympathy, forbearance, understanding; and we are always more or less irresponsible and—queer. In Nell's case"—she smiled grimly— "it was rather more than less. But she has done nothing really wrong, and if I ever hear of your saying anything to her—"

She paused and eyed Jimmie sternly.

"I won't," he promised. "But what do you mean? What's been the matter with her?"

And then, leaning forward in her chair and speaking in a low tone, his sister released the great secret.

As she continued Jimmie's face took on an expression of blank incredulity and astonishment, and when she had finished he sat and regarded her in speechless amazement.

His sister leaned forward and spoke again, and Jimmie found his tongue.

"Four months!" he shouted. "Why didn't she tell me?"

"Because she didn't know herself till I told her," his sister replied—to an empty room.

Jimmie had cleared her chair with one bound and disappeared within.

He left the doors open behind him and there issued therefrom for the next fifteen minutes a series of curious sounds and noises and the mingling of two voices, utterly unintelligible and yet somehow full of meaning.

Jimmie's sister sat, with a half-wistful, reminiscent smile, recalling a certain far-off period in her own life— the day when the amazing beauty and glory of a new and mysterious world had unfolded itself. Since then it had dimmed—but there was the memory.

Then Jimmie reappeared, his face radiant and joyous, and dragging after him—the white-enameled crib! His sister stared at him in wonder.

"What in the name of goodness are you going to do with that?" she demanded.

"Why," said Jimmie, visibly embarrassed, "I thought—er—to get it ready, you know."

His sister gasped; then she burst into an uncontrollable fit of laughter. Then she commanded Jimmie to take the crib back where it belonged.

Jimmie regarded her with an air of dignified importance.

"Mind your own business," said he. "This is mine. May I ask what you had to do with it?"

"Nothing whatever," said his sister meekly.

Whereupon Jimmie took out his handkerchief and began to dust the crib with minute care and particularity— the crib which was destined, some five months later, to become the rhythmic resting-place of the inevitable third.

For Mason, of course, had lost his job.

THE LIE

T HOMAS HANLEY HAD ALWAYS CONSIDERED HIM-
self, and been considered by others, as a man
without a heart. Firm, cold, entrenched behind the
rigid morality of a Puritan conscience, he had lived
wisely but not well.

He was the least loved and the most respected man in
Burrton. As the result of unremitting toil and unfailing
energy, he had come to be the owner of the lumber mill
in which he had begun as a day laborer, and in it was
all his life.

No man was so just, and none so entirely without
mercy. No man had so fairly earned all that he possessed, nor held it with a stronger hand.

Strength, however, is admirable, and may be forgiven;
but with it he had an idea. He hated shams, he hated
politeness, he hated compromises, and, above all, he
hated a lie. His strict and literal veracity was not a matter
of pride to him; it was too natural. If one saw the sun
rise at six o'clock, one still might doubt; one's watch
might be wrong; but if Thomas Hanley *said* the sun rose
at six o'clock it was so. It is something to have acquired
such an authority.

So extreme a practice of so stern a virtue excluded
the lighter ones. One neither expected nor received gen-

erosity or sympathy at the hands of Thomas Hanley. He had reached the age of forty without ever having performed one act of injustice or one act of kindness, hating nothing but a lie and loving no one.

The town had already begun to amuse itself by conjectures as to the future owner of the lumber mill. There was no one in Burrton who had reason to entertain any hopes of the legacy; Hanley despised charitable institutions, and there was certainly no chance of his marrying.

Jim Blood declared it to be his firm belief that Hanley would burn the mill down and himself with it before he would allow it to pass into the hands of anyone else. When a man's native town begins to jest about his death he might as well die.

And then, on a certain May evening, the inhabitants of Burrton experienced a shock from which they never recovered. The news traveled from one end of the town to the other as swiftly as the whirling of the great wheels in Hanley's lumber mill. It was amazing, unprecedented, unbelievable. Thomas Hanley had walked home with Marie Barber.

Burrton was prepared for the worst, and it came speedily. The courtship was a curious one. That Hanley was in love no one was willing to believe. He even half doubted it himself. But he knew that he wanted Marie more than he had ever wanted anything in all his life, and he set about the accomplishment of his purpose in his own stern and forceful manner.

Marie was pretty, young, and popular. At Hanley's first advances she was half frightened and half amused, then complacent. She never really loved him perhaps, but the devoted attention of a man who ignored the whole world beside was flattering to her vanity. In addition, she had a mother, and he owned the best business in Burrton. The combination proved irresistible; in September they were married.

Marie soon found that she need expect no gaiety or pleasure in her new home. Hanley loved as he had lived, sternly and honestly. Unsocial by nature and morose by habit, he would have found it impossible to enter into the little interests and frivolities that were Marie's chief delight, even if he had cared to try. He grudged her nothing and allowed her all the freedom she could ask, but held himself aloof from the idle and harmless pleasures which she had learned to enjoy.

The effect of this was exactly the opposite from that predicted by the good people of Burrton. Marie, whether from the mere pleasure of novelty, or from a genuine affection for her husband, began seriously to occupy herself with the task of making his home pleasant and his life agreeable.

She gradually dropped or neglected her large circle of friends and acquaintances, spent more and more of her time at home or at her mother's, assumed active care of the somewhat elaborate household Hanley had provided for her, and bade fair to become as severe a recluse and as rigid a moralist as himself.

Hanley regarded this change in his wife's attitude toward life with a sort of grim humor; otherwise with indifference. He had never either asked or expected anyone else to practice his own stern code of existence, least of all Marie, who had been spoiled.

The strict censorship which he maintained over his own tongue and actions was not extended to others; he simply ignored them. He loved Marie with an intensity which he kept locked in his own breast; he asked of her only that she be a faithful wife, and annoyed her with no eager demonstrations of his affection or curious inquisition of her conduct.

Marie, who was fast acquiring a philosophy of her own, had no inkling of the fire and passion that was hidden by this outward reserve. Consequently, when she returned one evening from a visit to her mother and whispered in her husband's ear the sweetest secret a wife may have, she was surprised at the fierce tenderness of his embraces and caresses.

Hanley recovered himself shortly and sat down to discuss the coming event with the seriousness it deserved. Marie answered his businesslike questions as well as possible, and when he was finished crossed over to his chair and put her arms round his neck.

"Dear," she whispered, "don't you hope it will be a little girl?"

Her eyes were moist with tears and her voice trembled with an anticipative tenderness.

Hanley rose to his feet.

"Why, certainly not," he answered; "it must be a boy."

And he passed out of the room and upstairs to his own chamber.

Marie sat down on the chair he had left and wept for the first time since her wedding. Afterward she was surprised at her own weakness. Why, she thought, should she expect Thomas Hanley to be otherwise than brutal? Since he had no feeling, she should not be surprised that he showed none.

Another man might at least have pretended to sympathize with her desire; but not Thomas Hanley, who had never lied even to himself. She remembered that her mother had warned her not to expect any tenderness from her husband, and she reflected somewhat bitterly that he was probably even now reproaching himself for the transient emotion he had exhibited in the first surprise at her announcement.

The months passed rapidly. Autumn disappeared, its bright reds and sober browns giving way regretfully to bare branches and dreary nakedness; the cold silences of winter came with the melancholy of their long nights and the false brilliance of their days, and in their turn were superseded by the sharp winds and muddy thaws of March; and then the world once more awoke to the glad call of spring.

How sweet the air! How green the grass! With what joyous notes did the birds salute the return of life, and how the little twigs with their fresh opening buds trembled with innocent delight!

Marie heard and saw this ever-recurring call of nature, and found an answering voice within her. In the first few months of her marriage, repelled by Hanley's coldness and tired of the idle amusements she had previously enjoyed, she had sometimes wondered what she had been born for. Now she knew.

As she sat by an open window, embroidering a tiny little dress that certainly was not intended for herself, she closed her eyes dreamily to hide from the world outside the wave of exquisite emotion that swept over her.

Marie, like the spoiled child that she was, was attempting to dictate to nature. These little garments spread about in delightful confusion were every one trimmed in blue. Blue ribbon was just now at a premium in Burrton; Marie was extravagant. She had even gone so far as to embroider a name on the little under slips that were safely tucked away in the bureau drawer. The name was Dorothy.

Hanley—I had almost said poor Hanley—was experiencing some difficulty in maintaining his stern indifference. He was, indeed, inclined to give up the whole thing as a bad job. When he came home of an evening to find Marie busily engaged on her endless task of love, when he saw the look of inexpressible tenderness with which she regarded every little indication of his cognizance of the expected arrival, he longed to take her in his arms and keep her there forever.

But the habits of a lifetime are not to be lightly shaken off, especially when they are fortified by all the strength of a stubborn will. Hanley forced himself to be satisfied with surrounding his wife with all possible comfort and care; and, indeed, believed he was doing well. He had ever found his own mind thoroughly capable of supporting itself, and could not realize the existence of a soul that required to be fed from without.

He was more or less irritated at Marie's insistence on what he considered a childish whim.

Though he avoided any further discussion of the subject, he could not understand how she could fail to realize the necessity that there should be a son and heir to perpetuate his name and carry on his business. Many times, on having her own preference intimated before him by some slight incident, he held his tongue with an effort.

The event which they both awaited with anxiety—Marie with a frank and tender eagerness, Hanley with a seeming coldness—came unexpectedly and almost without warning. It was an evening in June. Hanley, after an unusually hard day's work, had retired early and, as was his custom, had fallen asleep instantly. Awakened by the maid, he heard voices murmuring outside his door.

"What is it?" he asked, still half asleep.

"Mrs. Hanley wants you," answered the maid.

Hanley sat up. "Is it—" he asked.

"Yes."

The maid hurried out of the room, and Hanley dressed himself as quickly as possible and followed her. In the hall he found the cook and the laundress, whispering excitedly in a corner. All the rooms were lighted up. The door leading to Marie's room was open.

"What are you doing up here?" Hanley demanded. "Where's Simmons?"

They started at the sound of his voice.

"He's gone after the doctor and Mrs. Barber," the cook said. "We—we—can stay out here in the hall?"

Marie's voice sounded from her room, faint and sweet.

"Of course you may stay," she called. "Come here, Maggie."

The cook's homely face broke into a smile, and her eyes filled with tears. Sometimes even Maggies are wonderful.

"Can I?" she appealed to Hanley.

Without answering, Hanley passed through the hall and down the stairs. Hearing a noise in the kitchen, he went out to find the maid standing on a chair searching among the bottles on the top shelf of the cupboard.

"Why didn't you call me sooner?" Hanley demanded.

The maid continued her search without looking at him.

"Because we were busy," she answered.

Hanley watched her for a minute or two, then walked through the dining room out into the front hall. Why he did not go to Marie he could not possibly have told. Perhaps because of a fear of the tumultuous emotion he felt struggling within him; perhaps because she had not asked for him. Thomas Hanley found himself in the strange position of jealousy toward the cook.

Turning to go upstairs, his eye lighted on the telephone on its stand in the corner. He took up the receiver and called the number of Dr. Perkins's residence.

Dr. Perkins, he was told, had already left and could

be expected to arrive any minute. Then he called up the Barbers. Mrs. Barber was dressing, and would be over shortly. Hanley hung up the receiver and proceeded upstairs to his own room. As he passed over to a chair by the window and sat down he heard the outer door open below and the doctor's voice sounded from the hall.

The minutes passed slowly. Through the wall Hanley could hear the voices of the doctor and the maid in Marie's room. Later, that of Mrs. Barber was joined to them. It seemed that they would never get through talking.

"Why don't they do something?" Hanley growled.

Finally, when he could bear it no longer, he crossed to the door and opened it just in time to see the maid disappearing into the room opposite Marie's with a little white bundle in her arms. The doctor, following her into the hall, saw Hanley approaching, and leading him back into his own room, closed the door after him.

"Well?" said Hanley.

"You have a son," said the doctor. "A fine boy. But—"

"Well?" repeated Hanley impatiently.

"I am afraid it has killed your wife," the doctor said bluntly. One expected Thomas Hanley to bear anything.

Hanley's hands closed on the doctor's shoulders like grips of steel.

"Is she dead?" he asked calmly.

"No." The doctor winced under Hanley's grasp. "But I can give you little hope. I shall do my best."

Hanley turned without a word and passed to Marie's room. She was lying with her head propped up by a pillow, her face deathly pale, her eyes closed. Mrs. Barber sat on the edge of the bed, holding her daughter's hand. As Hanley entered she looked up and placed her fingers to her lips to enjoin silence.

Hanley crossed over to the bedside and stood looking down at his wife, his lips sternly compressed, his hands twitching nervously. Marie's eyes opened as though with an effort, and, seeing her husband, she tried to sit up. Mrs. Barber gently pressed her back on the pillow. Marie held out her hand, and Hanley awkwardly took it in his.

"Thomas," said Marie faintly; and then, with a shudder: "How I hate that name!"

"I—I don't like it very well myself," said Hanley.

"I want—you—to—tell me—something," said Marie. The words came with difficulty. "I know you—wouldn't lie. Mother told me it is a little girl, but she looked so queer, and she wouldn't let me—"

Her voice died away, but she kept her eyes on Hanley's face in mute appeal.

Hanley bent over to kiss the hand he held and saw Mrs. Barber's eyes full of tears. Then:

"It is a little girl," he said. "A little blue-eyed girl."

Marie sighed long and happily and closed her eyes, and as Hanley turned to leave the room Mrs. Barber caught his hand and kissed it. The doctor, meeting him at the door, asked him not to return till he was called, saying that Marie required absolute quiet. Hanley nodded and sought his own room.

Five, ten minutes passed. As before, the sound of voices came faintly through the wall. Would they never cease? He passed his hand across his brow and found it wet.

It is a painful thing to find one's heart at forty, and delightful. Of course, Marie would live. Hanley found himself making plans for the future with a boyish fancy. What would he not do for her? It would be pretty hard, he reflected grimly, for Thomas Hanley to learn how to play, but it was for Marie. She would be disappointed to find a son instead of a daughter, but still he would make her happy.

Then the present recurred to his mind and filled him with a redoubled fear. He listened; the voices in her room had ceased and he thought he heard someone sobbing. He could bear it no longer; he must go to her.

The doctor met him at the door of Marie's room. Hanley asked with his eyes. The doctor, who again felt that there was no need of gentleness with Thomas Hanley, used none.

"She is dead," he said simply.

Hanley stared at him, unbelieving. Then he walked over to the bed and, kneeling by it, gazed steadily at the pallor of death on the face resting heavily against the pillow.

"Mrs. Barber," he said, "I have killed your daughter. I have killed Marie." And again, as he rose to his feet: "I have killed Marie."

The doctor, not understanding, protested.

Hanley leaped toward him. The floodgates that had been closed for a lifetime burst suddenly.

"Curse you!" he screamed. "Don't you lie to me! I tell you I killed her with a lie! Because I lied, God has killed her! I killed her!"

He threw himself on the bed and took Marie's head to his breast in a wild embrace, sobbing like a woman.

Through the window came the breath of spring. Mrs. Barber was kneeling by the bed, weeping silently. From the hall came the sound of Maggie sniffling in the corner where Marie had said she could stay.

If He Be Married

🎼

I T WAS AN APRIL MORNING IN NEW YORK; THAT IS
to say, perfect. From the Battery there comes a
breath of the sea; from Westchester, a scent of the
country; and when the two unite the result is intoxica-
tion.

At such a time the strugglers of Manhattan are kept
to their daily tasks only by their native instinct to *herd*.
It is certain that if anyone of them should become tem-
porarily insane, pull on his coat, and start for the Cat-
skills the city would be depopulated in thirty minutes.

For if ever spring is spring, it is so in New York.

So thought Carl McNair, bookkeeper for Cohen &
Aduchefsky, manufacturers of ladies' dresses. And with
him the desire to attend Pan's symphony had nothing of
the vagueness of ignorance. He had heard it before.

In January he had arrived in New York with a capital
of two hundred dollars, a good education, a pleasing appearance, and an engaging manner. Also, he possessed
great expectations. But getting a start in the metropolis
is largely a matter of luck, and Carl had been unlucky.

At one time he was almost ready to give it up; but at
the thought of the smiles and I-told-you-sos that would
celebrate his return he strengthened his vows, burned
another bridge or two, and tried again.

He had at first determined to take no position unless it measured up to his powers and requirements as he figured them, but by the time his two hundred dollars had been cut in half he was considerably less squeamish; and, in place of "holding himself open for an advantageous offer," he began to look for a job.

That, of course, was simple. Nothing in New York is easier than getting a job, except, perhaps, getting out of one.

On the day that he began posting the ledgers of Cohen & Aduchefsky, manufacturers of ladies' dresses, he felt himself forever disgraced. But even that, he reflected, was better than returning to Caxton.

And besides, it was purely temporary. Which proves that he knew nothing of the awful power of the millstones of a metropolis.

Carl was twenty-two, lovable, able, and ambitious; and yet he was in a very fair way to become a head bookkeeper at thirty, go to the Hippodrome each year, marry a stenographer, and live in Brooklyn, if it had not been for an incredible piece of luck and the mysterious ways of the little naked god.

On this particular April morning he was more than usually lonesome and dissatisfied.

It was Saturday, the last day of his third week at Cohen & Aduchefsky's. As Miss Alteresko, the stenographer, entered the office he groaned audibly. It is true that Miss Alteresko was not beautiful, and she was a girl, and no girl should be forced to pound a typewriter in April. It is a crime against nature.

"You don't feel well, Mr. McNair," she observed.

Carl said that he felt as well as could be expected, and began billing the orders for the day before. Miss Alteresko sat regarding his back with a curious air of interest until the door opened to admit Mr. Cohen, when she started to bang the typewriter with a becoming zeal.

Mr. Cohen gave his usual good morning, half groan and half grunt, and proceeded to the sample room.

To Carl the morning passed with exasperating slowness. Through the open window came the alluring call of spring, little unmistakable breaths and cadences that reach to the most hidden vault and the deafest of ears.

Eleven o'clock found the billing still unfinished, with Carl gazing at the calendar above his desk in a sort of helpless resentment.

At sound of the chimes on the Metropolitan Tower he awoke with a start and fell to his task resignedly; and as he glanced through the latticed window which looked out on the salesroom he saw Mr. Cohen regarding him with an air of disapproval. An hour later he closed the sales book with a bang, stuffed the bunch of orders in the drawer of his desk, and, turning to look through the window for the ubiquitous Mr. Cohen, found himself gazing directly into the most beautiful pair of eyes in the world.

Carl grew red, then pale.

He started to turn away, then turned back again. He tried to speak, and couldn't. The girl at the window regarded him with silent sympathy. The symptoms evidently were by no means unknown to her.

By a gesture she directed Carl's attention to a card lying on the window ledge. He picked it up with fumbling fingers and read:

INSPECTOR
Bureau of Labor
City of New York

Then, looking into the eyes again, he stammered: "Yes—er—oh, yes!"

"I have come to inspect your loft. Your factory is here, isn't it?"

Even with its businesslike tone, the voice was sweetly modulated, as the call of spring.

Mr. Cohen, who heard everything, came bustling up. "What is it you want?" he demanded.

The girl flushed at his tone. "I want to see if the operators are working under proper sanitary conditions," she answered.

Mr. Cohen regarded her with an air of suspicion. "Well, why should—Oh, all right." To Carl: "Mr. McNair, the young lady wants to see the factory. You should go up with her, because I got a customer—Mr. Waldstein, from Yonkers."

And he hurried back to Mr. Waldstein as one ready and anxious for battle.

During the interruption Carl had somewhat recovered his wits; in thinking it over afterward, he was amazed at his own composure in conducting the girl courteously to the elevator and through the whirring maze of sewing machines and finishers on the upper floor.

He watched her silently as she talked with the foreman and gave him some final instructions as to the ventilation. When she turned to go he hastened before her to the elevator and pressed the button carefully and firmly, as though it were a most important ceremony, and entered the car after her.

Arrived at the first floor, they walked together to the outer vestibule. The girl turned and held out her hand. "Thank you so much," she said.

Carl hesitated, took the offered hand, and let it fall. Then, gathering himself together: "I—er—I—wanted to say something. May I?"

"Certainly. What is it?"

"You are sure you won't be offended?"

"Well," she hesitated in her turn, "that depends on what you have to say."

"I know I don't *want* to offend you," declared Carl, smiling with so engaging a frankness that she returned it involuntarily, "but I probably shall."

There could be no doubt about his sincerity. "Well?" the girl asked encouragingly.

"Of course," he managed to continue, "you won't, I know. But I thought—could—would you—go to lunch with me?"

He asked the commonplace question with a tragic earnestness that was completely ludicrous. The girl hesitated.

"Is it a lark?" she asked. And noting his surprise, "Oh, I beg your pardon," she continued. "What I meant was, I'll go."

Carl could scarcely believe his ears. He had asked her just as a gambler throws his last dollar on the wheel, sure of failure, on a hopeless chance. Which may seem exaggerated to those of my readers to whom spring means merely a time to plant cabbages.

"But—but perhaps you don't want to go," he stammered foolishly.

"Of course I do. But I *don't* want to stand in this vestibule all day," smiling.

Carl blurted out an excuse, and went to the office for his hat and gloves. He had no time to wonder why she had agreed to go, but he might have known. The reader may guess.

In less than a minute he returned, and they started up Fifth Avenue.

"Now"—as they neared Twenty-second Street— "the first thing is where to go. Is Martin's all right?"

"Certainly. But how did you happen to think of Martin's?"

Carl flushed at the implication. "Well, I *don't* eat there every day," he admitted.

"Oh!" exclaimed the girl, embarrassed. "I—why, you know I couldn't mean—"

"It doesn't matter the least bit if you did," he asserted. "I refuse to consider myself disgraced because I am rich. Anyway," meaningly, "I certainly can't expect you to be conventional. And now I'm even."

"That is very rude of you, and I've a mind to go back."

"Forgive me," humbly. "If I were to live a thousand years I couldn't tell you how very, *very* grateful I am."

They walked on in silence.

"Do you know," he continued, after they had entered the restaurant and seated themselves at a table over against the side wall, "I believe you were right, after all."

"How? What did I say?"

"It *is* a lark."

"I was wrong; it is nothing of the sort. At least, not for me."

"Well, what is it, then?"

"A—an act of charity."

"Oh, that is all forgotten," airily. "I was just pretending. Or if I was a little blue, now I'm gay as—as a *lark*."

" 'Hence, vain, deluding joys,' " the girl quoted solemnly.

For the next five minutes Carl was lost in the mazes of the menu. He felt sure that there was nothing on it— or anywhere—good enough for her; but something must be ordered. He ended by selecting those items with the longest names and the highest prices, and turned to the girl with a sigh of relief.

She was gazing out of the window at the passersby,

her elbow on the table, her chin resting in her hand, her lips curved in a thoughtful smile.

Carl watched her so for a full minute. If, he thought, he had collected all his vague longings of the morning into one wish, it would have been for this. She was perfect, no less. If he had been a nice observer, he might have thought the finely tailored suit and fashionable French bonnet rather out of place on a humble inspector of the bureau of labor; but all he knew or cared was that they were suited to her.

"Do you know," he remarked, "I don't even know your name."

She started and turned at sound of his voice. "Well, I—" hesitating, "a rose by—only I don't pretend to be a rose."

"But you are."

"That, Mr. McNair, was very clumsy—and obvious."

"I knew you knew mine," scornfully. "Mr. Cohen called me, and you heard him."

"You are dreadfully conceited," she retorted, cheated out of her surprise. "Of course I heard him call you; but why should I remember it?"

Carl meanly took advantage of the opening. "Well," he said, "you *did*."

"Oh, very well! Now I shall *never* tell you."

"Please."

"No."

"Please."

"Never."

There was a pause. Carl looked at her imploringly. She busied herself with a plate of clams. Finally:

"I wish *you* would tell *me* something," she said. "Will you?"

"Never," declared Carl firmly. They both laughed.

"Must I say 'please'?" she asked.

"Yes. Twice."

"No; I am in earnest. Please tell me."

"Anything." And he, too, was in earnest.

"I want to know all about you."

"Oh, then it wouldn't be a lark!" he protested.

"But I *really* want to know."

"Well—what, for instance?"

"Well," hesitating, "your college."

"How do you know I had one?"

"Oh, that is easy! Anyone could tell that."

Carl laughed, pleased. Nothing is more delightful to a man than such a tribute to his alma mater.

Perhaps the girl knew it; at any rate, she got from Carl all that she wanted to know. It is always dangerous to tell a man that you want to hear about himself. In thirty minutes you are sure to think him either a bore or a hero.

And they are equally uncomfortable, though for different reasons.

But the girl was certainly not bored. Carl told her of Caxton; its people, its play, its life; his friends, his mother, his ambitions. When once started, he spoke with an easy earnestness that was charming.

Besides, you can talk forever, and well, to a pretty girl who admits that she likes to hear you.

When he came to his departure for New York he stopped short. "The rest," he declared, "is funny. And I don't want you to laugh at me."

"You know I won't," she said earnestly. "Please."

And so he told of his high hopes and silly pretensions, his disappointment and shame, and finally of the ignominious fall that landed him in the office of Cohen & Aduchefsky.

"The truth is," he concluded, "that New York is too big for me. There's nothing for me to get hold of."

"The truth is," she contradicted, "that you are foolish

to expect to do anything in New York without knowing someone. No one *ever* has.''

Their luncheon was finished and they arose to go. As they left the restaurant and started toward Broadway, Carl remarked that on account of the Saturday half-holiday he need not return to the office.

''I'm so sorry I have an engagement,'' said the girl. ''Wouldn't it be pleasant to walk?''

Carl nodded. ''With you?''

''Of course, with me,'' she agreed. ''Because,'' smiling, ''I let you talk all you want to.''

But he was in no mood for badinage. What, he reflected, was he to do for the rest of the day, when she was gone? And the next, and the next, and all the others?

He turned and looked at her beseechingly. They had stopped on the platform of the elevated railroad station, waiting for her train. ''Won't you please tell me?'' he pleaded.

She returned his gaze steadily, smiling. ''No,'' she replied. ''I would, but—''

Her train rolled in alongside the platform.

''Here,'' she said, and handed him a card. Before he had time to move she was on the car, and gone. He gazed at the receding train stupidly, and when it had disappeared, looked at the card. It read:

INSPECTOR
Bureau of Labor
City of New York

He tore the card in pieces and threw them on the platform, then carefully picked them up again and put them in his pocket. Two or three waiting passengers stared at him in wonder. He returned the stare with indifference and made his way to the street.

His first impulse was to go to the offices of the bureau of labor; but he thought better of it, and went to walk in the square. After half an hour of indecision he went to a telephone and called up the bureau.

The office was closed.

"It's lucky they *were* closed," he commented to himself. "What could I have said? 'Have you an inspector in your office with brown hair and beautiful eyes?' Of course they'd tell me all about it."

He wandered down Broadway, musing. When a sudden impact with a lamppost made him realize that he was in no condition to take care of himself, he returned to his room and tried to read; but he could see nothing but a sweet, laughing face and teasing eyes.

He started to write a letter, and finished one paragraph in two hours. And yet, after all this, it was nearly eleven o'clock before he admitted to himself that he was in love.

Sunday passed, dull and eventless. On Monday morning he approached Mr. Cohen with an air of satisfaction and announced that he would leave on the following Saturday. Mr. Cohen was astonished and excited.

"That's the way!" he exclaimed. "After you learn the job a whole month's expenses you go at once. What do they give you?"

"Who?"

"Why, where you're going."

"Nothing. I have no other position. I am only leaving this one."

Mr. Cohen was called to wait on a customer, and Carl commenced his daily task with a light heart. Why, Heaven only knows.

At noon he went to the factory and asked the foreman what instructions had been given him by the labor inspector. The foreman was very obliging.

"Didn't she say the thing would be looked over?" Carl asked carelessly.

"Yes," answered the foreman. "Said she'd be around Tuesday." Which explains the light heart.

On Tuesday morning, therefore, Carl entered the office whistling. Miss Alteresko handed him a letter. He tore open the envelope and found, on an embossed sheet, the somewhat startling information that Mr. R. U. Carson of R. U Carson & Co., would be pleased to have him call and see him at his office on Tuesday morning after ten.

Mr. Carson was well known to Carl, as indeed he was to everyone who read the newspapers. In the war of finance, though perhaps not a general, he was at the very least a colonel. His name was one of the household words of the metropolis, and not the least important.

Carl wondered vaguely what the great Carson could want with *him*.

At ten o'clock he told Mr. Cohen that he wished to go downtown on business. Mr. Cohen eyed him suspiciously, but said nothing; and fifteen minutes later Carl entered the imposing offices of R. U. Carson & Co. and handed in the letter he had received.

The boy returned with the information that Mr. Carson was engaged, but would see him presently.

Carl seated himself, full of conjectures as to the purpose of this unexpected invitation. Five, ten minutes passed, and he began to feel worried; for the inspector—he smiled at the title—had promised to return on Tuesday, and he had decided that, Carson or no Carson, he would be back in the office by eleven.

By half past ten he was decidedly anxious, and was watching the clock.

"Mr. Carson will see you now, sir," announced the boy. "This way."

And Carl was led through a succession of passages and rooms to a large, elegantly furnished apartment overlooking the street. The great Carson himself was seated at a desk in the center of the room, dictating to his stenographer. At Carl's approach he arose and extended his hand.

"Mr. McNair," he said, "I am glad to know you."

"And I you, sir," taking the hand.

Mr. Carson dismissed the stenographer, and conducting Carl to an inner room, waved him to a seat.

"Now, my boy," he began abruptly, "to come to the point at once, you have been recommended to me as a very worthy young man. In the first place, would a position with our firm be agreeable to you?"

Carl concealed his surprise. "Certainly, sir. That is," he added, "it depends a little on the position."

"Of course," agreed Mr. Carson. "But that will be arranged to your satisfaction. What I want is the man. I prefer to teach him myself; the less he knows the better, if he isn't a blockhead. And now to details."

For a quarter of an hour Carl was kept busy answering questions. Finally Mr. Carson expressed himself as satisfied. He arose and again extended his hand.

"There is one thing, sir, that I would like to know," said Carl as he prepared to leave. "I can't imagine which of my friends has done me this favor. In fact, I didn't know that—"

He was interrupted by a voice from the outer room. "Oh, dear, he's *always* busy," someone was saying.

Carl's heart leaped; it was the girl's voice! Mr. Carson walked to the door, smiling. "Come in," he invited.

The girl, for it was she, hurried over to him.

"Oh, dad," she cried, "I haven't a minute. I just ran in to tell you that when you write to Mr. McNair—you know who I mean—you mustn't mention me. You see, I didn't tell him—"

Mr. Carson interrupted with a laugh. "Well, you've told him now. This is your friend, Mr. McNair."

The girl turned and saw Carl, who was gazing at her stupidly. "Oh!" she cried, and stopped short. Her cheeks became crimson. Then, recovering herself, "Good morning, Mr. McNair," politely.

"Good morning, Miss Carson," still more politely.

Carl walked across the room, hat in hand. Turning at the door, "I am greatly obliged to you, Mr. Carson," he said. "Good morning, sir." And he ran, rather than walked, through the corridors and down the stairs to the street door. Arrived there, he stopped to consider.

He understood it all, he assured himself, bitterly. He felt that he had been cheated and deceived. Of course it was all very plain. Miss Carson—the wealthy, the socially elect—had picked him out as a worthy object of charity.

She had probably decided to *elevate him.*

"Damned idiot!" he said aloud.

"Mr. McNair!" came a voice. He turned.

It was the girl. As she approached Carl stiffened perceptibly.

"I am going uptown," she said breathlessly, "and I supposed you were, too, so I wanted to ask you to ride up with me. Will you?"

"I am sorry," declined Carl, with finality and extreme dignity.

"But I—" she stopped, surprised. "Please."

Carl was silent. Just in front of them a footman was opening the door of a limousine.

"You may help me in," said the girl. Carl did so, politely, and stood by the open door.

"Now," she continued, "did you have to beg me to have luncheon with you?"

Carl could not speak. She was very, very sweet.

"Well, then," taking his silence for assent, "please."

Carl entered and seated himself at her side. To the waiting footman Miss Carson gave the address of Carl's office, and the car started uptown.

"Now," said the girl, "why were you in such a hurry to leave?"

"I—I had to catch a train."

"Oh!" A pause. Then, with calm impertinence, "Where were you going?"

"To Caxton. I am going back there to live." And then, as she started to interrupt, "There's no use pretending. You know *why* I am going."

There was a long silence.

Carl gazed out of the window, seeing nothing. He reproached himself that he had not refused obstinately to enter the car. He hated the soft luxuriousness of the cushions; he almost persuaded himself that he hated the girl.

Finally she spoke.

"I have an explanation to make, Mr. McNair. And a request. You see, I do settlement work. On Saturday one of the girls was ill, and I offered to do her work for her. That is why—that is how I met you. If my father knew of it he would be angry. I mean, if he knew I was an inspector," smiling. "I told him I met you at a reception. You won't tell him, will you?"

"Likely not, since I sha'n't see him again." Clearly, Carl was very unhappy.

The girl smiled. "Oh, but you will. I thought the one thing you wanted was a start. Well."

"So did I. But now I *know* what I want. And it is beyond me. You are very kind, Miss Carson—and charitable."

The car stopped at Carl's office.

He glanced up at it with a shudder, and leaving the car, stood at its door looking in at the girl. She looked at him questioningly. Plainly, he was ready to go without a word.

"What—" she began, and then finished bravely, "what if I, too, know what you want?"

Carl looked at her in wonder, unbelieving. She was bending toward him, face flushed and lips parted. And her eyes—but Carl was blind.

"*Please* stay," she whispered. "And now go— quick."

Carl mechanically lifted his hat and obeyed. He had walked all of five blocks before he understood anything.

That evening he wrote a letter to Caxton, telling of his new position with R. U. Carson & Co. After it was folded and sealed he tried for an hour to convince himself, and finally went to the mirror and examined himself critically.

"Why," he said aloud, and with emphasis, "the thing is impossible."

But it wasn't. It never is.

BABA

A HOUSE PARTY, BEING AN INSTITUTION ESTAB-
lished and maintained solely for the convenience
of storywriters and matchmakers, has no excuse
for existence unless it serves the purposes of one or the
other of these valuable members of society.

In real life no matron dreams of giving a house party
without inviting a man, preferably young, and a girl,
necessarily pretty, whom she wishes to bring together;
and no novelist ever puts one in his book if he can find
any other way out of it. With the hostess it necessitates
many indifferent guests, and with the novelist many un-
desirable characters. It belongs, therefore, to that species
of artificial phenomena known as last resorts.

Knowing all this—for she was a wise matron—Mrs.
T. M. S. Hartshorn had nevertheless invited fourteen per-
sons to a house party at her country home in Westchester
County during the last week of April.

This fact produces an alternative. Either she knew I
was going to write a story about it or she had certain
designs in connection with the fates of Edward Besant
and Sylvia Herrow; for he was the only young man in
the crowd and she the only pretty girl.

Mrs. Hartshorn was a wise matron!

But it would seem that her plan was doomed to fail-

ure. Consider: On the evening of the third day of the
party Mrs. Hartshorn, making a tour of exploration some
time after the dinner hour discovered Mr. Besant seated
in gloomy solitude in a dark corner of the library. She
paused, waiting for recognition.

He looked up and said: "Oh, is it you?" And buried
his face in his hands again.

"Ned, what on earth is the matter with you?" demanded his hostess. "Come on in front; we need you
for a fourth table."

Mr. Besant muttered something very uncomplimen-
tary to tables in general and fourth tables in particular,
and declared his intention of remaining where he was
forever. Then he looked up with an air of weary decision:

"I forgot. I wanted to speak to you, Dora. I'm going
home on the seven-ten."

"The seven-ten?"

"Tomorrow morning."

She exploded immediately. She declared that he
couldn't go; that everyone would know why, and laugh
at him; that she couldn't possibly explain his departure,
and wouldn't try; and that she would never give another
houseparty as long as she lived.

"Anyway," she finished, "it's perfectly silly of you.
I suppose Sylvia has refused you, just because she
doesn't happen to know what she wants. Good Heavens!
And you run away like this! Ned Besant, you're a coward!"

But all that the young man would permit himself was
a gloomy reiteration of his purpose to leave on the
seven-ten in the morning. His hostess presented a dozen
arguments—but what is the good of arguing with an oys-
ter?

And at length, convinced of the inflexibility of his

determination, she returned to the waiting tables in the drawingroom, announcing:

"We'll have to do without him. He's in the library writing letters. Just received a telegram and says he has to leave on the seven-ten tomorrow."

"Leave!" exclaimed the parrot of the party—a little, fat, red-faced man with eyeglasses.

"Telegram! It couldn't—" began Tom Hartshorn, the host; then subsided at a glance from his wife.

"Too bad!"

"It breaks up the game."

"Miss Herrow, you go after him—he'll come then, all right."

But Miss Herrow—a slender, graceful girl with fair, velvety skin and gray eyes shot with lights of green, merely continued toying with a pack of cards.

"We shall have to cut in," said Mrs. Hartshorn, advancing to a table. "Tom, give Mr. Nelson your seat. Mr. Graves, you will have to be a fifth. Higgins, take away the extra table."

And, after some confusion and chatter, they found their places and began the pleasant pastime of trying to win one another's money.

In the meantime Edward Besant remained in his dark corner in the library. The only light in the room entered through the open door leading into the hall, and it barely permitted him to see the deep outline of a chair here and a table there.

Occasionally an exclamation of triumph or annoyance or a burst of laughter floated down the hall from the room in front.

Mr. Besant seemed not to hear. For thirty minutes he sat staring straight ahead at nothing, then he arose, walked noiselessly to the door and down the hall, appropriated the first hat in sight, and sought the night without.

An hour later he returned, went directly to the library, and switched on the electricity.

By its light could be seen an expression on his face that belied the hopelessness of his words to his hostess a short time before. It wore an air of determination and resolve—the look of a man who has sought a decision and found it.

"It's the only thing to do," he muttered aloud, crossing to the desk and searching for a pen. "I'm tired of this faithful Fido business. This will end it for good."

He sat down and wrote four letters—one long, two medium, and one short. Then he rang for a servant.

"Higgins," he said, "I'm leaving on the seven-ten in the morning. I don't want to bother Mrs. Hartshorn about it; so will you see that the car is ready at six-fifty-five to take me to the village? And here are some letters. These three are to be posted; the other is for Miss Herrow. Please send it to her room."

Higgins took the letters and something else with them.

"Thank you, sir. Sorry you're going to leave. Mr. Besant. I'll see that the car is ready. And your luggage, sir?"

"I have only a bag. I'll attend to it myself. By the way, you'd better call me about a quarter past six. Good night."

"Very well, sir. Good night, sir."

When Higgins had gone Besant again passed noiselessly down the hall. At the door of the drawing room he halted a moment listening to the voices within. For a time nothing could be distinguished; then came:

"Two club."

"Two heart."

"Two royal."

"Two no trump."

And then, evidently from another table, a silvery girl-ish voice sounded suddenly:

"But Mr. Nelson! You had only led diamonds once, so how could I know?"

This was followed by a burst of laughter from many throats.

Besant sighed, turned to the stairs, and mounted to his own room. For a while he sat on the edge of a table, then rose and began to pace the floor.

But despite this his face still held its expression of determination and decision; and his lips were pressed together in a grim line as he undressed and prepared for bed. Fifteen minutes later he was sound asleep.

At exactly six-fifteen in the morning he was called by Higgins.

Again at six-twenty, and six-thirty, and this time he was informed in a respectful but firm voice that trains were stubborn things. Accordingly he leaped out of a bed, into a tub, and thence into his clothes.

Then he threw his things hurriedly but effectively into his bag and descended to the breakfast room. It was empty, except for a servant, who approached as the young man entered.

"Eggs, sir?"

"Yes. As usual," replied Besant absently as he stood looking out of the window.

April sunshine was just beginning to chase away the long shadows and transform the drops of cool dew into glittering jewels, but the young man did not see. The expression of his face would seem to imply that he was filled with regret for his decision of the evening before.

He sighed deeply twice, passed his hand wearily across his forehead, took a cigarette from his case, and turned to the table for a match.

Then suddenly he started back and uttered a sharp exclamation of surprise, while the cigarette fell from his fingers to the floor.

A girl had entered the room, stopping three paces from the threshold—a slender, graceful girl with gray eyes shot with lights of green.

"Miss Herrow!" exclaimed Besant, finding his tongue.

"Good morning," said the girl quite as though she were speaking to Higgins, advancing to the opposite side of the table.

But Besant was too agitated with surprise to notice her tone. Simple wonder and astonishment at her appearance shone in his eyes, to be followed soon by a sudden expression of embarrassment and hesitation.

"It is quite early this morning," he stammered, then wanted to bite his tongue off.

Miss Herrow did not smile; instead, she approached a step, holding out something white in her hand.

"It is," she agreed icily. "I got up," she continued, "to return something to you which—that is—something sent to me by mistake."

And she threw the something white on the table. Then she turned and started for the door—not too hastily.

"But Miss Herrow!" cried Besant. "What do you mean? What is it?"

She paused, turning her head and pointing to the table.

"It is there. You will understand when you read it." Then she turned full around. "Mr. Besant, I want to say that I am painfully disappointed in you. After yesterday—after what you said yesterday—I thought—"

She stopped, caught her breath, and went on: "When I went to my room last night I found an envelope on the dressing table. It contained *that!* I have never been so—so insulted before, and I showed it to Dora—to Mrs.

Hartshorn. I asked her to return it to you, but she said you deserved—that is—I should return it myself. I have done so.''

Besant was staring at her with an expression of the most profound amazement.

''Insult!'' he exclaimed finally. ''That is a hard term, Miss Herrow. Is it an insult for a man to tell a woman he loves her? Or is a farewell an insult?''

''That he loves her?'' repeated the girl scornfully. ''No. But that—read it and you will understand. It is— evidently—intended for some—some person.''

Besant stared at her for a moment, then turned to the table and picked up the sheet of paper. He read:

Baba, you were right. I cannot live without you.
NED.

''Good God!'' cried the young man in a tone of utter consternation, and sank limply into a chair.

''One can't be too careful with one's correspondence,'' observed Miss Herrow acidly. She seemed somehow unable to get to the door.

''This is horrible!'' groaned poor Besant from the chair. But he must have been keeping an eye on the girl, for as she turned again to leave he sprang to his feet. And, as though by a superhuman effort, he appeared suddenly calm.

''Miss Herrow,'' he said. Again she turned.

''I—you know—I'm dashed, of course. I would have given anything not to have this happen. I would like to cut off my hand for doing it. But I cannot agree that I have insulted you. Where is the insult?''

''Where?'' exclaimed the girl in withering scorn. ''But I am not surprised that you do not see it, Mr.

Besant. After what you told me yesterday—and then this—''

"What did I tell you yesterday?''

"Yes, worse than insult!'' She rode over the interruption. "You know very well what you told me yesterday. You love me! Bah! To write—'' she choked with scorn and indignation—"to write to another girl that you cannot live without her, and in the very room where you had said exactly the same thing to me not two hours before!

"If that is what your love is like, I am glad it is no longer mine. I wish it never had been. I wish I'd never seen you. What if I had believed you? What if I had admitted—that is—what if I had *pretended* to return your love? You, who cannot live without Baba. Oh, you—you monster!''

"It was true!'' exclaimed the young man as she paused for breath.

"Ah! You declare it to my face!''

"I mean,'' he stammered, "I mean that I love you.''

"Bah!'' Her eyes blazed. "As though you could write to another—to someone like that if you loved me!''

"I could and did,'' replied Besant, a little more calmly. "What is the use of pretending, Sylvia, when you know? Why, Baba—the girl I wrote to—*she knows I love you!*''

"She?''

"Yes. That is, she knows I love someone. That's why—she went away, you see—that's why I had to write. She told me to, if ever—And why not?'' he demanded fiercely. "If I cannot have your love, why should I not take what I can get? You say I insult you. Good Heavens! What do you care? If I insult anyone it is she who loves me—who will always love me—''

He stopped, swallowing hard, and walked to the window.

As he did so a servant appeared, bearing a platter and a pot of coffee, and Higgins's voice came from the doorway announcing that the car was waiting. But at the sight of Miss Herrow and the sound of Mr. Besant's sharp answer they both retreated in confusion.

Presently, as the young man stood looking out on the April sunshine, a voice came from behind:

"Who is she?"

He made no answer. Again the voice:

"Is her name Baba?"

At that he turned and observed dryly:

"Miss Herrow, you have no right to ask those questions. Her name is not Baba. I call her that. You do not know her."

Then, as the girl started back at the rebuff, he continued calmly:

"You see, you make a mistake if you think your indignation proceeds from a sense of insult. It comes from selfishness. For two years you tell me that you can never love me until you end by convincing me. Then, when I turn to one who loves me—Heaven knows why, but she does—then what happens? You don't want me; then what does it matter where I go, or to whom?"

"I didn't say I could never love you," replied Miss Herrow.

"I beg your pardon; the last time you said it was yesterday."

"I did not! I merely said that I didn't happen to love you at that moment."

"If there has been a more auspicious moment in the past two years, I have failed to find it."

"Perhaps you didn't try hard enough. But then—" a sigh—"that is all over now."

"Yes," the young man assented grimly, "it is."

"You have written to—to her?"

"I have." He crossed to the table, picked up the paper, and put it in his pocket.

"I suppose—she will come?"

"She will." He smiled—a smile of assurance, almost of happiness.

"She—she loves you?"

"Yes. Of course, you can't understand that; but she does."

"And what will you do when—when she comes?"

"What will I do?" He stared. "Go to meet her, I suppose."

"At the train?"

"Yes. She comes by train."

There ensued a long silence. Besant walked to the window; the girl seated herself abruptly in a chair, then abruptly got up again. For six seconds she gazed at the young man's broad back, then exclaimed suddenly and fiercely:

"I hate her!"

Besant turned in surprise.

"I mean," stammered the girl, flushing, "I mean—she has no right to love you! I mean, there is no earthly reason for it!"

"I admit it is inexplicable," agreed Besant. "But I assure you such is the case."

"Tell me her name."

"Miss Herrow!"

"Yes. Well—yes. I want to know."

"You know very well I will do nothing of the sort. You should not—" He stopped suddenly and glanced at his watch. "Good Heavens! It's seven o'clock! Only ten minutes. Miss Herrow—you'll pardon me—" He started for the door.

"But you haven't had your breakfast!"

"I'll have to go without it," came from the hall. "Higgins, bring my bag! Good-by, Miss Herrow!"

The girl stood motionless, amazed. He was actually going—like that!

She heard the outer door open and close with a bang; then, through the window, came the sound of a motor whirring and the voice of Besant urging someone to go like the devil. Miss Herrow hesitated no longer. One bound and she was in the hall; another carried her to the outer door.

The next instant she was running like a deer down the gravel walk that encircled the house; and just as Higgins started to close the door of the tonneau after throwing in the bag, a streak of blue rushed past him and deposited itself on the seat beside Mr. Besant.

"What—" began the young man, dazed with wonder. Then he spoke to the chauffeur: "Go on! We have only seven minutes."

The car leaped forward like a mad bull. It reached the gateway—a short, swift turn—then shot forward on the smooth, level road. Besant sat looking straight ahead, with the expression of one who is performing a painful duty.

"I don't see why we are hurrying so fast," observed Miss Herrow presently—if one may be said to observe anything when going at the rate of fifty miles an hour. "You aren't going to catch that train, you know."

"Yes, I am," shouted the young man without turning his head. "It's only five miles and we have six minutes. We'll make it easy."

"That isn't what I meant. I mean you're not going to get on it."

"On what?"

"The train."

He did not appear to think this worthy of an answer. She waited ten seconds, then added:

"Because I won't let you."

Still no answer. The car was eating up the road hungrily with great bounds and leaps; the fence posts and nearby landscapes were an indistinct blur. She waited till they had crossed a raised bridge, holding tightly to the seat to keep from bouncing out; then called:

"Mr. Besant!"

No answer.

"Ned!"

Even at that he did not turn. She saw the spire of the village church over some trees two miles away, and fancied she heard the whistle of a train—the train that was to carry him to Baba. She shouted in desperation:

"Ned, do you love me?"

Then, and then only, did the young man appear to find the conversation interesting. He turned.

"Yes!" he shouted back.

"Then don't go! Because I love you, too! I do, indeed! And she can't be very nice, or she wouldn't let you send for her like that. Please! I do love you! Don't go!"

Besant's face had turned white, and the wind had brought the tears to his eyes. But his voice was loud and firm enough:

"Will you marry me?"

"Yes."

"I can't hear you!"

"Yes!"

Besant reached forward, touched the chauffeur's arm, and shouted something in his ear. The car slowed down, stopped, backed, turned around, and headed back.

Then—it was a lonely country road, and the chauffeur, like all Mrs. Hartshorn's servants, was well trained—Besant firmly put his arms where they had wanted to be for two years, and at the same time something caused a delicious sensation of warmth to creep around his neck. And if there was no conversation on the homeward journey, it was because there are times when lips have something more important to do than talk.

Late that evening a girl and a young man sat on a wooden bench in a moonlit garden. As far as shades of expression were revealed by the dim silvery light, it might be seen that their faces were filled with the fire of triumphant happiness; but it might also have been observed that every now and then the girl's eyes were turned upward with a suggestion of mingled curiosity and hesitation.

"Ned," she said suddenly, "I want to know—you must tell me—who is she?"

Mr. Besant took his lips away from her fingers long enough to answer, "Who?"

"Why—the—Baba."

"Ah!" Mr. Besant looked up. "That's a secret, my dearest Sylvia. But no"—he appeared to consider—"I might as well tell you now. You're sure to find out some day. It is very simple. The word *baba* is Hindustani for *baby*. Speaking vulgarly and more or less metaphorically, you are certainly my baby. Therefore—"

"You don't mean—" began Sylvia, while her eyes danced with sudden comprehension.

"Yes, I do," interrupted Mr. Besant, again raising her fingers to his lips and preparing to resume operations. "Baba was what you might call a strategical creation—a figment of the imagination. There never was any Baba except you.

"And," he added, as something happened that caused him to forget all about the fingers, "there never will be."

WARNER & WIFE

LORA WARNER, AFTER A LEISURELY INSPECTION OF herself in the pier mirror next the window, buttoned her well-fitting blue jacket closely about her, put on her hat, and caught up a bulging portfolio of brown leather that was lying on the dressing table. Then she turned to call to her husband in the adjoining room:

"Timmie!"

When she had waited at least half a second she called again, this time with a shade of impatience in her voice: *"Timmie!"*

The door opened and a man appeared on the threshold. Picture him a scant three inches over five feet in height, weighing perhaps a hundred and fifteen or twenty pounds; in short, a midget. A thin forelock of reddish hair straggled over his left eyebrow; his mustache, also thin and red, pointed straight down in a valiant but abortive attempt to reach his full lips; his ears, of generous size, had an odd appearance of being cocked like those of an expectant horse.

The small and deep-set eyes, filled as they were with timidity and self-deprecation amounting almost to docility, seemed nevertheless to possess a twinkle of intelligence. This was Timothy D. Warner.

"Good morning, my dear!" said he, stopping three

paces from the threshold like a well-trained servant.

"Where were you at breakfast?" returned his wife, scorning the convention of salutation.

Mr. Warner blinked once, then said pleasantly:

"I haven't been."

"Indeed! I supposed as much, or I would have seen you. I told you last night I wanted to talk over this Hamlin & Hamlin matter at the breakfast table."

"I know. I'm sorry. But you see"—Mr. Warner appeared to hesitate—"I—the fact is, the beastly alarm clock failed to go off."

"Did you wind it?"

"No." This manfully.

Lora Warner sighed. "Timmie, you are unthinkable! What about Hamlin & Hamlin? Did you look it over?"

This simple question seemed to upset Mr. Warner completely. He grew red, hesitated, and finally stammered:

"No—that is—I read something—"

"Do you mean you didn't?"

He nodded reluctantly.

"Then what were you doing? There was a light in your room when I went to bed."

Mr. Warner gazed on the floor, and was silent.

"What were you doing?"

Still silence.

"I have asked you twice, Timmie, what you were doing." The tone was merciless.

Mr. Warner, seeing there was no help for it, raised his eyes and met her gaze. "I was playing solitaire," he announced bravely.

Then, before the storm had time to break, he continued apologetically:

"I didn't know there was any hurry about it, my dear, or I would have looked it over at once. The case doesn't come up till the twenty-fifth. Besides, you said you had it all worked up, and merely wanted my opinion on one or two minor points. If I had known you really needed—'' He stopped suddenly.

''Well? If you had known I really needed—''

''Nothing,'' said Mr. Warner lamely.

''What were you going to say?''

''Why—advice—if you needed my advice—''

''Your advice! Do you think by any chance I *need* your advice?''

''My dear, goodness no!'' exclaimed Mr. Warner, as though the idea were preposterous.

''I should hope not,'' his wife agreed. ''I am quite able to manage my business without you, Timmie. Only, as you do nothing but sit around and read, I thought you might have happened on something that would throw light on the question of annulled liens, which is intricately involved and has an important bearing on this case. But I believe I have it very well in hand.''

''There is plenty of time till the twenty-fifth,'' Mr. Warner observed diffidently.

''There is,'' assented his wife. ''But that has nothing to do with this. The case has been put forward. It is calendared for today.''

''Today! But what—then perhaps—I can look it over this morning and see you at lunch—at recess—''

''My dear Timmie,'' smiled Mrs. Warner, ''you appear to think I do need your advice. Don't trouble yourself. I have it well in hand. Play solitaire by all means.'' She moved toward the door.

''At ten dollars a point,'' announced Mr. Warner to her back, ''I am sixty-two thousand dollars ahead of the game.''

''Fine!'' She sent a derisive smile over her shoulder. ''By-by, Timmie!''

Mr. Warner gazed at the closed door for a full thirty seconds, then turned and went to his own room to complete his interrupted toilet. That done, he went downstairs to the dining room.

Sadie, the cook, appeared in the doorway.

"Good morning!" she observed unamiably.

"I see I am late," returned Mr. Warner with a weak attempt at cheerfulness. "Do you suppose I could have a couple of eggs, Sadie?"

"Fried or boiled?"

"Well—shirred."

Mr. Warner never ate his eggs any other way than shirred, and as Sadie never failed to ask him, "Fried or boiled?" he was forced to begin each day with the feeling that he was being somehow put in the wrong. A most uncomfortable feeling, but one to which he was so well accustomed that he shook it off almost immediately and fell to thinking of other things.

First of the case of Hamlin & Hamlin *vs.* the Central Sash and Door Company, which was to come up that day in court. No use to worry about it, he decided; no doubt his wife, as she had said, had it well in hand. His wife usually had things well in hand. No less could be expected of her, being, as she was, the ablest lawyer in the city of Granton, excepting neither man nor woman.

Everybody said so, including Mr. Warner; indeed, he had said it before anyone else. He had expected it of her from the first; and during all the fifteen years of their married life she had been mounting steadily, with never a faltering step, to the height of his expectation and her own ambition.

Mr. Warner often pictured her to himself as he appeared on that day when he had first seen her in the law school in New York. His attention, which had just begun to be solidly fixed on torts and evidence, had suddenly wavered, fluttered through the air, and settled inextricably in the fluffy brown mass of her glorious hair.

It had taken him just three seconds to discover that her face was as fresh and beautiful as any phrase in Blackstone—in fact, a little more so—which was quite a discovery for a man of the temperament and inclinations of Timothy D. Warner.

The puzzle of his life was, why had she married him? When, some years after the event, in a moment of astounding intrepidity, he had asked her this question directly, she had replied with cynical humor that every ship needs an anchor for safety. Mr. Warner understood quite well what she meant, but he was inclined to doubt.

He had at one time distinctly heard her pronounce the words, ''I love you,'' and, since there had been nobody else in the room but himself, he felt justified in believing that they were addressed to him. For six months after the wedding she had openly fed this belief; since then her time had been completely occupied with her own career.

They had been married within a week after the end of their three years in law school, and had gone immediately to Granton, a town of sixty thousand in the Middle West—Lora having declared there was no time to waste on a honeymoon.

Luckily, Mr. Warner had inherited an income of some three thousand dollars a year from his father, so they were not forced to dig for bread.

He had supposed, not unreasonably, that they would open an office together, for Lora had stipulated that her marriage should not interfere with her ambition. But she vetoed this idea without ceremony. No partnership for her. She would carve out her own future, unhampered and alone. So he rented an office for her in the finest building on Main Street, and another for himself two blocks farther down.

From the first she had been successful. The New Woman had just become fashionable in Granton, and the city received its first female lawyer with open arms.

Her first two or three cases, unimportant of course, she won easily. Then called in consultation as an experiment by the corporation which owned the largest factory in the city, she had saved them a considerable amount of worry and a large sum of money by showing wherein a certain annoying statute could be proved unconstitutional.

She and Mr. Warner had sat up every night for a week, studying this problem. It was, of course, by the merest luck that Mr. Warner happened to be the one who discovered the solution. So said Mr. Warner, and his wife politely agreed with him.

Nor could she see any necessity for mentioning her husband's name when she carried the solution to the board of directors in her own pretty head.

At any rate, it earned for her a share of the corporation's law business, and in addition the amazed respect of the solid businessmen of the city. They began to take her seriously. At the end of a year one of these men actually placed an important case entirely in her hands. She was half afraid to take it, and told her husband so.

"My dear," said Mr. Warner, "you are far too modest. You'll win it, sure as shucks." And he had straightway sat down and attacked the case on both flanks and in the center, with the result that in less than a fortnight he had it bound, gagged, and delivered into her hands.

Mrs. Warner acknowledged the obligation in private with a kiss—the first he had received in four months. That was his reward. Hers consisted of a fee in four figures, an immense gain in prestige, and the clamorous eulogy of the men higher up.

From that day forth her office was filled with clients and her portfolio with briefs.

As for Mr. Warner's office, it was never filled with anything but tobacco smoke, for Mr. Warner himself occupied a very small portion of space, and no one else ever set foot in it.

Nevertheless, for fifteen years he continued his habit of visiting it for an hour every day, usually about two o'clock in the afternoon. He would lean back in the swivel chair, cock his feet on the edge of the desk, and light his pipe. Thus he would remain, looking meditatively out on Main Street for the space of three pipefuls; the time varied from forty-five minutes to an hour and a quarter, according to the kind of pipe he happened to be smoking.

Then he would return home and bury himself in the library with the documents relative to some one of his wife's important cases which she had recommended to his study.

For it must be understood that Mr. Warner did all his wife's "preliminary work." That was what she called it—not inaccurately, for what he exactly did was to work up her cases for trial. That is, the difficult and doubtful ones.

"But," you will exclaim if you happen to be a lawyer, "that is all there is to the case. The preparation is the difficulty. Anyone with a little wit and common sense can do the court work."

That may be true. I am not a lawyer, and am not qualified to judge. You may take the facts as I give them for what they are worth.

To resume. Mr. Warner's time was so taken up with his wife's preliminary work that he had none left to search for clients on his own account. Besides, was he not the happy possessor of an exciting avocation? Any man who has won sixty-two thousand dollars from himself at solitaire, even at ten dollars a point, has had his hands pretty full.

Mr. Warner had been driven to solitaire by loneliness. The loneliness was a natural growth. His brilliant and beautiful wife, drawn more and more as her popularity increased into the whirl of Granton society, had at first attempted to take her husband along, and he had not been averse. But he soon had enough of it.

Two teas and one dinner were sufficient to make it plain to him that his position was perfectly analogous to that of the husband of a prima donna. His wife was courted, sought after, flattered, fawned upon, flirted with. She was beautiful, witty, graceful, and four inches taller than her husband. He was—well, he was Timmie.

So he went home and played solitaire.

He played for hours, days, weeks, months—whenever he could find a respite from the preliminary work. He played all the kinds he had ever heard of, and when they became tiresome, invented new ones.

Then, one day he had an idea. He had had it before, but never had it struck him so forcibly. All day it remained in the front of his brain, and that night after dinner he spoke to his wife about it. It was an embarrassing idea, and he grew red and stammered for a full ten minutes before Mrs. Warner grasped the meaning of his disconnected and halting sentences. When she did understand, she stopped him with an exclamation.

"My dear Timmie! You know very well it's impossible. I regret it as much as you do. I—I would like to have—to be a mother, too. But right in the middle of my career—it takes time, you know—and there is the danger—really, it's impossible. It's too bad, Timmie; but one can't have everything. Here are those Tilbury supply contracts; look them over, will you? They must be absolutely tight."

Mr. Warner took the contracts and went to his room. That night was the most uncomfortable one he had ever known. He had seen a glorious vision of a little Timmie sitting on his knee, and to have it so rudely snatched away was sadly bewildering. It was this experience that planted within him the germ of dissatisfaction with life which was destined to prove his salvation.

By this morning on which we have seen Mr. Warner descend to his breakfast this germ had grown and begotten a family. It stirred around within him as he consumed his shirred eggs, and made him gloomy. Even the remembrance of his brilliant victory at solitaire the night before could not bring ease to his mind.

"Something's wrong with me," he muttered to himself as he wandered into the library. "Something inside, I mean." He kicked viciously at a chair that had thoughtlessly gotten in his path. "Can't be stomach—breakfast tasted good. I guess I need some air."

He went out for a walk. Down the broad residential-street, lined with great trees and extensive lawns, he strolled aimlessly; but as soon as the fresh morning air got well into his lungs he quickened his pace, and soon found himself on the outer edge of the city.

After another half-hour of brisk walking he was surrounded by woods and fields and green meadows; and, turning down a narrow, winding lane, entered a shady wilderness. Somewhere quite near he could hear a brook. He found it, and flopped down on the bank.

For two hours he lay there, dozing.

Three o'clock found him at home again, feeling a little guilty that he had not been there to lunch with his wife. He always liked to hear her talk of the proceedings at court on days when she attended, not to mention the fact that she liked him to listen. Besides, was there not something in particular he wanted to ask about?

Something—to be sure. The Hamlin & Hamlin case, of course. No doubt it would be all right, but he really should not have neglected it, and she should have told him sooner that it had been put forward. A glance at the clock showed him that it was past four; too late now, anyway. He wandered aimlessly around the house for a while; then took a book from the library and went up to his room to read.

An hour later he heard the hall door leading into the adjoining room open and close, followed by the patter of quick footsteps to and fro, barely audible through the thick wall. Mr. Warner laid down his book and leaned forward attentively, trying to discover the temperature of the room beyond the wall by whatever sounds might reach his ear.

Suddenly his wife's voice came:

"Timmie!"

He jumped hastily to his feet, crossed to the mirror and arranged his tie, cleared his throat twice and walked reluctantly, by a circuitous route, to the door. There he stood.

"Timmie!"

He opened the door and went in.

"Good evening, my dear," said he, stopping three paces from the threshold.

Mrs. Warner was seated at the dressing table arranging her hair. Her lovely face, wearing an unwonted flush, looked across at her husband from the mirror. There was also an unusual redness about her eyes, which he noted and wondered at.

"I didn't see you at lunch," she began abruptly.

Mr. Warner blinked. "No," he said, and stopped.

"Where were you?"

"Why—I—the fact is, I went for a walk."

Mrs. Warner turned around to look at him.

"A walk?"

"Yes, in the country. The jolliest woods out on the Wakarusa Road. Perfectly full of trees."

"That is a habit of woods, isn't it?" suggested Mrs. Warner sarcastically. Then she had the grace to laugh at herself; but Mr. Warner thought she was laughing at him and became uncomfortable.

"I was sorry to miss lunch," said he, to change the subject. "I wanted to ask about Hamlin & Hamlin. I suppose it came out all right."

"Well, you suppose wrong. It didn't."

"What!" Mr. Warner took a step forward. "You don't mean—"

"Yes. We lost."

"But that's impossible!" cried the little man, aghast.

"No. It's true. Good heavens, Timmie, do you think I can always win?"

He answered simply:

"Yes."

At that tribute she turned again to look at him, and her eyes softened. "I believe you really do think so," she said. "You're a dear, Timmie." Then she exploded with sudden violence: "I just wish old Hamlin had heard you say that!"

Her husband blinked at her, utterly bewildered.

"What?" he stammered.

"What you just said." She turned about to face him. "Timmie, do you think I am a woman naturally inclined to give way to tears?"

"My dear goodness, no!" Mr. Warner actually smiled, the idea was so very amusing.

"Well, I did this afternoon. It was old Hamlin's fault.

I hate him! Do you know what he said? He said that you win my cases for me. At least he intimated it. 'My dear Mrs. Warner, it is quite evident that we have not had the benefit of your husband's advice in this case. I shall pay your fee with reluctance.' That was the way he put it. Just because he was angry at losing! I won't take a cent!''

''But why on earth should he say such a thing?'' demanded Mr. Warner.

''I don't know. Of course, it's absurd. But he'll shout it all over town, and I have enough enemies to make it embarrassing.''

''No one will believe it.''

''Oh, yes they will. The envious are easily persuaded. But not for long. I'll show them.'' Mrs. Warner's pretty lips narrowed to a thin line. ''As far as old Hamlin is concerned,'' she continued, ''it is easy enough to understand him. He hasn't forgotten ten years ago, when he had the impudence to try to make love to me. I told you about it at the time.''

''I know,'' said the little man, looking away. He was thinking that old Hamlin was not the only one, and telling himself that this was a good opportunity to say something that had been on his mind for months, if he could only find the courage. He ended by blurting out:

''There is young Nelson, too.''

Mrs. Warner looked up, frowning. ''What do you mean by that?''

''Why—you know—he is—that is, you see him—''

''Don't be a goose, Timmie.'' The pretty lips parted in a smile, possibly at the idea of her husband being jealous. ''Of course I see him. I can't very well snub the son of the man who owns the Granton Electric Railway Company—they are my best clients. But don't get any silly notions in your head. You know very well I haven't time to allow myself to be in love with Jack Nelson or anyone else. Not even you, Timmie, dear. Now off with you; I must get ready for dinner. It's nearly time.''

''But people are bound to talk—''

''Timmie!''

Mr. Warner went. The germ of dissatisfaction was stirring within him, and he wore a gloomy countenance as he took off his brown tweed suit and got into a dinner jacket. He wondered why it should render him utterly speechless to hear his wife say ''Timmie!'' like that.

Then the dinner bell sounded, and he gave it up with a sigh.

II

During the month that followed, Mrs. Warner found abundant justification for her prophecy that old Mr. Hamlin would ''shout it all over town.'' More accurately, he whispered it, which in such cases is far more effective.

The first rumor of his pernicious utterances came to her ears from the lips of her friend Mrs. Lodge, at a dinner party at the latter's home. It appeared that Mr. Hamlin had assured Mr. Lodge—strictly *sub rosa*, of course—that the brilliant and eminent Mrs. Warner was really nothing more than a pretty dummy whose strings were worked by the subtle brain of her insignificant-looking husband.

''Of course,'' said Mrs. Lodge in conclusion, ''it's all the veriest bosh. Haven't we all heard you make the most wonderful speeches? Thomas Hamlin is an old crank. But it is really too bad, because some people are going to believe it.''

And a week later, at a meeting of the city bar association, of which she was vice president, Mrs. Warner overheard several unpleasant witticisms that were quite evidently intended for her ears. They were actuated, she told herself, by the contemptible envy of disgruntled lawyers who hated her for her preeminent success. Nevertheless, they left their mark.

She began to fear for her prestige.

Fed for ten years on a rich diet of eulogy and adulation, the horrible thought entered her mind that she might end by finding a seat at the table of ridicule. As for a shrinkage in fees, she did not care about that, having made herself independently rich.

But the fees, instead of shrinking, were augmented, and new clients came while old ones stayed. She naturally considered this a good sign and her fear dwindled. And when President Nelson, of the Granton Electric Railway Company, informed her that the defense of the famous Holdup Suit, as the conservative press had nicknamed it, was to be left entirely in her hands, she felt herself able to laugh at her enemies and detractors.

The Holdup Suit, brought by the City of Granton against the Granton Electric Railway Company, to collect thirty thousand dollars in profits in accordance with a clause of the franchise, was a political move on the part of the new liberal city administration.

Everyone knew that the city could not possibly win. Every lawyer in Granton had declared both in public and private that the case had not a leg to stand on. But the administration was making an immense hit with the people by bringing it, and it was being gloriously front-paged by the press.

No wonder Mrs. Warner felt proud that she had been selected to defend it, though she was naturally a little vexed that it should be so universally known that her task was absurdly simple. As she overheard one lawyer say, ''Nelson won't even have to defend the action. As soon as the city presents its case the judge will throw it out of court.''

It was in connection with the Holdup Suit that Mrs. Warner conceived her great idea.

One sunny afternoon in August as she was being carried swiftly down Main Street in her motorcar on her way to the offices of the railway company, her face suddenly took on an expression of deep thought, then lighted up with a victorious smile.

''I'll do it!'' she said to herself with prompt decision. ''It's just the thing! Nobody could talk after that.''

She spent two hours with President Nelson in his private office, examining innumerable documents and pamphlets. When they had finished, and Mr. Nelson had expressed his admiration of her sagacity and penetration, she informed him that she had a question to ask.

''Fire away,'' said the great man genially.

''I want to know,'' returned Mrs. Warner, rising and putting on her gloves to indicate that the point was really unimportant, ''if it would make any difference to you if Mr. Warner—my husband—should be chosen to represent the city in this case?''

Mr. Nelson stared for a moment, then permitted himself a smile of surprise. ''Of course not,'' he ended by declaring. ''But why—I didn't know—''

''It isn't decided yet,'' Mrs. Warner explained. ''But I have reason to believe he is going to be retained. Of course, this is in the strictest confidence.''

Mr. Nelson, still smiling, assured her that he would keep the secret. ''I don't care if they retain Satan himself,'' he declared. ''We can't lose.'' Then he added hastily, ''with you.''

Mrs. Warner thanked him for the expression of confidence and departed. At the door of the outer office she found herself suddenly confronted by a tall young man, hat in hand, bowing and smiling.

"Mrs. Warner, I've been waiting here two endless hours for a word with you. I had begun to fear Father was going to keep you locked in there forever. Won't you let me drive you home? My car is outside." This all came out in a breath.

"My car, too, is outside," smiled Mrs. Warner.

"Please," said the young man persuasively.

She ended by accepting. No sooner had they seated themselves on the soft leather cushions than the young man pulled out his watch and proferred a second request.

"Couldn't we drive round awhile?" he pleaded. "It's only four o'clock, and such a jolly day."

But this met with a firm refusal. "I am not good-for-nothing like you, Jack. I have work to do. Straight home!"

"Please?"

It was difficult to resist the pleading brown eyes, for he was a good-looking and pleasant youth, besides being the son of Henry Blood Nelson. But Lora Warner was not the woman to make even so slight a mistake as this would have been. She repeated, "Straight home!" in a firmer tone than before, and shook a menacing finger at him. The car shot off down Main Street.

Twenty minutes later, as she stood on the steps of her home shaking hands with her escort, she looked up to see a familiar figure turn in from the street and come up the walk. Nelson, noting her raised eyes, turned and caught sight of the newcomer.

"Good evening, Mr. Warner," he said pleasantly.

"Good evening," replied the husband, coming up to them. The men shook hands. "Home so early, my dear?" he continued, turning to his wife. Then, without waiting for an answer, he went into the house.

"Thank you for bringing me home," said Lora; and the young man lifted his hat and departed.

At the dinner table that evening Mr. Warner wore the appearance of one who has communed with himself in sorrow. His constitutional cheerfulness had been slipping away from him for some time now, thanks to the ravages of the germ of dissatisfaction; but on this occasion he was absolutely dumpish. Lora noticed it with surprise and a little discomfort.

"Is there something wrong, Timmie?" she demanded.

"Everything," he replied rashly, without thinking; and then, aghast at his own nihilism, he stammered something about not feeling well.

"I'm sorry," said his wife, not without feeling. "Is there anything I can do?"

He replied with a simple "No," and attacked the roast.

After dinner Mrs. Warner led the way to the library, saying she had an important matter in mind which it would be necessary to discuss at length. In dreary silence Mr. Warner followed her to a divan between the windows and seated himself on the arm of a chair.

This in itself was a revolution. Only a free and bold man, a man of initiative, deposits himself on the arm of a chair. Mr. Warner had never done it before save in the privacy of his own room, having, like all others who are timid, weak, or downtrodden, invariably chosen the seat.

He went still further. Before his wife had time to introduce her important matter he opened his mouth and said distinctly:

"I saw old Mr. Hamlin today."

Lora, feeling the electricity in his tone, looked up quickly.

"Well? Is there anything so very strange about that?"

"He came to see me at the office."

"At the office?"

"At my office."

"Oh, he did ! What about?"

"About his case against the Central Sash and Door Company. You know, he appealed."

"But why should he go to see you?"

Mr. Warner appeared to hesitate. The fact was, he hadn't intended to mention this affair at all. What was it that forced the words to his lips? Perhaps the memory of seeing his wife standing on the steps with her hand in that of young Nelson; perhaps merely—and this is a better guess—the germ of dissatisfaction within him. He continued:

"He wanted me to take the case. In spite of the fee he seemed to think it wasn't necessary—that is, to think about you."

"Did you take it?"

"Of course not. No. Hadn't he insulted you? I told him so. I told him some other things, too. He's a very energetic man."

"Energetic?"

"Yes. He actually tried to throw me out of the office. Must be fifty years old if he's a day. But then I'm not so very big, and he thought he could do it. I pushed him out and locked the door."

Mrs. Warner smiled. "It must have been a very exciting encounter."

"It was. Quite hot for a minute. I thought you might want to know about it."

"Of course. I'm glad you told me. I didn't know you were a fighter, Timmie."

"Well"—the little man was evidently trying not to look pleased with himself—"to tell the truth, I didn't, either. But I couldn't stand still and let him put me out of my own office."

"I'm glad to know it," continued Mrs. Warner. "That you're a fighter, I mean. Because it will make it all the more interesting. You have to fight me now."

Mr. Warner blinked three times before he could find his tongue.

"Fight you!" he exclaimed finally, quite as though he had been informed that he was about to charge on the German army.

"Yes. That is what I wanted to talk to you about. My dear Timmie, you are to represent the city in the Holdup Suit."

"The city! Me! What—why—" He was staggered out of coherence.

"Exactly. The city and you. You are to handle the case for the City of Granton."

Mr. Warner was blinking at the rate of fifty times a second.

"My dear Lora," said he—and you may believe he was strongly agitated when he called his wife his dear Lora—"my dear Lora, I haven't the slightest idea what you are talking about."

Mrs. Warner began her explanation. "It's very simple," she declared. "In fact, there's nothing more to say. As you know, I am retained for the railway company. You will represent the city. We will be opponents. It is my own idea."

"But why?" He was still bewildered.

"Silly! Don't you see it will put an end to all these absurd rumors about my being—what old Hamlin says?"

"Oh !" said Mr. Warner, suddenly comprehending.

"They can't very well say we are in partnership when we are opposed to each other," continued his wife. "It will work out beautifully. The only difficulty is to get the brief for you. But you ought to be able to manage it. Mayor Slosson is still a good friend of yours, isn't he?''

Mr. Warner nodded.

''Then it shouldn't be so difficult. Besides, they know very well there isn't a chance in the world of winning, so they won't care who handles the case. If necessary, you could offer your services without fee. You had better see the mayor in the morning.''

''But—''

''Well?''

''Would it be professionally correct?''

''Correct? How?''

''For us to take retainers in opposition.''

''Good Heavens! Why not?''

''I don't know. I thought perhaps—I suppose it would be all right.'' He hesitated for a minute, then added diffidently, ''Naturally, you know, I don't like to take a hopeless case.''

''I know. I thought of that. But nobody expects you to win. Every one knows you can't win.''

''True.'' The little man walked across to a window and stood looking out on the night. This for perhaps ten seconds; then he returned to the chair and sat down, not on the arm, but in the seat. He looked up at his wife and found her regarding him expectantly; he kept his eyes steadfast, noting her fresh velvety skin, her pretty parted lips, her mass of glorious brown hair. Then he looked away, blinked and sighed.

''I'll see Mayor Slosson in the morning,'' he said.

Lora sprang up from the divan, ran to his chair and threw her arms about his neck. ''You're a dear, Timmie!'' she cried.

When he got to his room ten minutes later his face was still flushed with the remembrance of her kiss.

III

At ten o'clock the following morning Timothy D. Warner called on Mayor Slosson at the city hall, and was shown at once into the private office.

Mayor Slosson, a square-jawed, athletic-looking man of thirty-two or-three, had been carried into office by a wave of liberal sentiment that had swept the city at the last election.

He had been a factory hand, had risen to the position of superintendent, and some five years before had started a factory of his own with capital borrowed from one Timothy D. Warner. He had paid back the money, but it will be seen that he considered himself still in debt.

"Pretty busy?" inquired Mr. Warner, dropping into a chair. "There's a crowd outside. I supposed I'd have to wait."

"Beggars, most of 'em," commented the mayor. "I'm never too busy to see you, Mr. Warner. Thank God, I haven't reached the point yet where I forget my friends. I've discovered that most people have. How's everything?"

Mr. Warner replied in a somewhat doubtful tone that everything was all right. Then, because what he had to say tasted badly in his mouth, he got it out at once, without preamble.

"Jim, I want to represent the city in the Holdup Suit."

The mayor whistled in mild surprise; but before he had time to put it into words his visitor continued:

"I know it's a great deal to ask, and I'd rather bite my tongue off. But—that is—I have a personal reason. I ask it as a favor. It isn't as though you were endangering your case, because everyone says you haven't any."

Some inward thought had brought a grin to the mayor's face.

"Isn't Mrs. Warner representing Nelson?" he asked curiously.

The other replied simply: "Yes."

"Then—would it be professional?"

"I think so. We are not partners, you know."

There was a pause, while the mayor gazed thoughtfully at a paperweight on his desk.

"I don't see why you shouldn't have it," he said finally. "Gray, the city attorney, could appoint you as temporary assistant and give you the assignment. He'd be glad of the chance, for I'm afraid they're right when they say we haven't a case. It's a pity, too. The people are entitled to that money and they ought to have it. I know they say we are trying to make political capital, and maybe we are, but it's a just claim for all that."

"Then do you think—shall I see Gray?"

"Yes. Wait a minute." The mayor looked at his watch. "He ought to be in now. Come on—we'll go round there together."

Thus it happened that at two o'clock that afternoon Mr. Warner entered his office on Main Street with a huge bundle of papers under his arm and a worried frown on his brow. The papers he had got from City Attorney Gray, who had evidently been glad to get rid of them; the frown came from a certain newfound perplexity that was destined to give him many uncomfortable hours in the immediate future.

Mr. Warner's trained legal mind had shown him at a glance that Mayor Slosson was indisputably correct in his contention that the city's case was a just one. Also, that it was as hopeless as it was just. But the curious thing was that, finding himself thus accidentally the leader of a lost cause, he felt suddenly freed from his immemorial timidity and diffidence. Instead, he felt a new instinct stirring within him—a glorious, breathtaking instinct—the instinct to fight.

He sat down at his desk, untied the bundle of papers, and read over the clause in the franchise that was the center of dispute.

ARTICLE 14—It is further agreed that whenever the net profits of the party of the first part for any fiscal year, beginning on the first day of July and ending on the thirtieth day of June following, shall be shown to be in excess of eight per centum of the amount of capital stock as stated in the papers of incorporation, the party of the second part shall receive an amount not less than fifty per centum of such excess, to be paid within sixty days from the expiration of the fiscal year in which such excess was realized. (Net profits defined below.) Furthermore, that the party of the second part, through its representatives, shall at all times have access to the books, papers and accounts of the party of the first part, in order to determine such excess.

"Not a chance," Mr. Warner muttered to himself. "We can't win. It's as simple as A B C. That part of the railway which runs to Vinewood Park, being without the city limits, is not covered by the franchise, and the city can't collect a cent on its profits. And yet it's the city people that use it and they're certainly entitled to their share. The man that signed this franchise for the city was either a crook or a brainless fool!"

He read on through the articles to the end, including the stipulation for fines for violation of franchise and the conditions of revocation. Then he returned to Article 14 and read it over several times, shaking his head dismally. Then—suddenly he stopped short, uttered a sharp exclamation, and glanced up at a calendar on the wall.

"August thirtieth," he observed, while his eyes shone with excitement. "I wonder—but they wouldn't be such fools. They're too sharp for that. Anyway—"

He turned to the telephone. A short wait—then:

"Hello! Mayor Slosson? This is Mr. Warner. Warner. I want to see you for a minute. Will you be in? I'll run right over. Yes. Something important."

These were the sentences—short, snappy—of a man of ability and decision in action. Mr. Warner had not talked like that for fifteen years. Some such thought crossed his mind as he ran out to hail a Main Street car. He felt dazed and intoxicated, but thoroughly alive.

His interview with Mayor Slosson was a short one. As soon as they were alone in the private office he fired a question:

"Jim, has the Granton Electric Railway Company sent the city a check for its share of the excess profits last year?"

The mayor looked surprised. "Why no, of course not," he replied. "That's what they won't do. We claimed thirty thousand"—the mayor looked at a paper on his desk—"$31,254.65 for our share, including the profits on the Vinewood Park line, and they refused to pay it."

"I know," said Mr. Warner impatiently, "but have they paid the ten thousand they admit they owe?"

"No."

"Are you sure?"

"Positive."

"Have they offered it?"

The mayor thought a moment. "I don't know," he said finally. "I think not. Metcalf, at the city treasurer's office, could tell you. Why? Is it important?"

"Rather," said the lawyer dryly.

"Well, here's the telephone."

But Mr. Warner was already halfway to the door. "No telephone for this," he declared. "It has too many leaks. I'll go and see Metcalf. And listen, Jim, don't breathe a word of what I've asked you. Not a word to anybody."

And he was gone before the astonished mayor could frame a reply.

Metcalf, at the city treasurer's office, proved to be a thin, sorrowful-looking young man with an immense white brow and a mass of coal-black hair. When Mr. Warner had explained his errand, after swearing the young man to the strictest secrecy, he turned to a large book and examined its pages attentively, after which he turned over one by one the contents of a bulging letter file. Then he turned to the lawyer:

"They have never sent a check, Mr. Warner. I was sure of it, anyway, but I thought I'd better look it up. On July twentieth we wrote demanding the payment of $31,254.65. They returned a refusal and a denial of the obligation on July twenty-third. On the twenty-fourth we replied that if the amount were not paid by the end of the month we would bring suit. On the twenty-fifth they told us to go ahead. The correspondence, with our copies, can be placed at your disposal at any time."

"Who signed the letters?" Mr. Warner's eyes positively glittered.

"John Henry Nelson, the secretary of the company— old man Nelson's son," replied the young man.

Mr. Warner returned to his office. His eyes shone more than ever, but the frown had deepened. His perplexity was great and intolerably painful, and it entirely overshadowed his elation.

He knew one thing for certain—he could not face his wife with defiance in his heart and get away with it. At least, not at home. The fighting instinct had done valiant

work within him in the past hour, but he had not reached
so sublime a height as that.

So, lacking the firmness of moderation, he adopted the
only course left to a desperate man. He burned his
bridges. In other words, he went to a Main Street restaurant and ate two mutton chops and some fried potatoes; and on his way back to the office he stopped at a
furniture store and made certain purchases, stipulating
that they be delivered within the hour.

Ten minutes later he stood before his desk regarding
the telephone that stood upon it with an expression of
fearsome dread. He was saying to himself, "I am about
to perform the bravest act of my life—that is, I hope I
am."

He coughed twice for courage, whistled aloud, pressed
his lips firmly together and stretched out a trembling
hand toward the receiver. As he did so the bell rang
violently. He jumped backward halfway across the office, knocking over a chair and bumping his head on the
chandelier.

But it was only Mayor Slosson calling up to ask if he
had seen Metcalf. Mr. Warner replied that he had.

"What did he have to say? Had they sent the check?
What's the game, Mr. Warner?"

"I can't tell you over the telephone," replied the lawyer; and hung up with a bang.

After a wait of a few seconds he took the receiver
down again and gave the operator the number of his own
home.

"Hello!"

Mr. Warner recognized the voice of Higgins, the maid.
He requested in a firm tone that Mrs. Warner be called
to the phone.

"Who is it wants to speak to her?" came the voice
of Higgins.

"Mr. Warner."

"Who?"

"Mr. Warner!"

"I can't hear you."

"Her husband—Timmie!" shouted the unhappy man.

"Oh—wait a minute!"

And then, in much less than a minute, came a well-known voice, clear and pleasant:

"Hello! Timmie?"

"Good evening, my dear," said Mr. Warner.

"It would be a better one if you would come home to dinner." There was a smile in the voice. "Where on earth are you? It's nearly seven o'clock."

Mr. Warner took his courage between his teeth. "I'm at the office. I'm going to sleep here. I'm having a cot sent in. I want to know if you could send Higgins or somebody over with my bag—a comb and brush—my things, you know—"

"My dear Timmie!" Mr. Warner could feel her astonishment and incredulity oozing through the wire. "Are you crazy? Come home at once."

"No. I'm going to sleep here."

"In the name of goodness, why?"

"Because I don't think it would be exactly right for us to—that is, live together—while we—while this case—the Holdup Suit, you know. I'm retained for the city. I saw the mayor this morning. I'm going to stay here till the case is decided."

"My dear Timmie"—his wife's voice was becoming deliberate—"of all the silly notions you've ever had, this is certainly the silliest! What possible difference does *that* make?"

"It makes lots of difference. Will you send the bag?"

"No, I won't! Come home!"

"Will you send it?"

"No!"

"Then I'll do without it," declared Mr. Warner with strange calmness; and again he hung up with a bang. Never in all his life, before that day, had he hung up with a bang even once.

He dropped into a chair, mopping his brow with a handkerchief. The deed was done. Strange, bizarre emotions were leaping wildly about in his breast. He felt capable of anything. Suddenly he looked up quickly, while an expression of apprehension shot into his eyes. Suppose she did ! It would be just like her. He walked to the door and locked it and put the key in his pocket.

As he sat down again the telephone bell rang. He turned around and eyed it malevolently. It rang again—a long insistent jingle. He reached out, took the receiver from the hook and set it on the table. Then, grinning, he took out his pipe, filled and lighted it, and cocked his feet upon the desk.

He had been in this position, puffing jerkily, for half an hour, when a knock sounded on the door. He jumped up, startled; then, remembering his purchase at the furniture store, crossed leisurely, taking the key from his pocket. But before he inserted it in the lock he called out:

"Who is it?"

Silence; then another knock.

"Who is it?" he repeated.

A well-known voice came:

"It's I—Lora. Let me in!"

Mr. Warner felt his knees come together. He had not really expected this. He hoped the door was good and thick. Clutching the key firmly in his hand as though it were a weapon of defense, he called huskily:

"I won't!"

"Timmie, open the door!"

"I tell you I won't," repeated Mr. Warner. Some of the huskiness left his voice. "I can't, Lora. The mayor wouldn't want me to. It wouldn't be right. Did you bring the bag?"

"Yes. I want to give it to you." The voice sharpened a little. "Don't be an ass, Timmie! Open the door!"

But the brilliant Lora had made a mistake. At her confession that she had brought the bag Mr. Warner felt his heart leap with an intoxicating thrill. She had admitted to herself the possibility of defeat, then. He pressed his lips tightly together.

"If you've got the bag," he said finally, between his teeth, "leave it in the hall and I'll get it when you're gone. I can't let you in. I'm—I haven't any clothes on." This was a lie, but the poor man needed it. "Anyway," he continued, "why should you want to come in? What do you want?"

"I want you to come home, of course." The tone could not be called one of appeal, but neither was it that of command. "I honestly believe you need someone to look after you, Timmie. You've been acting queerly for weeks. Please open the door!"

"No!"

"Please!"

It was awfully hard; he could not remember that she had ever said please to him before. He gritted his teeth. "Go away!" he shouted savagely.

Silence followed for perhaps ten seconds; on the part of Mr. Warner, a breathless silence. Then came a sound as of something heavy dropped on the floor outside, and retreating footsteps. He ran to the window and looked out, and saw his wife cross the sidewalk and enter her car at the curb. The car started forward with a jerk and disappeared down Main Street. Mr. Warner dropped into a chair as one exhausted.

A little later he went into the hall and got the bag, which he found outside the door. Soon after that the cot came, and he put it up in a corner and went to bed, to dream strange dreams.

IV

The following morning Mr. Warner received a call from Mayor Slosson, who appeared to be slightly irritated at the discourtesy he had been subjected to the evening before. But he accepted the lawyer's apology without reservation, and proceeded at once to inquire into the reason for the mysterious questions concerning the check the railway company hadn't sent.

"There's no reason why I shouldn't tell you," replied Mr. Warner, glancing up at the calendar. "It's August thirty-first, and it doesn't matter now if the whole town knows it. Only we might as well keep the secret till we get in our work."

"What is it?" inquired the mayor. "A puzzle?"

"Why, yes. It's a puzzle to me, and a joke, too. But it won't be a joke to Mr. Henry Blood Nelson. Listen."

And Mr. Warner leaned forward and began to whisper. He whispered steadily for five minutes, save when he was interrupted by an exclamation of astonishment and delight from the mayor, which was often. When he had finished the mayor's face was a study in exultation, glee, and triumph.

"By God, we've got 'em!" he cried; and he was not naturally a profane man.

"I think so," agreed the lawyer.

"It's certain. Certain! I'll leave all details to you, Mr. Warner. But make the appointment for tomorrow if you can, and call me up as soon as you know. Of course, I won't say a word to anyone."

The mayor stayed half an hour longer, discussing the

case from every possible angle. When he had gone Mr. Warner drew forth a sheet of paper from a drawer of his desk, took up a pen and wrote as follows:

MRS. LORA WARNER,
621 Main Street,
City.

DEAR MADAM:

I am writing to ask if it would be convenient for yourself and a representative of the Granton Electric Railway Company to receive a call from the undersigned in your office sometime tomorrow (Friday, September 1). Mayor James L. Slosson will probably be with me. We wish to confer concerning the suit brought by the City of Granton against the Granton Electric Railway Company.

Yours very truly,
TIMOTHY D. WARNER.

A grim smile hovered about Mr. Warner's lips as he signed this letter, sealed, and stamped it. Then he put on his hat and went out to the mailbox on the corner.

The following morning brought a reply, typewritten:

MR. TIMOTHY D. WARNER,
417 Main Street,
Granton.

DEAR SIR:

Replying to your favor of August 31, I wish to say that Mr. John Henry Nelson, secretary of the Granton Electric Railway Company, and myself will expect you and the mayor at my office at 11 A.M. tomorrow (Friday). But I also wish to say that if it is your intention to offer any compromise in this matter the conference will be fruitless. My client has too high a confidence in the justice of his case to submit to any compromise whatever short of an unconditional withdrawal of the suit.

> Yours truly,
> LORA WARNER.

Up to the receipt of this letter Mr. Warner had been conscious of a stubborn disinclination to do what he felt to be his duty both to the city and to himself. But the mention of young Nelson's name drove away the last vestige of a qualm. Indeed, when he called up Mayor Slosson to tell him the hour of appointment there was a note of vindictiveness in his tone that caused the mayor to grin to himself. He thought he knew the reason for it, and perhaps he was not so far wrong at that.

At exactly one minute to eleven Mr. Warner and Mayor Slosson turned in at the entrance of 621 Main Street and mounted a flight of stairs to the most luxurious suite of law offices in Granton. The door at the end of the hall bore the inscription in gold letters:

LORA WARNER
Attorney at Law

"This way, gentlemen," said a neatly dressed female clerk; and they were ushered through a door on the right into a large, sunny room facing on Main Street. At one end of a shining mahogany table sat Mrs. Lora Warner; behind her chair stood John Henry Nelson.

Everyone said good morning at once, and young Nelson placed chairs for the newcomers. None of the four appeared to be exactly at his ease; constraint was in the air. Mrs. Warner, who had remained seated at the end of the table, motioned young Nelson to a chair at her right; her husband, seated at the other end, was busily fumbling among some papers in a portfolio. His face was flushed.

"We await your pleasure, gentlemen," said Mrs. Warner in a most professional tone.

The mayor glanced at Mr. Warner, who cleared his throat and looked around the table with steady eyes.

"In the first place," he began, "we wish to announce our intention of withdrawing our suit against the Granton Electric Railway Company for excess profits. I speak for the City of Granton"—he looked at the mayor; the mayor nodded—"and we admit that under the terms of the present franchise our claim cannot be justified at law."

An involuntary exclamation of surprise came from the lips of young Nelson; but Mrs. Warner maintained her professional gravity.

"Will you give us a notice of this withdrawal in writing?" she inquired coolly.

"Certainly. I have it here." Mr. Warner tapped his portfolio. "But I wish first to speak of another matter." He opened the portfolio and took from it a sheet of paper, which he unfolded. "This is a copy of the franchise under which the Granton Electric Railway operates. No doubt you are familiar with it, but I shall take the liberty of reading a portion of Article Fourteen.

" 'It is further agreed that whenever the net profits of the party of the first part for any fiscal year, beginning on the first day of July and ending on the thirtieth day of June following, shall be shown to be in excess of eight per centum of the amount of capital stock as stated in the papers of incorporation, the party of the second part shall receive an amount not less than fifty per centum of such excess, to be paid within sixty days from the expiration of the fiscal year in which such excess was realized.'

"You will notice it is provided and agreed that the excess of profit shall be paid within sixty days after the end of the fiscal year. Obviously, an infraction of this rule would constitute a violation of franchise. Such violation has been consummated. The Granton Electric Railway has admitted in writing an excess of profits amounting"—Mr. Warner consulted a slip of paper— "to $10,604.20, and no payment, or offer of payment has been made. This is the first day of September. The sixty days have terminated."

"Of course not!" cried young Nelson, springing to his feet. "Of course we haven't paid! You know very well we have merely been waiting till the dispute was settled. We've been willing to pay the ten thousand at any time. The sixty-day clause has nothing to do with it. As a matter of fact, only last year we didn't send the city a check till well in October. I signed it myself."

"Pardon me, Mr. Nelson," put in Mrs. Warner, whose face had suddenly gone white. She turned to her husband and stretched out a hand that trembled. "Will you please let me see that franchise?" she asked, with an evident effort at control.

"With pleasure," replied the lawyer. "But just a moment, please." He turned to young Nelson. "The fact that your check last year was not sent till October proves merely that the preceding city administration were better friends of yours than they were of the city's." Then again to his wife, holding up the franchise:

"You will notice, here at the bottom, it is provided that any violation of franchise shall be deemed sufficient cause for revocation. We wish to announce our intention to take full advantage of this technical violation. Here are our terms:

"The Granton Electric Railway Company is to pay the city $31,254.65, the full amount of its claim for excess profits. It is to submit to the revocation of the present franchise and accept a new one which shall include the Vinewood Park line in the computation of future profits. The alternative is that we will revoke the present franchise by law and refuse to grant a new one.''

"It's blackmail!" cried young Nelson, again starting to his feet; but at a glance from Mrs. Warner he sat down again.

"Will you please let me see that franchise?" she repeated, and this time her voice plainly trembled.

Mr. Warner handed the paper across the table.

"You may keep it," he said politely. "It's only a copy."

Then he gathered the rest of the papers into the portfolio and rose to his feet. The mayor also rose.

"We will wait till noon tomorrow for your decision," said Mr. Warner. "Unless our demands are met by that time, we shall at once enter an action to annul your franchise." And he turned to go.

Mrs. Warner looked up from the paper; the print was dancing before her eyes.

"But—wait!" she cried. "Timmie!" She stopped short, while her face reddened to the tips of her ears. Then her head went up proudly. "I mean Mr. Warner," she amended. "Will you give me time to get in communication with Mr. Nelson?"

Mr. Warner turned at the door. "Mr. Nelson is here," he said, dryly.

Again his wife's face grew red. "I mean Mr. Henry Blood Nelson," she explained. "The president of the company."

"He can communicate with me at my office at any time," replied the lawyer. "But our terms, as I have given them, are final." With that he departed, followed by the mayor.

"The blackmailers!" cried young Nelson at the closed door.

"Mr. Nelson," came Mrs. Warner's voice, curiously steady, "you are talking of my husband."

The young man turned, flushing. "I'm sorry, I—really, I forgot."

"Very well. I understand. Now go—your car is outside, isn't it?—go to your father's office and tell him I shall be there in half an hour. Don't say anything about what has happened. I'll tell him myself. I deserve it."

She sent him away, in spite of his remonstrances. When she found herself alone she sat down with the franchise before her on the table and began to read Article Fourteen.

V

That night Mayor Slosson and Mr. Warner sat up till eleven in vain expectation of a word from the hostile camp. Then, considering it useless to wait longer, the mayor arose to go.

"We'll hear in the morning," he observed hopefully. "You don't think it possible they've found a loophole?"

"Not a chance," declared the lawyer confidently.

As soon as his visitor had departed he undressed and lay down on the cot. He felt that he had done a good day's work, both for himself and for others. But somehow this feeling brought no comfort. His wife's face, white with consternation and dismay, would not leave his vision. He wondered if she had gone to bed, and if so, whether she slept.

For an hour he lay thus, uneasy, in torment. Suddenly he sprang up from the cot, turned on the light, took a pack of cards from a drawer of the desk and sat down. He began to lay them out for his favorite game of Canfield: One up, six down, one up, five down, one up, four down, one up, three down. He had nearly completed the pleasant task when his face suddenly filled with an expression of disgust.

"Silly fool!" he muttered aloud, brushing the cards onto the floor and rising to his feet.

Again he sought the cot and lay there, with eyes alternately open and closed, till morning. Then he arose, dressed and went out to a restaurant for breakfast.

The first word from the enemy came a little before nine o'clock in the form of a telephone message from Mr. Henry Blood Nelson. He wished to know if he could call on Mr. Warner at his office at a quarter past nine.

"We've got 'em," said Mr. Warner, hanging up the receiver and turning to Mayor Slosson, who had just come in.

"We have," agreed the mayor. "Shall I leave?"

"No. I may want you."

The mayor sat down and lit a cigar.

The little office at 417 Main Street saw more bustle and excitement in the next three hours than it had witnessed in all the fifteen years of its uneventful career.

First came Mr. Henry Blood Nelson, to depart sputtering with wrath. Then his son, John Henry Nelson, who departed likewise. Then different officers of the Granton Electric Railway Company, singly and in bodies, armed with books, arguments, and protestations. Then Mr. Arthur Hampton, of the firm of Hampton and Osgood, who had been the G. E. R. lawyers before the advent of Mrs. Warner.

And, finally, came again Mr. Henry Blood Nelson, with hatred in his heart and a check for $31,254.65 in his hand. It was surrender.

"Mr. Warner," said the mayor, when he found himself again alone with the lawyer, "I want to congratulate and thank you on behalf of the people of Granton. You used sharp weapons against the enemy, but it is the only kind that will pierce their dirty, thick skin. And I thought I was doing you a favor when I gave you the case!''

Late that evening Mr. Warner, after dining at the Main Street restaurant, walked wearily up the two flights of stairs that led to his office. In his hand were two evening newspapers, and on the front page of each was a three-column picture of Mr. Warner himself. He had not read the accompanying articles, but their tenor may easily be guessed.

As he ate his dinner he had marveled somewhat at the pictures. To his certain knowledge there was not a photograph of himself anywhere in the world except the one he had given to his wife some fifteen years before, and he had supposed it had long since been destroyed. Yet here it was, staring him out of countenance from the columns of a newspaper!

He wondered vaguely how they had managed to get hold of it. He remembered now that when he returned from a long walk late that afternoon the man in the office next door had told him that some reporters had been hanging around since one o'clock.

He sat down at his desk, turned on the light—it was nearly eight o'clock—and opened one of the papers. So that was how he had looked fifteen years ago! Not so bad—really, not so bad. Silly mustache, though—kind of funny-looking. Had time improved it any? He got up and looked in the mirror over the mantel. As he turned again to the desk he was startled by hearing the telephone bell.

He took up the receiver.

''Hello.''

''Hello. Is this Mr. Warner?''

He recognized the voice at once. ''Yes. What is it, Higgins?''

A pause followed, during which a mumbling of voices came over the wire. Then Higgins:

"Mrs. Warner wants to know if you're coming home to dinner."

"I'm not coming—" began Mr. Warner impulsively, then he stopped short. He reflected that such a message should not be given to a servant. But why not? The whole town would be talking of it in a day or two. He turned to the transmitter and spoke distinctly:

"Tell Mrs. Warner I'm not coming home at all."

Then he hung up.

He opened a paper, sat down and tried to read. But the print was a vacant blur to his eyes, though he tried hard for five minutes.

"What the devil!" he muttered angrily, aloud, "am I losing my eyesight? Am I a baby?"

He threw the paper on the floor and picked up a law book, but with no better success. Somehow the page bore a distinct resemblance to a tangled mass of brown hair.

"If I'm going to do this I may as well do it like a man," he growled; and to show that he meant what he said he got up and began to pace up and down the room. This for half an hour; then he crossed to the window and stood looking out on dimly lighted Main Street, two stories below.

In the show windows of the Thayer Dry Goods Company, directly opposite, wax dummies stood simpering at the passersby. Half a block down were the red and blue lights of Rowley's drugstore; a block in the other direction was the arc over the entrance of the restaurant of which he had become a patron two days before. The street itself was nearly deserted; perhaps a dozen pedestrians were in sight, and now and then a carriage or buggy came along.

The whirr of an automobile sounded from the north, and soon the car itself appeared around the corner of Washington Avenue. It crossed, and came up the west side of Main Street; slowed down, and stopped in front of 417, directly beneath the window.

Mr. Warner felt something catch in his throat. "It can't be," he muttered. But he knew it was, and hence felt no additional surprise when he saw a familiar figure leap from the tonneau and start for the entrance. But he felt something else. What was it? What was the matter with him? He only knew that he seemed suddenly to have been paralyzed, that he could not move a muscle to save his life. He remained staring stupidly out of the window, feeling as though he were about to be shot in the back.

A moment passed that seemed an hour, and then he heard the door open and close and a voice sounded behind him:

"Timmie."

He turned slowly, as on a pivot. Lora, with flushed face and strange eyes, stood with her back to the closed door.

"Good evening, my dear," said Mr. Warner. Then he wanted to bite his tongue off. Next he tried, "Won't you be seated?" and felt more foolish than before. So he kept still.

"I've come," said Lora, advancing a step, "to take you home."

The lawyer found control of his tongue. "I'm not going home," he declared calmly.

"Yes, you are. You have to."

"Why?"

"Because I want you."

"Is my own inclination to be disregarded?"

"Oh!" She caught her breath. "Is that it? Don't you want to live with me anymore?"

"Yes, that's it. That is—See here, Lora. Sit down. Let's talk it over."

She crossed to the chair he placed for her with a curious hesitancy in her step he had never seen before, and waited for him to speak.

"You say you want me," he began abruptly. "You don't mean that. You mean you are used to me—miss me, like you would Higgins. Just now you asked me if I didn't want to live with you. That's just it. I've been living with you for fifteen years. If I were to say what I wanted, I'd say that I want you to live with me for a while."

"It's the same thing—" began Lora, but he interrupted her:

"Pardon me." He caught her eye and held it. "Do you know what I meant?"

Her gaze fell. "Yes," she admitted.

"Then don't pretend. You see, the trouble is you shouldn't ever have married me. Perhaps you shouldn't have married anyone. But don't think I'm saying you're a great lawyer. I used to think that, but I don't anymore. Any smart lawyer, even, would have seen that sixty-day clause in that franchise the first time he glanced at it. And you didn't see it at all."

He stopped; his wife raised a flushed face.

"You are pretty hard on me, Timmie."

At that, moved by a swift, uncontrollable impulse, he sprang to his feet and shouted:

"Don't call me Timmie!"

Lora looked amazed. "Why not?"

"Because it's a fool name. *'Timmie!'* No woman could think anything of a man with a name like that.

That's why I don't blame you. It's the most idiotic name I ever heard.''

"It's your name. That's why I like it."

"And that's why I hate it." Mr. Warner actually glared. "I should never have let you call me Timmie. I shouldn't have let you do lots of things—at the beginning, I mean—but I was so crazy about you I couldn't help it. I thought—"

She interrupted him:

"You were crazy about me?"

"Of course."

"Do you mean you were in love with me?"

"I do."

"It's funny you never said anything about it."

"Good Heavens!" Again the little man glared. "It was you who wouldn't let me say anything! Simple enough, since you weren't in love with me."

"That isn't true."

"It is."

"I say it isn't."

Mr. Warner advanced a step. "What do you mean by that?" he demanded. "*Were* you in love with me?"

Silence. He advanced another step, and repeated his question. "*Were* you in love with me?"

Lora nodded her head slowly up and down, and there came to Mr. Warner's ears a barely audible: "Yes."

That, entirely unexpected, brought him to a halt. He didn't know what to say, and ended by dropping back into his chair and muttering "Too bad it ended so soon."

Five seconds passed in silence, then Lora suddenly fired a question.

"Timmie, why do you think I came here for you to-night?"

"Because you missed me," he replied moodily.

"Worse than that. Because I couldn't live without you. I know now, because I've tried it."

She rose from her chair, crossed to his side and laid a hand on his arm. "Listen, dear." He stirred uneasily. "No, don't move. I'm not going to make love to you, and I don't want to argue. I just want to ask you once more to come home with me, and tell you why.

"Last night I nearly cried my eyes out. I was miserable and unhappy and I couldn't go to sleep. I tried for hours, and then I got up and went to your room and cried all over your pillow. I don't know whether I love you or not, but I do know that unless you come home with me I don't want to live. You said something just now—I know I'm not a lawyer; that is, your kind of a lawyer. I found it out last night. I'll admit I'd hate to give up my office, because there are parts of the work I love. But—couldn't we make it Warner & Warner? Of course, the first Warner would be you. Or even"—she smiled—"Warner & Wife."

It would seem that so extended and gracious a speech as that would deserve a careful and thoughtful answer. But Mr. Warner appeared to think otherwise. All he said was:

"Why did you cry last night?"

"Because I wanted you. I wanted you worse than I've ever wanted anything in my life."

"And you—cried on my pillow?"

"Yes."

"Which one? The one on the outside?"

"Yes. It seemed to bring me nearer to you. I kissed it, too. I—I wished it was you, Timmie. Wasn't I silly?"

"No." Something seemed to be wrong with Mr. Warner's voice. "No, I don't think you were silly."

JONATHAN STANNARD'S
SECRET VICE

W HEN MRS. STANNARD SAW HER HUSBAND
with a woman in a yellow hat one night at
Courin's Restaurant, she thought she had
solved the mystery which was making her life miserable.
Then, watching from her secluded corner, she had seen
a tall, middle-aged man with a brown mustache walk
over to their table and join them.

Him she recognized. So her husband had not lied to
her, after all, when he had said that he was going to dine
that evening with John Dupont, of the Academy.

And she was further assured when he observed casu-
ally, in their own home three hours later:

"By the way, Dupont brought his wife along. Did you
ever see her?"

"No," replied Mrs. Stannard.

"Nice-looking woman, but a bit flashy. Had on a lot
of yellow stuff. Dupont's getting to be tiresome. I
wished myself at home with you. What did you do with
yourself all evening?"

She murmured something about reading, thereby
achieving her second falsehood within sixty seconds.

But though her husband thus stood acquitted of this
particular malfeasance, the mystery remained. It was not
of long standing. She had married Jonathan Stannard

twelve years before, when he was still an underprofessor at the university.

Three years later he had become suddenly famous by his lengthy essay, "The New Homer." Others had followed; his reputation grew and solidified; and since he was financially independent he had been able to give up his professorship and devote himself entirely to writing.

He was a conservative.

Classicism was his sacred word. His books and lectures were divided into two equal parts: appreciations of the classic and attacks on the modern; the latter were the most interesting, for he was a hard hitter.

He could belabor the Futurists or motion pictures or Eugene Brieux for three hundred pages, with what effect! Assuredly not in vain, for he was taken seriously.

As a husband he was as near perfection as any reasonable woman could expect. He had never neglected his wife; for over eleven years he had even appeared to continue to love her, which is admittedly something unusual in the case of a literary man who hangs around the house all the time. Indeed, for any positive act of his to the contrary, she had every reason to believe that he loved her still.

But there was the mystery.

Though she had previously noticed a rather unusual amount of absence on his part, it had really begun one January evening some six months before. After dinner he had appeared restless, a rare thing with him; and finally, after an hour of books picked up and thrown down again, he had announced abruptly that he had an appointment at the Century Club.

A hasty kiss and he was gone.

Two hours later, about eleven in the evening, an important message had come for him and she had telephoned the club, only to be told that he had not been there. That was all very well; men do change their minds. But when he returned shortly before midnight he replied to her question:

"Why, I've been at the club. I said I was going there, didn't I?"

"That's odd," said Mrs. Stannard. "I called up to give you Selwyn's message and they said you hadn't been there all evening."

"Absurd!" he exclaimed. "Of course I was there! Why, of course I was there! If they had only searched properly—"

But his wife, noting his ill-concealed embarrassment, felt the shadow of doubt enter her mind. She entertained it most unwillingly, for she was not of a suspicious nature, and there had been eleven years of mutual trust to justify her confidence in him; so she had almost succeeded in obliterating the incident from her mind when, a week later, something happened to remind her of it.

He had taken tickets for them for a Hofmann recital, and at the last moment a headache had put her on her back, so he had gone off alone. The next morning she had asked him:

"And how was the new Debussy tone poem?"

"Awful," he replied emphatically, after a second's hesitation. "The man has no ears or he couldn't write such stuff."

And ten minutes later, going through the morning paper, her eye had fallen on the following paragraph:

. . . Salammbo, the new tone poem by Debussy, which was to have been rendered for the first time in America, was dropped from the program on account of the late arrival of the manuscript, leaving Mr. Hofmann insufficient time to study the composition. A group of Chopin was substituted . . .

Obviously, her husband had not attended the recital at all! Mrs. Stannard drew her lips together and hid her face behind the paper to think unseen. Should she confront him with the evidence of his falsehood and demand an explanation? Yes. No.

If he had lied once he would lie again. Useless. Better to hide her knowledge of his guilt. But she found it extremely difficult to hold her tongue, and it was with a sigh of relief that she saw the door close behind him as he went out for his morning stroll.

Her feeling was chiefly one of discomfort, for she could not as yet bring herself to believe that her husband, Jonathan Stannard, the man who above all others stood for rectitude in morals as well as in art, could be guilty of any misdeed.

But he had lied—she pronounced the word aloud in order to get a better hold on it—he had lied to her twice within the week. And now that she thought of it, he had been absent from the house considerably more than usual for the past month or so.

Tuesday afternoon he had gone out at two o'clock and stayed till dinnertime without saying a word of where he had been. Wednesday evening he had gone out for a walk after dinner and returned at a quarter to eleven.

Clearly, he was up to something.

That was her first conclusion. After an hour's reflection she reached her second, and her eyes flashed as she said it aloud:

"There's a woman in it somewhere."

Thenceforth she took good care not to ask where he was going or where he had been. And he, abandoning a habit closely followed for more than eleven years, did not take the trouble to tell her. His absences grew more frequent.

Two or three afternoons and as many evenings each

week he would go out and remain several hours without a word to her. She suffered considerably, but she told herself that the only possible course was to sit and wait in dignified sorrow for whatever might come.

Then, on a sudden impulse, she had gone alone to Courin's Restaurant one night when he had told her he was to dine there with John Dupont, the painter; and she thought she had discovered her enemy in the woman with the yellow hat, only to find later that she was Dupont's wife.

But she resolved to sit and wait no longer.

Dignity or no dignity, she would find out who or what it was that was taking her husband away from her. She had lost six pounds in a month, and her eyes were acquiring a permanent and unattractive redness from frequent tears.

When her husband left the house at eight o'clock the next evening she followed him. But not very far. At the corner of Broadway and Eighty-seventh Street he boarded a downtown car, and she stood helplessly in the middle of the pavement watching the thing whiz out of sight.

The next time, two days later, she had a taxi ready.

She saw him, a block ahead, as he darted into the subway station; but by the time she had reached the spot and leaped out and paid the driver and rushed breathlessly down the steps, a train had gone through and the platform was empty.

Then she awoke to the absurdity of her course. If she did keep close enough to follow him, he would certainly see and recognize her, even through her heavy veil.

By now she was too enraged to cry. She went home, consulted the Red Book, and in a firm and resolute voice asked central for a certain number found therein.

Within thirty minutes her maid ushered in a short, fat

man in a brown suit and straw hat, with enormous hands and feet and twinkling eyes. Mrs. Stannard received him in the library.

"You are—" she began in a timid voice, as the man stood in the doorway with the straw hat in his hand.

"Mr. Pearson, of Doane, Doane & Doane," he replied amiably. "You telephoned for a man, I believe. This is Mrs. Stannard?"

"Yes. You are"—her voice faltered—"you are a detective?"

"I am."

Mrs. Stannard looked at him much as she might have looked at a strange and ferocious animal from the zoo. Then, partially recovering herself, she asked him to be seated. He did so, jerking up his trousers and balancing the straw hat on his knee.

"You follow people?" she declared abruptly.

Mr. Pearson smiled.

"I sure do," he admitted proudly.

"Well"—she hesitated—"of course, I know that there's nothing really wrong, but I am a little worried about it, and I thought if you could—"

"Pardon me," the detective interrupted, "but are you speaking of your husband?"

"Certainly!" said Mrs. Stannard indignantly.

"Just so. You want to know where he goes. Natural curiosity. Day or night?"

"Why—both."

"Ah!" Mr. Pearson elevated his brows. "That's bad. Now, if you will permit me to ask a few questions. What is his full name?"

"Jonathan Stannard."

Mr. Pearson wrote it down in a little leatherbound book.

"Business?"

"Why—the writer."

"Writer?"

"Yes. He writes."

"U-m. Does he drink?"

"No."

"Gamble?"

"No!"

"Er—fond of—er—women?"

"Well! Well—"

But seeing the foolishness of it, she swallowed her indignation and replied calmly:

"No."

"I see." Mr. Pearson was frowning as he wrote. "Evidently he's a bad un. Always been a good husband?"

"Yes."

"U-m. The worst kind. Like Wooley. I handled that case. I suppose now you've got some particular woman in mind?"

"I have told you my husband does not run after women," said Mrs. Stannard with dignity.

"No?" Mr. Pearson winked at a chair. "Now, madam, please give me the particulars of his absence."

She did so; the hours, the dates, the duration. He filled two pages of the book with them.

"You say he's a writer. Stories?"

"No. Mr. Stannard writes essays and criticisms. He is a man of high morals and serious purpose. I can't imagine why he is deceiving me—"

"No doubt. You aren't expected to. We find out and let you know. We always find out. I'd like to go through his desk."

She demurred, but he insisted. She sat trembling, with an eye on the hall door, while Mr. Pearson opened drawer after drawer of her husband's desk and examined the contents. But he found nothing but typewritten sheets with headings like, "Chiaroscuro; the Lost Art," or "The Deleterious Effect of the Motion Picture on the Literary Sense."

"I take it," said Mr. Pearson, closing the bottom drawer and standing up—"I take it that Mr. Stannard is one of them serious guys. Moody and a kicker. I see here where he says he has about as much respect for the modern school of illustrators as he has for a paper hanger. Also, he seems to have a grudge against the movies."

"He stands for the noble in art," said Mrs. Stannard. "He has conducted a campaign against the cinema because it appeals only to the lowest function of our mentality."

"Just so," Mr. Pearson agreed. "I remember him now. I've heard my daughter speak of him. He hates things that other people like. Take this, for instance."

He picked up a sheet from the desk and read:

"The real danger of the poison—for the motion picture is a poison—lies in the ease and frequency with which it is administered. One dose would be harmless, but repeated day after day it is slowly corroding the intellect of the nation.

"We hear much criticism nowadays of the modern craze for wealth, of materialism in art, of the undermining of Christianity by science; but more pernicious than any of these, or of all of them put together, is the subtle and insidious virus of the cinema.

"I see," muttered Mr. Pearson, replacing the paper on the desk. "Probably a shifty customer. Secret vice. Will you please sign this order, madam, for our protection. On the bottom line."

Mrs. Stannard did so.

"I take it," said the detective, pocketing the slip,

"that you want a complete report of your husband's movements outside this house. Including everything?"

"Including everything," she agreed, her lips tight.

"All right." He picked up the straw hat. "You may depend on us, madam. You will hear developments. Good day."

A bow from the door and he was gone.

Mrs. Stannard lived a year in the week that followed.

For the first day or two she reproached herself bitterly for what she had done. To have one's husband followed by a detective! So vulgar! So mean, somehow! However he was wronging her, was it not better to remain in ignorance than to stoop to the role of spy, even by proxy?

If it transpired that some creature had ensnared him with unlawful charms—and she no longer had doubt of this—what could she do, anyhow? And if it were something else?

What, then? She remembered the detective's words, "secret vice." There was something sinister, something horrible about them. Yes, there were worse things even than a woman.

Each day she gazed at her husband's back with alarm and dread as he left the house. To what dreadful place was he going? What revolting deed was he about to commit?

"Secret vice!" Yes, it would be something truly, grandly horrible. There was nothing petty about Jonathan Stannard. Even in his vices he would not be as other men.

On the third morning after the detective's visit, seized with insatiable curiosity, she telephoned the office of Doane, Doane & Doane. No, they had nothing to communicate as yet.

Mr. Pearson, one of their best men, was working on

the case day and night. They would probably not report before the end of the week, when all possible evidence would have been gathered.

Really, Mrs. Stannard must have a little patience.

So she waited, brooding, scarcely sleeping at all, tormented by her fears. When her husband told her at the breakfast table that she was not looking well, and advised a trip to the mountains or seashore, she could hardly refrain from replying: "Yes, you want me out of the way." She was, in fact, working herself into a pretty state.

Her husband was absent nearly every afternoon and evening, and she would sit in her room, at the window, gazing dully into the street for hours. Several times she saw a man start from somewhere in the block to follow her husband as he descended the stoop. It was Mr. Pearson.

And then at five o'clock, Friday afternoon, the detective called to make his report.

She received him, as before, in the library. He wore the same brown suit and straw hat—the former, indeed, looked as if he had never taken it off—and he wiped his brow with his handkerchief as he took a seat at her invitation.

She saw something ominous in the deliberate manner with which he turned to face her, drawing the leather-bound book from his pocket with one hand and placing his hat on the floor with the other.

She trembled.

"You—you—"

She could not go on.

"Madam," said Mr. Pearson impressively, "I am able to give you a full and complete account of your husband's actions. I may say the thing has been done thoroughly. I did it myself. Are you prepared to listen?"

She nodded, unable to speak.

"In my judgment," continued the detective, opening the leatherbound book, "your husband is the finest example of a Dr. Jekyll and Mr. Hyde I have met in my professional career. Also, he is a clever man. I would have lost him the first day but for my ability to hang onto the tail of a subway express. Evidently he has gone in fear of being followed. But he could not elude me."

"Tell me! Tell me!" Mrs. Stannard implored.

"Certainly. I am coming to it. I take it, madam, that you do not care to hear the details of the chase. What you want to know is what your husband has done and where he has gone. I have here a list of the dates and places, if you will be so good as to give me your attention."

He pulled out his handkerchief to mop his brow, cleared his throat, and read as follows in a loud, rhetorical voice:

REPORT ON JONATHAN STANNARD,
WRITER, 318 RIVERSIDE DRIVE

Friday, July 9, 2.24 P.M., entered Empire Moving Picture Theater, Third Avenue and Thirty-ninth Street. Remained three hours and eleven minutes.

Friday, July 9, 8.15 P.M., entered Royal Moving Picture Theater, Third Avenue and Grand Street. Remained two hours and thirty-four minutes.

Saturday, July 10, only appearance in company with client, Mrs. Stannard.

Sunday, July 11, A.M., attended church with client.

Sunday, July 11, 7.09 P.M., entered Circle Moving Picture Theater, Ninth Avenue and Fifty-ninth Street. Remained three hours and fifteen minutes.

Monday, July 12, 3.03 P.M., entered Louvre Moving Picture

Theater, Third Avenue and 149th Street. Remained two hours and one minute.

Tuesday, July 13, only appearance in company with client.

Wednesday, July 14, 10.48 P.M., entered Columbia Moving Picture Theater, Eighth Avenue and 117th Street. Remained four hours and twenty-one minutes.

Thursday, July 15, 9.10 A.M., went to Long Beach with client.

Friday, July 16, 1.55 P.M., entered Mecca Moving Picture Theater, Broadway and Ninety-eighth Street. (Evidently getting bolder.)

Left him there to report to client.

Mr. Pearson closed the book and looked at his client with an air of triumph.

She sat motionless, gazing at him stupidly as though she had not comprehended. Then suddenly she was aware of a shadow on the threshold, and she looked up to see her husband standing in the doorway, a puzzled expression on his grave, handsome face at the sight of his wife seated talking to a man he had never seen.

He came toward them and saw the look on his wife's face.

"What's the matter?" he demanded.

She struggled for a moment to find her voice, and finally succeeded.

"Jonathan," she said, "I know all. This is Mr. Pearson, a detective. He will tell you—"

Stannard's face paled a little as he looked from one to the other.

"A detective!" he repeated. "What for? What is it?"

Then Mr. Pearson spoke.

"Mr. Stannard," he announced, rising to his feet, "I have just informed your wife that during the past seven days you have spent twenty hours and two minutes in moving picture theaters, *with* the dates and places."

There was a silence. Stannard's face grew white as chalk, and it could be seen that he trembled from head to foot.

The detective gazed at him sternly. His wife had cast her eyes on the floor, as though she could not bear to look at him in that moment.

"I am ruined!" groaned the stricken man, sinking into a chair.

"And I thought it was some kind of a woman," whispered his wife. Profound regret was in her voice.

The detective stooped to pick up his hat.

"Well," he said as he started for the door, "I guess you're through with me."

Mrs. Stannard nodded her head in silence, then said suddenly:

"But I must pay you; how much is it?"

"That's all right," replied the other genially from the threshold; "we'll mail our bill and you can send a check. I trust the job has been satisfactory?"

Again Mrs. Stannard nodded. "Quite satisfactory."

"Good. Good day, madam." He started to go, then turned again to add, "You'll have to excuse me for hurrying off like this, but I got a date to go to the movies."

Alone with her husband, Mrs. Stannard turned to look at him with an expression of mingled incredulity and sorrow. The unhappy man sat with his face buried in his hands, moaning piteously; great beads of perspiration stood out on his brow. Thus do strong men, overtaken by their sins, bend under the awful burden of remorse.

Suddenly he looked up and showed her his haggard countenance.

"It is the end," he whispered miserably. "The end of everything—I cannot—it is too much to expect—Vera, tell me—tell me—can you ever forgive me?"

And then it was that Vera Stannard shone forth in all

the glory of her womanliness. She gazed at her husband and saw the dumb pleading of his eyes fastened on her; she heard the agonized despair in his voice, and she felt something come up in her throat, while the hot tears came to her eyes. It is ever woman's part to forgive. She smiled at him.

"We are one, Jonathan," she said in a sweet voice that trembled. "Who am I to judge you. I will even"—she hesitated and faltered, then went bravely on—"I will even share your sin. Yes, I will share it and glory in it."

She stepped forward and laid a hand on his arm.

"Come, dear; let us dress for dinner. Afterward we shall attend the cinema—together."

SANÉTOMO

ON THE DAY THAT HENRY BRILLON TOOK A wife, he renounced—with a pang here and there—the habits and possessions of his single life.

Most important of all was the change from the luxurious bachelor apartments on Forty-sixth Street to a still more luxurious home on Riverside Drive; it he furnished in a style calculated to strain the purse even of a successful broker. Besides his clothing and some paintings and bric-à-brac, he kept only three articles from the downtown apartment: a lacquer-wood humidor, a case of books, and his Japanese manservant, Sanétomo.

He could bring himself to part with none of these.

Poor Sanétomo! He was lost in the great house on the drive. He could still dress his master; he could still arrange the shining linen, the trousers, the jackets, in neat rows for a hasty selection; but that was all. No longer was he called on to prepare those savory midnight repasts, those dainty breakfasts, those perfect little teas, which had made Harry Brillon's rooms the Mecca of all jaded palates.

The house on the drive had a butler, a great man whom Sanétomo detested and feared, to attend to such things. Sanétomo was no longer a factotum and an artist; he was the merest valet.

And he could remember the time he had overheard the beautiful Nella Somi say to his master: "My dear M. Brillon, I do not come here for love of you, but to taste this *gibelotte* of Sanétomo's!"

So it is not a question which of the two men, the master or the servant, most regretted the old free life. It may be doubted, in fact, whether Henry Brillon regretted it at all; at least in the first year or two of his marriage.

His wife, who had been Dora Crevel, daughter of old Morton Crevel, was fair—fair to divinity; and in her large, dark eyes, with their shadowy depths, Brillon found happiness and the recompense for his sacrifice of freedom.

Her face was noted for its beauty; she was young and healthy; she was intelligent; she was in love with the man she had married—small wonder if she filled his thoughts.

So they prospered and were happy. If now and then a tiny cloud appeared on the horizon, they rushed together to drive it away.

One or two small irritations there were, of course. Brillon's favorite painting, a copy of a Degas, which hung in the reception hall, was an eyesore to his wife, though he never knew it. He was more frank in his disapproval of her activities—feeble and innocent enough, goodness knows—in the interests of women's rights.

Of more importance, perhaps, than either of these, since it did cause them some slight inconvenience, was the unaccountable dislike Mrs. Brillon had taken to the Japanese valet.

She had said to her husband one night, a month or two after the wedding.:

"Ugh! Everytime I see him I shudder."

"Who? Sanétomo?" asked Brillon in surprise.

"Yes."

"But why?"

"I don't know." Already Dora was sorry she had spoken. "He seems so snaky, so silent—I don't know just what. It makes me feel creepy to know he is near me."

"In point of fact, he isn't very pretty to look at," Brillon admitted. "He's even ugly. But you see, darling, I've grown attached to him; he's been with me ten years now, and he saved my life once in Brazil. I don't believe I could get along without him. You don't mean—are you really annoyed by his being here?"

Of course, Dora replied "No," and punctuated it with a kiss. For the moment Sanétomo was forgotten.

But as time went on her repugnance for the little yellow man increased until she could scarcely bear the sight of him; not that this caused her any great discomfort, since he scarcely ever left his master's dressing room. She would probably not have seen him oftener than once or twice a month but for the fact that she had contracted the habit of spending a half-hour or so before bedtime in that very room with her husband; it had been begun by her desire to read aloud to him a novel of Dreiser's.

One evening as she read she became suddenly aware that the Japanese was sitting on a stool at the farther end of the room, absolutely motionless, with his little, expressionless eyes gazing straight ahead. Sometime later, when he had gone, she had said to her husband:

"Really, Harry, I don't think it's a good idea to allow the servants to sit around like that."

But he had only laughed, and replied that Sanétomo was not a servant, but a seneschal.

Every evening thereafter the yellow man could be seen on his stool in the corner; and when the sight of him became an irritation too strong for Dora's nerves, she solved the difficulty by simply turning her chair the other way. There she would sit for an hour or so, usually after midnight, three or four times a week, reading aloud from a novel or play, or conversing with her husband, who would lie stretched out in a big Turkish chair in front of her.

And Sanétomo would squat on his stool in the shadow, unnoticed and unheard. Not a sound would come from him during the whole hour; not a cough, nor a movement of the body, nor even a deep breath; none of those little noises by which a human being reveals its presence even in sleep.

Heaven only knows what he was thinking of, or why he sat there. He gave no evidence of any interest in the story that was being read; Brillon might roar with laughter at a humorous passage, or Dora's voice tremble and her eyes fill with tears at a tragic or pathetic one, but Sanétomo gave no sign.

After learning that her husband was genuinely attached to the Japanese, and that it would give him real pain to part with him, Dora said no more about it. But her feeling of aversion increased, in spite of her desire to ignore it.

She would feel his eyes on the back of her head, and then, turning suddenly, would see plainly that his dull and impassive gaze was either fixed straight before him or on the floor, and she would become impatient with herself for her childishness.

"Certainly I am not afraid of him," she would argue with herself; "then why in the name of common sense do I think of him at all? It's absurd; mere stupid fancy; the poor, harmless thing!"

Then she began to come across him in other parts of the house; in the corridors, in the servants' room downstairs, once even in the reception hall; and though she never once succeeded in catching his eye, she persuaded herself to the belief that his gaze was constantly on her.

The day she met him in the reception hall she turned in a sudden flash of anger and said:

"What are you doing down here? Why aren't you upstairs?"

"Yes, ma'am. I sorry," replied Sanétomo, backing off.

"I suppose you know you should not be here," said Dora quietly, ashamed at having shown temper with a servant.

"Yes, ma'am."

And he backed clear to the door and disappeared without turning.

These were small incidents, of course, in the life of the wealthy and fashionable Mrs. Brillon; the little yellow man was for her merely one of those petty annoyances of existence which meet us in so many forms and disguises, and he probably would have remained so indefinitely—for she had finally decided to tolerate his presence out of consideration for her husband—had it not been for the curious adventure which explained Sanétomo and finished him all at once.

Early in the summer of the year which saw the second anniversary of his wedding, Brillon took it into his head that he wanted to see the Rocky Mountains; the idea having been suggested by a friend who offered him the use of a bungalow on a ranch near Steamboat Lake, some three hundred miles west of Denver.

Mrs. Brillon, having looked forward to a season at Newport, made some objections, but was won over with little difficulty, and toward the middle of July they departed for the West, accompanied only by Mrs. Brillon's maid and Sanétomo.

They found the ranch, consisting of a few hundred

acres of wild forest and tumbling streams—for everything from a cabbage patch to a mountain range is called
a ranch in Colorado—sufficiently delightful to repay
them for their tiresome journey. More important still to
these New Yorkers, the bungalow was furnished completely throughout its nine or ten large rooms, and had
been kept in excellent order by the caretaker, an old griz-
zled veteran of the mountainside who called himself
Trapper Joe.

There were some difficulties at first. They had brought
several articles with them from Denver: a case of guns
and tackle, three donkeys, a cook, and an automobile.
The guns were useless, since it was closed season on
everything but chipmunks and small birds. As for the
donkeys, Steamboat Lake—the village—was already
full of them.

The automobile had beautiful lines and its engine was
smooth as butter; but it refused to climb hills, and the
Rockies *will* slope.

But worst of all was the cook. In his sober moments—
that is to say, for the first day or two—he was bad
enough; but the third morning— He had evidently decided that Mr. Brillon had brought along just one too
many cases of champagne, and attempted to remedy the
error in one heroic coup.

When they found him he was frightfully drunk, even
for a cook. Brillon packed him off with a ticket back to
Denver.

And that was how Sanétomo came into his own again.

"You don't object to cooking for us, do you,
'Tomo?" asked his master.

A swift gleam appeared in the eyes of the yellow man.
"No, sir. I like."

"All right. Thank the Lord! Luncheon at one. Come

on, Dora, let's see if we can push that confounded car uphill.''

Many pleasant days followed. There were peaks to be climbed, trout to be caught, cañons and forests to be explored; and best of all, Brillon finally succeeded in persuading the automobile that it was the duty of a Christian car to toil upward.

After that they made delightful daily excursions. They would coax the motor through some winding valley or along a narrow road at the brink of a precipice until the way became steep beyond all reason, and then they would get out and open a hamper; and there, on the cool grass beside a little tumbling mountain stream, with the light, winey air in their nostrils and the songs of birds in their ears, they would sit and eat good things and perhaps while away a whole afternoon reading or talking, or merely gazing in silence at the soft green of the valleys below and the dim gray and purple peaks in the distance.

They usually took Sanétomo along to look after the hamper. Brillon insisted on it, and Dora kept her objections to herself.

It was really a sacrifice on her part, for the yellow man's presence took away a good half of her pleasure. It sounds unreasonable enough, and indeed she thought it so herself; but she hated the very sight of him. Instinctive aversion is stubborn, and grows.

There was certainly nothing in Sanétomo's behavior or appearance to warrant dislike, beyond the fact that his skin was yellow. He was always quiet, always efficient, and never impudent or obtrusive. In the automobile he sat in front with his master, who drove; and not once would he turn his head; nor would he betray the slightest sign of anxiety or fear when they crept along at the edge of a chasm and Dora would be begging her husband to stop with every turn of the wheels.

Arrived at a halting place, Sanétomo would unstrap the hamper and find a shady spot of green to spread the cloth—and with what a feast would he cover it! The meal over, he would pack up again; and then he would sit down somewhere against a tree and—what?

That was a question. What was in his mind? Dreams of far-away Nippon? Considerations of the ragout to be served at dinner that evening? Or simply nothing at all?

He would sit for hours without moving a muscle of his face, with his little black eyes staring dully, apparently at nothing. Sometimes he would turn them on his master, more seldom on his master's wife. But they would remain utterly expressionless; no one could have guessed his thoughts, or whether he had any.

Once Dora, happening to turn and meet his gaze, addressed her husband in a tone of irritation:

"Harry, I wish you would tell Sanétomo to stop looking at me. He annoys me."

Brillon, who was lying on his back in the grass, laughed good-humoredly.

"Is he looking at you? I don't blame him. You grow more bewitching every day here in the mountains."

"I say he annoys me," repeated Dora angrily, ashamed of her petulance, but too irritated to keep the words back.

"Really?" Brillon turned lazily. " 'Tomo, you hear what your mistress says. Don't annoy her. Look the other way."

The Japanese had turned the offending eyes on the ground.

"*Tatta Sanétomo,*" he said quietly. "I sorry."

And after that Dora met his gaze no more. But yes—once.

One day toward the end of August they had left the bungalow quite early in the morning, intending to reach Cotton Pass, about sixty miles north of Steamboat Lake, by midday. But the latter half of the way was unknown to them, and they met more hills and dangerous roads than they had bargained for.

Several times Brillon was forced to stop the car and walk some distance ahead to see if a passage was safe, or even possible; and when noon came they found themselves still twenty miles short of their destination.

Soon after they came across a clearing at the roadside where even the scrub oak had not found sufficient soil for its tough roots; and Brillon turned the wheels to the left and stopped the motor with a sigh of relief.

"Come on, 'Tomo, break out the grub," he directed, jumping down. "Here you go, Dora. Gad, I'm hungry! And I haven't a nerve left in my body. What an infernal road!"

Beyond the clearing they found a grassy spot under some trees, and there Sanétomo carried the hamper and spread out its contents on a dazzling white cloth.

Brillon was in ill-humor, and Dora, badly shaken by the rough and dangerous journey, was enjoying a well-developed attack of nerves; also they were disappointed at being forced to give up the visit to Cotton Pass.

Naturally they took it out on Sanétomo. Nothing was right. Why hadn't he brought Fantori instead of Megauvin? He should have known that Megauvin will not stand shaking. The bread was too dry; surely he ought to be able to wrap bread properly. And are these the best olives to be procured? Better, a thousand times better, no olives at all!

Sanétomo merely kept repeating: "I sorry," without the slightest change of countenance, filling and refilling their glasses and plates.

"For Heaven's sake don't say that again!" cried Dora suddenly dropping her napkin. "You'll drive me crazy!"

"Yes," agreed Brillon; "keep still, 'Tomo."

"I sorry," said the Japanese gravely.

" 'Tomo!"

"Yes, sir."

"Tell him to go away," said Dora crossly. "I wish you wouldn't bring him along at all Harry. Creepy little yellow thing!"

"Oh, come now—" Brillon began to protest, but she interrupted him:

"Yes, he is! He gets on my nerves."

"Dora!"

Brillon glanced at Sanétomo, who was gathering up the dishes and bottles without any indication that the conversation concerned him in the slightest degree; so he merely shrugged his shoulders and took another sandwich.

When the meal was finished they lay on the grass for half an hour, Brillon smoking cigarettes and Dora trying to rest, while Sanétomo repacked the hamper and strapped it in the car. Then Brillon rose to his feet, saying that they must make sure of reaching Steamboat Lake before nightfall or they might not reach it at all.

He helped Dora to the tonneau, then took the wheel with Sanétomo at his side.

There was barely room in the clearing to turn the car, and after a great deal of backing and starting Brillon managed to get its nose pointed south. With a sigh he settled to his task, cursing himself for having undertaken a road avoided by everyone else for its discomfort and danger.

As soon as Dora reached her seat in the tonneau she had settled back against the cushions and closed her eyes, as if to say: "Let it come if it's going to!"

As for Sanétomo, he sat as always with his arms folded, looking straight ahead with stoical eyes, except now and then when he would turn them aside to follow the line of a distant purple peak or one nearer crowned with white.

They crawled along thus for two hours, occasionally speeding up a little as they entered a pass between two cliffs with the walls rising almost perpendicularly above their heads on either side; but for the most part barely going forward as they cautiously followed the narrow road, often no more than a path, coiling around the side of a mountain like a huge snake.

But at least they made better time than they had in the morning, when Brillon had been forced to reconnoiter on foot every mile or so to avoid getting caught in a *cul de sac*; and five o'clock found them within ten miles of Steamboat Lake, with the worst passed.

They began to liven up a little; Brillon chatted with Sanétomo, and Dora had opened her eyes to follow the wonderful changing colors of the sun on the snow-capped hills to the right. Then a great cliff obstructed her view, and she turned to the other side and looked into the valley far below; not ten feet from the wheels of the car a precipice yawned, its bank so straight that she could see only the jagged edge, with here and there a spot of green where a scrub oak clung stubbornly to the granite with its scanty foot of soil.

But ten feet was enough and to spare—many times that afternoon they had had a margin of only two or three—and the accident that befell them was directly and entirely the fault of Brillon himself.

The contributing cause was his desire for a smoke; and presumably it was overconfidence that induced him to reach in his own pockets for cigarette case and matches instead of getting Sanétomo to do it, as he had done before.

So it happened.

Even after the wheel struck a rock and turned he could have kept the road if he had only retained his presence of mind. But his nerves were already shaken by the trying journey, and his frantic pull at the steering wheel was in the wrong direction.

There was a startled oath, a flying leap, a cry of fright from the tonneau, and the next instant the car had flopped over and was rolling down the precipice.

No one could possibly have told afterward just how it happened, Dora least of all. She tried to jump, but was on the left side of the car and thus could not reach the road. She shut her eyes as the thing went over.

Then she felt blows all over her body and a fearful din in her ears, as something seemed to be pressing her mercilessly against the hard rock. Then she felt herself released, pawing at the air frantically, wildly, and her hands closed on something small and round that seemed to hold. She clung on desperately.

She opened her eyes and saw that she was hanging to a limb of a small scrub oak, suspended on the bank of the precipice. A frightful clatter came from below; it was the automobile rolling to destruction. She felt the branch bending dangerously with her weight.

She called in terror and agony:

"Harry! Harry! Harry!"

Immediately a frenzied voice came from above:

"Dora! Thank God!"

She looked up and saw her husband's face peering over the edge of the precipice, ten feet away.

"Hold on, hold on!" he was shouting. "I'll make a rope of something Just a minute, dearest! For God's sake hold on!"

"Yes—" she shouted back, then stopped. She became suddenly aware of a form on her right, not five feet away.

It was Sanétomo, clinging to the same branch as herself!

She looked at the little yellow man dangling there beside her, and, while her arms were aching with the strain and her ears rang with her husband's shouts of encouragement from above, an irresistible desire to laugh seized her. He looked so funny hanging there! There they were, like two vaudeville acrobats on a trapeze!

Suddenly Sanétomo's eyes met hers. She felt the branch giving way as it bent under their weight. An ominous snap sounded. She felt herself going down, slowly down. Another snap!

"My God!" she cried in horror.

She heard Sanétomo's calm voice:

"It break. We too heavy."

She looked into his eyes as if fascinated. And as she looked there appeared in them a sudden flame of passion that seem to leap out and scorch her.

It was all in an instant; it must have been, for the branch was cracking and snapping now under their hands. It was all in an instant, but the impression of those glowing eyes was imprinted on her brain forever.

Then Sanétomo's voice came clearly:

"For the master—*seppuku! Sayonara!*" ("Suicide! Good-by!")

Dora met a gleam of wild joy from his eyes; she saw his hands loosen their grasp, and his body dropped like a shot from her sight. She heard noises on the rocks below, and she grew so faint and sick at the sound that she nearly lost her own grip and followed Sanétomo in his fall to death.

But by that fall she was saved. The branch, relieved

of half its load, held firm; it even sprang up a little. And two minutes later she was dragged to safety by a line made from strips of cloth from her husband's coat.

It was eight o'clock when they reached Steamboat Lake after a walk of nearly ten miles, tired, bruised, and sore.

The following morning Brillon took some men from the village and went to look for Sanétomo's body. And when they found the mangled and shapeless heap at the foot of the precipice, the master gave his faithful servant the tribute of a few tears before they covered the little grave on the mountainside.

But he never learned how and why the little yellow man had saved the life of the one dearest to him: Dora Brillon never told. In the flame of Sanétomo's eyes, in the greatness of his sacrifice, her dislike for him was burned up, and from its ashes rose an admiration that would not sully the memory of a hero.

For is he not a hero who at the cost of his own life gives back to one he loves the life of another—whom he hates?

JUSTICE ENDS AT HOME

Chapter One
The Plea

THE COURTROOM OF NEW YORK COUNTY GENeral Sessions, Part VI, was unusually busy that April morning. The calling of the calendar occupied all of an hour, delayed as it was by arguments on postponements and various motions, with now and then a sound of raised voices as opposing attorneys entered into a wrangle that colored their logic with emotion.

Judge Fraser Manton cut off most of these disputes in the middle with a terse, final ruling on the point at issue. He seemed to have been made for the bench of justice. Rather youngish-looking for a judge of New York General Sessions, with bright, dark eyes and clear skin, he possessed nevertheless that air of natural authority and wisdom that sits so gracefully on some fortunate men.

Perched high above the others in the great leather chair on the daïs, black-gowned and black-collared, his was easily the most handsome face in the room. He was liked and admired by lawyers for his cool, swift decisions and imperturbable impartiality; and he was even more popular off the bench than on, for he was a wealthy bachelor and somewhat of a good fellow. He was a prominent clubman, and came from a family of high social position.

The first business after the calling of the calendar was a batch of indictments sent over from the Grand Jury.

Three gunmen, accused of holding up a jewelry store on Sixth Avenue, entered a plea of not guilty; they were represented by a large, jovial individual who was known to be high in the councils of Tammany. Then the attorney of a little black-haired Italian who was alleged—as the newspapers say—to have planted a bomb in his neighbor's hallway, asked permission to withhold his plea for twenty-four hours, which was granted. Two others followed—a druggist charged with illegal sales of heroin, and a weak-faced youth, whose employer had missed a thousand dollars from his safe. The clerk called out the next case, and a seedy-looking man was led to the bar by a sheriff's deputy, while Arthur Thornton, assistant district attorney, arose from his seat at a nearby table.

The prisoner—the seedy-looking man—was about forty years of age, and his clothing seemed nearly as old, so worn and dirty was it. His face, shaven that morning in the Tombs, had the hollow and haggard appearance that is the result of continued misery and misfortune, and his gray eyes were filled with the heroic indifference of a man who knows he is doomed and cares very little about the matter.

He gave his pedigree to the clerk in a low, even voice: William Mount, no address, age thirty-eight, American born, occupation bookkeeper.

Judge Fraser Manton, who had been gazing with keen interest at the prisoner during the questioning, now cleared his throat.

"William Mount," he said, "you have been charged before the grand jury with the murder of your wife, Mrs. Elaine Mount, known as Alice Reeves. Do you wish the indictment read?"

The prisoner looked up at the judge and the eyes of the two men met.

"No, sir; I don't want to hear the indictment," Mount replied.

"Very well. You are brought before me to enter a plea. You understand, this is not a trial, and you are not expected to say anything except a plea to the indictment. Are you guilty of the crime charged?"

A little light appeared in the prisoner's eyes, but speedily died out as he replied simply:

"I didn't do it, sir."

"Then you plead not guilty?"

"Yes, sir."

The judge turned to the clerk to instruct him to enter the plea, then his eyes went back to the prisoner.

"Are you represented by counsel? Have you a lawyer?"

The shadow of a scornful and bitter smile swept across Mount's lips.

"No, sir," he replied.

"Do you want one?"

"What if I did? I couldn't pay a lawyer. I haven't any money."

"I suppose not. Just so." The judge appeared to be examining the prisoner with attentive curiosity. "It's my duty, Mount, in the case that a man charged with a capital crime is unable to retain counsel, to assign an attorney to his defense. The attorney will be paid by the State, also all legitimate and necessary expenses incurred by him up to a certain amount. The State takes this precaution to safeguard the lives and liberties of its children. I will assign counsel to your case this afternoon, and he will probably see you tomorrow.''

"Yes, sir," replied the prisoner without a show of interest. It was evident that he expected little assistance from any lawyer.

Judge Manton beckoned to the clerk, who handed him a file to which two or three sheets of paper were attached. The judge looked over them thoughtfully, then turned to the assistant district attorney.

"I'll set this case for May eighteenth, Mr. Thornton. Will that be all right?"

"Perfectly, your honor," replied the prosecutor.

"Well. Mount, you will be tried on Tuesday, the eighteenth day of May. Your counsel will be notified to that effect. That's all."

As the prisoner was led from the courtroom his face wore exactly the same expression of resigned hopelessness that it had shown when he entered twenty minutes before.

Late that afternoon, in his chambers adjoining the courtroom, Judge Fraser Manton was enjoying a cigar and a chat with his friends, Hamilton Rogers, proprietor and editor of the *Bulletin*, and Richard Hammel, police commissioner, when his clerk approached with some letters and other documents to be signed.

"By the way," observed the clerk as he blotted the signatures, "there will be another, sir. Who are you going to give the Mount case to? He must be notified."

"Oh, yes," replied the judge. "Why, I don't know; let me see. I looked the list over this afternoon, and I thought of assigning it to Simon Leg." He hesitated. "Yes, give it to Leg. L, E, G, Leg; you'll find his address in the book."

"What!" exclaimed Police Commissioner Hammel; "old Simmie Leg?"

The clerk had stopped short on his way out of the room, while an expression of surprise and amusement filled his eyes.

"Yes, sir," he said finally as he turned to go. A minute later the click of his typewriter was heard through the open door.

Chapter II
The Attorney for the Defense

I N A NICELY FURNISHED OFFICE, CONSISTING OF TWO rooms, on the eighteenth floor of one of New York's highest buildings, situated on Broadway not far south of City Hall, a stenographer was talking to an office boy at nine o'clock in the morning. (Heavens! How many stenographers are there talking to office boys at nine o'clock in the morning?) This particular stenographer was, perhaps, a little prettier than the average, but otherwise she held strictly to type; whereas the office boy appeared to be really individual.

There was a light in his eyes and a form to his brow that spoke of intelligence, and he was genuinely, not superficially, neat in appearance. He was about twenty years of age, and his name was Dan Culp. As soon as the morning conversation with his coworker was finished, he took a heavy law volume down from a shelf and began reading in it.

The door opened and a man entered the office.

The office boy and the stenographer spoke together:

"Good morning, sir."

"Good morning, Mr. Leg."

The newcomer returned their greetings and hung his hat and spring overcoat in a closet. He was a middle-aged man of heavy build, with an elongated, sober-looking countenance, which formed an odd contrast with his pleasant, twinkling eyes.

"Any mail, Miss Venner?" he asked, turning.

"Yes, sir."

He took the two letters which the stenographer handed him and passed into the other room. The office boy returned to his law volume. Miss Venner took a piece of embroidery from a drawer of her desk and started to work on it. From within came various small sounds as their employer opened his desk, pulled his chair back, and tore open his mail. Silence followed.

Presently his voice came:

"Dan!"

The office boy stuck a blotter in his book and went to the door of the other room.

"Yes, sir."

"Come here." Mr. Leg had wheeled himself about in his swivel chair and was gazing with an expression of puzzled astonishment at a typewritten letter in his hand. "Just come here, Dan, and look at this! Of all the—but just look at it!"

The youth's face took on a sudden expression of eager interest as he read the letter through to the end.

"It's a murder case, sir," he said with animation.

"So I see. But why, in Heaven's name, has it been assigned to me? Why should any case be assigned to me?"

The youth smiled. "It is surprising, sir."

"Surprising! It's outrageous! There's no reason for it! A murderer! Why, I wouldn't know how to talk to the fellow. They know very well I haven't had a case for ten years. Dan, it's an outrage!"

"Yes, sir."

"I won't take it."

"No, sir."

Mr. Leg got up from his chair with a gesture of indignation and walked to the window. Dan stood regarding him hesitatingly, with eagerness in his eyes, and finally inquired diffidently:

"Would that be ethical, Mr. Leg?"

The lawyer wheeled with a sharp: "What?"

"To refuse the case, sir."

"I don't know. No, it wouldn't. Hang it all, I suppose I'm in for it. But where's the sense in it? I don't know the first thing about murder. What if he's innocent? How could I prove it? Whoever this Mount is, God help him. I suppose I'll have to go and see him."

"Yes, sir."

Though Mr. Leg talked for another half-hour, while Dan listened respectfully, he could arrive at no other conclusion. There was no way out of it—he must go and see the man, Mount. Heavens, what a frightful, unexpected thing, to have a murderer thrown on one's hands! Really, there ought to be a public defender.

At ten o'clock he put on his hat and coat and started for the Tombs.

Let us talk about him while he is on his way. Mr. Simon Leg was known among the members of his profession as well as any lawyer in the city, but not as a lawyer. In fact, he wasn't a lawyer at all, except in name. He hadn't had a case in ten years.

He had inherited a large fortune, and thus, seeing no necessity for work of any kind, he refused to do any.

It was apparently to maintain his self-respect that he kept an office and spent his days in it, for all he ever did was to sit in the swivel chair and consume novels and tales of adventure at the rate of five or six a week, with now and then a game of chess with Dan, who gave him odds of a rook and beat him. At first sight it would appear that Dan and Miss Venner had absolutely nothing to do, but they were in fact kept pretty busy picking up the novels and tales from the floor as their employer finished them, and sending them to the Salvation Army.

As for Mr. Leg's wide popularity among the members of his profession, that was accounted for by the fact that he was a member of all the best clubs, a good fellow, and a liberal friend.

He is now at the Tombs. Entering the grim portals with an inward shudder, he explained his mission to the doorkeeper, and was at once ushered into the office of the warden, to whom he exhibited the letter from Judge Manton by way of credentials. The warden summoned the attendant, who conducted the lawyer to a small, bare room at the end of a dark corridor, and left him there. Five minutes later the door opened again and a uniformed turnkey appeared; ahead of him was a man with white face and sunken eyes, wearing a seedy black suit.

The turnkey pointed to a button on the wall.

"Ring when you're through," he directed, and went out, closing the door behind him.

The lawyer rose and approached the other man, who stood near the door regarding him stolidly.

"Mr. Mount," said the attorney in an embarrassed tone of voice, holding out his hand. "I'm Mr. Leg, Simon Leg, your—that is; your counsel."

The other hesitated a moment, then took the proffered hand.

"Glad to meet you, Mr. Leg," he said. He appeared to be also ill at ease. It is a curious thing how the lighter emotions, such as ordinary social embarrassment, continue to operate even when a man is in the shadow of death.

"Well—" began the lawyer, and stopped.

The other came to his rescue.

"I suppose," said Mount, "you've come to hear my side of it?"

"Exactly," Mr. Leg agreed. "But here, we may as well sit down."

They seated themselves, one on either side of the wooden table in the center of the room.

"You see, Mr. Mount," began the lawyer, "I don't know the first thing about this case. I was assigned to it by Judge Manton. And before you give me any confidences, I want to tell you that I have had no criminal practice whatever. To tell the truth, I'm not much of a lawyer. I say this so that you can ask the court to give you other counsel, and I think you'd better do it."

"It doesn't matter," returned Mount quietly. "There's no use putting in a defense, anyway."

Mr. Leg glanced at him quickly. "Oh," he observed. "What—do you mean you're guilty?"

The lawyer shrank back from the quick, burning light that leaped from the other's eyes.

"No!" Mount shouted fiercely. Then suddenly he was quiet again. "No," he continued calmly, "I'm not guilty, Mr. Leg. My God, do you think I could have killed her? But there's no use. I was caught—they found me there—"

"Wait," the lawyer interrupted. "I really think, Mr. Mount, that you'd better ask for other counsel."

"Well, I won't."

"But I'm incompetent."

"It doesn't matter. Nothing matters. She's dead, and that's all there is to it. What do I care? I tell you that I haven't any defense except that I didn't do it. No, I won't ask the judge for anything. Let it go."

Mr. Leg sighed.

"Then I'll do the best I can," he said hopelessly. "Now, Mr. Mount, tell me all you know about it. Tell me everything. And remember that my only chance to help you is if you tell me the whole truth."

"There's no use in it, sir," said the other in a dull tone of misery.

"Go on," returned the lawyer sternly.

And William Mount told his story.

Chapter III
The Amateur Detective

IT WAS WELL PAST TWO O'CLOCK WHEN MR. LEG returned to his office, having stopped at a restaurant for lunch on the way. As he entered, Miss Venner and Dan looked up with faces of expectant eagerness, and a faint smile of amusement curled the stenographer's pretty lips. Dan sprang to his feet to hang up his employer's coat, and a shadow of disappointment fell across his face as the lawyer nodded his greetings and thanks and passed without a word into the other room. But it was not long before his voice came:

"Dan!"

The youth hastened to the door.

"Yes, sir."

"Come here." Mr. Leg was seated at his desk with his feet upon its edge and his chin buried in his collar—his favorite reading attitude. "Dan," he said as the other stood before him, "this Mount case is a very sad affair. I'm sorrier than ever that I'm mixed up in it. As sure as Heaven, they're going to convict an innocent man."

"Yes, sir."

"He's innocent, beyond any doubt; but I don't know

what to do. Sit down there and let me tell you about it. You're a bright boy; you play a good game of chess; maybe you'll think of something.''

"Yes, sir," returned the youth eagerly, bringing forward a chair.

"You know," the lawyer began, "Mount is accused of murdering his wife. Well, she was his wife only in name. He hadn't been living with her for four years. He hadn't even seen her in that time. He married her seven years ago when he was thirty-two and she was twenty-one. He was head clerk in an insurance office, getting a good salary, and she had been a stenographer in a law office. For two years they lived together happily. Mount worshiped her. Then she seemed to become discontented, and one day, a year later, she suddenly disappeared, leaving a letter for him which indicated that she had found another man, but not saying so in so many words. He searched—''

"Has he got that letter?" interrupted Dan, who was listening intently.

"What letter?"

"The one his wife left."

"Oh, I don't know. I didn't ask him."

"All right, sir. Excuse me."

"He searched for her everywhere," the lawyer continued, "but found no trace whatever. He went to the police, but they had no better luck. By that time, he had lost his position, having continually absented himself from the office for two months. His heart was broken, and with his wife gone, he didn't care whether he lived or not. He went from bad to worse, and became practically a vagabond. Half mad from misery and grief, he tramped around looking vaguely for his lost wife. More than three years passed, and the edge of his sorrow dulled a little. He obtained a position as bookkeeper in a coal office, and held it faithfully for four months.

"One evening—this was April 2, a week ago last Friday—he was walking across One Hundred and Fourth Street on his way home from work, when a woman, coming in the opposite direction, stopped suddenly in front of him with a cry of surprise. It was his wife.

"Mount, of course, was staggered.

"He remembered afterward that she was very well dressed, even expensively, it seemed to him. She told him she had been searching for him for the past six months; she had discovered that she really loved him and no one else, and she wanted to come back to him. Mount called attention to his pitiable condition, physical and sartorial, but she said that she had a great deal of money, enough to last them a very long time, many years. Poor Mount didn't even dare ask her where the money came from. He said he would take her back.

"She arranged to meet him the following night at nine o'clock at a drugstore on the corner of One Hundred and Sixteenth Street and Eighth Avenue. He begged her to go with him then, at once; but that she said she couldn't do. Finally they separated. But Mount couldn't bear to let her get out of his sight, and he followed her.

"She took the subway at One Hundred and Third Street, and he managed to get on the same train without being discovered. At One Hundred and Fifty-seventh Street she got off, and he followed her to an apartment house near Broadway. Soon after she entered he saw a light appear in the east flat on the third floor, so he supposed she lived there. He stayed around till after eleven, but she didn't come out again.

"The next night Mount was at the drugstore ahead of time. She wasn't there, nor did she arrive at nine o'clock. He waited nearly two hours. At twenty minutes to eleven he went uptown to One Hundred and Fifty-seventh

Street. From the pavement he saw a light in her windows.

"He entered the building; the outer door was open.

"A man was standing in the lower hall. Mount barely glanced at him as he passed to the stairs; he doesn't remember what the man looked like, only he has an indistinct recollection that he had a suitcase in his hand. Mount went upstairs to the third floor and rang the bell at the flat to the east. There was no answer, though he rang several times, and finally, finding the door unlocked, he pushed it open and entered.

"On the floor, with the electric lights glaring above her, was the dead body of his wife with the hilt of a knife protruding from her breast and blood everywhere. Mount screamed, leaped forward, and pulled out the knife; blood spurted on his hands and sleeves. His scream brought adjoining tenants to the scene. In ten minutes the police were there, and when they left, they took Mount with them."

Mr. Leg took one foot down from the desk, reached in his pocket for a packet of cigarettes, and lit one.

"That's Mount's story," said he, blowing a column of smoke into the air, "and I'm certain it's a true one. The man has an appearance of honesty."

A slight smile appeared on Dan's lips.

"You know, sir, you believe everything people tell you," he suggested diffidently.

"True." Mr. Leg frowned. "Yes, I suppose it's a fault not to be suspicious sometimes. But that's what the man told me, and I'm his counsel. I don't mind confessing to you, Dan, that I'm absolutely helpless. I haven't the slightest idea what to do. I thought of several things, but they all seemed absurd on analysis. I had it in mind during luncheon. I've put a lot of thought on it."

"Yes, sir."

"But I arrived nowhere. As I said before, Dan, you're a bright boy. Maybe you might suggest something—"

The youth's eyes were alive with eager intelligence. "I could think it over, sir. It's a mighty interesting case. There's one curious thing about it—very curious—"

"What is it?"

"I wouldn't like to mention it, sir, till I've examined it more. Maybe I can suggest something then."

"All right, Dan. If you're as good at detective work as you are at playing chess, Mount might do worse after all. Exercise your ingenuity, my boy. We'll talk it over again tomorrow."

"Yes, sir."

After Dan had returned to the other room Mr. Leg sat for some time thoughtfully regarding his inkwell. Presently he shook himself, heaved a sigh, and reached across the desk for a book bound in red cloth with a gilt title, *The Fight on the Amazon.*

He opened it at the first page and began to read. An expression of pure content appeared on his face. The minutes passed unheeded. His chin sank deeper in his collar and his hands gripped the book tightly as he came to the fourth chapter, "The Night Attack." At the end of an hour he had reached the most thrilling point of the fight and his eyes were glowing with unrestrained joy.

"Mr. Leg."

The lawyer looked up to find Dan standing before him.

"Well?"

"Why, this Mount case, sir."

"What about it?"

"I've been thinking it over, sir, but before we can get anywhere we must obtain more information. Somebody ought to go up and examine the scene of the murder. I'd be only too glad to do it."

"All right, that's a good idea," agreed Mr. Leg, whose fingers were twitching impatiently as they held the place in his book.

"And there are other things we must do, too, sir. Things absolutely essential. I've made a little list of questions, if you'd like to look it over."

With a gesture of impatience the lawyer took the sheet of paper which Dan handed him. Evidently he had been making use of the stenographer's machine, for it was covered with typewriting:

First, to verify Mount's story:

1. Has he kept the letter his wife left when she ran away? If so, get it from him.

2. Where was he employed as bookkeeper during the four months previous to the crime? Verify.

3. Did he wait inside the drugstore at the corner of One Hundred and Sixteenth Street and Eighth Avenue on the night of April 3, or merely in its neighborhood? Find out if there is anyone in the store or near it who remembers seeing him.

4. Does he drink to excess?

5. Does he appear nervous and excitable, or stolid and calm?

Second, from the police:

1. With what kind of a knife was the crime committed? Were there fingerprints on it other than Mount's?

2. Exactly at what hour were the police summoned to the scene, and how long had the victim been dead, according to doctor's report, when they arrived?

3. Did they take any papers or articles of any kind from the flat? If so, examine them, if possible.

4. Has either Mount or his wife any criminal record?

5. Get a photograph of Mount.

6. Did the body show any marks of violence besides the wound in the breast?

Having reached this point, halfway down the sheet, the lawyer stopped to look up at his office boy with an expression of admiration.

"All this is very sensible, Dan," he observed. "Remarkably sensible. These are serviceable ideas."

"Yes, sir." The youth smiled a little. "Of course, Mr. Leg, you won't be able to see Mount again till tomorrow morning, but you can get the information from the police this afternoon. I suppose headquarters—"

"You mean for *me* to go to the police?" interrupted Mr. Leg in dismay.

"Certainly, sir. They wouldn't pay much attention to me, and besides, I'm going uptown to the flat."

"Well, but—" Mr. Leg appeared to be dumfounded to discover that there would actually be work for him to do. "All right," he said finally, "I suppose I'll have to. I'll go first thing in the morning."

"To see Mount, yes, sir. But you must go to the police this afternoon, at once."

"This afternoon!" The lawyer glanced in helpless consternation at the book in his hand. "Now, Dan, there's no use rushing things. I'll go tomorrow. Anyway, what right has this Mount to upset my whole office like this?"

"He's your client, sir. This is April sixteenth, and the trial is set for the eighteenth of May. There's no time to be lost."

"Yes, hang it all, he's my client," the lawyer agreed. "So much the worse for him, but I suppose I ought to do the best I can. All right, I'll go this afternoon."

"Right away, sir."

"Yes. You want answers to all these questions, do you?"

"Yes, sir. And tomorrow, besides seeing Mount, you

must go to the office where he says he worked, and other places. I'll see about the drugstore myself. There'll be a lot to do.''

''There sure will, if we follow your orders.'' Mr. Leg was beginning to recover his good humor.

''Yes, sir. I'm going up to the flat now, and I—'' the youth hesitated—''I may need some money for janitors and people like that. They talk better when you give them something.''

''Dan, you're a cynic.'' Mr. Leg pulled out his wallet. ''How much?''

''I think fifty dollars, sir.''

''Here's a hundred.''

''Thank you, sir.''

Fifteen minutes later, having waited to see his employer safely started for police headquarters, Dan took his hat from the closet. On his way to the door he stopped beside the stenographer's desk, where that proud damsel was seated at work on her dainty embroidery.

''Maybe pretty soon you'll think I'm not just a boy anymore, Miss Venner.''

The lady looked up.

''Oh! I suppose you think you're going to do something great.''

''You bet I am.'' Enthusiasm and confidence shone from Dan's eyes. ''You'll see. And then, when I want to tell you—er—tell you—''

''Well, tell me what?'' Miss Venner smiled with sweet maliciousness.

But Dan appeared to have no finish for his sentence. Suddenly he bent over and imprinted a loud kiss on the dainty piece of embroidery, and then, his face burning red, he made for the door.

Chapter IV
A Slip of Paper

I T WAS NEARLY FOUR O'CLOCK WHEN DAN ARRIVED
at the apartment house on One Hundred and Fifty-
seventh Street, the address of which he had obtained
from Mr. Leg. He first stood across the street and ran
his eye over the exterior. It was a five-story stone building, the oldest and smallest in the block, with fire es-
capes in front. Dan picked out the three east windows
on the third floor as those of the flat in which Elaine
Mount had met her death.

He crossed the street and rang the janitor's bell. After
a minute's delay there appeared in the areaway below a
hard-looking customer with a black mustache.

"What do you want?" he demanded gruffly, looking
up at the boy on the stoop.

Dan smiled down at him.

"Are you the janitor?"

"Yes."

Dan descended to the areaway.

"I'm from Mr. Leg's office, the lawyer for the man
held for the murder committed here. I want to look
through the flat. Is there a policeman in charge?"

"In charge of what?"

"The flat."

"No."

"Is it sealed up?"

"No. They took the seal off day before yesterday. But
I don't know who *you* are, young fellow."

"That's all right. I have a letter here from Mr. Leg.
See." As Dan pulled the letter from his pocket a five-

dollar bill came with it. The letter was soon returned, but the bill found its way to the janitor's grimy palm.

"I'd like to go through the flat, if you don't mind," Dan repeated.

"All right," the other agreed more amiably. "There's no reason why you shouldn't, seeing as it's for rent."

He turned and led the way through the dark hall and up the stairs. Dan observed as they passed that the corridor on the ground floor was quite narrow and deserted, there being neither telephone switchboard nor elevator. This was evidently one of the old houses erected on the Heights between 1890 and 1900, with its entire lack of twentieth-century middle-class show.

"Here you are," said the janitor, stopping at the door on the right two flights up. He selected a key from a bunch, unlocked the door and passed within, with Dan at his heels.

With one foot across the threshold, Dan stopped short in amazed consternation. What he saw was a flat bare of furniture, with discolored wall paper and dirty floors; in short, that dreariest and dismalest of all sights on earth, a vacant and empty apartment.

"But—but—" the youth stammered in dismay. "But there's nothing here."

"Nope. All empty," returned the janitor placidly.

"But how—do the police know of this?"

"Sure. I told you they was here day before yesterday and took the seal off. They said we could take the stuff out. One of the cops told me they had the man that did it, so there wasn't any use keeping it locked up any longer."

"Where's the furniture and things?"

"In storage. Hauled away yesterday."

For a minute Dan gazed at the dismantled flat in dismayed silence. If there had been anything here which

would have been of value to his untrained eye it was
now too late.

"Spilt milk," he finally observed aloud. "No use crying." He turned again to the janitor.

"Who got the stuff ready?"

"I did."

"Did you take away anything, did you leave papers
and everything in the desks and drawers, if there were
any?"

"Sure I did." The janitor appeared to be a little net-
tled at this slight aspersion on his integrity. "I didn't
take nothing. Of course there was a lot of papers and
trash and stuff I cleaned out."

"Did you throw it away?"

"Yes. It ain't gone yet, though; it's still down in the
basement."

"Do you mind if I take a look at it?"

So they returned downstairs, and there, in a dark corner of the basement the janitor pointed out a dirty old
bag filled with papers and all sorts of trash. With a feeling that he was making a silly fool of himself, Dan
dragged the bag out into the light and dumped its contents on the cement floor. Then he began to pick the
articles up one by one, examine them, and replace them
in the bag.

There was a little bit of everything: magazines and
newspapers, a broken inkwell, stubs of lead pencils, writing paper, banana skins, combings of hair, bills from
butchers and delicatessen shops.

There was a lot of it, and he pawed through the stuff
for an hour before he came across anything that appeared
to him worthy of attention. This was a small piece of
white paper, rectangular in shape. In one corner was an
imprint of the seal of the County of New York, and
across the middle of the sheet was written in ink:

Bonneau et Mouet—Sec.

Dan carried the paper to the window and examined it attentively, and ended by sticking it in his pocket.

"I'm crazy, I suppose," he murmured to himself. "It's all right to have an idea, but there's no sense in expecting—However, we'll see."

In another thirty minutes he had finished with the heap of trash, having found nothing else of interest. He found the janitor in the front room of the basement, smoking a pipe and reading a newspaper. On a table before him was a bucket of beer. Already Mr. Leg's five-dollar bill was cheering humanity.

"Through?" asked the janitor, glancing up with a grin that was supposed to be amiable. "Find anything?"

Dan shook his head. "No. And now, mister—I didn't get your name—"

"Yoakum, Bill Yoakum."

"I'd like to ask you a question or two, Mr. Yoakum, if you don't mind. Were you at home on the night of Saturday, April third, the night of the murder?"

"Yep. All evening."

"Did you hear or see anything unusual?"

Mr. Yoakum grinned, as though at some secret joke. "I sure didn't," he replied.

"Nothing whatever?"

"Absolutely nothin'."

"When did you first know of the murder. What time, I mean."

"Let's see, Monday morning," replied the janitor, still grinning.

"Monday morning!" exclaimed Dan in amazement. "Do you mean you didn't hear of it till thirty-six hours afterward?"

"I sure didn't."

"How was that?"

"Well, you see," replied Mr. Yoakum slowly, as though regretful that his joke must end, "I didn't get here till Monday morning."

"But you said you were at home—"

"Sure, I was home, so I wasn't here. I was janitor down on Ninety-eighth Street then. You see, I've only been here about ten days. I came after the murder was all over, though I had to clean up after it."

Mr. Yoakum cackled. Dan interrupted him:

"So you weren't here a week ago Saturday?"

"I sure wasn't."

"Do you know who was janitor here before you?"

"Nope. Don't know a thing about him, only he sure put the hot-water boiler on the bum. He was ignorant, that's all I know."

So there was nothing to be learned from Mr. Yoakum, except the name and address of the agent of the apartment house. Dan wrote this down in a memorandum book, refused Mr. Yoakum's offer of a glass of beer, and left to go above to the ground floor, where he rang the bell of the tenant on the right. By then it was nearly seven o'clock, and quite dark outdoors, but the amateur detective had no thought of halting his investigations for anything so trivial as dinner.

His ring was answered by a woman in a dirty blue kimono, who informed him that she had lived in the house only two months; that she had never seen the murdered woman, and that she didn't want to talk about so disgusting a subject as murder anyhow. The other flat on the ground floor was vacant.

Dan mounted a flight of stairs and tried again.

Here he had better luck. He was told by a pale young woman in a kitchen apron that she had spoken many times to the murdered woman, who had lived there under

the name of Miss Alice Reeves. Miss Reeves had been
an old tenant; she had been there when the pale young
woman came, and that was over two years ago.

She had been very pretty, with dark eyes and hair, and
a beautiful complexion; she was always quiet and reserved, not mixing with anyone; she had sometimes had
callers, especially one gentleman, who came quite often.
The pale young woman had never got a good look at
him, having seen him only on the dark stairs; besides,
he had always worn a sort of a muffler over the lower
part of his face, so she couldn't describe him except to
say that he was rather tall and very well dressed and
distinguished-looking. She wouldn't recognize him if
she saw him.

Yes, said the pale young woman, they had a new janitor. She didn't know what had become of the old one,
who had been a little gray-haired Irishman named Cummings. He had been there Saturday evening to take off
the garbage, but at midnight, the time of the murder, he
could not be found, nor did he return on Sunday; they
had been compelled to go without hot water all day.
Monday morning the new man was sent up by the agent.
He wasn't as good as Cummings, who had been very
capable and obliging.

It took an hour for the pale young woman to tell Dan
all she knew.

At the other flat on that floor he found a new tenant,
who could tell him nothing. Another flight up and he
was on the floor on which Mrs. Mount, or Alice Reeves,
had lived. Here, in the flat across the hall from hers, he
met a Tartar in the person of an old music teacher who
said that he lived there alone with his wife; that he never
poked his nose into other people's business, and that he
expected them to do the same.

Dan retreated in good order.

On the two top floors he had no better luck; he found no one who had known Miss Reeves, though some had seen her often; nor could he get any description of the mysterious caller who, according to the pale young woman, had always worn a muffler across the lower part of his face. He did find the persons who had arrived first at the scene of the murder, a young husband and wife on the floor above.

Their story tallied with Mount's; they had been attracted by his scream, which they described as piercing and terrible, and, running down to Miss Reeves's flat, they had found her lying on the floor in a pool of blood, with Mount, the dripping knife in his hand, standing above her. It was the young husband who had summoned the police. According to him, Mount had appeared absolutely dazed—half mad, in fact. He had made no attempt whatever to get away, but had remained kneeling over the dead body of his wife until the arrival of the police.

But Dan's greatest disappointment was that he was unable to find among the tenants any trace of the man who, according to Mount's story, was standing in the lower hall with a suitcase in his hand when Mount entered. No one had seen him or knew anything about him.

It was a quarter to nine when Dan found himself again on the street.

A block or two down Broadway he entered a dairy lunchroom for a sandwich and a glass of milk, after which he sought the subway on the downtown side. The train was well filled, though it was too late for the theater crowd, for everybody is always going somewhere in New York. At the Ninety-sixth Street station Dan got out, walked two blocks north on Broadway, and over to West End Avenue, and entered the marble reception hall of an ornate apartment house.

"I want to see Mr. Leg," he said to the West Indian at the switchboard. "Tell him it's Dan Culp."

The negro threw in a plug and presently spoke into the transmitter:

"Thirty-four? Don Koolp to see Mr. Leg. All right, sir."

He disposed of Dan with a lordly gesture toward the elevator.

Mr. Leg appeared to be surprised, even alarmed, at the unexpected visit from his office boy. Dan, ushered in by the manservant, found his employer entertaining four or five friends in a session of the national game—not baseball.

"What is it, Dan? Something happened?" queried the lawyer, advancing to meet the youth at the door with a pair of kings in his hand.

"No, sir. That is, nothing important. I just wanted to find out if you got a photograph of Mount."

"Yes, the police let me have a copy of the one taken for the gallery."

"May I have it, sir? I'm going up to the drugstore to see if they remember seeing him there."

"By Jove, you are certainly on the job," smiled the lawyer. "Yes, of course you can have it." He went to a desk at the other end of the room and returned with a small unmounted photograph. "Here you are. But what's the hurry? Couldn't you have gone tomorrow just as well?"

"No, sir. You see, he was there at night, just about this time, so I'm more apt to find somebody who saw him. I didn't want to wait till tomorrow night." The youth appeared to hesitate, then continued, "There was something else, sir. May I have your night pass to the office building? I want to go down and look at something."

The lawyer's smile became a little impatient. "Well, really now, Dan, isn't that a little bit unnecessary? It isn't long till tomorrow morning."

"All right, sir, if you don't want—"

"Oh, I don't care. Wait a minute. I don't know where the blamed thing is."

This time Mr. Leg had to search for what he wanted, and it was finally found hidden under some papers in the bottom drawer of his desk.

Back uptown went Dan, to One Hundred and Sixteenth Street and Eighth Avenue, one of the busiest spots in Harlem, where he found a drugstore on the southwest corner. He failed to get any satisfactory information. The two clerks and the boy at the soda fountain declared that they had been on duty all evening on Saturday, April 3, but they had no recollection of seeing anyone who resembled the photograph of William Mount. The man at the newsstand outside said that he had an indistinct memory of such a man, but that he couldn't tell just when he had seen him.

"It's been two weeks, so I suppose I shouldn't expect anything," thought Dan as he turned away.

As he boarded a downtown train he was telling himself that Mr. Leg had stated the case mildly when he said that it was a little bit unnecessary to make a trip down to the office so late at night. It was worse than that, it was absurd.

Not for worlds would Dan have disclosed to anyone the extent of its absurdity by confessing the nature of his errand; he was himself trying to scoff at the wild idea that had entered his head that morning, and he felt that he was doubly a fool to entertain it as a possibility. Nevertheless, he was so completely possessed by it that he felt he couldn't sleep till he had sought the slight corroboration chance had offered him.

"But even if it's the same it won't really prove anything," he muttered, gazing out of the window down at the never-ending row of lighted shops as the elevated train rumbled along through the night.

At the office building he was admitted and passed into the night elevator by the watchman on showing Mr. Leg's card. He carried a key to the office, since he was always the first to arrive in the morning. A queer sense of strangeness and loneliness came over him as he switched on the electricity and saw his desk and Miss Venner's, all the familiar objects, revealed by its cold rays.

What a difference artificial light, with the night outside, makes in a room which we have previously seen illumined only by the soft, natural light of day!

Dan passed into the inner room, went straight to Mr. Leg's desk, turned on the electric reading globe, and cast his eye over the accumulation of books and papers. There were publishers' announcements, social invitations, personal letters, and other things. Almost at once, with an exclamation of satisfaction, he pounced on a typewritten sheet of paper with a name written at the bottom.

He spread this out on the desk, pulled from his pocket the slip he had found in Mr. Yoakum's bag of trash bearing the words "Bonneau et Mouet—Sec," and, sitting down in Mr. Leg's chair, began to examine with minute attention first the name on the letter, then the words on the slip. He did this for a full half-hour, with his brows wrinkled in concentration and the glow of discovery in his eyes.

"Of course," he muttered finally aloud, as he put the typewritten sheet back where he had found it, "I may not be a handwriting expert, but those were written by the same man as sure as my name's Dan Culp. He's mixed up in it somehow.''

He placed the slip back in his pocket, and going to a case devoted to law volumes and similar works at one side of the room, took out a large blue book and carried it to the desk. He opened it at the front, ran his finger down the list of illustrations, stopped about the middle, and turned over the pages till he came to the one he wanted. It showed a full-page reproduction of a photograph of a man. He looked at it a moment, then carefully tore it out of the book, folded it, and placed it in his pocket.

There was a scared look on the youth's face as he turned out the lights and turned to leave the office. As the lock of the door clicked behind him there came faintly the sound of Trinity's midnight chimes.

Chapter V
The Police Commissioner

DESPITE THE FACT THAT HE DIDN'T GET TO BED till nearly two o'clock, having consumed half an hour explaining his late arrival to his mother and accepting her good-natured banter on his coming career as a great detective, Dan arrived at the office at half-past eight the following morning. He sat at his desk reading till nine, when Miss Venner appeared.

"Well, did you find the murderer?" she inquired sweetly, as he drew out her chair for her.

"Maybe," Dan replied in a tone so professionally cryptic that she burst into a peal of laughter.

"All right," continued Dan calmly, "wait and see."

"I'll tell you what I'll do," remarked Miss Venner as

she sat down and took her embroidery from the drawer. "If you win Mr. Leg's case for him—for, of course, he can't do it—I'll give you this scarf I'm working on."

The splendid vanity of this proposal appeared not to occur to Dan. "No; do you mean it?" he exclaimed.

Miss Venner's reply was lost in the sound of the door opening to admit Mr. Leg. Greetings were exchanged. Dan sought his own desk.

A few minutes later, called into the other room by his employer, he proceeded to give him an account of his activities of the day before. He told him all that he had learned at the apartment house, from the janitor and tenants, and of his failure to find anyone at the drugstore who remembered seeing Mount. But there was one thing he did not mention: the slip of paper he had in his pocket; nor did he inform the lawyer that one of his books had been disfigured by having a photograph torn from it.

"And now I suppose you're ready for my report," observed Mr. Leg with an amused smile when Dan had finished.

"If you please, sir."

"Well, to begin with, I had a hard time to find out anything." The lawyer took a sheet of paper covered with writing from his pocket. "First I went to the office of Police Commissioner Hammel, who is a personal friend of mine, to get his authority, but he was out of town and wasn't expected back until this afternoon.

"I was afraid you'd call me down if I put it off, so I went to Inspector Brown, and he referred me to another inspector, Lobert, who is in charge of the case. Naturally, I suppose, they regard it as their business to convict Mount, but Lobert certainly didn't want to tell me anything. I got most of my information from a record of the testimony at the coroner's inquest and before the Grand Jury, of which I secured a copy.

"The police arrived at the scene of the murder at twenty-five minutes to twelve. Their story of what happened after they got there is the same as Mount's. They say that the body of the victim was still quite warm; it wasn't examined by a doctor until the next morning at nine o'clock, and then all he could say was that she had died between eight o'clock and midnight.

"They took nothing from the flat except the knife, and nothing from Mount's person of any significance. The knife was an ordinary steel paper knife with an ivory hilt, presumably the property of Mrs. Mount, or Alice Reeves, under which name the murdered woman was living there. The police didn't examine the hilt for fingerprints, as it was found in Mount's hand. Besides the wound in the breast, the body showed no marks of violence. Neither Mount nor his wife has any criminal record."

The lawyer handed the sheet of paper to Dan as he finished.

"So," observed the youth, "the knife doesn't tell us anything. I was hoping—"

"Well?" the other prodded him as he stopped.

"Nothing, sir. That is, nothing that is worth telling. But that doesn't matter; we've only begun. Of course, we can't expect any real help from the police; all they want is to convict somebody. Are you going to see Mount this morning, sir?"

"I suppose so." Mr. Leg frowned. "The Tombs is an extremely unpleasant place to visit, Dan. Extremely. But, of course, if it's necessary—"

Mr. Leg suddenly smiled, arose to his feet, drew himself up, and performed a clumsy imitation of a military salute.

"At your orders, Captain Culp."

When, a little later, the lawyer departed on his way to the Tombs, Dan remained behind to go over the testimony at the inquest. But he found nothing in it of importance except what Mr. Leg had already told him, and, having finished it, he left the office in care of Miss Venner and descended to the street.

A Broadway streetcar took him to a certain address near Union Square which he had got the day before from Mr. Yoakum. He entered a door marked in gilt lettering, "Levis & Levis, Real Estate," and, after explaining his errand to a clerk, was admitted to the private room of a junior member of the firm.

"Yes," replied the agent, in answer to his question; "we had a man named Cummings working for us. Patrick Cummings. Yes, he was janitor of the house where the murder took place. But we don't know where he is now."

"Isn't he with you any longer?"

"No. It was mighty curious. He disappeared suddenly, and the funny part of it is we still owe him fifteen dollars wages, which makes it really mysterious. All we know is that when one of our men went up there Sunday, on account of the murder, Cummings was nowhere to be found, although the tenants said he had been there Saturday evening. We haven't heard anything of him."

"I should think," observed Dan, "that you might have suspected his disappearance was connected with the murder."

The real estate agent smiled condescendingly. "You're a great little thinker, my lad. We did suspect it, and we communicated the fact to the police. I myself told Inspector Lobert about it. He said he'd let me know if they found him, but I haven't heard."

"Would you mind describing him to me, sir?"

"He was a little gray-haired man, about fifty, I should say, with light-colored eyes—I don't know if they were blue or gray—and a scraggly mustache. He was about five feet seven and weighed about one hundred and thirty-five pounds."

"Had he been working for you long?"

"About three years."

"Thank you, sir. One other thing; I'd like to get permission to go through Mrs. Mount's furniture and things—Miss Reeves, you know. The janitor says it is in storage. A letter from you, sir—"

"Nothing doing," returned the agent. "It's under the jurisdiction of the probate court, and I couldn't give you permission if I wanted to. You'll have to get a court order."

So Dan went back down to Chambers Street, where, after interminable delays and examinations of his credentials from Mr. Leg, he obtained the sought-for permission. Then he had to wait another hour until a court officer was ready to accompany him to the storage warehouse; and in the end he had all his trouble for nothing. Among the hundreds of papers and books and other articles which he examined till late in the afternoon, he found absolutely nothing of significance.

"It's mighty curious," he muttered disgustedly, "that I shouldn't find one letter, or one book with his writing in it, or anything."

It was after four o'clock when he handed the court officer a two-dollar bill out of Mr. Leg's diminishing hundred and left him to go farther uptown. His destination was the house on One Hundred and Fifty-seventh Street, and when he arrived there he once more made a round of the tenants, from the top floor to the bottom.

To each of them he showed the photograph which he had torn out of the book in his employer's office, but no one remembered ever having seen the man; and when he asked the pale young woman on the second floor if the photograph resembled the man of whom she had spoken as a frequent caller at Miss Reeves's apartment, she replied that she really couldn't say, as she had never had a good look at him.

But most of Dan's questions on this occasion concerned Patrick Cummings, the missing janitor. He learned little from the tenants; and then, realizing his mistake, he left the house and sought the basement next door.

The janitor here was a broken-down Scotchman with watery eyes. Yes, he replied, he had known Paddy Cummings well: and, urged on by another appropriation from Mr. Leg's hundred, he furnished a great deal of miscellaneous information concerning the character and habits of his missing confrère.

He said he had been a happy-go-lucky individual, much given, however, to unexpected fits of sullenness.

He had been unmarried, with no apparent relatives or friends whatever. Despite the fact that there was always money in his pocket, he had invariably cheated at pinocle. He had possessed the tastes of a gentleman, preferring whisky to beer. During the past year, however, he had contracted a disgusting fondness for motion pictures, having attended at least three times a week at the nickelodeon around the corner.

The Scotchman knew nothing of where he had gone; he missed him unspeakably, all the more on account of the insufferable Yoakum, who had taken his place.

Dan went back next door to see the insufferable Yoakum, from whom he learned that the former janitor had evidently departed unexpectedly and in a great hurry, as he had left his household goods behind him. Yoakum had found cooking utensils, a bed, two tables, some chairs, et cetera, in their places in the basement when he arrived; presumably they were the property of Cummings. Dan went through the place half a dozen times, but found nothing that gave any trace of the missing man's reasons for departure.

By the time he emerged again into the street the day was gone; a clock in a window at the Broadway corner said ten minutes past six. He entered and sought a telephone booth to call up the office, thinking it barely possible that Mr. Leg would be awaiting his return, but he got no answer.

He went home to sleep over the developments of the day.

At the office the next morning Mr. Leg submitted his report of the previous day's activities immediately upon his arrival. He had written down the answers to Dan's questions in their order:

1. Mount hasn't got the letter his wife left when she ran away. It was destroyed two years ago.

2. He was employed as bookkeeper at the office of Rafter & Co., coal dealers, foot of One Hundred and Twelfth Street, for the four months previous to the murder.

3. He was inside the drugstore only a few minutes. The rest of the time he waited outside on the corner. He bought a paper from the man at the newsstand and talked with him a little. He says this man might remember him.

4. He drank a great deal for the two years following his wife's disappearance, but not since then. He swears he didn't touch a drop that night.

5. He appears solid and calm, with a lifeless indifference that is extraordinary, except when speaking of his wife, when he nearly breaks down with grief.

"There," said Mr. Leg, "that's what you wanted to know. I went to Rafter & Co., and they corroborated

Mount, saying that he had worked for them a little over four months, and that he had been very satisfactory. He never drank any as far as they knew."

"I'm glad to hear that, sir," replied Dan. "That settles it as far as Mount's concerned. He's out of it, anyway; only I thought he might have done it in a fit of drunkenness. You see, sir, he couldn't have had any possible reason to kill his wife. The police supposition is that he found that she had been receiving another man in that flat, and killed her for revenge and jealousy.

"But, according to his story, he had agreed to take her back only the night before, knowing that in all probability she had done wrong. The reason I believe him is because of what he said about the money. He was even willing to make use of the money she was going to bring with her. No man would make up a thing like that about himself, even to save his own neck."

"Humph!" the lawyer grunted. "So you're a student of human nature, are you, Dan?"

"Yes, sir. I'm just beginning. I've had very little experience, but there's something else just as good. The people who say experience is the best school don't know what they're talking about. Most people could learn more about human nature in one week by studying Montaigne's *Essays* than in a lifetime of observation, because hardly any one knows how to observe. Not that I don't need experience; I'm just beginning to get it. I always keep my eyes and ears open. You remember, sir, it was you who told me to read Montaigne."

"Yes, I believe I did," agreed the lawyer. "I never got much out of him myself."

"No, sir; I suppose not. But to go back to Mount. I am certain now that he's innocent."

Mr. Leg frowned. "But that doesn't get us anywhere."

"No, sir. But I am also pretty certain that I know who is responsible for the murder."

"What?" shouted Mr. Leg, nearly falling out of his chair in his surprise.

"Yes, sir."

"You know who the murderer is!"

"No, sir, I didn't say that. I only know who is responsible for it, though it may be that he actually did it himself. I wouldn't think it possible, only I remember that Montaigne says, 'The passions smothered by modern civilization are doubly ferocious when awakened,' and that was nearly four hundred years ago."

"But, good Heavens, Dan, how did you—who is it?"

But that the boy wouldn't tell, saying that he might be wrong, and that he had no real evidence to support his suspicion. Mr. Leg insisted, but finally gave it up, and listened attentively while Dan recounted the story of the missing janitor, with all the details.

"There's just one thing we've got to do," finished the boy, "and that is find Patrick Cummings. It won't be easy, because it's certain that he's in hiding, if something worse hasn't happened to him. I looked around for a photograph of him, but couldn't find any."

"The thing to do is get the police after him," suggested Mr. Leg.

"Yes, sir," agreed Dan, but there was a curious expression in his eyes. "That's what I wanted to ask, will you go to Commissioner Hammel himself, since you know him?"

"Yes, I will," said the lawyer, "and I'll go right now."

And ten minutes later he was off, with a detailed description of Patrick Cummings, typewritten by Dan, in his pocket. A taxicab got him to headquarters for eighty cents.

This time he found the police commissioner in, and, being Simmie Leg, Dick Hammel's friend from college days, he was passed in ahead of a score of others who had been waiting anywhere from ten minutes to three hours.

Police Commissioner Richard Hammel was a tall, well-built man of middle age, with a fine-looking head, well carried, and piercing, cynical eyes. He was well connected socially, being a member of an old New York family that had been prominent in the life of the city for over a century.

"How are you, Simmie?" said he, rising from his chair with outstretched hand as Mr. Leg was ushered in. "Something new to see you around here."

"Hello, Dick!" The visitor took the proffered hand. "Yes, but you know what Devery said."

They chatted for ten minutes before the lawyer came to the purpose of his call. Then, pulling Dan's description of the missing janitor from his pocket, he explained the circumstances to the commissioner saying that he wished a general alarm sent out for him all over the country.

Commissioner Hammel did not reply at once. He was apparently making a careful study of the length of a pencil he held in his hand, as he continued to gaze at it thoughtfully for some moments after Mr. Leg had stopped speaking. Finally he turned to his visitor.

"Simmie," he said slowly, "I'm sorry, but I can't do it."

"Why not?" demanded the lawyer in surprise. "Of course, I know you might be working against yourself in case Cummings's testimony should free Mount, but justice—"

"It isn't that." The commissioner frowned. "Our esprit de corps doesn't go so far as to want to convict an innocent man of murder. But Mount isn't innocent." He eyed his visitor speculatively. "If it were anyone else, Simmie, I'd turn him off with evasion, but with you I can be frank.

"Of course Mount is guilty; the evidence is conclusive. I don't mean it's merely sufficient to convict; it's absolutely conclusive of his guilt. You know that as well as I do. But you think this man Cummings could throw new light on the affair. Well, you're right. He could."

The commissioner stopped to clear his throat.

"The fact is," he continued, "if Cummings were found and allowed to tell his story, he would bring notoriety on somebody. I don't know who. I really don't know, Simmie. But it's somebody that has a voice in high places, for word has come that Cummings must not be found. You appreciate the circumstances. There's no use kicking up a scandal when it will do good to nobody."

There was a silence.

"Humph," grunted Mr. Leg finally, casting a thoughtful eye on the floor. "Of course, Dick, I don't like scandal any more than you do, especially when it hits one of my friends. But, in the first place, I don't know that this unknown person is my friend, and I don't admire this mystery stuff except in stories. And secondly, how do you know it wouldn't do any good?"

"Oh, come now, Simmie," replied the commissioner with a smile, "you know very well Mount's guilty. Don't be foolish."

"On the contrary," retorted the lawyer, "I believe he's innocent. And Dan—that is, a detective I've employed—believes it, too. I tell you, Dick, scandal or no scandal, Cummings must be found."

"If he is," said the commissioner decisively, "it will be without the help of the police."

"But, Dick—"

"No. A good friend of mine, and a valuable member of this community, has asked me to stay off, and that's all there is to it. I don't know who he spoke for, and he wouldn't tell me; but since we unquestionably have the guilty man—"

"I tell you he's innocent!" repeated Mr. Leg warmly. He got up from his chair and put on his hat; he was dangerously near losing his temper for the first time in five years.

"Don't be an ass!" was the commissioner's reply.

"Is that so?" retorted Mr. Leg inelegantly. "I'll show you who's an ass, Dick Hammel! And let me tell you something: Patrick Cummings is going to be found if I have to hunt for him myself!"

And, leaving this awful threat to shake the walls behind him, he departed.

Chapter VI
The Name on the Screen

IN THE WEEKS THAT FOLLOWED, MR. SIMON LEG experienced for the first time in his life the sensation of mingled rage, helplessness, and doubt that attacks a man when he grimly swears to do a thing and then fails in the execution. He had said: "Patrick Cummings is going to be found if I have to hunt for him myself."

He hunted. Dan hunted. They hired detectives, and the detectives hunted. But three weeks after Mr. Leg had hurled his ultimatum at the commissioner of police the missing janitor was still missing.

The detectives were also set to work on other aspects of the case. They investigated the past lives of both

Mount and his wife, but found out nothing of real value. They discovered that for at least a year previous to her disappearance Mrs. Mount had been a more or less frequent visitor to cabarets, and once they thought they had found the man with whom she had run away, but he proved an alibi.

In all, Mr. Leg hired more than a dozen detectives, including the great Jim Dickinson himself, at a cost of several thousand dollars, but all he really got out of it was a huge stack of elaborate daily reports which, in fact, were absolutely useless.

They advised Mr. Leg to advertise a reward of five thousand dollars for Patrick Cummings, since he had expressed his willingness to spend ten times that sum if necessary, and Mr. Leg himself favored the idea. But Dan, who had surprised the lawyer on his return from the commissioner's office by not being surprised at what the commissioner had said, vetoed it, saying that it might be all right to offer a reward if the police were on their side, but utterly futile under the circumstances.

"Besides," argued the youth, "the first time Cummings saw the reward posted he would fly to cover, if he isn't there already. Public rewards are never any good, except to stimulate the police. And, besides that, I have a reason of my own."

Dan was the busiest of all. He spent a whole day going inch by inch through the basement where Cummings had lived, though he had previously searched it; he interviewed the Scotchman next door several times; he found and talked with everyone in the neighborhood who had ever seen the missing man; he pursued vainly a thousand avenues of information. It seemed that Patrick Cummings had come from nowhere and gone back to the same place.

His first appearance in the discoverable world had

been the day when, nearly three years back, he had called at the office of Levis & Levis to ask for a job as janitor; his last, the evening of the murder. It got so that one thing, one name, one person, occupied Dan's mind like a mania; he thought, ate, slept, and breathed Patrick Cummings.

He forgot to open Miss Venner's desk for her of mornings; he forgot to comb his hair; he forgot to look when he crossed the street.

He came near having cause to regret this latter neglect when one afternoon, hearing a warning honk, he jumped in the wrong direction and was knocked flat on his back by a touring car as it whizzed by. He scrambled to his feet in time to see the well-dressed figure of Judge Fraser Manton in the tonneau.

Finally, when there appeared to be nothing else to do, Dan would walk the streets for hours at a time, cudgeling his brain for a scheme to find a man that evidently didn't want to be found, and meanwhile watching the passersby. He had followed many a gray-haired man with a scraggly mustache in the past three weeks; once he had found one named Cummings, but not Patrick.

The number of suspects rounded up by the detectives mounted into the hundreds, so eager were they, for Mr. Leg had let it be known that the successful man would get a good-sized check.

Late one afternoon, a week before the date set for Mount's trial, Dan was walking down Eighth Avenue, tired, dejected, and ready to give up, but, nevertheless, with his eyes open. As he passed the tawdry front of a motion picture theater he stopped to glance over a group of men standing near, and then half unconsciously began to glance over the flaring posters displayed at the entrance to the theater. "The Scotchman said Cummings was a movie fan," he was thinking. Suddenly he gave a start, stopped still, as if transfixed by a sudden thought, and uttered an ejaculation of discovery.

"I never thought of that!" he exclaimed aloud, so that the girl in the ticket booth looked over at him with an amused grin. He stood for several minutes, lost in consideration of the scheme that had entered his mind. Suddenly he pulled himself together, dashed into the avenue, and hopped on a downtown trolley car.

Fifteen minutes later he was in the office, explaining his plan to Mr. Leg with eager tongue. His enthusiasm was somewhat dampened by his employer's lack of it.

"All right," said the lawyer indifferently; "try it if you want to, though I don't think much of it. I'll foot the bill and stand for the reward if you find him. Write the letter yourself."

Dan went into the other room to ask Miss Venner for permission to use her machine. She granted it politely; she had had very little to say to Dan lately, since he had begun to neglect the thousand little attentions he had always paid her. He sat down with a frown and began to click.

Half an hour later he submitted the following letter to his employer:

MANAGER OF THE EMPIRE MOTION PICTURE THEATER,
2168 Eighth Avenue, New York.

DEAR SIR:

I am trying to find a man whom I need as witness in an important case. I make you the following proposition:

You are to flash on your screen at every performance the words: "Patrick Cummings, formerly of 714 West 157th Street, is wanted on the telephone." If Cummings appears in response, tell him that the party rang off after asking that he wait till they call again. Then telephone at once to my office, 11902 Rector, and report that Cummings is there; and you are to hold Cummings, if possible, until someone from my office arrives. If it is impossible to hold him, have him followed by one of your employees when he leaves.

In case I find Cummings with this assistance from you, I will pay you five thousand dollars cash. As to my reliability and integrity, as well as ability to pay that amount, I refer you to the Murray National Bank of New York.

I am enclosing a detailed description of Cummings. *This offer is good for only ten days from the date of this letter*.

Yours truly,

"It's a pretty good idea," admitted Mr. Leg when he had finished reading it; "but what makes you think that Cummings will be fool enough to walk into the trap, provided he sees the bait?"

"That's just it," explained Dan. "I'm counting on his being somewhat of a fool. Put yourself in his place, sir. Here he is, sitting in the movies, when suddenly he sees his own name thrown on the screen, and, so that there may be no mistake about it, even the address where he lived. It won't occur to him that it is merely an attempt to find him; he will immediately conclude that whoever is asking for him must already know where he is, and the chances are that he'll be mighty anxious to find out who the call is from. At any rate, it's worth trying. It won't cost much unless we find him, and you won't care then."

"I certainly won't," agreed the lawyer grimly. "I didn't tell you, Dan, that I went to see Hammel again yesterday. Nothing doing."

"Of course not, sir." Dan took back the letter. "I'm going to take this right downstairs and have them run off ten thousand copies on the multigraph. Then I'll telephone to the Trow people for a list of motion picture theaters, and to an agency for ten or twelve girls to come and help us send them out. I think it would be best, sir,

if you would sign the letters. If the signature were mul-
tigraphed perhaps they wouldn't feel so sure of the reward.''

"By Jove, you've got it all down," observed Mr. Leg.
"Yes, the letters ought to be signed, but you can do it
as well as I. They won't know the difference." He
glanced at his watch. "I have to be uptown for dinner."

Thus was Dan's scheme set to work. Somewhat to his
surprise, Miss Venner volunteered to stay and help; and,
with the assistance of some dozen girls sent in by an
agency, they had the ten thousand letters signed, addressed, sealed, and stamped by midnight. Dan carried
them to the main post office, after which he escorted
Miss Venner home.

Meanwhile, Mr. Leg was acquiring a fresh stock of
indignation. His dinner engagement uptown was only
half social; it was an informal meeting of a special committee of one of the most exclusive clubs of the city to
arrange for a dinner to be given in honor of one of their
members on the occasion of his return from a high dip-
lomatic position abroad. The membership of the committee included James Reynolds, the banker; Alfred
Sinnott and Corkran Updegraff, capitalists; Judge Fraser
Manton, and two or three others.

Although Mr. Leg had met Judge Manton several
years before, and had of course seen him many times
since, they had never got beyond a bowing acquaintance.
So when, after dinner was over and they retired to the
club library, Mr. Leg approached the judge with a view
to conversation, there was a slight tinge of formality in
his manner. They talked a little on a topic that had been
discussed earlier in the evening, on which they had dis-
agreed.

"By the way, Judge," observed Mr. Leg when a
chance offered itself, "I want to thank you for assigning

me to that Mount case—the murder case, you know—though I certainly can't guess why I was selected.''

"Ah!" Judge Manton's brows lifted. "Is it a matter for thanks?"

"It certainly is. Most interesting three weeks I've ever had. I've worked day and night. Spent ten thousand dollars, and there's a chance I'll win it."

"M-m-m! Of course you know I can't discuss the case out of court."

"Oh, no! I understand that," agreed Mr. Leg hastily. "Only I just thought I'd let you know that I'll probably be in court tomorrow with a request for postponement."

"Ah!" Again Judge Manton's brows were lifted. "I suppose you have a good reason."

"No, I haven't. That is, no particular reason. But I haven't been able to get hold of my most important witness, and I believe there is usually no difficulty in getting a postponement when a man's life depends on it. I believe the district attorney will make no objection."

For a moment there was no reply. Judge Manton took from his pocket a silk case embroidered with gold, extracted a cigarette, and lit it. He blew a long column of smoke slowly into the air, and another. Then he turned with startling suddenness and spoke rapidly in a low voice, looking straight into Mr. Leg's eyes:

"I don't know if the district attorney will object, Mr. Leg. But I do know that I will. The calendar is too far behind already to permit of further postponements, except for the most cogent reasons. You've had a month to prepare your case and find your witnesses. Of course you may come to court and enter your petition for a postponement if you wish. But, my dear Leg, speaking merely as a private citizen, I wouldn't advise you to bank much on it."

Judge Manton stopped abruptly, blew a third column

of smoke into the air, turned on his heel, and walked away.

"Well!" ejaculated Mr. Leg to himself in astonishment. "I'll be damned if they haven't got to Manton the same as they did Dick Hammel! Lord, how I'd love to show 'em all up!"

And he walked all the way home from downtown, a distance of over two miles, in order to inspect the faces of the passersby in search of Patrick Cummings. He was deadly in earnest, was Mr. Simon Leg. Think of walking over two miles when a mere uplifting of a finger would have brought a spirited taxi dashing to the curb!

The following morning at the office Mr. Leg lost no time in telling Dan of his conversation with Judge Manton. His indignation had increased during the night; he denounced the entire police force and judiciary of the city.

"Think of it!" he exclaimed. "They are willing to throw away an innocent man's life merely to save the good name of a friend! Or there may be politics in it. Whatever it is, it's rotten! I didn't think it of Dick Hammel, and now the judge himself—"

"I'm not surprised, sir," observed Dan. "I've half a mind to tell you—but it would do no good. Our only hope now is the movies. We've got ten thousand of them working for us. We've covered everything within five hundred miles of New York; the only trouble is, he's nearly as apt to be in San Francisco."

"Or dead."

"Yes, sir. For Mount's sake I hope not."

"Well, we've got just six days left. I'm going to call up Dickinson and tell him to send out more men. I don't know, Dan; I'm about ready to give up."

A little later telephone calls began to come in from the motion picture theaters. They asked every conceivable question under the sun, from the number of hairs on Patrick Cummings's head to the color of his shoestrings. Dan finally gave up all thought of leaving the office, and all day long he sat at his desk with the telephone receiver at his ear. Toward the middle of the afternoon he made two calls on his own account: one to his mother to tell her that he would not be home that night, and the other to a furniture dealer on Fourteenth Street. An hour later Mr. Leg, hearing a most unusual noise in the outer office, stepped to his door to see a man setting up a cot with mattress, covers, and pillows.

"I sent for it," explained Dan to his astonished employer. "I'm going to sleep here, sir, to answer the telephone."

After that he refused to leave the office; he had his meals sent in from a nearby restaurant. The truth was, Dan's conscience was troubling him; he had begun to fear that he had done wrong not to tell his suspicions and his reasons for them to his employer, though he tried to console himself by reflecting that he would only have been laughed at.

But the poor boy felt that his desire for glory had jeopardized the life of an innocent man, and he was miserable. His whole hope now lay in the telephone. Would the word come? Everytime the bell rang his nerves quivered.

The next day Mr. Leg went to court and requested a postponement of two weeks, having first gained the acquiescence of the district attorney's office. Judge Manton denied the petition, and the lawyer left in a rage.

Only five days were left before the trial.

Several false alarms came in from the motion picture theaters. Most of them were obviously mistakes, but one sent Dan flying for a train to Stamford. When he got there he found the manager of the theater seated in his office, chatting with a little, redhaired Irishman, whose name indeed proved to be Patrick Cummings, but who was certainly not the one wanted.

"Didn't you read the description of him?" Dan demanded.

"Sure," replied the manager, "but I wasn't taking any chances."

"You're a fool!" retorted the boy shortly as he started at a run to catch the next train back to New York.

That was Monday afternoon, and the trial was set for Wednesday.

Later that same afternoon Mr. Leg, wandering into the outer office, approached Dan's desk. The boy was seated there with the telephone at his elbow, apparently buried deep in contemplation of some object spread out before him on the desk. Mr. Leg, going closer and looking over his shoulder, saw a white slip of paper with the words, "Bonneau et Mouet—Sec," written on it in ink, and beside it a large reproduction of a man's photograph.

"What in the name of goodness are you doing with that?" demanded Mr. Leg, pointing to the photograph.

Dan jumped with surprise.

"Oh, I—I didn't know you were there, sir!" He flushed. "Why, I—er—I was just looking at it." He managed a smile. "Studying human nature, sir."

The lawyer grunted. "If you ask me, Dan, I think you're getting kind of queer."

"Yes, sir." The boy folded the photograph with the slip of paper inside and placed it in his pocket. The lawyer regarded him sharply for a moment, then returned to the other room.

Tuesday morning came, the day before the trial. Dan did not move from his desk all day and evening. The telephone rang over and over, and each time he took up the receiver it was with a hand that trembled so it could scarcely hold the receiver to his ear. The fact was, he had persuaded himself, or, rather, he felt that the little wire was certain to bring him the word he wanted. But it did not come.

The following morning at ten o'clock William Mount was called before the bar to stand trial for the murder of his wife.

The courtroom was not crowded, for the case was not a celebrated one; but there was a good-sized gathering of those people who may always be counted on to turn up at a murder trial, and there was much twisting of curious necks when the prisoner was led in. There was little change in Mount's appearance since the day a month previous, when he had been called before Judge Manton to plead.

His face was slightly paler and his cheeks more sunken; but he wore the same air of heavy, stolid indifference, and his eyes were sullen and devoid of hope.

Mr. Leg started proceedings by asking again for a postponement, declaring that he had been unable to locate his most important witness. Assistant District Attorney Thornton, for the prosecution, refrained from argument. Judge Manton denied the request, saying that counsel for the defense had had ample time to prepare his case.

There was little difficulty in selecting the jury, as neither side appeared to be particular, and the box was filled by noon. The addresses to the jury were short, and by the time court reconvened after lunch they were ready for the witnesses.

The prosecution opened with the young man who had been called to the scene of the murder by Mount's scream, and had found him standing over the body with the knife in his hand. His testimony, with that of three other tenants and as many policemen, consumed the afternoon.

When court adjourned a little before six Mr. Leg returned to his office to find Dan seated at his desk, staring moodily at the telephone.

"Nothing doing, Dan?" said Mr. Leg grimly.

"No, sir."

"Been here all day?"

"Yes, sir."

"It's funny you can't see," put in Miss Venner with sudden sharpness, "that he's getting sick over it. He sits and stares at that telephone like a crazy man. He hasn't eaten a bite all day. Of course, not that I care, only I— I—"

She flushed and stopped.

"Can't help it," remarked Mr. Leg gloomily. "Come on in the other room, Dan, and I'll tell you how it went in court. Or wait, I'll sit here."

The following day at noon the prosecution finished. They had presented evidence that the murdered woman was the wife of the prisoner, and had left him, furnishing—as the assistant district attorney had said in his opening address—the strongest possible combination of motives—jealousy and revenge. When the prosecution's last witness left the stand it was easy to see from the expression of the jurors' faces as they stole glances at the prisoner that they regarded the case as already proven. Mr. Leg, following Dan's instructions, had attempted to gain time by prolonging the cross-examinations; but he was anything but an adept at the game, and several times he had been prodded by Judge Manton.

The first witness called by the defense was the prisoner himself. Aided—and sometimes retarded—by questions from Mr. Leg, he merely repeated the story he had previously told to the police, the coroner, and his lawyer. Again Mr. Leg attempted to drag out the proceedings by prolonging the examination; but at length his invention ran out and he was forced to let the witness go, reflecting, however, that the cross-examination would occupy another hour or two.

Therefore, was he struck with consternation when he heard the prosecuting attorney say calmly:

"I will not cross-examine, your honor."

"Call your next witness, Mr. Leg," said Judge Manton sharply.

Luckily Mr. Leg had one—a Mr. Rafter, of the firm by whom Mount had been employed as bookkeeper. He was followed by two men who had known the prisoner in his earlier and happier days, and who testified to his good character and mild temper. At that point court was adjourned till tomorrow.

Mr. Leg missed his dinner that evening. Long after darkness had fallen and windows had begun to make their tens of thousands of little squares of light against the huge black forms of the skyscrapers, the lawyer sat in his office talking with Dan between patches of silence, trying to invent something that could be applied as a desperate last resort.

Jim Dickinson, chief of the best detective bureau in the city, whose men had been employed on the case for the past month, was called in by telephone, but he had nothing to suggest, and soon left them. The lawyer had told Dan of the failure of the prosecution to cross-examine Mount, observing bitterly that their case was so strong they could afford to appear compassionate.

Trinity's chimes rang out for ten o'clock. Mr. Leg arose and put on his hat.

"Well, I guess we're done for," he observed. "We've only got two more witnesses, and they don't amount to anything. Three hours for the summing-up; it will probably go to the jury by three o'clock tomorrow afternoon. It's no use, Dan. You're taking it too hard; it's not your fault, my boy. See you in the morning. Good night.''

After his employer had gone, Dan sat motionless at his desk with his eyes on the telephone. He felt that it had betrayed him. Curious, how confident he had felt that the wire would bring him the word he awaited!

"Bum hunch," he muttered.

The little black instrument was distasteful to his sight. He hated it. An impulse entered his mind to seize the thing, jerk it from its cord, and hurl it out of the window; an impulse so strong that he actually got up from his chair and walked over and sat down on the cot for fear he would give way to it. He sat there for some time. Finally he bent over and began unlacing his shoes preparatory to lying down. The knot was tight and he jerked angrily at the string.

As he did so the telephone bell rang.

He hastened to the desk, took up the telephone, placed the receiver to his ear, and said ''Hello!''

"Hello!" came a female voice. "Is this Rector 11902?"

"Yes."

"Wait a minute, please. This is long distance. Albany wants you."

There was a moment's wait, while Dan trembled with impatience. Then a man's voice came:

"Hello! Is this Simon Leg's office?"

"Yes," Dan replied.

"The lawyer, Broadway, New York?"

"Yes."

"This is the Royal Theater, No. 472 Jefferson Avenue, Albany. Four, seven, two Jefferson Avenue. I've got your man, Patrick Cummings."—"Yes, I tell you,

I've got him. He's here—wait—wait a minute—I'm afraid he'll beat it—''

The last words came faintly. There was a buzzing on the line, a series of clicks, and the wire sounded dead. Dan moved the receiver hook frantically up and down; finally he got a reply from the local operator, who informed him that Albany had rung off. Yes, she could get them again, probably in a quarter of an hour; would he please hang up his receiver?

He did so, but took it off again immediately and asked for Grand Central Station. From the information bureau he learned that there would be no train to Albany for two hours, and then a slow one. Dan grabbed up his hat and, without stopping even to turn out the light, dashed from the office. He ran all the way to the subway station, where he boarded an uptown express train. At Fourteenth Street he got off and rushed up the steps to the sidewalk three at a time, and started east at breakneck speed, knocking over pedestrians and leaping across the path of streetcars and automobiles. Two minutes later he appeared, breathless and trembling, before two men who were seated in the entrance of a garage near Third Avenue.

''The fastest car in the place!'' he hurled at them. ''Quick!''

He thrust a bunch of twenty-dollar bills under the nose of one of the men.

''Don't look, get busy!'' he commanded. ''The fastest car you've got, and a chauffeur that can drive!''

Finally they were moved to action. Lights were turned on in the rear of the garage, a limousine was wheeled to one side, disclosing to view a big touring car, and a sleepy-looking young man, wearing a cap and drab uniform, appeared from somewhere.

''Here's a hundred dollars!'' cried Dan to one of the

men, thrusting a roll of bills into his hand. "If that isn't enough, I'll pay the rest when I get back."

He scrambled into the tonneau and the chauffeur mounted his seat in front. The powerful engine began to throb.

"Where to?" asked the chauffeur.

"Albany," replied Dan as the car started forward. "And there's a fifty-dollar bill in it if we get there by four o'clock!"

Chapter VII
The End

MR. SIMON LEG ARRIVED AT HIS OFFICE EARLY the following morning. After reaching home the night before he had stayed up for four hours working on his address to the jury, though he felt it to be a hopeless task, and when he did go to bed, he slept fitfully. That was the explanation of his red eyes and general appearance of discomfort as he opened his office door.

He found Miss Venner with her hat and coat still on, gazing at the cot in the corner.

"Where's Dan?" demanded Mr. Leg, stopping short after a glance around.

"I don't know." The stenographer turned a troubled countenance on him. "He wasn't here when I came in." She pointed to the cot. "The covers haven't been disturbed. I guess he didn't sleep here. And the electric lights were all turned on."

The lawyer grunted. "Strange. I left him here late last night, and he intended to stay then. There's no message anywhere?"

"No, sir; I looked." Miss Venner appeared to hesitate, then continued: "You don't think—he's done anything, do you, Mr. Leg? He acted queer yesterday. I know he felt responsible, somehow, about Mr. Mount. I—I'm afraid, sir."

Even Mr. Leg, who didn't pretend to be a student of human nature, realized suddenly that the quiver in the stenographer's voice and the expression in her eyes betokened more than ordinary concern. He crossed over and laid a fatherly hand on her shoulder.

"Don't you worry, Miss Venner," said he. "Nothing has happened to Dan and nothing is likely to happen. He's fully able to take care of himself, and someone else into the bargain."

And then, as Miss Venner caught the significance of his last words and began to flush indignantly, he speedily retreated into the other room.

He looked through the drawers of his desk, thinking Dan might have left a message there, but there was nothing. He glanced at his watch; it was 8:20, and court was to convene at nine.

"I suppose I ought to go over and have a talk with Mount first," he thought as he sat down at his desk and began to stuff some papers into a portfolio. "Poor devil! Well, we've tried, anyway. I wonder where the deuce Dan can be? At that, I've got a pretty fair speech here, though I don't suppose it will do any good. It isn't possible Dan has gone somewhere after—but there's no use trying to guess."

A little later he departed for the courthouse, leaving Miss Venner alone in the office.

The door had no sooner closed behind him than the stenographer rushed to the telephone and asked for a number.

"Hello, Mrs. Culp?" she said presently. "This is Miss

Venner, at the office."—"Yes. I—that is, Mr. Leg wants to speak to Dan."—"He isn't there?"—"I didn't know, only he went uptown some time ago, and I thought he might have gone home."—"You haven't seen him for four days?"—"Yes, I know he has been sleeping in the office."—"Yes, it's dreadful; I'm so glad it will be over today."—"Yes. Thank you, Mrs. Culp."

Slowly she got up and returned to her own desk, where she sat gazing at the cot in the corner. "I wish Mr. Leg never *had* got a case," she said aloud vehemently. She took out her embroidery and started to work on it. The minutes passed draggingly. She felt that an hour must have gone by when the sound of chimes entered at the open window. "Good Heavens, it's only nine o'clock!" she thought.

She went to the window and stood for some time looking down into the street far below, then returned to her sewing. Suddenly she stopped and gazed in astonishment at what she had done, then threw the thing down on her desk with a gasp of irritation. She had embroidered two whole figures on the wrong side of the cloth.

"I don't care!" she snapped. "I don't see how I can expect myself—"

She was interrupted by the ringing of the telephone bell.

She sprang to the instrument. "Hello."

"Hello," came the response. "Is this you, Miss Venner?"

"Oh!" The light of joy that leaped into her eyes! "Oh, Dan, it's you!"

"Yes." It was indeed Dan's voice, eager and rapid. "Has Mr. Leg gone to court yet?"

"Yes, half an hour ago. Where are you?"

"Yonkers. In an automobile. I've got Patrick Cummings."

"*No!*"

"Yes, I have. Found him at Albany. I got a call at the office last night, and I certainly didn't lose any time getting there. Made it in a little over four hours. A fellow named Saunders, manager of a moving picture theater, had him locked up in his office. Saunders was certainly out for that five thousand, and he deserves it. I would have been down there when court opened only we were held up near Peekskill for speeding. Fool policeman wouldn't listen to reason."

"But, Dan, have you really got that Cummings? The right one?"

"I sure have. Listen, Miss Venner, here's what I want you to do. Go over to the courthouse as fast as you can—take a taxi—and tell Mr. Leg I'm coming. Tell him to hold things off—put some more witnesses on, do anything—till I get there. I'll come as fast as the police let me."

"All right, I'll hurry. Oh, Dan, I'm so glad!"

"So am I. Good-by."

Miss Venner hung up the receiver and sprang to her feet. Her eyes, dancing with excitement, and her flushed and joyous face were good to look at as she ran to the closet and took down her coat and hat. Of course, she had to examine herself in the mirror above the washbasin, but nevertheless she was out of the office and on the street in less than five minutes after Dan's last words had come over the wire.

She found a taxi in front of Raoul's and gave the driver the address of the courthouse. North, they crawled on Broadway; the crowds of hurrying people on the sidewalk, the noise of the traffic, and the May sunshine, all answered to Miss Venner's mood and made her feel that she was a part, and not the least important, of this busy world. She leaned forward and spoke over the driver shoulder:

"I'm in a hurry, you know."

He nodded and made a quick turn to the left to get around a slow-moving truck. Skillfully and swiftly he made his way through Broadway's crowded traffic as far as Grand Street, where he turned east, and after that it was easier. Soon he drew up at the entrance of a large, gloomy building whose granite pillars had been blackened by time.

"Thank you, miss," said he, touching his cap as his fare alighted and handed him a dollar bill.

Inside the courthouse, Miss Venner was forced to ask the way of a uniformed attendant, who obligingly accompanied her up two flights of stairs and down a long, dark corridor, finally halting before a pair of double swinging doors bearing the inscription in plain black letters: "General Sessions, Part VI."

"There you are," said the attendant.

She pushed the door open and entered. At first she was bewildered by the unexpected spaciousness of the room as well as the throng of people—men and women—seated on the benches and chairs; but finally she saw Mr. Leg. He was standing at one end of the attorneys' table, listening to a reply to one of his questions from the witness in the chair, who was a young woman in a blue dress.

Miss Venner timidly made her way up the aisle, feeling two hundred eyes staring at her, and through the little swinging gate in front of the public benches. There she halted, hesitating, wondering what would happen to her if she dared interrupt Mr. Leg while he was examining a witness. Finally she sat down at the table, on which were lying some scattered sheets of paper, pulled a pencil from her hair, and scribbled a few lines.

She walked over and handed the paper to Mr. Leg. He took it with a glance of surprise at finding her there. He motioned her to a chair and she sat down, not ten feet from the prisoner. But she didn't notice that, for she was busy watching Mr. Leg's face as he read the slip of paper. It expressed doubt, stupefaction, incredulous joy; his face grew pale at the unexpectedness of it, and he stood looking at the paper, hardly believing his eyes.

"Go on with the witness, Mr. Leg," came the voice of Judge Manton from the bench.

"Yes, your honor—I—what—" the lawyer stammered. "That is, I'm through with the witness, your honor."

The prosecuting attorney bobbed up from his chair to say that he would not cross-examine, and sat down again. Mr. Leg hastened over to whisper to Miss Venner, pointing to the slip of paper:

"Is this true, is it possible?"

"Yes, sir," she whispered back. "He just telephoned from Yonkers. I came right over—"

She was interrupted by the voice of Judge Manton:

"Call your next witness, Mr. Leg."

He had just one left—a young woman who, like the preceding witness, had known Mrs. Mount during the time she had lived with her husband, and whose function it was to testify to the prisoner's excellent character during that period and the unfailing tenderness and affection he had shown his wife, even when she had begun to neglect her home. Mr. Leg asked many questions; he made them as long as possible, and he drawled his words.

In the past two days he had learned something about the art of killing time, and though the testimony of this particular witness would ordinarily have occupied barely fifteen minutes, he succeeded in keeping her on the stand almost an hour. Finally he was forced to stop, and the witness was dismissed.

"Have you any more witnesses?" asked Judge Manton.

Mr. Leg hadn't, but he did have an idea.

"I would like to recall Mount for a few questions, your honor."

The judge nodded impatiently, and the prisoner was summoned to the witness chair. Mr. Leg began questioning him concerning the disappearance of his wife four years before. Then he switched to the night of the murder, and once more Mount told of his entry into the apartment house, of the man he saw in the hall, and of the finding of his wife's body. This consumed some time, until finally an interruption came from Judge Manton:

"This has all been gone over before, Mr. Leg."

"Yes, your honor, I—"

The lawyer stopped and turned. His ear caught the sound of the almost noiseless opening of the swinging door of the courtroom. Every eye in the room followed the direction of his gaze, and what they saw was the entrance of a little, gray-haired man with a scraggly mustache, followed by a twenty-year-old youth, who had a firm grip on the other's arm.

Mr. Leg turned to address the court:

"I am through with the witness—"

Again he was interrupted, this time by a cry of amazement from the lips of the gray-haired man who had just entered. There was an instant commotion; the spectators rose to their feet and craned their necks to see the man who had uttered the cry, and who was now saying to the youth:

"You didn't tell me—you didn't tell me—"

The face of Judge Manton had turned pale with irritation at this disorder in his court. He rapped on the desk with his gavel and called out sharply:

"Order! Silence! Sit down!"

But by this time Mr. Leg had met Dan's eyes and read their message of assurance and triumph. He turned to the judge:

"Your honor, that man is my next witness. I apologize for the disturbance." Again he turned to look at Dan.

"Patrick Cummings to the stand!"

The spectators sat down again, though whispers were still going back and forth over the room. The prosecuting attorney was leaning back in his chair with the amused and bored smile he had worn throughout the presentation of the defense. (It must be admitted that Mr. Leg had shown himself a fearful tyro.) William Mount was looking indifferently across the table at Miss Venner; as for her, she was gazing with bright eyes at Dan as he led Patrick Cummings up to the rail and turned him over to the court attendant, who conducted him to the witness chair.

Dan crossed over to Mr. Leg and murmured in his ear:

"Just get him started on his story. He'll do the rest. I'll prompt you if you need it."

Then he took a chair at the lawyer's elbow.

The witness gave his name to the clerk and was sworn in. His voice trembled, his hands were nervously gripping the arms of the chair, and his eyes were shifting constantly from side to side with an expression of fear. In answer to Mr. Leg's first question, he said his name was Patrick Cummings, his address No. 311 Murray Street, Albany, and his occupation janitor, though he was not working at present.

"Did you ever work in New York City?" asked Mr. Leg.

"Yes, sir."

"As janitor?"

"Yes, sir."

"At what address?"

"No. 714 West One Hundred and Fifty-seventh Street."

"When did you start work there?"

The witness thought a moment.

"I don't know exactly; but it was sometime in July 1912."

One of the jurors in the last row interrupted to say that the witness was not speaking loud enough for him to hear. Judge Manton, who had been gazing directly at Cummings ever since he took the chair, admonished him to speak louder.

"Where did you work before that?" continued Mr. Leg.

"In Philadelphia, sir. That was my first job in New York."

"How long were you janitor at No. 714 West One Hundred and Fifty-seventh Street?"

"Nearly three years."

"Were you there on April 3, 1915?"

"Yes, sir."

Dan got up from his chair to whisper something in Mr. Leg's ear. The lawyer nodded and returned to the witness.

"Cummings, did you ever see Mrs. Elaine Mount, known as Alice Reeves, a tenant in the house where you were janitor?"

"I knew Miss Reeves, yes, sir."

"She lived there quite a while, didn't she?"

"Yes, sir. I don't know how long; she was there when I came."

"Did you see Miss Reeves often?"

"Oh, yes, I saw her every day; sometimes two or three times." Again Dan got up to whisper a suggestion in the lawyer's ear; from this time on, indeed, half the questions were suggested by him. As for the witness, he was losing, little by little, the nervous fright that had possessed him when he took the chair. His voice was becoming stronger and louder, and his eyes had gained an expression of determination and defiance.

"Now, Cummings, do you know if Miss Reeves ever had any callers?"

"Yes, sir."

"Well, did she?"

"She had one."

"Only one?"

"There were others, sir, but not very often; but this man came every two or three days, sometimes oftener than that."

"So it was a man?"

"Yes, sir."

"Can you describe him?"

The witness hesitated, then spoke in a louder voice than before:

"He was a man about thirty-eight or forty, with dark hair and dark eyes. He was a good-looking man."

"And you say he would call often on Miss Reeves. How do you know he was calling on her?"

"Why, he would go in her flat."

"Did you see him go in?"

"Of course I did. And besides, he would often send me out for something at the restaurant or delicatessen; and I'd take it up, and he'd be there in the flat, and he'd give me a dollar, or sometimes even five."

"So he was liberal, was he?"

"Sir?"

"He was good to you, was he?"

"Oh, yes; he always gave me something. He always had lots of money."

"Do you know who this man was?"

"No, sir. That is, I don't know his name."

"Do you know where he lived?"

"No, sir."

"I see. And did he continue to call on Miss Reeves all the time you were there?"

"Yes, sir. Two or three times a week, except toward the last, when he didn't come quite so often."

The lawyer stopped to confer with Dan a moment. Then, with a nod of satisfaction, he turned again to the witness.

"Now, Cummings, do you remember whether this man whom you have described called at No. 714 West One Hundred and Fifty-seventh Street on the evening of Saturday, April 3, 1915?"

The witness's answer was lost in a sudden stir which passed over the courtroom as the spectators leaned forward. Judge Manton took advantage of the interruption to beckon to an attendant for a glass of water. When it came he drank a little and placed the glass, still half full, before him on his desk. The last question was reread by the clerk, and the witness repeated his answer:

"Yes, sir; he was there."

"What time did he arrive?"

"I don't know; I didn't see him come in."

"Did you see him at all that evening?"

"Yes, sir."

"What time?"

"About half past eight, I think it was, the bell rang for the dumbwaiter. That was the way he always sent for me to come up when he wanted something. I went up and rang the bell at Miss Reeves's door, and he opened it.''

"How was he dressed?''

"Why, he had on a black suit, except he had taken off his coat and put on a smoking jacket. He always did that.''

"Did you see Miss Reeves?''

"Yes, sir; I went inside the hall to wait, while he went to the desk to write something, and I saw Miss Reeves in the front room. She was sitting by the table, crying. She had her handkerchief up to her eyes.''

"Did she say anything to you?''

"No, sir; she didn't even look at me.''

"I see. What did the man go to the desk for?''

"He went for some paper to write down something. I remember he didn't find any there, and he took a piece out of his pocket. He wanted to write down the name of some wine he wanted me to get. He wrote it down and gave it to me, and gave me a ten-dollar bill to get it with.''

Mr. Leg turned to find Dan at his elbow with a slip of paper in his hand. The lawyer took it, and examined it while the boy whispered in his ear. By this time every spectator in the room was listening intently to the witness's every word. The prosecuting attorney had leaned forward in his chair with a new expression of interest for this unexpected Irishman. Judge Manton sat up straight, gazing at the prisoner Mount with an expressionless countenance.

"I have here,'' Mr. Leg resumed, "a slip of paper bearing in ink the words, *Bonneau et Mouet—Sec*. Now, Cummings, is this the paper which this man in Miss Reeves's apartment handed to you on the night of April third?''

The witness took the slip and examined it. "Yes, sir; that's it," he said finally. "That's the name of the wine he wanted me to get."

"And that's the paper he wrote on and handed to you?"

"Yes, sir; it's the same one," answered Cummings. "It's got that funny thing in the corner."

Mr. Leg turned to the judge:

"Your honor, I wish to introduce this paper in evidence."

Judge Manton merely inclined his head. The clerk took the slip and marked it.

"Now, Cummings," went on the lawyer, "after this man gave you the slip of paper, what did you do?"

"I went out after the wine."

"Did you get it?"

"Yes, sir, but I had a hard time. I always went to a wine store at the corner of One Hundred and Fifty-eighth Street and Broadway, but they didn't have this kind, so I went down to One Hundred and Twenty-fifth Street, and I had to go to four or five stores before I could find it. I was gone about an hour, or maybe more, because when I got back it was nearly ten o'clock."

"All right, go on. You took the wine upstairs?"

"Yes, sir. I went up to Miss Reeves's apartment, and I was about to ring the bell when I heard her crying inside. She was crying and talking very loud."

"Could you hear what she was saying?"

"Some of it, yes, sir. I heard her say, 'Let me go! I love him! Let me go!' Then I heard the man's voice, only he didn't talk as loud as she did; but I could hear him even plainer than her. He was saying, 'You'll stay right here; do you hear? I won't let you go back to him; do you hear? Let him wait all night if he wants to.' I didn't want to ring the bell while they were going on like that, so I stood and listened for a long while. Miss Reeves kept crying, and the man kept swearing at her. He kept saying, 'I won't let you go back to him!'

"Finally I got tired waiting and rang the bell. I guess I stood there half an hour. The man opened the door, and he told me to come in, and go and put the wine in the refrigerator. I went back to the kitchen and unwrapped it, and put the bottle on the ice. Then I went out again. As soon as I closed the door behind me I heard them begin fighting again inside."

"Do you remember what became of the slip of paper on which this man had written the name of the wine?"

"Yes, sir; I remember they had wrapped it up with the wine. I threw it on the floor with the wrapping paper."

"I see. What did you do after you left the apartment?"

"I turned down the lights in the halls, and then went down to the basement and got ready to go to bed."

"Do you know what time that was?"

"Yes, sir; when I wound my clock it was twenty minutes past ten. I put some coal on the hot-water furnace and locked the basement doors and went to bed."

"Well?"

"Well, I'd been in bed, I guess, about half an hour and was nearly asleep when there was a knock on the door. I went—"

"You mean the door of your room?"

"Yes, sir; the room in the basement where I was sleeping. I got up and lit the gas and opened the door, and there stood the colonel."

"The colonel?"

"That's what I called the man who called on Miss Reeves. He stepped inside the room, and I saw that he had a big bundle of papers and things in his hand. He had on his hat and light overcoat, and the muffler he always wore around the lower part of his face. He told me to close the door because he had the bundle in his hands, and then he said, 'Hurry up, Cummings; dress yourself. Don't ask me any questions.' "

"I knew at once from his funny voice and the way he looked at me that something had happened. I didn't say a word, but dressed myself as quick as I could. When I was done he said, 'Where's the furnace? I want to burn this stuff.' I went back and opened the furnace door, and he threw the papers and things on the fire. He wouldn't let me help him."

"Did you see any of the articles? Do you know what they were?"

"No, sir; only there was a lot of letters and other papers. I supposed they came from Miss Reeves's—"

"Never mind what you supposed. Go on."

"Well, after the stuff was burned up we went back in front. He had me sit down in a chair, and then he said, 'Cummings, I've got a proposition to make to you. I'll give you a thousand dollars cash to leave New York immediately and put yourself where nobody can find you.'

"I didn't know what to answer, I was so surprised, and he went on to say that that was all he happened to have with him, and that it was lucky he had that much. He said he wouldn't tell me who he was, but he told me how to have something printed in the *Herald* if I ever needed money, and he would send me some. He said I'd have to take his word for that. I decided to do it when I saw him count out the thousand dollars on the table. I promised to leave right away, in ten minutes, without stopping to take anything but my clothes."

Mr. Leg interrupted:

"Didn't you suspect that a crime had been committed?"

"Yes, sir; of course I knew something had happened, but all that money was too much for me. After he had gone—"

"Didn't he wait to see you go?"

"No, sir; he went right away. I guess he knew that I'd certainly beat it with the money. I let him out at the basement door, and in less than no time I had my clothes packed and was all ready. I went out by the basement door, too, but I couldn't make myself go. I stood there on the sidewalk maybe two minutes calling myself a fool, but I couldn't help it. I wanted to see what had happened in that flat upstairs.

"I went up to the ground floor by the front steps, leaving the outer door open as I entered, dropped my suitcase in the front hall, and went up two more flights to the door of Miss Reeves's flat. It was locked. I ran down to the basement for my duplicate key, came back up and unlocked the door. The flat was dark. I switched on the lights, and there on the floor I saw Miss Reeves. The hilt of a knife was sticking from her breast, and there was blood on her dress, and her face looked awful. It scared me so I didn't know what I was doing. I ran out without turning off the lights, and I think I forgot to lock the door.

"I ran back to the ground floor as fast as I could and picked up my suitcase. I started for the outside door, and then I suddenly saw a man coming up the stoop. I was so scared I didn't know what to do. I stepped back into the corner of the hall as the man entered the door, and, scared as I was, I was surprised to see that it wasn't one of the tenants, or anyone I had ever seen before. He came in and started upstairs without saying anything, just glancing at me. I picked up—"

"Just a minute, Cummings," Mr. Leg interrupted. He turned and pointed at William Mount. "Is that the man you saw enter and go upstairs, *after* you had seen Miss Reeves's dead body on the floor?''

The witness examined the prisoner a moment.

"Yes, sir, I think so. The light in the hall was dim, so I couldn't be sure, but it looks like him."

"All right. Go on."

"That's all, sir. I picked up the suitcase and ran. I took the subway to the end of the line, and there I got on a trolley for Yonkers. The next day I went on to Albany, and I've been hiding there ever since."

"And don't you know that you have made yourself an accessory to this murder and are liable to punishment?" asked the lawyer.

"Yes, sir, I know that. I didn't care at first, until I saw in the papers that some man that I knew was innocent had been arrested for it. Then I wanted to come and tell all I knew—I really did, sir—but I was afraid, and I couldn't ever make myself start. When that young man came after me this morning"—he pointed to Dan—"I was only too glad to come, sir. Ask him. I hope I won't be punished, sir."

At this point Judge Manton interrupted the examination. He leaned forward in his chair as he spoke, while the fingers of his right hand were toying with the edge of the glass which had remained on his desk, half full of water.

"I think we had better adjourn for luncheon, Mr. Leg," he observed. "It's one o'clock. You may continue with the witness after the recess."

Dan sprang up to murmur something in Mr. Leg's ear. The lawyer looked astonished and bewildered, but finally nodded in acquiescence.

"Very well, your honor," he said to the court. "But I would like to ask the witness just two more questions before adjournment, if your honor please."

"Let them be short," the judge said curtly.

Mr. Leg turned to the witness.

"Cummings, I want to ask you if this man whom you called the colonel, whom you saw and heard quarreling with Alice Reeves, and who gave you a thousand dollars to flee from the scene of the murder—I want to ask you if that man is now in this courtroom?"

Cummings hesitated a moment and glanced from side to side, then suddenly straightened up and said in a loud and distinct tone:

"Yes, sir, he is here."

A gasp of amazement came from every side.

"Will you point him out to the judge and jury?"

For reply, Cummings turned and leveled his finger straight at the face of Judge Manton.

But the wave of astonishment and incredulity that swept over the courtroom was swiftly drowned in a great cry of alarm. Judge Manton, looking over the accusing finger straight into Cummings's face, had lifted the glass of water to his lips; and Dan, springing up and knocking Mr. Leg out of his way, had leaped like a panther over the rail to the daïs and with one sweep of his arm dashed the glass from the judge's hand to the floor.

Court attendants ran forward, shouting; the jury stood up in their box; several of them leaped over the partition and rushed onto the platform of justice; the spectators tumbled over the rail by scores, trampling one another; screams were heard from a hundred throats. Dan was hanging desperately on to Judge Manton's gown, calling at the top of his voice:

"The water was poisoned! Quick! Hold him! You fools! He'll kill himself! Help!"

But the officers and attendants shrank back before the look of mad rage and passion on Judge Manton's face. With a violent movement he threw Dan off; the boy fell on his knees on the platform, still calling out for help. Judge Manton seized the heavy wooden gavel from his desk and raised it high.

"Damn you!" he snarled in a voice of savage fury, and brought the gavel down on Dan's head. The boy toppled over with a moan.

The next moment a dozen men had sprung forward and borne Judge Manton to the floor.

The following morning Mr. Leg and Dan sat talking in the lawyer's office. Nearby was Miss Venner, listening to them; her eyes never left Dan's face. The blow from Judge Manton's gavel had, luckily, not seriously injured him; he had been unconscious for more than an hour, but when he finally came to, was none the worse for it.

"Yes, I let Mount have two thousand dollars," Mr. Leg was saying. "He's going to buy a little cigar store or something somewhere and try to forget things. Poor devil! I hope he succeeds."

"Yes, sir," Dan agreed. "But he really hasn't anything left to live for." And quite unconsciously the boy's eyes turned to meet those of Miss Venner, who flushed and looked the other way.

"And so you saw Manton take something from his pocket and put it in that glass of water," Mr. Leg observed in a voice filled with undisguised admiration.

"Yes, sir. Of course, I was watching him all the time."

"And you think it was with him that Mount's wife left home. But why wouldn't some of his friends have known about her?"

"Perhaps they did," was the reply. "But it's evident that the judge was pretty cagey; he doesn't seem ever to have taken anybody up there. He probably met her in a cabaret, or somewhere, and simply fell in love with her.

As for his willingness to sacrifice Mount, well, some men are made that way. He probably said to himself, 'What does this broken-down creature amount to compared with a man like me—wealthy, intellectual, cultured, of high position?' You must remember that he murdered her in a fit of passion, just as when he hit me with that gavel.''

"There's one thing I don't understand yet," observed Mr. Leg. "I've got to believe you when you say you thought it was Judge Manton all the time, because I saw you carrying his photograph around. And you say you found that slip of paper was in his handwriting by comparing it with his signature and the postscript on the letter he sent me assigning me to the case. But what the dickens made you compare it with *his* handwriting? What made you suspect him in the first place?"

"You remember what I quoted from Montaigne," replied Dan, with a smile. " 'The passions smothered by modern civilization are doubly ferocious when awakened.' "

"Yes; but what made you suspect *him*?"

"What's the difference, sir, so long as we got him? It certainly made a fuss, didn't it?" Dan grinned with delight as he glanced at a pile of morning papers on his desk, the front page of each of which carried under scare headlines pictures of Manton, the murderer, and Dan, his boy Nemesis, side by side.

"There's no doubt about his being convicted," Dan went on, "unless he manages to find some way of committing suicide before his trial, which is likely. We have a dozen corroborative items for Cummings's story. By the way, I'm glad the district attorney has offered him immunity."

"So am I," Mr. Leg agreed; "but don't try to change the subject, young man. Clever as you are, you can't evade me. What made you first suspect Judge Manton?''

"I see I'll have to tell you, sir," grinned Dan. "Well, it was on account of you."

"On account of *me*?"

"Yes, sir. I wondered about it from the very first, when you called me in that morning and told me the judge had assigned you to the case. I couldn't understand it, because I know the practice in such cases is to give it to a man fairly well up in the profession. And men, especially judges, don't play jokes in murder cases. So I knew there must be some good reason why he assigned you to Mount's defense, and the most probable one was that he wanted him convicted."

"But I don't see—"

Again Dan grinned. "You know I think you're a mighty fine man, Mr. Leg. You've been awfully good to me, sir. But you hadn't had a case in ten years, and you certainly are a bum lawyer."

Mr. Leg frowned. A peal of mischievous laughter came from behind him in Miss Venner's silvery voice. And Dan, because he was looking at her dancing eyes and parted lips and wavy hair, and found it such an agreeable and delightful sight, began to laugh with her. Mr. Leg looked from one to the other, trying hard to maintain his frown; but who can frown at a boy and a fun-loving girl when they are looking at and laughing with each other?

And so Mr. Leg joined in and began to laugh, too.

It's Science that Counts

"I GUESS I NEVER COULD LEARN TO DO THAT," Peter Boley, the grocer, declared admiringly. Jone Simmons, to whom the remark was addressed, paused to clear his brow of perspiration, which came from the strenuous exercise of knocking a leather punching bag from one side to another of an inverted board platform about four feet square, suspended from the ceiling.

"It ain't half as hard as hittin' a man," he observed, as one who should know.

"I'm not so sure about that," Boley objected. "I guess you wouldn't have much trouble hittin' me."

Jone Simmons seemed to find this observation absurd. "I meant a fightin' man," he explained. "Of course I could probably floor you maybe once a minute. But you take a man that's had training and studied the science, and maybe I could hit him and maybe I couldn't. I'm not what I used to be."

"Well, you're mighty quick at knockin' that bag around," declared the grocer, moving his cigar from the right corner of his mouth to the left. "I wish you'd teach me some day. I was saying to Harry Vawter last week, it's too bad there's not somebody in town could put on the gloves with you, and we could have a regular match at the Annual Picnic.''

''Huh!'' Simmons snorted. ''I guess there's nobody would want to take that job. I'm not what I used to be, but you can see I'm still a little too lively for anybody in Holtville.''

He hauled off and gave the punching bag a smash that caused it to rebound madly back and forth against the boards.

In order to avoid a misconception, it is best to explain at once that Jone Simmons was not, and never had been, a pugilist. He ran the only hardware store in Holtville, Ohio, whither he had come three or four years before from some town up the river, and in action he was the most peaceful and easy-going citizen imaginable. Within two weeks after his coming to Holtville everybody in town knew him and liked him—all the more because his predecessor in the hardware store had been the most unpopular member of the community.

Jone Simmons had only one weakness in conversation, and that a mild one. The subject was fistic prowess, or more correctly, fistic science; and particularly the fistic science of Jone Simmons. No sooner had he got the stock inventoried and in place in the hardware store than he put up a punching bag in the back room; and Peter Boley, the grocer next door, led to investigate by mysterious and insistent thumpings which he could not logically connect with the hardware trade, had been the first to discover this curious fad of the new inhabitant of Holtville.

He found, as all Holtville did later, that Jone was anything but averse to talk on the subject. He told stories of himself. It appeared that in his youth he had been a pretty bad customer. He wished he had a nickel for every nose he'd broke before he was twenty. Now that he was twice that age, of course he wasn't as spry as formerly, but still it was science that counted—bang! against the punching bag.

Then Jone would produce an old number of the *Police Gazette* containing an article by Bob Fitzsimmons on the relative merits of the uppercut and the half-swing.

When midsummer came Jone's fame was such that he was invited to give a punching bag exhibition at the Eleventh Annual Picnic of the Holtville Merchants' Association, and the performance had proven so popular that it was repeated the two following summers.

It must not be thought that Jone made use of his prowess in any unjust or cruel manner. He was no bully. Two or three of his fellow townsmen had at one time or another put on the gloves with him to learn something of the defensive art, but they had frankly been scared half to death by Jone's professional attitudes and gestures, and he had merely dealt them gentle taps on the chest as they danced around with their hands waving frantically to and fro in front of their faces.

Nobody in Holtville wanted to "go up against" Jone Simmons.

One afternoon in the early part of July Pete Boley, the grocer, entered Simmon's hardware store with his face alight with the excitement of discovery.

"Hello, Pete, where you been since noon?" called Simmons from the rear of the store, where he was wrapping up a package of nails for Mrs. Pearl's little boy.

When the customer had gone the grocer approached and said with the importance of one who brings news:

"Jonas, our picnic is going to be a bigger success this year than ever before."

"What's up?" demanded Simmons, stopping to pick up a nail and throw it in the bin.

"Something new *and* good," declared the grocer. "I

guess they won't be sorry they chose me chairman of the entertainment committee.''

"You goin' to have a circus?''

"No. Wait till I tell you. I was just down to Bill Ogilvy's store. Went down to get some muslin for the Missis. You know, Bill has a new fellow in there clerkin' for him, a fellow named Notter that he got from Columbus about a week ago. Well, this Notter waited on me, and I noticed he lifted down a big bolt of muslin, must have weighed thirty pounds, just like it was a feather.

" 'You must be pretty strong,' says I.

"He just nodded, measuring off the muslin. " 'Funny, too, because you don't get much exercise in a job like this,' says I.

" 'I don't need it,' he says, looking at me. 'I've always been strong. I'm an athlete. I was amateur champion of Columbus once.'

" 'Champion of what?' I asked.

" 'Why, just champion,' he says. 'Lightweight champion. I licked everybody in town under a hundred and forty pounds.' ''

At this point the grocer broke off his narrative to ask the other abruptly:

"How much do you weigh, Jonas?''

"About a hundred and thirty-seven,'' Simmons replied. His voice was rather low.

"I thought so. Well, this Notter got started talkin'. Bill Ogilvy came up and he told both of us about how he was champion down at Columbus. That was some years ago. There was one man he knocked clear out of the ropes, he said, and he was unconscious for two days. Of course I was thinkin' of you all the time.

"Finally I says to him, 'Well, Mr. Notter, I'm mighty glad you come to Holtville. You've come just in time to give us a boxing match at our Merchants' Association Annual Picnic.'

" 'But there's nobody in Holtville to box with,' he says.

" 'Oh yes there is,' says I, 'there's Jone Simmons that runs the hardware store. He knocks a punching bag two hours every day. You ought to see him! He'll box with you and welcome.'

" 'Well,' says he, 'I'd just as soon knock his block off as anybody else's, but I have to be here in the store every day and evening too, and I wouldn't have time to train.'

" 'That's all right, Mr. Notter,' Bill Ogilvy puts in. 'I reckon I can hold the fort here an hour or so every day so you can have time for training. I'll be more than paid for it by seeing you and Jone Simmons box.'

"So we fixed it up," the grocer concluded. "Bill and I didn't know anything about the rules or anything, but Mr. Notter helped us. It's to be a match for ten rounds, with six ounce gloves. I told 'em you'd have some in the store. To tell the truth, Jonas, I don't like this fellow from Columbus very much, and I'll be right glad to see you kind of hurt him a little."

The grocer finished. A silence followed. Simmons had opened a showcase and was carefully picking an assortment of files and wrenches from a box and putting them into another one exactly similar. The operation appeared to interest him intently.

"What kind of a lookin' man is this Mr. Notter?" he asked finally, without looking up.

"Oh, medium-like," was the reply. "About your size, I guess; maybe a little bigger. He's got a mustache and he looks kind of pinched in the face, but he's got a good muscle on him. He rolled up his sleeve and showed us.

I should say he's about thirty-eight or nine, maybe a little older."

Simmons was silent.

"Of course you'll have to train," continued the grocer. "He's goin' to."

"Of course," Simmons agreed. His tone was entirely without enthusiasm. After a moment he added thoughtfully: "You know, Peter, maybe it wouldn't be wise to have a boxing match at the picnic after all. It's a mighty brutal thing, and all the children will be there—it's a bad example—"

"But it's not exactly a *fight*," the grocer protested. "It's an exhibition. It's more like science. You ain't exactly goin' to hurt each other."

Simmons shook his head dubiously. "I don't know. Of course I know it's science, but you must remember there might be an accident. For instance, say I aim an uppercut for his cheek and it happened to hit his jaw instead. The jaw's a dangerous spot, Peter. It might kill him."

"Shucks, you're not going to hit as hard as all that," the grocer snorted. "You ain't going to be mad."

"No," Simmons agreed slowly, "no, we're not going to be mad."

"It'll do the children good," declared Peter Boley heartily. "I've often heard you say every boy ought to know how to fight without pullin' hair and kickin'. I tell you, Jonas, it'll be the greatest attraction we ever had at Holtville. I stopped in at Riley's, and Harry Vawters on the way up and told 'em about it, and they each gave five dollars more for the refreshment fund. Why, people'll come from all over the county just to see it. Holtville is going to be proud of you, Jonas!"

And at that, fired by this flattery and rosy vision of

the glory to come, Simmons closed the showcase with a bang.

"All right, Peter," said he, firmly. "I'll begin training tomorrow."

By the following afternoon the boxing match between Jone Simmons and Bill Ogilvy's new clerk was the only topic of conversation on Holtville's street.

Almost at once, much to Peter Boley's painful surprise, opposition made itself felt. The Ladies' Reading Circle, at their weekly meeting on the following Wednesday, passed resolutions condemning the projected match in unmeasured terms. The most striking phrase of the document was that which referred to the affair as a "brutal, inhuman and degrading exhibition of the lowest instinct in man."

In a body, reinforced by the pastor of the Methodist Church, they carried the resolution, carefully typewritten by the pastor, to Peter Boley in his capacity as Chairman of the Entertainment Committee of the Merchants' Association at Holtville.

Poor Boley was flabbergasted out of speech. By pure luck Harry Vawter, the druggist, happened to be there at the time, and he spoke as follows:

"Ladies, this isn't going to be a fight. It is a scientific exhibition by two gentlemen, one of whom has been known and respected in this city for three years. There will be blows struck, but purely in the interests of science. There may even be a bloody nose, but that happens when your little boy falls against the woodbox, so it cannot justly be termed brutal. Mr. Boley and myself, as a majority of the Entertainment Committee, must respectfully refuse your request."

The indignant ladies departed to argue the matter with their husbands over the supper table, where they met with no better success.

The following morning about nine o'clock the citizens of Holtville were astonished to see a man with his legs bare to his knees and his arms and shoulders entirely so, clad apparently in white muslin drawers and an abbreviated shirt of the same material, run down the length of Main Street at a goodly pace, looking neither to right nor left, and turn at the end into the lane that led to the country. His hair streamed in the wind behind him and his bristly moustache poked ahead.

Holtville gasped.

"It's Mr. Notter getting up his wind," explained Slim Pearl, the barber, standing in the door of his shop with a shaving mug in his hand. "Looks like he'd have to take off eight or nine pounds."

Jone Simmons, letting down the awning in front of his hardware store, stopped and turned to watch the runner go by. Then, happening to encounter the grin on the face of Peter Boley, whose grocery was next door, he hastily turned away and set to work fastening the awning ropes.

An hour later the grocer came in to find his neighbor, naked to the waist, standing before the punching bag with a frown on his face and a book in his hand.

"One thing I'd like to know," said Boley as he sat down on a nail keg, "how does it help a man to fight to go runnin' around the country in his underwear?"

The reply was a terrific smash of Simmons's fist on the punching bag.

"I think that's it," said he, disregarding the other's question. "It says that a full swing on the ear should be landed with one foot drawn back and the body weight thrown all on one side. Watch, Peter. Does this look right?"

He stopped the punching bag from swinging, stepped

back, trailed his right foot, lunged forward and swung on the bag with all his might.

"I don't know whether it's right or not," said the grocer feelingly, "but it looks mighty dangerous. I hope, Jonas, you ain't going to hit Mr. Notter as hard as that."

"I may not hit him at all," the other returned gloomily. "I tell you, Peter, I've got to have a sparring partner. Nobody ever trained for a fight without one."

This expression of a need on the part of Simmons led no later than the following afternoon to a regrettable occurrence. Since no one suitable for the position of sparring partner was to be found in Holtville, Peter Boley decided to sacrifice himself for the good of science. They put on the gloves in the back room of the hardware store. Within the first ten seconds Simmons landed a savage swing on the grocer's nose, and the blood spurted out as from a miniature fountain.

"Good Lord, Jonas, why did you hit so hard?" groaned Peter, holding his face over a basin of water.

"I got to train, haven't I?" demanded Simmons. "You should have dodged, Peter. You should have side-stepped and countered with your right. Didn't I tell you that was the defense for a body swing?"

Thenceforth Simmons was forced to get along without a sparring partner. He spent hours daily with the punching bag, and he also indulged in an exercise which he found explained in detail in a chapter of his book on pugilism. Entering the rear of the hardware store one afternoon, Peter Boley found its proprietor, stripped to the waist, dancing madly around in front of a large mirror, making a bewildering succession of lunges and swings and uppercuts at his reflection in the glass.

Simultaneously he skipped agilely from one foot to the other, jerking his head with wary quickness to the right or left and throwing now one arm, now the other, in a defensive position before his face.

"Good Lord, Jonas, what you tryin' to do?" exclaimed the grocer, halting in astonishment.

"Shadowboxing," returned Simmons grimly, without stopping to look around.

Thus the month passed, and the eve of the picnic arrived. On that Friday night, a little after ten o'clock, which was quite late for Holtville, Jone Simmons sat alone on a box in the back room of the hardware store, holding his chin in his hands and gazing broodingly at the darkness in a corner of the room. It had been a strenuous month. He had trained hard and long. Lively tales had run down the main street of the town concerning the past glory of the career of Mr. Notter.

The expression on Jone Simmons's face as he sat there was not one of pleasurable expectation.

"Amateur champion of Columbus," he mused finally, aloud.

Another brooding silence followed. After a time he rose to put out the light and go upstairs to join his wife in bed, and as he gave a vicious kick at the box on which he had been sitting he spoke again aloud:

"And Columbus is a mighty big town, too!"

The following day all Holtville was up early. The Annual Picnic of the Merchants' Association was the great outdoor event of the season, having even become of more importance than the Republican Rally. Wellman's Grove, a little over two miles from the center of the town, was the spot which had served as the scene of festivals for many years, and thither, in wagon and buggy, by auto and on foot, Holtville and the whole countryside made their way on this bright July morning, having first locked their doors and windows and put out the cats.

The families of Jone Simmons and Peter Boley, which included only themselves and wives, since neither had any children, went together in the grocer's five-passenger gasoline runabout. Boley had already made the trip half a dozen times since six o'clock that morning, carrying sundry paraphernalia for the entertainments and games of the afternoon.

Among them was a clothesline from his own back yard, which, stretched around four stakes driven in the ground to form a square, was to inclose the "ring" for the unique and principal event of the day. Jone Simmons, as he sat on the driver's seat beside the grocer, held on his knees a carefully wrapped parcel, which contained two sponges, four towels, a set of boxing gloves and his own costume for the encounter.

The costume had been much admired by the two or three select friends who had been permitted a glimpse of it. It had been made by the fair hands of Mrs. Simmons herself from red silk and white-and-blue muslin, and it was an exact replica of the one worn by Jess Willard in his triumph over Jack Johnson, having been copied from a picture discovered by Slim Pearl, the barber, in an old number of the *Police Gazette*.

Jone Simmons was the center of all eyes that morning at Wellman's Grove. Farmers from all over the country, some of whom he had never seen before, sought him out and started conversation. Young country girls, fresh-faced and laughing as they strolled past in groups, would glance at him with shyly interested eyes, giving Jone a curiously pleasurable thrill that he had not experienced for years.

As the sun reached the top of the heavens and the grove filled with its hundreds of pleasure seekers, parties were formed to make excursions down the little river, shady and sparkling, that wound its way between grassy banks at one end of the grove, and here and there a group of young men and girls would start some country game.

Jone was surprised out of speech when one such group broke up at his approach and ran to ask him to join the fun in "drop the handkerchief." It was their tribute to a fighting man.

Among the men there was only one topic of conversation. Politics and crops were put aside for once to discuss the great event of the afternoon, and more often than not the discussions warmed into arguments. Slim Pearl, the barber, having witnessed several professional prize fights in Cincinnati, suddenly assumed a new importance, being called upon to settle endless disputes on some nice point or other of the technicalities of pugilism. As far as the outcome of the match was concerned, opinion was pretty much one way; nearly everybody favored the chances of Simmons as against the newcomer from Columbus, and there was very little betting.

It was well toward noon before Simmons caught his first glimpse that day of his opponent. He had approached a group of men who appeared to be in the midst of an animated discussion, and suddenly, in the center of the group, he saw a medium-sized, bare-headed man with a little bristly mustache and sharp gray eyes.

It was Mr. Notter. He was talking in a half-bored, half-lively sort of manner with the farmers and village men who had gathered about him.

"He looks mighty cheerful," muttered Simmons to himself, turning hastily away before Mr. Notter should see him.

It is time now to admit that Simmons himself was far from being cheerful. It would be unjust perhaps to say that he had any feeling of fear, but he was at least mentally uncomfortable.

As he walked away from the group which contained

Mr. Notter toward the other end of the grove, where preparations were in progress for the picnic feast, a feeling of indignation mounted slowly and steadily within him. What did Peter Boley mean by dragging him into this thing, anyway? Of course, he thought bitterly, it meant nothing to Peter; it meant nothing to all these people, gathered together from a morbid curiosity to see the flowing of blood; *they* weren't going to stand roped in a ten-foot ring and let an ex-champion of Columbus smash them in the face! He hated them.

How absurd it was, anyway, for two grown men to deliberately set about punching each other! Perfectly silly. Oh, what an awful fool he had been to let it go so far as this! The scorn of the whole country would fall on his head if he should back out now. He gritted his teeth. He would *have* to see it through!

What an ugly look there was about that fellow Notter's eyes . . . Sort of bestial . . . Perhaps he had been a *professional!* . . .

These were the thoughts that coursed through Simmons's head throughout the picnic feast, to which all were soon summoned by the jangling of a string of cowbells. He couldn't eat, and he hated the others for eating. How utterly heartless they seemed, laughing and talking and munching their sandwiches and pickles and cake! Didn't they realize the seriousness of a fistic contest between two trained men? Didn't they know that a full swing on the jaw, scientifically delivered, was very apt to prove fatal?

After the feast the program of amusements began. There was a potato race and a bag race and other games and contests peculiar to the country. Simmons stood aside, leaning against a tree, trying to remain unnoticed. He felt faint, as though if he didn't lean against some-

thing he would be unable to stand. Really, he didn't feel
well.

He was telling himself fiercely that he was no coward.
It wasn't that. He just thought it was silly, and anyway
he shouldn't be expected to fight an ex-champion. Probably Mr. Notter knew just how to land a blow so as to
knock a man out.

Suddenly he heard Peter Boley's stentorian tones calling out:

"This way, entries for the greased pig contest! This
way, entries for the greased pig contest!"

Simmons felt an immense lump rise in his throat. The
greased pig contest! According to the program of the
Entertainment Committee, the boxing match was to follow that. The hour had come!

He heard his name pronounced from behind. He
turned and saw Harry Vawter, the druggist.

"Come on, Jonas, you'd better get ready while they're
running down the pig. Here's your stuff. Peter told me
to help you. We've got the ring all fixed, buckets and
towels and sponges and everything. Slim Pearl's putting
down the sawdust now."

Simmons got himself clear of the tree. Over toward
the middle of the grove he saw the ring on a raised
platform, surrounded by a crowd of the curious, not to
be pulled away even by anything so exciting as a greased
pig contest. And people were standing around, looking
at him.

"Where's Mr. Notter?" he asked in a hoarse voice.

"He's gone over to the shanty to get ready," replied
Vawter. "Come on, here's your stuff. You can dress
over in the tent."

"All right; but I'm going down to the creek first."

"You'll have to hurry."

"I'll be back in a minute. Go on over to the tent and wait for me. I'll be there in a minute."

Simmons had been seized by panic. Was the ghastly thing really going to happen? He must have a minute to think.

He walked down toward the little river. The path there was almost deserted, since the greased pig contest was on the other side of the grove. He reached the bank and stood looking down at the clear, rippling water. Vawter had said he would have to hurry—the time had actually come—in twenty minutes now, maybe fifteen, he would be standing in that roped-off ring, with that brutal Notter facing him, waiting for a chance to land a fatal blow—

He looked around. There was nobody in sight. He sneaked slowly down the bank of the creek, away from the grove. He began to walk faster, glancing back over his shoulder. Still there was nobody in sight.

He broke into a run.

He ran with short, jerky steps, on his tiptoes, almost noiselessly, and every minute he ran faster. Soon he left the bank of the creek, for that was dangerous—some of the picnickers might be rowing and see him—and broke into the woods to the left. Then he left caution behind and went forward in great, broad leaps, like a startled jackrabbit. He stumbled over logs and was scratched in the face by low-hanging branches, but he paid no attention to these things. He dashed blindly on.

At length, figuring that he had left the grove and the roped ring at least a mile behind, he came to a halt in the midst of a tiny clearing surrounded by trees and shrubbery. He glanced warily in every direction, and for a full minute he stood perfectly still, listening intently. The only sound was the cry of blackbirds from above the woods. Exhausted, panting, he sank down on the grass and stretched himself out to rest and think.

He had run away. All right, he said to himself fiercely, what of it? What was anybody going to do about it? Of course he had run away. Who wouldn't? If everybody was so anxious to see a fight, why didn't they fight themselves? They'd laugh at him, would they? Well, they wouldn't laugh very long. He'd leave Holtville, that's what he'd do. He'd never liked the town very well, anyhow.

One thing, he'd like to hear anybody say he was a coward. He'd just like to hear 'em. He'd smash their face, that's what he'd do. In fact, if he was back there right now he'd walk up to Mr. Notter and smash *his* face. That was different from letting 'em rope you in a ring. That's what he should have done in the first place.

The day Peter Boley came and told him that Bill Ogilvy's new clerk had said he'd box him at the Annual Picnic he should have gone right down to Bill Ogilvy's store and walked up to Mr. Notter and said to him, "So you want to fight me, do you?" and smashed him in the face. That would have been—

At this point the course of Simmons's thoughts was abruptly halted. He heard a noise somewhere to the right—no, the left. A sound of something moving.

Instantly he was on the alert. He rose cautiously to his hands and knees and crawled across the grass to the shrubbery. Noiselessly pulling a branch aside, he looked through—

And found himself face to face with Mr. Notter!

Simmons stopped short, squatting there on his hands and knees, gazing into Mr. Notter's eyes not three feet away. Mr. Notter, too, appeared to be startled out of speech. He had forced his way half through the shrubbery, when the apparition of Simmons burst suddenly upon him, and now he stood there, surrounded by the leaves and branches, with a stupid, amazed stare in his usually keen eyes, like a steer that has just been felled with an ax.

For several seconds the two men gazed at each other, silent and motionless. Suddenly a new look flashed into the eyes of each; a look of comprehension, of mutual understanding.

"Hello," said Jone Simmons weakly.

Mr. Notter nodded. Then he removed his eyes from the other's face to glance hastily behind him, as though he contemplated retreat. But appearing to think better of it, he moved forward instead, pushed his way through the tangled shrubbery and stood within the clearing. Simultaneously Simmons backed in again and rose to his feet.

"Hello," said Mr. Notter then, as though he had just remembered that he had not returned the other's greeting.

Simmons nodded. There was a silence. Suddenly a grin appeared on Mr. Notter's face. He looked about him for a nice grassy spot, selected one near the trunk of a tree at the edge of the clearing and deliberately sat down on it, stretching his legs out comfortably and leaning against the tree.

"Very nice here," he observed pleasantly.

Simmons felt that he didn't want to sit down. He thought that he would feel silly if he sat down, and he tried to think of something else to do. No go. He couldn't very well stand there like a man ready to run.

So he sat down, somewhat abruptly, a little distance away. He was trying to decide whether he ought to reply to Mr. Notter's observations. After all, there was no reason why he shouldn't.

"Nice and shady," he declared, plucking a blade of grass and placing it between his teeth.

All at once a great burst of laughter came from Mr.

Notter. He kicked up his heels and roared. He rocked to and fro, shaking all over, reveling in mirth, waking the forest.

"What you laughin' at?" Simmons demanded.

"Oh, all them people," the other managed to get out between gasps.

"All what people?"

"Why, back there waitin' and lookin' for us. Waitin' to see a bloody nose. And here we sit, laughin' at 'em!"

"Well, if you're going to make so much noise they'll soon find us," Simmons observed. But he grinned in spite of himself. It *was* funny. He could see Peter Boley and Slim Pearl and the rest running around like chickens with their heads cut off.

"It's queer we should both come to the same spot," observed Mr. Notter presently. "One of life's calm incidents."

That was the way Simmons understood it at first, then he realized that the other had meant to say "coincidences." He nodded in agreement. But another thought was occupying his mind, and after a moment he gave it speech.

"You know," he said abruptly, "if I was an ex-champion I think I'd just as soon fight as not."

"So would I," chuckled Mr. Notter.

"But you are," Simmons objected in surprise.

"You mean what I told old Boley," the other grinned. "I was just stringin' him. I used to belong to an athletic club, all right. Up in Columbus."

"Then you wasn't a fighter?"

"Not so as you could notice it."

Silence. Simmons cursed himself mentally. *This* was the kind of man he had run away from! A liar and braggart! A bag of wind! He, Jone Simmons, man of science, absolute master of the punching bag, had run away from this little, white-faced city dry-goods clerk!

"Of course," he said contemptuously, "then it's not much wonder you was afraid to fight."

"I didn't say I was afraid," returned Mr. Notter, glancing at him. "I just didn't want to."

"Well, it's easy enough to see why you didn't want to."

"I don't know whether it is or not."

"I do."

"I don't."

Simmons opened his mouth to say "I do" again, but reflected that the remark would seem pointless on repetition. He substituted another—

"Anyhow, you run away."

"I suppose *you* didn't," retorted Mr. Notter sarcastically.

"That's my business."

"And mine's mine."

"If I did come away it wasn't because I was afraid of you, I tell you that!"

Mr. Notter laughed coldly. "No," he returned, "I suppose you was afraid of the greased pig."

Simmons rose to his knees, trembling a little. "Are you lookin' for trouble?" he demanded.

"What if I am?" retorted the other crushingly.

"I say, are you lookin' for trouble?"

"And I say what if I am?"

"You coward, you, are you lookin' for trouble?"

Mr. Notter's face grew suddenly red. "I'm a coward, am I?" His voice was raised hoarsely. "That's a lie!"

There was a silence. A tense, pendent silence, while the two men, glaring at each other, breathed heavily. And then, surprising even himself by the suddenness of it, Jone Simmons lunged forward and swung at Mr. Notter's jaw. A vicious, full swing, and it nearly hit him.

"You would, would you?" Mr. Notter cried furiously, leaping to his feet. Simmons followed him. But before he could get set for another blow Mr. Notter had reached out and grasped his hair with both hands, jerking with all his strength.

"Wow!" screamed Simmons, tears of pain starting to his eyes. He drew back his right foot and delivered a well-placed-kick on the other's shin. It had the desired effect. He felt the grasp on his hair loosen.

The next moment he had jumped forward to throw his arms around Mr. Notter's neck, and together the two men went to the ground in a savage embrace.

They landed with Simmons on top, but Mr. Notter somehow got hold of his ear and pulled him beneath, wriggling out from under. Both were kicking frantically, and Simmons managed to get a hand fastened in the other's hair. He was at a disadvantage there, for Mr. Notter's scalp was not sensitive.

Over and over they rolled on the grass from one side of the clearing to the other and back again, pulling hair, scratching, kicking, both boiling with rage. Once they rolled against a tree, knocking Simmons's head against the trunk, and he thought the other had hit him.

"You damn coward!" he yelled.

He released his hold around his opponent's neck, doubled his fists and pushed them savagely against Mr. Notter's nose. That brought first blood for Simmons, and moved Mr. Notter, wild with fury, to superhuman efforts. He wriggled on top and pinned Simmons down with his knees, and began raining blows all over his face.

More blood. Simmons felt it on his face and thought he was being killed. With a sudden mighty upheaving of his body he unseated his opponent and sent him tumbling to one side, and then rolled over on top of him.

Again they closed in an embrace, each with his fingers fastened in the other's hair.

"Leggo my hair!" screamed Simmons in agony.

"You leggo mine!" yelled Mr. Notter in return.

Simmons pulled harder, but it was quite evident even to his frenzied brain that his opponent's scalp was the toughest part of him. Accordingly, he released his hold on Mr. Notter's hair and gripped his nose instead. He clutched the nose, sore and bleeding, with the fingers of both hands, and jerked it savagely from right to left and back again.

Mr. Notter emitted a fearful yell, but pulled harder on the hair, rolling over meantime so that he was on top. In desperate fury Simmons let go of the nose and closed his fingers around the other's throat.

"Let go my hair!" he screamed again, blinded with tears.

Mr. Notter began to gurgle, and his grasp weakened. They began to roll again, first one on top and then the other, mad with frenzy. Simmons got his knuckles against Mr. Notter's eye and bored in with them, twisting his fist from side to side. Mr. Notter jerked away and butted his forehead against Simmons's nose, causing the blood to spurt afresh.

Simmons let out an awful oath and began pounding his opponent's face with both fists—his eyes, his nose, his mouth. They rolled over once, twice, toward a tree at the edge of the clearing, Mr. Notter coming out on top.

They were both about exhausted by that time, and the end would have come soon in any event, but the chance of their rolling close to the tree hastened it.

Mr. Notter reached out again for Simmons's hair; Simmons, anticipating the maneuver, closed his fingers firmly around the other's nose; Mr. Notter jerked violently backward to free himself, his head struck against the trunk of the tree, and he rolled over limp and unconscious.

For a moment Simmons didn't know what had happened. But as he saw his opponent lying there beside him still and motionless, comprehension came, and he was seized with a sudden, terrible fright. He scrambled frantically to his feet. Mr. Notter was dead! He had killed him! Good heavens! He stood looking at the prostrate form in speechless horror, scarcely able to keep on his feet from fatigue and the exhaustion of rage—

"Here they are!" came a sudden shout from behind.

Simmons jumped half out of his skin, whirled around and saw a man pushing his way through the shrubbery into the clearing. It was Peter Boley.

"Here they are!" Boley shouted again, and Simmons heard answering calls from the wood in all directions.

The grocer entered the clearing, and his glance fell on the form of Mr. Notter on the ground; as he looked it stirred a little.

"Here they are!" he shouted a third time. "Come quick! Quick! Jonas has knocked him out!"

Toward noon of the following day Peter Boley and Jone Simmons were seated talking in the back room of the hardware store. Simmons looked considerably the worse for wear. His nose was swollen to twice its usual size, there was a bandage over one eye and innumerable scratches made his face look something like a railroad map.

Still his expression, as far as it could be ascertained underneath these disfigurements, was not exactly unhappy.

"It's not that I blame you for, Jonas," Peter Boley was saying. "If you and Mr. Notter decided to go off in the woods together and fight it out because there was too many women and children around, I don't blame you a bit. When you found out you was mad at each other, that was the only thing to do. But what I say is, you might have let some of us come along—at least Slim Pearl and Harry Vawter and me. You might have told us. By jumpers, Jonas, I tell you I wouldn't of missed that fight for twenty dollars! It must of been an awful blow when you knocked him out. He didn't come to for five minutes. A swing on the jaw, eh?''

Simmons nodded negligently. ''He put up an awful good fight,'' he admitted magnanimously. ''He's no slouch, Peter, I tell you that. I guess it was the hardest fight I ever had. He's stronger than I am.

''But,'' he added, producing a plug of tobacco, ''you see how much good it did him. It's science that counts!''

THE ROPE DANCE

I T WAS ON A BRIGHT OCTOBER AFTERNOON THAT
Rick Duggett got off at Grand Central Station, New
York, with eight hundred dollars in the pocket of his
brand-new suit of clothes. But first of all it is necessary
to explain how he got there and where the money came
from.

He was one of those men who never do anything by
halves. He ate prodigiously or fasted, he slept eleven
hours or not at all, he sat in a poker game only when it
was expressly understood that the roof was the limit and
you might blow that off if you had enough powder.

Whatever he did he went just a little farther than anyone else, so it was only natural that he should reach the
top of his profession. He was the best roper in Eastern
Arizona, which is no mean title even in these days when
good ropers are as scarce as water holes in a desert.

When a prize of one thousand dollars cash was hung
up in the great roping contest held at Honeville last October everybody expected Rick Duggett to win it, and he
did not disappoint them. He roped and tied ten steers in
fourteen minutes and twenty-eight seconds, seven full
minutes better than the nearest competitor.

There had been considerable speculation as to what
Rick would do with the money. Of course he would

entertain the crowd at Ogilvy's, but even a gang of
thirsty ranchmen can't drink a thousand dollars' worth
of whisky. The rest would probably find its way into a
poker game; but then Rick Duggett was a surprising sort
of fellow and you couldn't tell. He might get married,
or even take a trip to Denver.

As a matter of fact, Rick bought one round of drinks
at Ogilvy's, made arrangements for his horse to be returned to the ranch, and entrusted a comrade with the
following note to the foreman:

Dear Fraser:
   I won the big prize all right. I'm going to take a month off
for a little trip to New York. I've never been there.
                                              Yours truly,
                                              R. Duggett

Even from Rick, that was amazing. Denver or K. C.,
yes. People did go to those places, and sometimes even
to St. Louis. Indeed, it was understandable that a man
might conceivably undertake, for pleasure, a journey to
Chicago.

But New York!

Absurd.

You might as well say Constantinople and be done
with it. However, it was just like Rick Duggett. Having
decided to visit a big city, you might know he would
choose the biggest. He never did anything by halves.

Thus it was that Rick arrived in New York, with a
roll of bills amounting to eight hundred and eighteen
dollars in his pocket, about two o'clock of a sunny October afternoon.

Having stopped off in Chicago to buy a suit of clothes,
his outward appearance, as he emerged from the Grand
Central Station onto Forty-second Street, was not as star-

tling as you might have expected of the champion roper of Arizona. But he had not thought of discarding the floppy broad-brimmed Stetson, and the ruggedness of his brown countenance and the flashing clearness of his eye were patently not of Broadway.

So it was that before he had even reached Times Square, threading his way through the throng westward on Forty-second Street, he was accosted by a dapper white-faced person in a blue serge suit who murmured something, without preamble, concerning "the third race at Latonia," and a "sure thing," and "just around the corner."

"Listen, sonny," said Rick, not unkindly. "I don't bet on horses unless I can see 'em. Besides, if I'd wanted to gamble I'd of stayed in Honeville. I came to New York to see the sights, and I guess you're one of 'em. Much obliged. Here's two bits."

And he thrust a quarter into the hand of the astonished "runner."

After he had tramped around for a couple of hours and got his eyes full he took a taxicab to the Hotel Croyville, which had been recommended to him by someone on the train.

It is too bad that I can't describe his timidity on entering the cab and his novel sensations as the engine started and the thing shot forward. The trouble is that the owner of the ranch on which he worked was also the owner of two automobiles, and Rick was a pretty good hand at driving a car himself. Yet he was indeed impressed by the cab driver marvellous dexterity in threading his way through the maze of whirling traffic down Fifth Avenue.

Rick ate dinner, or supper, as he called it, at the Croyville, and a little later sallied forth for a look at the town by electric light. He had a sort of an idea that he might go to a show, but, having perused the amusement columns of an evening newspaper, found himself embarrassed by the superabundance of material. His final decision rested between a performance of *Macbeth* and a Broadway dancing revue, and about half-past seven he dropped into a café to consider the matter over a little of something wet.

It was there that he met a person named Henderson. One thing Rick must admit, it was he himself who addressed the first words to the stranger. But then it is also a fact that the stranger, who was standing next to Rick at the bar, started things by observing to the bartender and whoever else might care to hear:

"We don't use those nonrefillable bottles out West, where I come from. We don't have to. We know the men that sell us our drinks, and by——, they know us. But that's the way it is in New York. You got to watch everybody, or you'll get your insides all filled up with water."

Rick turned and asked the stranger—a ruddy-faced, middle-aged man in a gray sack suit and soft hat—what part of the West he came from. That was enough. Ten minutes later they were having their second drink together.

Mr. Henderson, it appeared, was from Kansas, where he owned an immense wheat farm. He was much interested in what Rick had to say about Arizona. They discussed the metropolis, and Rick, by way of comment on Mr. Henderson's observation that "you got to watch everybody in New York," told of his encounter with the poolroom runner on Forty-second Street. Then, as it was nearing eight o'clock, he remarked that he was intending to see the revue up at the Stuyvesant Theater, and guessed he would have to trot along.

"That's a bum show," declared Mr. Henderson. "I

saw it the other night. Lord, I've seen better than that out in Wichita. Why don't you come with me up to the Century? A fellow at the hotel told me it's the real thing.''

So after Mr. Henderson had paid for the drinks—despite Rick's protest—they left the café and took a taxi to Sixty-second Street, where Henderson allowed Rick to settle with the cab driver while he entered the theater lobby to get the tickets.

Rick liked the man from Kansas. He appeared to be an outspoken, blunt sort of fellow who liked to have a good time and knew where to go for it. Lucky thing to have met up with him. Mighty pleasant to have for a companion a chap from the right side of the Mississippi.

The show was in fact a good one, and Rick enjoyed it hugely. Pretty girls, catchy music, funny lines, clever dancing. Rick applauded with gusto and laughed himself weak. The only drawback was that Mr. Henderson appeared to have an unconquerable aversion to going out between the acts. It was incomprehensible. The man actually seemed to prefer sitting in the stuffy, crowded theater to stepping out for a little air. But then he was a most amusing talker and the intermissions were not so very long.

After the final curtain they pushed out with the crowd to the sidewalk. Rick felt exhilarated and a little bewildered in the whirlpool of smiling faces and the noise of a thousand chattering tongues.

''This is certainly New York,'' he was saying to himself, when his thoughts were interrupted by his companion's voice:

''What do you say we go downtown for a little supper? I know a good place. Unless you'd rather turn in—''

''I should say not,'' declared Rick. ''I had my supper

at six o'clock, but I'm always ready for more. Lead me to it. This is on me, you know.''

So they found a taxi at the curb and got in, after Mr. Henderson had given the driver the name of a cabaret and supper room downtown. A little delay, and they were out of the crush in front of the theater; a minute later the cab turned into Broadway, with its glaring lights and throngs of vehicles and pedestrians, and headed south.

Suddenly Mr. Henderson pulled himself forward, thrust his hand into his hip pocket and brought it forth again holding something that glistened like bright silver as the rays of light through the cab window reflected on it. Rick's curious glance showed him that it was a nickel-plated whisky flask. He watched with a speculative eye as the other unscrewed the top, turned it over and poured it full of liquid.

''Some stuff I brought with me from Kansas,'' explained Mr. Henderson. ''The real thing, this is. I always keep it in the sideboard. If you'd care to join me, sir—''

Rick hesitated. Then he blushed for the base thought that had entered his mind. It was all right to be cautious and all that, but it was carrying it a little too far to be suspicious of a man like Henderson. Still—

''Sure,'' said Rick. ''After you. I'd like to sample it.''

The other proffered the tiny nickel-plated cup.

''After you,'' Rick repeated with a polite gesture.

''Here's how, then,'' replied Henderson, and emptied the cup at a gulp. ''Nothing to rinse with, you know,'' he observed as he filled it again from the flask. ''The stuff's too good to waste it washing dishes.''

''That's all right.'' Rick took the cup, brimful, in his fingers. ''Here's looking at you.''

And, following the other's example, he swallowed it with one draught.

About three hours later, a little after three o'clock in the morning, the lieutenant at the desk of the Murray Hill Police Station was conducting an investigation. The chief witness was a taxicab driver, whose face was flushed with indignation at the iniquity of a wicked world, and whose tone was filled with injured protest.

"I was in front of the Century," said the driver to the police lieutenant, "when two guys took me. One of 'em, a short, red-faced guy, told me to hit it up for Shoney's cabaret. I got 'em there as quick as I could, of course bein' careful, but when I pulled up in front of Shoney's the red-faced guy leaned out of the window and said they'd changed their minds and guessed they'd drive around a little. 'Maybe an hour,' he said, and told me to go up the Avenue to the Park. So I beat it for the Park.

"I drove around till I got dizzy, nearly two hours, and it seemed funny I wasn't hearing sounds of voices inside. They had the front curtains pulled down. Finally I slowed down and took a peep around the corner through the side window. I couldn't see no one. I stopped and jumped down and opened the door. The red-faced guy was gone and the other guy was sprawled out half on the seat and half on the floor. I yelled at him and shook him around, but he was dead to the world. So I brought him—"

"All right, that'll do," the lieutenant interrupted. "You've got a license, I suppose?"

"Sure I have. I've been three years with the M. B. Company—"

"And you don't know when the red-faced man left the cab?"

"No. Unless it was at Sixth Avenue and Forty-second Street. They was a jam there and we was held up a long time. He might of ducked then—"

"All right." The lieutenant turned to a policeman. "See if that man is able to talk yet."

As the policeman turned to obey, a door leading into an inner room opened and Rick Duggett, champion roper of Eastern Arizona, appeared on the threshold. His face was pale and his eyes were swollen and dull, like those of a man roused from a long sleep; his necktie was on one side and his hair was rumpled into a tangled mass.

"Here he is now," said the policeman.

"Oh, so you've come to." The lieutenant looked the newcomer over. "What's the matter with you? What kind of a game is this?"

Rick Duggett approached the desk.

"Listen here," he said, gazing at the lieutenant with a melancholy eye. His voice was slow and labored, but he made it distinct. "Listen here," he repeated. "I see by the clock yonder that it's after three. So I've been knocked out for three hours. I came to in there fifteen minutes ago, and they told me where I was. I guess I'm straightened out now. A gazabo named Henderson gave me a drink of something from Kansas, and when I closed my eyes because I enjoyed it so much he lifted a roll of eight hundred dollars and a return ticket to Arizona from my pants pocket. You got to watch everybody in New York. It was Henderson said that. Perhaps he meant—"

"Wait a minute." The lieutenant arranged the blotter and dipped his pen in the ink. "What's your name?"

Rick achieved a weary smile. "My name is Billy Boob. Write it down and let me see how it looks. That's all you'll get, because I'm not exactly anxious to get myself in the papers in this connection. My name is Billy

Boob, and I come from Ginkville on Sucker Creek. If that's all I guess I'll trot along."

"I guess you won't," said the lieutenant sharply. "How do you expect us to get your money back for you if you don't tell us anything? What kind of a looking man was this Henderson? Where did you meet him?"

"Nothing doing." Again Rick smiled wearily. "Strange to say, I forgot to brand him. He wore a gray suit of clothes, and he had a red face and white teeth, and I met him somewhere talking about nonrefillable bottles. No use writing anything down, because I'm not making any holler. I've always had a theory that if a man can't take care of himself he's not fit to have anyone else do the job. The boys would run me off the ranch if they heard of this. I guess I'll trot along."

The policeman grinned. The lieutenant expostulated and argued. But Rick was firm.

"No, Cap, nothing doing on the complaint. You wouldn't catch him, anyway. I'm going home and get some sleep. So long and much obliged."

He made for the door. But on the threshold he hesitated, then turned.

"There's one thing I'd like to know," he said slowly. "Henderson took a drink just before I did, and it didn't seem to make him sleepy. Is it a general practice around here to carry two kinds of booze in one horn?"

At that the lieutenant grinned, too. "Oh, that's one of our eastern refinements," he explained. "You see, the flask is divided in the middle. If you press the button on the right side you get Scotch and if you press the one on the left you get something else. Men like Mr. Henderson have them made to order."

"I see," said Rick. "Much obliged."

And with a farewell nod he turned again and disappeared into the street.

*   *   *

It was noon when he awoke the next day in his room at the hotel. He first felt a vague sense of depression, then suddenly everything came back to him. He jumped out of bed, filled the washbowl with cold water and ducked his head in it, then washed and dressed. That done, he descended to the dining room and ate six eggs and two square feet of ham. After he had paid the breakfast check he went into the lobby and sank into a big leather chair.

"Let's see," he said to himself, "that leaves me fourteen dollars and twenty cents. Thank heaven Henderson didn't look in my vest pocket, though he did take my watch out of the other one. That watch would have got me back to Honeville. The fare is fifty-eight dollars. I'll starve before I'll telegraph Fraser. Well, let's see."

He spent the entire afternoon loitering about the hotel, trying to get his mind to work. How to make some money? The thing appeared impossible. They don't hold roping contests in New York. He considered everything from sweeping streets to chauffeuring. Could he drive a car around New York? No money in it, anyway, probably. But surely a man could do *something*.

By evening he had decided on nothing. After dinner he strolled up Broadway and bought a ticket for the revue. He was determined to find it amusing, for Mr. Henderson had said it was a bum show. It really bored him to death. But he stayed till the final curtain. Then he found himself on Broadway again.

Just how he got into Dickson's is uncertain. He wanted a drink, and he wandered into the place and found himself in the presence of "the most famous cabaret in America." Rick sat at a small table at one end of the immense, gorgeous room, watching the antics of the dancers and singers and other performers on the platform, and it was there that his idea came to him. Before he went to bed that night he had decided to give it a trial the very next day.

Accordingly the following morning he sought out a hardware store on Sixth Avenue and purchased thirty yards of first grade hemp rope and a gallon of crude oil. The cost was eight dollars and sixty cents. These articles he took back to the hotel, and for three hours he sat in his room rubbing the oil into the rope to bring it to the required degree of pliancy and toughness.

Then he spliced a loop in one end, doubled it through and made a six-foot noose—the size of the room would not permit a larger one—and began whirling it about his head. A sigh of satisfaction escaped him. Ah, the nimble wrist! And the rope would really do very well; a little limbering up and he would ask nothing better.

He pulled his traveling bag from under the bed, dumped out its contents and put the rope, carefully coiled, in their place. Then, with the bag in his hand, he descended to the street and made his way uptown to Dickson's. At the entrance he halted a moment, then went boldly inside and accosted one of the young women at the door of the cloakroom.

"I want to speak to the manager of the show," said he, hat in hand.

"You mean the headwaiter?" she hazarded.

"I don't know," replied Rick. "The man that runs the show on the platform. I saw it last night."

"Oh," she grinned. "You mean the cabaret."

"Do I? Much obliged. Anyway, I want to see him."

"It ain't so easy," the young woman observed. "The boss tends to that himself. I'll see. Come in here."

She led the way down a narrow, dark corridor to an office where stenographers and bookkeepers sat at their desks and machines, and turned Rick over to a wise-looking youth with a threatening mustache. The youth surveyed the caller with ill-concealed amusement at his ungraceful appearance, and when he finally condescended to speak there was a note of tolerant sarcasm in his voice.

"So you want to see Mr. Dickson," he observed. "What do you want with him?"

"Listen, sonny." Rick was smiling, too, quietly enough. "No doubt we're having a lot of fun looking at each other, but my time's valuable just now. I'm Rick Duggett from Arizona. Report the fact to your Mr. Dickson."

Thus did Rick make his way into the presence of Lonny Dickson, the best known man on Broadway and the owner of its most famous cabaret. He was a large, smiling individual, with a clear countenance and a keen, penetrating eye. As Rick entered the inner office where he sat at a large flat desk heaped with papers, smoking a long thin cigar, he got up from his chair and held out a hand in greeting.

"Jimmie just told me," he observed genially, looking Rick in the eye, "that a wild guy from the West wanted to see me. I'm kind of wild myself, so I don't mind. But Jimmie didn't get the name—"

"Duggett," said Rick, taking the proffered hand.

"Glad to meet you, Mr. Duggett. What can I do for you?"

Rick hesitated.

"It's this way," he said finally. "I'm from Arizona. I'm a son of misfortune. Two days ago I had a roll big enough to choke a horse, but night before last I let it out to pasture, as though I wasn't green enough myself. So I'm broke, and it's a long, long way to Arizona. Last night I happened in here and saw your show, and an idea came to me. It's a new stunt for the show, and it ought to be pretty good. So I thought I'd—"

"What is it?" interrupted Mr. Dickson, whose cordiality had rapidly disappeared as he became aware of the nature of the visitor's errand. This was just some nut looking for a job.

"Something new," said Rick placidly. "I can't tell you very well; I've got to show you. It'll take five minutes. All I want is a room with plenty of space, say twenty feet on each side, and a high ceiling—"

"But what is it?" the other repeated impatiently.

Rick looked at him.

"Gosh, you're not wild," he observed with a twinkle in his eye. "You're just plain sassy. Didn't I say I had to show you? Haven't you got a room around here somewhere of the general size I indicated? Haven't you got a pair of eyes to look at me with?"

The frown left Dickson's brow, and he laughed.

"Well, you're wild enough for both of us," he declared. "I guess you'll get back to Arizona all right, someway or other. As for your stunt for the cabaret, it's a thousand to one that it's rotten. Naturally you can't be expected to know anything about cabarets. However, I'll take a look. Come on, we'll go up to the banquet room on the next floor; I guess you'll find it big enough."

"Much obliged," said Rick.

He picked up his traveling bag and followed the restaurant proprietor out of the office.

The evening of the following day the patrons of Dickson's of Broadway were treated to a surprise.

Do you know the main room at Dickson's?

The first thing you notice about the place is the light—dazzling, glaring, bold; a perfect riot of light, whitish yellow, that comes from four immense chandeliers suspended from the ceiling and innumerable electric lamps on the marble pillars, attached to the walls, on the tables, everywhere.

Then your ears are assaulted, and you hear the clinking of glasses, the muffled footsteps of waiters, the confusing hum of conversation from half a thousand tongues, and mingled with all this a sound of music, now suppressed, now insistent, that comes from the orchestra on the rear of the raised platform at one side. On the front of this platform, of which a fair view may be had by each of the hundreds of diners and drinkers packed in the immense room, the cabaret performers appear in turn.

It was the height of the dinner hour, a little after seven. A young woman in a low-necked blue dress with cow-like eyes had finished three verses and choruses of a popular sentimental song, and the orchestra had rested the usual three minutes. Then they struck up again for the next "turn," and a girl appeared on the platform, followed by a man.

The girl—a lively little black-haired creature with sparkling eyes and a saucy, winning smile—was no stranger to the habitués of the place; she had been dancing there for several months. But always alone. Who was this fellow with her? They opened their eyes at his strange appearance.

He was a tall, ungainly chap, wearing the costume of a moving picture cowboy, and in his hand he carried a great coil of rope. There was an expression of painful embarrassment on his brown face as he glanced from side to side and saw five hundred pairs of eyes looking into his from all parts of the large, brilliantly lighted room.

The girl began to dance, swinging into the music with a series of simple, tentative steps, and the man roused himself to action. He loosened the coil of rope and began pulling it through a loop at one end to form a noose. Then slowly and easily, and gracefully, he began whirling the noose in the air. It was fifteen feet in diameter, half as wide as the platform.

The girl, quickening her steps with the music, swerved suddenly to one side and leaped into the center of the whirling coil of rope. Then the music quickened again and the rope whirled faster, while the dancer circled round and round its circumference in a series of dizzy gyrations. Suddenly the man twisted to one side, with a quick and powerful turn of the wrist, and the rope doubled on itself like lightning, forming two circles instead of one. The girl leaped and danced from one to the other.

The music became more rapid still, and the rope and the dancer, whirling with incredible swiftness in the most intricate and dazzling combinations, challenged the eye to follow them. The nooses of the rope, which had again doubled, came closer together, until finally two of them encircled the girl at once, then three, then all four, still whirling about her swiftly revolving form.

All at once the orchestra, with one tremendous crash, was silent; simultaneously the man gave a sudden powerful jerk with his arm and the dancer stopped and became rigid, while the four nooses of the rope tightened themselves about her, pinning her arms to her sides and rendering her powerless. One more crash from the orchestra, and the man ran forward, picked the girl up in his arms and ran quickly from the platform.

The applause was deafening. Dickson's had scored another hit. All Broadway asks is something new.

Back of the platform the man had halted to place the girl gently on her feet and unwind the coils of rope. That done, she took him by the hand to lead him back to the platform for the bow. He hung back, but she insisted, and finally she dragged him on. They were forced to take another, and a third. When they returned from the last one they found Lonny Dickson himself waiting for them at the foot of the platform steps.

"Great stuff, Duggett," he said enthusiastically. "You put it over fine, especially with only one day's rehearsal. It'll improve, too. I've been paying Miss Carson fifty a week. I'll make it a hundred and fifty for the turn, and you and she can split it fifty-fifty."

"Much obliged," replied Rick calmly. His face was flushed and his brow covered with perspiration. He turned to his partner.

"Shall we have a drink on it, Miss Carson?"

They found a table in a corner back of the platform. Miss Carson, a rarity among cabaret performers, was even more pleasing to look at when you were close to her than on the stage. Her sparkling eyes retained all their charm, and the softness of her hair, the daintiness of her little mouth, the fresh smoothness of her cheeks, became more apparent. She was panting now from her exertions, and her flushed face and disarranged hair made a lovely picture.

"Really," she said, as she sat down, "I ought to ask you to wait till I go to the dressing room and repair damages."

"Oh, that can wait," declared Rick. "If you knew how nice you look right now you wouldn't want to fix up anyway. I suppose we ought to drink to each other with a bottle of champagne, but to tell the truth I was kind of hungry this evening and I'm afraid I about finished my little stake. I'll corral Dickson for an advance tonight and we'll have the wine later."

But Miss Carson protested with a gay smile that she never drank anything stronger than mineral water, so that was all right. More, a little exclamation of horror escaped her when she saw Rick swallow three fingers of whiskey straight, after clinking glasses with her.

"That awful stuff!" she exclaimed. "It'll kill you. I thought you mixed water with it or something."

"I haven't got that low yet," Rick declared. "But there's a funny thing, I was thinking just then that I've been drinking too much since I came East. Out home I don't touch it oftener than once in two months, though I do fill up pretty well then. You know—" he hesitated—and blushed! "You know," he went on, "I'm glad you don't drink."

"Yes? Why?"

"Lord, I don't know. I'm just glad."

"Well, so am I. I never have. But listen, Mr. Duggett. Mr. Dickson said he was going to give us a hundred and fifty and we could split it fifty-fifty. I won't do that— divide it even, I mean. I was only getting fifty alone, so it's quite evident that the hundred belongs to you."

"You don't say so," Rick smiled at her. "Now, that's just like you." (How in the world could he have known what was just like her, having met her only twenty-four hours before?) "But you've got it wrong. The hundred is yours. I wouldn't be worth two bits without you."

"Mr. Duggett, the increased value of the turn is due entirely to you, and you must take the extra money. I insist."

"Miss Carson, you really ought to have the whole thing, only I need a stake to get back home, so I'll agree to take one-third. Not a cent more."

They argued about it for twenty minutes, and at the end of that time compromised on an even split.

"It must be terribly exciting out in Arizona," observed Miss Carson after a pause.

Rick lifted his eyebrows.

"Exciting?"

"Yes. That is—well—*exciting*."

"Not so as you could notice it. Oh, it's all right. I

don't kick any. Plenty to eat, a good poker game whenever you're loaded and a dance every once in a while. And of course lots of work—''

"But I didn't mean that," Miss Carson put in. "Working and eating and playing cards and dancing— why, that's just what the men do in New York. I meant Indians, and things like that."

"Yes, the Indians are pretty bad," Rick agreed. "You've got to keep your eye on 'em all the time. They'll get anything that's loose. Worst sneak thieves in the world. But I don't call that very exciting. In fact, I guess I'm having the most exciting time of my life right now."

"Oh, so you like New York?"

"I should say not. That is, I didn't mean New York. I meant right now, here at this table."

"My goodness, I don't see anything very exciting about this," the girl smiled.

"Of course not. You're looking in the wrong direction. You're looking at me and I'm looking at you. You know, it's a funny thing about your eyes. They look like the eyes of a pony I had once, the best that ever felt a saddle. The only time I ever cried was when he stumbled in a prairie dog hole and had to be shot."

This was not the first compliment Rick had ever paid a woman, but you may see that he had not practiced the art sufficiently to acquire any great degree of subtlety. It appeared nevertheless not to be totally ineffective, for Miss Carson turned away the eyes that reminded Rick of his lost pony. She even made inquiry about the pony's name and age, and why his stumbling in a prairie dog hole necessitated his death; also what is a prairie dog and a hole thereof?

At their next appearance on the platform they repeated their former success. There seemed little doubt that they were to be talked of on Broadway, and that meant profitable popularity. Miss Carson was delighted, and Rick found himself echoing her pleasure. Besides he was pleased on his own account, for two reasons: he was going to have no difficulty getting back to Arizona without revealing his disgraceful adventure to the boys, and he was going to get back from Broadway itself at least a part of that which Broadway had taken from him.

After this second performance they would not be needed again for more than two hours, and Rick changed into his street clothes and went out for a walk. It may as well be admitted that his thoughts during this long stroll were mainly of his cabaret partner, but there was another idea in his mind at the same time. He did not leave Broadway, and his eye ran ceaselessly over the faces of the passersby; also he stopped in every café, though he drank not at all. He was hoping that he might run across Mr. Henderson.

At eleven o'clock he was back at Dickson's. Miss Carson found him in front of the dressing room and informed him that their call would be at 11:24. The immense dining room was filling up rapidly with the supper crowd from the theaters.

Waiters and omnibuses trotted swiftly up and down the aisles, there was a continuous line of new arrivals streaming in from the doors at both ends, and corks were beginning to pop. Two numbers of the supper cabaret had already done their turns, and the sentimental soprano was standing at the rear of the platform squeezing the bulb of an atomizer and half choking herself.

When the time came for the Rope Dance, as Lonny Dickson had decided to call it in his advertising copy for the following day, Rick Duggett was surprised at the ease with which he walked out on the platform, bowed and began loosening his coil of rope.

Miss Carson was daintily performing her short opening dance to the music of the orchestra. Rick got his noose arranged, stepped forward to his position in the center of the platform and started the rope slowly whirling. This was easy. He got it a little higher and went a little faster. There would still be at least a minute before the music cue came for the dancer to leap into the whirling circle, and Rick allowed his gaze to wander over the throng of faces turned toward him from every side. The scene spread out dazzlingly from the raised platform.

All at once Rick's head became rigid and his eyes fixed themselves in an unbelieving stare. This lasted for half a moment; then suddenly he started and jumped forward and shouted at the top of his voice: *"Damn!"*

Miss Carson stopped short with amazement in the middle of her dance. The orchestra wavered and was silent. The clinking of knives and forks and the hum of conversation was suddenly hushed all over the room. Rick stood at the front edge of the platform, still staring at something with a wildly inquiring eye, his arm still moving mechanically around his head as the noose whirled in a great circle.

And then those who followed the direction of Rick's gaze saw a man—a stout, red-faced, middle-aged man— suddenly rise to his feet from a table near the center of the room, cast one quick, startled glance at the cowboy on the platform and dart madly down the aisle toward the door.

The rest happened so quickly that no eye was swift enough to follow it. There was a lightning gleam from Rick's eye, a powerful, rapid movement of his arm, and the whirling circle of rope shot out and whizzed through the air over the heads of the amazed throng, leaving behind it, like the tail of a comet, the line whose other end was firmly grasped in Rick's hand.

It was a perfect throw, worthy of the champion of Eastern Arizona. Straight as an arrow the noose went to its mark, dropping with precision over the head of the red-faced man, far across the room. Rick lunged backward, jerking in his arm, and the noose tightened about the man's body, below his breast.

Rick leaped from the platform and dashed down the aisle, pulling in the rope as he ran to keep it taut. In a second he had reached the side of his captive, thrown him to the floor and sat on him.

"Hello, Henderson," said Rick calmly to the prostrate form under him. "I want eight hundred dollars and a ticket to Honeville, Arizona, and I want it quick."

Henderson, panting with exertion, glared and was silent. Not so the other diners. Women were screaming, and two or three of them were trying to faint. Men were calling out, "Get the police!" at the same time crowding down the aisles to be in at the death. Waiters were running distractedly in every direction; their chief pushed his way through, calling meantime to his lieutenants to get the police.

"You'd better act quick, Henderson," said Rick, shaking the head waiter off. "Somebody's gone to get a policeman. I don't like 'em any better than you do, and they'll have to catch you if they want you. Better come across."

"D'ye mean that?" gasped Henderson.

"I sure do."

There was some more quick action then. Rick arose and pulled the noose off. Henderson scrambled to his feet, thrust his hand in his pocket and handed his captor a roll of bills. Rick skinned back the edges, nodded and released his hold. And then you should have seen Mr. Henderson of Kansas get out of that restaurant. He overturned three or four tables and knocked down a dozen men and half as many women, but he certainly got out.

"Much obliged!" Rick yelled after him as he disappeared through the door.

Of course Rick lost his job. Worse, Lonny Dickson had him arrested for disturbing the peace, and he was taken to the night court. But the magistrate released him, after a reprimand for not having turned Henderson over to the law.

And what did he care for his job with nine hundred and thirty dollars in his pocket? That is an actual fact; instead of diminishing, the roll had grown. Perhaps Mr. Henderson had made another haul. And the railroad ticket was there too. Rick pocketed the hundred and thirty dollars profit without a word; you who understand ethics, which I don't, may argue about it if you want to.

Another thing. One o'clock the following afternoon found Rick Duggett eating luncheon—yes, luncheon—with a young lady named Carson. I wouldn't be surprised if it ended by his marrying the girl and taking her back to Arizona with him. He never did anything by halves.

An Officer and a Lady

B ILL FARDEN HAD HAD HIS EYE ON THE BIG BRICK
house on the corner for some time.

He had worked one in that block—the white
frame with the latticed porch farther down toward Mad-
ison Street—during the early part of March, and had got
rather a nice bag. Then, warned off by the scare and
hullabaloo that followed, he had fought shy of that part
of town for a full month, confining his operations to one
or two minor hauls in the Parkdale section. He figured
that by now things would have calmed down sufficiently
in this neighborhood to permit a quiet hour's work without undue danger.

It was a dark night, or would have been but for the
streetlamp on the corner. That mattered little, since the
right side of the house was in deep shadow anyway. By
an oversight I have neglected to place the scene of the
story in the vicinity of a clock tower, so Bill Farden was
obliged to take out his watch and look at it in order to
call attention to the fact that it was an hour past midnight.

He nodded his head with satisfaction, then advanced
across the lawn to that side of the house left in deep
shadow.

Two large windows loomed up side by side, then a

wide expanse of brick, then two more. After a leisurely examination he chose the second of the first pair. A ray from his flashlight showed the old-fashioned catch snapped to.

Grinning professionally, he took a thin shining instrument from his pocket, climbed noiselessly onto the ledge and inserted the steel blade in the slit. A quick jerk, a sharp snap, and he leaped down again. He cocked his ear.

No sound.

The window slid smoothly upward to his push, and the next instant his deft accustomed hand had noiselessly raised the inner shade. Again he lifted himself onto the ledge, and this time across it, too. He was inside the house.

He stood for a time absolutely motionless, listening. The faintest of scratching noises came from the right.

"Bird," Bill observed mentally, and his experienced ear was corroborated a moment later when the light of his flashlight revealed a canary blinking through the bars of its cage.

There was no other sound, and he let the cone of light travel boldly about the apartment. It was a well-furnished library and music room, with a large shining table, shelves of books along the walls, a grand piano at one end, and several comfortable chairs. Bill grunted and moved toward a door at the farther corner.

He passed through, and a glance showed him the dining room. Stepping noiselessly to the windows to make sure that the shades were drawn tight, he then switched on the electric chandelier. There was promise in the array of china and cut glass spread over the buffet and sideboard, and with an expectant gleam in his eye he sprang to open the heavy drawers.

The first held linen; he didn't bother to close it again.

The second was full of silver, dozens, scores of pieces of old family silver. In a trice Bill flew to the ledge of the window by which he had entered and was back again with a suitcase in his hand.

When the silver, wrapped in napkins, was safely in the suitcase, Bill straightened and glanced sharply around. Should he leave at once with this rare booty so easily gathered? He shook his head with decision and returned to place the suitcase on the window ledge in the library; then he came back, switched off the light in the dining room, and entered the kitchen.

By unerring instinct he stepped to the refrigerator. A flash of his pocket-lamp, and he gave a satisfied grunt. He turned on the light. From the recesses of the icebox he brought forth a dish of peas, some sliced beef, half a chicken, some cold potatoes, and part of a strawberry shortcake. In a drawer in the kitchen cabinet he found a knife and fork and some spoons.

From a common-sense viewpoint the performance was idiotic. Having broken into an inhabited house in the dead of night, rifled the silver drawer and deposited the loot on the windowsill, I for one would not be guilty of the artistic crime of tacking on an anticlimax by returning to the kitchen to rob the refrigerator and grossly stuff myself.

But Bill Farden was an old and experienced hand, thoroughly versed in the best burglar tradition. Also, perhaps he was hungry. He ate as one who respects food but has no time for formalities.

He had finished the meat and vegetables and was beginning on the shortcake, when all of a sudden he sprang noiselessly from his chair to the electric button on the wall. A tiny click and the room was in darkness. He crouched low against the wall, while the footsteps that had startled him from above became louder as they began to descend the back stairs.

There might still be a chance to make the door into the dining room, but he decided against it. Scarcely breathing, he pulled himself together and waited. The footsteps became louder still; they halted, and he heard a hand fumbling at the knob of the stairway door. The noise of the opening door followed.

Bill's mind was working like lightning. Probably someone had been awake and seen the light from a slit through the window shade. Man or woman? He would soon know.

The footsteps sounded on the floor, advancing, and his eyes, accustomed to the darkness, caught a dim outline. Noiselessly his hand sought the side pocket of his coat and fumbled there. The figure approached; it was now quite close, so close that all Bill had to do was rise swiftly to his feet and close his fingers in their viselike grip.

A curious penetrating odor filled the air and a sputtering, muffled cry came from the intruder. A short, sharp struggle, and the form sank limply to the floor. Kneeling down, Bill pressed the damp sponge a little longer against the nostrils and mouth until the body had quite relaxed, then returned the sponge to the pocket that held the chloroform tube.

He switched on the light and surveyed his prostrate anesthetized victim. It was a powerful-looking woman in a blue flannel nightgown; feet large and red, face coarse in feature and of contour Scandinavian; probably the cook. Bill wasted little thought on her. The point was that his blood was up now. He had had the taste of danger and his eyes gleamed. He shot a glance at the open stairway door.

A moment later his shoes were off, strung from his

belt by their laces, and he was on his way up—silently, warily. The eleventh step creaked a little and he stopped short.

Two minutes and no sound.

He went on to the top of the stairs and halted there, standing a while to listen before risking his flashlight. Its rays showed him a long wide hall with two doors on one side and three on the other, all closed, so he moved noiselessly on to the farther end, the front of the house, listened a moment at the crack of a door and then cautiously turned the knob and entered, leaving the door open behind him.

His ear told him instantly that he was not alone; the room was occupied; he heard someone breathing. His nerves were drawn tight now, his whole body alert and quivering with the pleasurable excitement of it, like a thoroughbred at the barrier.

A faint reflection of light from the streetlamp came in through the window, just enough to make out the dim forms of furniture and the vague lumpy outline under the covers on the bed. He heard a watch ticking; it became less audible when he had moved swiftly to the dressing table and transferred the timepiece to his own pocket. He turned as by instinct toward the door of the closet, but halted sharply halfway across the room.

There was something queer about that breathing. He listened tensely. Most irregular. Surely not the respiration of a sleeper—and he was an expert on the subject. Suspicious, to say the least.

Like a flash he was at the bedside, and his sharp gaze detected a shuddering movement all over the form that lay there under the sheets. His hand flew to the side pocket of his coat, then he remembered that the chloroform tube was empty. In a fit of rashness he pressed the button of his flashlight, and there on the pillow, in the center of the bright electric ray that shot forth, he saw the face of a man with mouth wide open and eyes staring in abject terror—a man wide awake and petrified with fear.

Bill had seen such countenances before, and experience had taught him to waste no time in taking advantage of the wide-open mouth. So, moving with swift sureness, he filled that gaping aperture with the corner of a sheet, stuffing it in with conscientious thoroughness. Then, while the man made feeble attempts to get loose, which Bill impatiently ignored, he tied his hands and feet and made the gag secure.

Gurglings barely audible came from the victim's nose; our hero made a threatening gesture, and they ceased. He proceeded calmly and methodically to rifle the room and closet. When he finished ten minutes later, he had deposited in various places about his person two silver cigarette cases, three scarf pins, five rings, a jeweled photograph frame, and ninety-four dollars in cash.

He looked to see that his captive was securely tied, scowled ferociously into his face, tiptoed out of the room and closed the door behind him. He had been in the house not more than thirty minutes, and already two of the enemy had been rendered hors de combat, a bag of booty was waiting for him below, his stomach was full, and his clothing was loaded with money and jewelry. His chest swelled with pardonable pride. On with the dance!

Inflated and emboldened by success, he flashed his light impudently up and down the hall, finally deciding on the next door to the right on the opposite side. He advanced, noiselessly turned the knob and entered. The light from the streetlamp did not enter on this side, and the room was pitch dark.

For a moment he thought it unoccupied, then the

sound of faint breathing came to his ear—quite faint and regular. He took a step toward the bed, then, magnificently scorning danger, turned to the wall near the door and felt for the electric button. He pushed; a click, and the room was flooded with light.

On the instant Bill sprang toward the bed, to forestall any outcry of alarm from its occupant. But he halted three paces away, with his arms half outstretched, at the sight that met his gaze.

There, under the silken coverlet, in the glare from the chandelier, he saw a sleeping child.

It was a girl of eight or nine years; her little white arm was curved under her head, and her soft brown hair spread in glorious curled confusion over the pillow. Her breast moved regularly up and down with her gentle breathing, and her sweet red lips were opened a little by the smile of a dream.

Bill stood still and gazed at her. He felt all of a sudden big and dirty and burly and clumsy and entirely out of place, and turning slowly to glance about the room, he saw that it was well suited to its occupant.

There was a small dressing table, a chest of drawers, a writing desk, and two or three chairs, all in dainty pink with delicately figured covers. On one corner of the desk stood a silver telephone instrument. The wall was pure white, with pink flowers and animals scattered in profusion along the border. A low wide bookcase, with full shelves, stood at one end. A pair of little white shoes were in the middle of the floor; on a chair nearby were the stockings and other garments.

Bill looked at them, and at the beautiful sleeping child, and at the child's beautiful room, and he felt something rise in his chest. Slowly his hand went to his head, and off came his cap.

"My little girl would have a place like this," he muttered half aloud.

The fact that Bill had no little girl or big one either, that he was indeed quite unmarried, is no reason to suspect the sincerity of his emotion. Some fathers might argue that it is in fact a reason to believe in it; but we are interested only in what actually happened. Undoubtedly what Bill meant was this, that if he had had a little girl of his own he would have wanted for her such a room as this one.

He moved close to the bed and stood there looking down at its occupant. What he was thinking was that he had never before realized that a creature could be so utterly helpless without thereby incurring the contempt of a strong man. There was something strangely stirring in the thought. Perhaps after all physical force was not the only power worth having. Here was this little child lying there utterly helpless before him—utterly helpless, and yet in fact far more secure from injury at his hands than a powerful man would have been.

No, force was not made to be used against helpless beings like her. What would he do if she should awake and cry out? He would talk to her and quiet her. According to the best burglar tradition, it would even be allowable to take her on his knee, and if a tear or so appeared in his eye it would be nothing to be ashamed of.

But what if she would not be quieted? What if in her fright she should persist in spreading the alarm? Force, then? No. In that case he would simply beat it. He would drop a kiss on her soft brown hair and make his escape. He did, in fact, bend over the pillow and deposit an extremely clumsy kiss on a lock of her hair, probably in order to have that much done and over with.

He turned away, for he felt one of the tears already

halfway to his eye. A shiny something on the dressing table caught his attention and he moved across to inspect it. It was a tiny gold wristwatch with enameled rim. He picked it up and looked at the name of the maker, and his eyes widened with respect.

Expensive trinket, that. Absurd to trust a child with it. No doubt she was very proud of the thing. He put it down again, spared even the impulse to put it in his pocket. He knew it would be useless to debate the matter with himself. What burglar would take anything from a sweet helpless child like—

"Hands up!"

The words came from behind him. They were uttered in a thin treble voice, as crisp and commanding as the snap of a whip. Bill wheeled like lightning and stood petrified.

The sweet helpless child was sitting up straight in bed, and in her extended hand was a mean-looking little revolver, with the muzzle directed unerringly one inch above the apex of Bill's heart.

"Lord above us!" ejaculated our hero, as his jaw dropped open in astonishment.

There was a short silence. The burglar's attitude of stupefaction became less pronounced, and his jaw came up again to take part in an amused grin as he relaxed, but the steady brown eyes facing him were unwavering in their direct and businesslike gaze.

"I would advise you to put your hands up before I count ten," said the sweet, helpless child calmly. "One, two, three—"

"Really, now," Bill put in hastily, "I wouldn't advise you to shoot, little girl. You might scare someone. I won't hurt you."

"I don't shoot to scare people. I see you don't take me seriously. It may interest you to know that yesterday at the gallery at Miss Vanderhoof's Academy I got nine straight centers from the hip. I am much better with the eye. I am Major Wentworth of Squadron A of the Girls' Military Auxiliary, and I am the crack shot of our regiment. Four, five, six—''

Bill was speechless. He calculated the distance to the bed. Easily ten feet. That revolver barrel was certainly aimed level. Nine straight centers from the hip, and much better with the eye. Coldish business. He hesitated. The brown eyes held his steadily.

''Seven, eight, nine—''

His keen eye saw the muscles of the little wrist begin to tighten. Up went his hands above his head.

''That's better,'' said the sweet, helpless child approvingly. ''I would have pulled the trigger in another half second. I had decided to get you in the right shoulder. Now turn your back, please, but keep your hands up.''

Bill did so. Almost immediately came the command to turn about again. She had clambered out of bed and stood there on the rug with her pink nightgown trailing about her feet and her soft brown hair tumbling over her shoulders. She looked more tiny than ever. But the muzzle of the revolver wavered not a fraction of an inch as she stepped sidewise to the wall and pressed her finger against a button there. Nothing was said while she repeated the operation three times. More silence.

''Look here, little girl,'' Bill began earnestly, ''there's no use gettin' your arm all tired with that toy gun. I ain't going to hurt you.''

''You may call me Major Wentworth,'' was all the reply he got.

''All right, major. But come, what's the use—''

''Stop! If you move again like that I'll shoot. I wonder

what's the matter with Hilda. She sleeps very lightly."
This last to herself.

Bill looked interested.

"Is Hilda a big sort of a woman in a blue night-gown?"

"Yes. Have you seen her?" The brown eyes filled with sudden alarm. "Oh! Where is she? Is she hurt?"

"Nope." Bill chuckled. "Kitchen floor. Chloroform. I was eatin' strawberry shortcake when she come in."

The major frowned.

"I suppose I must call my father. I hate to disturb him—"

"He's incapable, too," announced Bill with another chuckle. "Tied up with sheets and things. You see, major, we're all alone. Tell you what I'll do. There's a suitcase full of silver down on the library windowsill. I'll agree to leave it there—"

"You certainly will," the major nodded. "And you'll leave the other things too. I see them in your pockets. Since my father is tied up I suppose I must call the police myself."

She began to move sidewise toward the silver telephone on the desk, keeping the revolver pointed at Bill's breast.

I transcribe Bill's thought: the little devil was actually going to call the police! Action must come now if at all, and quickly. He dismissed the idea of a dash for freedom; she would certainly pull the trigger, and she had a firm eye and hand. Bill summoned all his wit.

"My little girl's mama is dead, too," he blurted out suddenly.

The major, with her hand outstretched for the telephone, stopped to look at him.

"My mother isn't dead," she observed sharply. "She's gone to the country."

"You don't say so!" Bill's voice was positively explosive with enthusiastic interest. "Why didn't you go along, major, if I may ask?"

"I am too busy with the Auxiliary. We are pushing the campaign for preparedness." She added politely: "You say your wife is dead?"

Bill nodded mournfully.

"Been dead three years. Got sick and wasted away and died. Broke my little girl's heart, and mine, too."

A suggestion of sympathy appeared in the major's eyes as she inquired:

"What is your little girl's name?"

"Her name?" Bill floundered in his stupidity. "Oh, her name. Why, of course her name's Hilda."

"Indeed!" The major looked interested. "The same as cook. How funny! How old is she?"

"Sixteen," said Bill rather desperately.

"Oh, she's a big girl, then! I suppose she goes to school?"

Bill nodded.

"Which one?"

It was a mean question. In Bill's mind school was simply school. He tried to think of a word that would sound like the name of one, but nothing came.

"Day school," he said at last, and then added hastily, "that is, she moves around, you know. Going up all the time. She's a smart girl." His tone was triumphant.

Then, fearing that another question might finish him, he continued slowly:

"You might as well go on and call the cops—the police, I suppose. Of course, Hilda's at home hungry, but that don't matter to you. She'll starve to death. I didn't tell you she's sick. She's sick all the time—something wrong with her. I was just walkin' past here and thought I might find something for her to eat, and I was lookin' around—''

"You ate the strawberry shortcake yourself," put in the major keenly.

"The doctor won't let Hilda have cake," Bill retorted. "And I was hungry myself. I suppose it's no crime to be hungry—''

"You took the silver and other things."

"I know." Bill's head drooped dejectedly. "I'm a bad man, I guess. I wanted to buy nice things for Hilda. She hasn't had a doll for over ten years. She never has much to eat. If I'm arrested I suppose she'll starve to death."

The sympathy in the major's eyes deepened. "I don't want to cause unnecessary suffering," she declared. "I feel strongly for the lower classes. And Miss Vanderhoof says that our penal system is disgraceful. I suppose little would be gained by sending you to prison."

"It's an awful place," Bill declared feelingly.

"You have been there?"

"Off and on."

"You see! It has done you no good. No, I might as well let you go. Turn your back."

Bill stared.

The major stamped her little bare foot.

" 'Turn your back, I say! That's right. I do wish you wouldn't make me repeat things. Walk forward near the dressing table. No, at the side. So. Now empty your pockets and turn them inside out. All of them. Put the things on the dressing table. Keep your back turned, or— as you would say in your vulgar parlance—I'll blow your block off."

Bill obeyed. He could feel the muzzle of the revolver pointed directly at the back of his head, and he obeyed. He lost no time about it either, for the anesthetized Hilda would be coming to soon.

Methodically and thoroughly the pockets were emptied and their contents deposited on the dressing table: a gentleman's watch, two silver cigarette cases, three scarf pins, five rings, a jeweled photograph frame, and ninety-four dollars in cash. The articles that were obviously Bill's own she instructed him to return to the pockets. He did so.

"There!" said the major briskly when he had finished. "You may turn now. That's all, I think. Kindly close the front door as you go out. I'll attend to the suitcase on the windowsill after you're gone. I wouldn't advise you to try any tricks on me. I've never got a man on the run, but I'd love to have a crack at one. That's all."

Bill hesitated. His eye was on the neat roll of bills reposing beside him on the dressing table. It traveled from that to the gold wristwatch he would not take because it belonged to the sweet, helpless child. Would he take it now if he had a chance? Would he!

The major's voice came:

"Go, please. I'm sleepy, and you've given me a lot of trouble. I shall have to revive Hilda, if it is possible. I have doubts on the subject. She refuses to keep herself in condition. She eats too much, she will not take a cold bath, she won't train properly, she is sixty-eight pounds overweight, and she sleeps with her mouth open. But she's a good cook—"

"She is that," Bill put in feelingly, with his memory on the shortcake.

"—and I trust she has not expired. There is my father, too. To put it mildly, he is a weakling. His lack of wind is deplorable. He sits down immediately after eating. It is only three miles to his law office, and he rides. He plays golf and calls it exercise. If you have gagged him scientifically he may have ceased breathing by now.

"In one way it would be nothing to grieve over, but

he is my father after all, and the filial instinct impels me to his assistance against my better judgment. You do not seem to be in good condition yourself. I doubt if you know how to breathe properly, and it is evident that you do not train systematically. There are books on the subject in the public library; I would advise you to get one. You may give my name as reference. Now go.''

Bill went. The door of the room was open. He started toward the back stairs, but the major halted him abruptly and made him right about; she had switched on the lights in the hall. Down the wide front staircase he tramped, and from behind came the major's voice:

"Keep your mouth closed. Head up! Arms at your side. Breathe through your nose. Chest out forward! Hep, hep, hep—the door swings in. Leave it open. Lift your foot and come down on the heel. Turn the corner sharply. Head up!''

She stood in the doorway as he marched across the porch, down the steps, and along the gravel path to the sidewalk. A turn to the right, and thirty paces took him to the street corner. Still the major's voice sounded from the doorway:

"Hep, hep, hep—lift your feet higher—breathe through your nose—hep, hep, hep—''

And as he reached the street corner the command came sharply:

"Halt! About-face! Salute!''

A glance over his shoulder showed him her nightgown framed in the doorway. There were trees in between. Bill halted, but he did not about-face and he did not salute. It was too much. Instead, after a second's hesitation, he bounded all at once into the street and across it, and was off like a shot. And as he ran he replied to her command to salute by calling back over his shoulder, as man to man:

"Go to hell!''

HEELS OF FATE

I FIRST BEGAN TO DROP IN AT DAL WILLETT'S LIVERY
stable for an hour's chat, on my way home from the
office in the evening or sometimes during the long
hours of a dull afternoon, about five years ago. I had
known him long before that, but had not appreciated
him. He was a tall, loose-jointed man, about forty then,
with a red leathery countenance and keen little gray eyes;
and as I gradually discovered, he was an extraordinarily
observant fellow, with a sharp knowledge of humans and
understanding of them, while his abstract opinions were
correspondingly generous and tinged with humor. With
his knowledge, he has helped me more than once in the
solution of some problem or other when I myself was
badly tangled; for though the cases that fall to us country
lawyers may be small ones they are often really difficult
and complicated. Of course I always hired a rig from
Dal on the rare occasions when I had to visit a client on
some farm not too far away. His livery stable was the
only one in town, and he was prosperous.

Of evenings we would sit out in front with our chairs
tilted back against the wall, Dal in his shirt sleeves, myself in a linen duster, and smoke and talk; or in the
winter we would hug the stove in the office. It was interesting to hear Dal discourse on any subject whatever,

from local politics to poetry. His favorite topic was the habits and peculiarities of his four-footed animals; he loved horses, and I am convinced understood them better than any other man that ever lived. At the time of this story, I remember, he had in the stable a "kicker," a magnificent black beast, clean of limb and of glossy coat, but with a most vicious eye. Dal called him Mac; a contraction, as I remember it, of Machiavelli.

Dal had love in his heart even for Mac, and he would spend hours working with incredible patience to cure him of his vicious habit. His understanding of the creature's psychology, or instinct, was almost uncanny. Without any apparent reason he would say to the hostlers some morning, after a leisurely tour of the stable, "Look out for Mac today, boys, he's ready to fire." And sure enough on the slightest provocation, or none whatever, the horse's iron-shod hoofs would fly out most unexpectedly like a shot from a cannon, with the force of a dozen sledgehammers.

His method with balkers was simple but invariably effective; I had a chance to observe it once in the case of a bay mare he had got from a farmer north of town. We would be driving along at a slow trot or a walk when suddenly Dal would pull on the reins with a commanding "Whoa!" The mare would stop with apparent reluctance, and after we had sat there a minute or two Dal would slacken the reins and slap them on her back and off we would go.

"The idea of balking always enters a horse's head when it is in motion, never when it's standing still," Dal would explain. "It is a double idea: 1—stop; 2—balk. The thing is, don't let them stop, and the way to avoid it is to stop them yourself before they get a chance to do it of their own accord. That gets 'em confused, and naturally they give it up as a bad job."

"But how do you know when they're ready to begin operations?"

"I don't know—something—the way they hold their head—you can tell—"

That is, *he* could tell. I grew to regard him as infallible on any question concerning an animal in harness or under a saddle. One thing was certain: he loved his horses better than he did his hostlers, though he understood them equally well; and I am not ready to quarrel with the preference.

It was one July afternoon, when Dal and I were seated together out in front that the individual known as H. E. Gruber first appeared on the scene. That was the name he gave Dal. We marked him for a new face in the town the moment we saw him glide past us with a curious gait, half furtive, half insolent, in through the door of the runway to the livery stable. I replied to Dal's inquiring glance:

"Never saw him before."

In a minute the stranger emerged again from the stable, approached me and spoke:

"The boys sent me out here. You the boss?"

I designated Dal by a nod of the head, and the stranger turned to him with the information that he wished to hire a rig. I took advantage of the opportunity to look him over. He had a sly, hard face, with mean little colorless eyes that shifted vaguely as he talked; his voice had a curious way of changing suddenly from a purry softness to a grating, rasping snarl. He looked to be somewhere in the fifties, and was dressed well, in a gray sack suit and black derby.

"Where do you want to go?" Dal inquired with a frown. It was plain that he, too, was unfavorably impressed with the man's appearance.

The stranger replied that he wished to drive out to

John Hawkins's farm; and finally, after taking his name and inquiring concerning the extent of his experience with horses, Dal called to one of the boys to tell him to get out a single buggy. While that was being done the stranger, Gruber, inquired the way to his destination, and Dal described the route with the greatest care. He was always particular about those things; not so much, I believe, to serve his customers, as on account of the fact that when a man loses his way he becomes angry and usually takes it out on the horse.

"It's good road all the way," said Dal, as the rig was led out and Gruber climbed in. "You ought to make it in an hour. If you're kept over suppertime John'll look after the horse. John Hawkins always feeds his animals before he does himself."

The stranger nodded, shook the reins and was off, with Nanny, one of the best mares in town, breaking into a smart trot the moment she hit the road.

Dal and I puffed for a couple of minutes in silence. The buggy had disappeared down the street when I took my cigar from my mouth to observe speculatively:

"Queer specimen."

Dal nodded. "Yes. Can't quite figure him out. Drummer? No. Looks like a backdoor politician. Probably from Denver. What the dickens does he want with old John Hawkins?"

The same query was in my own mind, for two men more totally different than the stranger Gruber and the farmer he was going to see would have been hard to find. John Hawkins had come to our part of the country some five years before, from where nobody knew, and bought the old Miller farm, paying all but a thousand dollars in cash. That last is a bit of inside information, for I was the lawyer who drew up the deed.

People laughed at him while they pitied him, for the

Miller farm was the most notoriously bad quarter section in the township. But Hawkins soon showed them that if he possessed no knowledge of farmland and farming he at least knew how to work and learn. He found a book somewhere on fertilizers, and the second year he got a fair crop of corn on his west forty, though he nearly starved doing it. The third year was better still, and he began then to make money from his poultry, too. People learned to respect and admire him, all the more because he had earned the reputation of being the hardest worker in the country; and yet he couldn't have been a day less than fifty-five, with his medium-sized stooping figure, gray hair, and furrowed careworn countenance. He was a silent, reserved man, with a look of grim submission in his steady brown eyes that at times startled you with its pathos.

A certain portion of the community was particularly interested in his poultry; and you will understand what that portion was when you learn that the poultry was under the special care of Hawkins's daughter. Her name was Janet. The best possible advertisement for the purposes of the "back to the farm" propagandists would be a card containing photographs, after the fashion of patent medicine ads, of Janet Hawkins "before" and "after." When she first appeared—I remember seeing her walk down Main Street with her father the day they arrived— she was a dark, shrinking little thing with muddy cheeks and dull, stony eyes that refused to look at anybody. Seeing her from a little distance you would have thought her an underfed twelve-year-old; close up she looked nearer twice that age. Really she was then just nineteen.

In a year she was a totally different creature. My enthusiasm makes me fear the attempt to describe her, for I myself have not reached the age of senility and for three years I held certain hopes with regard to Janet

Hawkins which finally proved vain. Though the change in her appearance was startling and complete, it took place so gradually that it would be hard to say when it began or what it consisted of. Her complexion became all milk and roses, her eyes alive with the fire and happiness of youth, her figure supple and incredibly quick and graceful in movement; but there was something deeper than any of these, a rebirth of her spirit that made her laughter thrill you from head to foot and her glance pierce you with joy. She was wonderful. I know.

It was not long, of course, before she was the object of a mad pursuit ; as pretty a race as you would care to see. Two or three young farmers were the first entries, besides old Jerry Pratt, who owns some fifteen hundred acres in the southern part of the county; soon they were joined, one by one, by a dozen of us from the town. Dal Willett was among the number; during one whole summer he drove out to the Hawkins farm every evening, but he spent little time with Janet. He was too reserved in the matter; the others rushed him off his feet, and I believe he never really entertained any hope. He used to sit out on the back porch with old Hawkins, talking horses and crops, and in that way the two men became intimate. About nine o'clock Janet would come out with a pitcher of lemonade, having first served those in front—there was always somebody—and a little later we would all leave together. Many a time I've seen two or three buggies and as many automobiles file out one after another through the Hawkins gate.

When we learned that Walter Rogers had entered the race the rest of us were about ready to give up. Rogers, a man about thirty, was president of the local bank and by far the wealthiest citizen of the country. He was a good, hard-working fellow, too, and well liked. Most of us admitted bitterly that he was just the man for Janet

Hawkins, and feeling that our chances were gone we soon capitulated. We should have known that Janet was not the kind of girl to be attracted by an eight-cylinder motor and three servants; but at that we were right in a way. Our chances were gone.

Late in September she was married to Roy Nelson, a struggling young farmer who lived five miles away and who had walked that distance and home again twice a week to see her, because he had been working his horses all day and thought they needed rest more than he did.

So Janet became Mrs. Nelson, and at the end of autumn her husband sold out his small interest in his forty acres and the newly married couple came to live with old man Hawkins. Nelson soon proved that Janet had made no mistake. During the following two years he nearly doubled the crops, and yet found time to make his wife happy. I got to know him pretty well, and discovered that he was an admirable fellow in every way. He worshiped Janet, and she thought him perfect. It was a mighty happy family. Nelson wouldn't let John Hawkins do anything except look after the poultry, but the old man did that with such success that at the end of the second year he had a profit of four figures and half a dozen blue ribbons to show for it. I remember the naïve pride with which he showed me his photograph one day, published in the *Utah Poultry Bulletin*.

After this explanation of our acquaintance and friendship with the Hawkins family, you will understand the curiosity that Dal Willett and I felt that afternoon when the stranger Gruber appeared to request a rig and the way to the Hawkins farm. As Dal had observed, the fellow had the appearance of a backdoor politician. We speculated at length on the possible nature of his errand, as two gossiping males will, but of course fruitlessly. The mere sight of Gruber was enough to make a decent man apprehensive, and it was perhaps that fact, rather than any particular premonition of trouble, that caused me to walk back down to the livery stable that night after supper. It was after ten o'clock when Gruber drove in, left the rig and paid for it, and went off with his shuffling gait toward Main Street.

When I got to my office the following morning I found John Hawkins there waiting for me.

The old man was standing in the hallway in front of the locked door; it was rather dark there and I didn't recognize him at once. He didn't speak as I approached, but merely moved to one side so I could get at the keyhole; as he turned I saw his face, and an ejaculation of amazement escaped me at sight of it.

"Why, it's John Hawkins," I exclaimed.

He nodded and mumbled, "Yes, I want to see you on some business."

I opened the door and we entered. In the light from the windows I gazed at him in astonishment; in the week since I had seen him last the man had apparently aged twenty years. He trembled as he walked over to a chair and sank down in it, and though the old grimness had not entirely departed from his face it was almost obliterated by a new look of despair and unmistakable fear. That was my most vivid impression, that he was terribly in fear of something. After I had unlocked my desk and pulled up a chair I asked him what the trouble was.

His eyes blinked rapidly and he opened his lips two or three times before he could get any words out. I barely caught his stammering reply:

"I want to get some money."

I glanced at him sharply.

"How much?"

"Eight thousand dollars."

That rather stunned me. Eight thousand dollars! In Holton County that's a pretty good-sized sum.

"Eight thousand," I repeated stupidly.

The old man leaned forward in his chair. "Yes, I've got to have it," he said. His voice suddenly became firmer and more distinct. "You can see I'm in trouble, Harry, but don't ask me any questions, because I can't answer them. I've got to have eight thousand dollars right away. There oughtn't to be much trouble about it. I only paid six thousand for the farm, but it's worth easy twice that much now and there ain't a cent owing on it. If I have to I'll give a mortgage on the stock, too, and my chickens. They're worth a lot of money. I thought maybe you could see Mr. Rogers and fix it up today. That's why I came in so early."

I looked at him awhile in silence. Twenty questions were on the tip of my tongue, and of course the stranger Gruber was in my mind. But all I said was:

"You're sure that you've got to have this money?"

There was a flash from his eyes. "Would I be asking for it if I didn't?" he exclaimed with a touch of angry exasperation. Then also instantly he stretched a trembling hand out to me. "I didn't mean anything, Harry. But I've got to have it."

"It's not so easy as it sounds," I replied slowly. "You know when anybody makes a loan, especially one of that size, they want to know what it's to be used for. You'd have to explain why you want it. The farmers around here have been getting a little reckless, buying automobiles, and so on, and Rogers has shut down on them."

Again the old man's eyes flashed. "I'm an honest man," he said. "And the farm's worth it. I didn't think there'd be any trouble."

"There probably won't be," I agreed, "if you'll explain what you want it for."

There was a little silence, while the farmer regarded me with a growing expression of despair, and then suddenly a look of shrewdness came into his face.

"It's a debt I owe," he declared almost triumphantly. "To a man—" he hesitated a second, then went on— "a man named Gruber. I've owed it over five years now, before I came here."

I nodded. "I saw Gruber yesterday. I was at Dal Willett's when he came there to hire a rig to go out to your place. Funny-looking man, that Gruber. I may be only a country lawyer, Mr. Hawkins, but one look at his face is enough. And besides, you're not a man to be ashamed of any honest debt. There's only one thing you could want to give money to this Gruber for, and that's blackmail."

The old farmer started a little and I saw his hand grip the arm of the chair. He was surprised out of his shrewdness, too, for he merely repeated stubbornly, after a moment, "I tell you it's a debt, Harry." In another second he added, "What could he blackmail me for?" Then a sudden look of fear drove everything else from his face and he half rose out of his chair as he repeated in a shrill trembling voice:

"What could he blackmail me for?"

I got up and crossed over to lay my hand on his shoulder. Under my touch I could feel a tremor all over his frame.

"That's just what you're going to tell me," I said quietly. "Listen to me. I'm a lawyer, and this sort of thing is my business. Maybe we can find a way out and maybe we can't, but at any rate if you expect me to help you, you must tell me about it. A decent lawyer doesn't betray a confidence, and I think I may say I'm decent. Why do you have to give this Gruber eight thousand dollars?"

In the end he told me. Garrulous, old men may be as a rule, but John Hawkins's words came hard that morning. He hung off for more than an hour, and when he finally told his story I could see that every word was wringing blood from his heart, where the thing had been so long locked up. But though it was sad enough there was nothing really base in it, and the old man's tough reluctance may be charged to his blind adoration of his daughter. It may be set down here baldly in a few words.

Six years before, John Hawkins, whose real name was Timothy Ryder, had been proprietor of a saloon in New York. His wife had died at the birth of their daughter; and Janet, spoiled by her father and not properly looked after, had gotten into bad company. There were details here that Hawkins passed over; he swore that Janet had not done anything really wrong, but through the misdeeds and treachery of her companions had been arrested and sentenced to three years at Bedford. I, who knew Janet, believed him. Hawkins had sold his saloon, spent half the proceeds in arranging his daughter's escape, and come west with her.

"Gruber—Nosey Gruber we called him—is a ward-heeler and a crook," said the old man toward the end. "I chased him out of the district once. I would have killed him last night, only there was no way. Unless I give him ten thousand dollars tomorrow he's going to telegraph the New York police. I've got about two thousand in the bank that I've made off of my chickens. It was through them he found out about me; he was in Denver and saw my picture that I showed you in the paper."

I remember as Hawkins finished the thought in the front of my brain was one of wonder at a man like Gruber reading a copy of the *Utah Poultry Bulletin*, and happening on that particular copy. My mind caught at that, I suppose, in an instinctive avoidance of the greater problem, how to save this old man from ruin, for I saw at once that the thing was insoluble. Nothing practicable could be done. We sat in silence, Hawkins with his fingers endlessly kneading themselves together and unfastening again, with so bitter a despair in his eyes as they met mine that I looked away.

At length we talked, but aimlessly. As a lawyer I had held the belief that no man should pay blackmail under any circumstances, but I faltered before the simple, hard facts. Refuse to pay, and Janet's life would be ruined; pay, and it would probably be the same in the end anyway. Blackmailers, like cats, always come back. I said these things and many others to old Hawkins, and he merely sat and nodded his head miserably.

"What can I do," he mumbled hopelessly. "I've got to pay. I could kill him, I suppose, but that would be just as bad for her. They'd find out who I was and it'd be the same thing. It's only Nosey Gruber would do this. There's never been any search for Janet—why was it Nosey saw that picture?"

I tried to get him to tell me what the offense was for which Janet had been committed, but he wouldn't talk about it; he would only say that she was innocent and that it was all his own fault. He began again on the subject of the mortgage. He was half-crazed by fear; the thing must be done that day, at once, or Gruber would wire New York. Of course that was absurd, but the old man was unable to think clearly. In the end I refused pointblank to do anything unless he would consent that I first go to Dal Willett for advice. This was a sudden impulse, and nothing but a move of weakness on my part; the responsibility was more than I was willing to assume alone; but, on the other hand, I had come to believe greatly in Dal's shrewdness and he might, after all, suggest something. To that I succeeded in getting Hawkins to agree, and leaving him there in the office I departed.

I've never seen Dal Willett worked up except that morning. The way I blurted the thing out in a breath had something to do with it, I suppose, but I have an idea that it was more the feeling he had for Janet. It opened my eyes to what passions and aches there had been behind his always quiet manner; I guess after all there was one human being he loved even more than he did his horses. I was astounded at the way he blazed up into fury; and then suddenly he was quiet again.

"Of course," he observed, "it isn't open to discussion. John can't refuse to pay. It would mean Janet's ruin and his own death, for the thing would certainly kill him. And he can't pay either. Gruber would come back again and again, and when the old man dies he'll keep after Janet. That would be just as pleasant as hell."

I mumbled something about there being nothing else to do but pay. Dal glared at me.

"I said it wasn't open to discussion, didn't I?" he returned testily. "It's a case of only two alternatives and both of them impossible."

That appeared to me somewhat absurd. It must be either yes or no. Dal walked to the window of his little office and stood there with his back to me for a long while. I was conscious mostly of a great relief at having gotten half the burden off my shoulders, and I merely sat in silence and waited. Outside in the stable I could hear the boys calling to each other as they hauled the rigs up to the runway for cleaning, and the stamping of the horses' feet in their stalls. Mot, Dal's black and white coach dog, wandered in through the door and came up to stick his nose in the palm of my hand, and then ambled out again. Ten minutes passed without anything being said.

Suddenly Dal turned from the window, and I saw immediately from the look on his face that there was something in his mind.

"John's over in your office?" he asked abruptly.

I nodded. "I left him there."

"All right. Go and tell him to go back to the farm and stay there. Tell him to leave this thing to me. If Gruber telephones he must refuse to talk to him. If he'll do that everything will be all right. Tell him I said so."

"But what—" I began, bewildered.

"Do what I tell you. And tell the old man not to worry."

That was all he would say, and a minute later I was trotting back to my office to carry out his instructions.

I anticipated a hard job of it, but old Hawkins was surprisingly amenable, and the secret of it was the unlimited confidence he felt in Dal Willett. As soon as I told him that Dal had given his word that "everything would come out all right" the old man meekly agreed to do just as he had said. He wanted to go around to the livery stable to talk with Dal, but finally I persuaded him to carry out the instructions to the letter. I went out to the street and unhitched his horse for him and watched him head south and disappear in the direction of the farm.

I hadn't any idea what Dal was up to, and I'm not sure even now that he had figured it all out that morning in his office, though I think it likely. It was easy even for me to see that there was only one way out; and having decided to do the thing it remained merely to find the means. It was characteristic of Dal that he let it happen as naturally as possible.

I stopped at the livery stable on my way home that

evening. Dal was seated out in front as usual with a cigar in his mouth. I had telephoned him at noon that Hawkins had agreed to obey instructions, and now as I halted in front of him I had fifty questions on the tip of my tongue. I asked if he had seen Gruber.

"No, and I'd rather not talk about him," he replied; and since I saw that none of my questions would be answered I went on home without asking them.

The following morning I, myself, saw Gruber as I walked down Main Street to my office. He was seated on the piazza of Charley Smith's Commercial Hotel, reading a magazine and smoking a cigarette. I looked at him curiously, and in the light of what I knew the man appeared more repulsive and snaky than before. He looked up and stared at me, and I hastened my step to get past the place.

A little before noon I had a telephone call from John Hawkins. At the first sound of his voice I could tell that the security he had felt from Dal Willett's assurances had become considerably weaker; the old man was almost in a state of panic again. Gruber had called up the farm twice that morning; Janet had answered the phone and told him her father would not speak to him. Janet was beginning to suspect some kind of trouble—luckily she had not seen Gruber—and Hawkins had evaded her questions with difficulty. I tried to reassure him, and he finally agreed to hold fast.

All that day I seemed to myself to be hanging in the air. A dozen times the impulse seized me to go to Dal's and find out if anything had happened. It was Thursday, the day on which Gruber had said the money must be paid; and though I knew that was merely a bluff I somehow felt that before the sun went down that night the thing would be settled. By the middle of the afternoon I was quivering with expectation so I could hardly stay in my chair. I pictured Dal walking calmly down the street to where Gruber was perched on the Commercial Hotel piazza, drawing a revolver and filling him full of bullets; I could see Gruber topple over with his ugly face knocking against the rail. Dal would then go down and give himself up to Tom Connolly, and they would send for me. My mind went forward to the courtroom, to the trial, and I saw myself opening for the defense—it would be a tremendous speech—

I shook myself and got to my feet, and crossing to the window saw Gruber walking down the street on the other side. I started as though I had seen a ghost. He was going along at a good pace, like a man who intends to get somewhere. I watched him till he disappeared around the corner two blocks down. Then I went back and sat down again at my desk.

I had a picture of Janet there in a drawer, and I pulled it out and looked at it. Old Hawkins's words protesting his daughter's innocence were in my mind, and I smiled. They had been so perfectly superfluous. To think of a girl like that in the clutches of a Gruber! I began to indulge in memories, and was soon lost in a sentimental reverie.

Fifteen minutes later I was brought to myself by hearing an automobile stop out in front.

I turned in time to see Jim Rowley, the doctor, jump out of his runabout and dash for the door of my office. Instantly I knew. I had the door open by the time he reached it. He blurted into my face:

"Dal Willett just phoned me—there's a man hurt down there—he told me to stop and get you—"

Without stopping for a hat I rushed out and leaped in the car. Jim must have been surprised at the readiness with which I grasped his unusual information, but I had no idea there was need of discretion. Almost immediately he was at the wheel beside me and we were off at a leap, tearing down Main Street.

"What is it—who is it—how was he hurt?" I shouted at Jim, but he was busy turning a corner and didn't answer. It was only a ten-minute walk from my office to the livery stable, and it took the car only a space of a dozen breaths. Before I knew it we were there.

Tom Connolly's buggy was out in front, with his mare breathing hard, and a crowd of boys was peering in at the big door of the stable, with a woman or two among them, while others came running down the street from both directions, shouting to one another. As the car came to a stop opposite the door and Jim leaped out with his black case in his hand, I caught sight of a group of men standing within, gathered in a close circle, and one of the stable boys running from the rear with a pail of water.

I got out of the car and started toward the crowd at the door, which was being reenforced every moment by new arrivals. The doctor had disappeared inside, and I saw the circle of men make way for him, calling, "Here he is!" There was confusion everywhere, those coming up being greeted by a chorus of cries so that nothing could be understood. I had started to enter the stable, but halted on the threshold. Somehow I didn't want to see what was in the center of that group of men—

At that moment I heard somebody behind me say to somebody else:

"It was Mac—you know, Mr. Willett's horse—he kicked a man—it was a stranger come to hire a rig; I don't know his name—he kicked him clear across the stable—"

Suddenly the group of men stirred and parted, and I saw the doctor rising to his feet. One of the men turned to the throng at the door, and before he spoke I knew by the expression on his face what the doctor had said.

Into the sudden silence about the doorway came the whisper:

"He's dead."

That evening after I came back from a ride out to old man Hawkins's farm I sat with Dal Willett in his office. We didn't talk much; I could see that Dal didn't want to, though he was glad to have me there. And when I asked a question—forced out of me by curiosity—which I perhaps should not have asked, Dal shook his head.

"Of course I knew," he said with a certain grimness. "And I sent him back there. But somehow I don't feel responsible. Those iron-shod hoofs were the heels of fate, that's all. Anyway, it's between Mac and me."

After a long pause he added:

"And God."

CARROLL & GRAF

MYSTERY / SUSPENSE
AVAILABLE FROM CARROLL & GRAF

☐ Charteris, Leslie / The Saint: The Saint & Mr. Teal	4.50
☐ Eberhart, Mignon G. / Message from Hong Kong	3.95
☐ Gilbert, Michael / The Crack in the Teacup	3.95
☐ Gilbert, Michael / Roller Coaster	4.95
☐ Kitchin, C. H. B. / Death of His Uncle	3.95
☐ Kitchin, C. H. B. / Death of My Aunt	3.50
☐ Lansdale, Joe R. / Act of Love	4.95
☐ Lansdale, Joe R. / The Nightrunners	4.95
☐ Lansdale, Joe R. / Writer of the Purple Rage	5.95
☐ McGivern, Wiliam P. / Odds Against Tomorrow	4.95
☐ Millhiser, Marlys / Willing Hostage	4.95
☐ Muller, Marcia and Bill Pronzini / Beyond the Grave	3.95
☐ Muller, Marcia and Bill Pronzini / The Lighthouse	4.50
☐ Pronzini, Bill / Dead Run	3.95
☐ Pronzini, Bill / Snowbound	4.95
☐ Sandra Scoppettone / A Creative Kind of Killer	4.50
☐ Sandra Scoppettone / Donato & Daughter	6.95
☐ Sandra Scoppettone / Razzamatazz	4.95
☐ Sandra Scoppettone / Some Unknown Person	5.95
☐ Stevens, Shane / The Anvil Chorus	4.95
☐ Stevens, Shane / By Reason of Insanity	5.95
☐ Stevens, Shane / Dead City	4.95
☐ Stout, Rex / A Prize for Princes	4.95
☐ Stout, Rex / Under the Andes	4.95
☐ Symons, Julian / Bogue's Fortune	3.95
☐ Westlake, Donald / Pity Him Afterwards	4.95
☐ Waugh, Hillary / A Death in a Town	3.95